The Lawyer in Medellín

Richard Hedlund

Published by New Generation Publishing in 2018

Copyright © Richard Hedlund 2018

First Edition

The author asserts the moral right under the Copyright, Designs and Patents Act 1988 to be identified as the author of this work.

All Rights reserved. No part of this publication may be reproduced, stored in a retrieval system or transmitted, in any form or by any means without the prior consent of the author, nor be otherwise circulated in any form of binding or cover other than that in which it is published and without a similar condition being imposed on the subsequent purchaser.

www.newgeneration-publishing.com

 New Generation Publishing

For Maria Luisa and her family for their friendship and hospitality when I visited Colombia.

Prologue

Stuart Gleeman found himself sitting inside a luxury villa, nestled on the hillside inside a deep valley. Outside, the sun was shining brightly, as it had done every day since Stuart had arrived in Colombia. The heat inside was pressing down on him and pearls of sweat were lining his forehead. Stuart was seated in a large, comfortable chair, just inside from a spacious veranda, which was accessible through a large wooden door that had been rolled in its entirety to one side.

A light gust of wind blew in from outside and for a second he felt cool. Stuart looked up and stared at the wonderful and mesmerising vista beyond. The veranda opened up to a lush, green valley framed by rising mountains, the tops of which were disappearing into the heat haze. Birds of all colours were nesting in the trees and bushes. What had captured Stuart's mind ever since his arrival at the house were the countless eagles soaring in the sky. They were a reminder of majesty and freedom, both of which Stuart had just lost.

The paradise beyond the house was an illusion and Stuart found himself ill at ease. His mind was drawn to something that his newfound travelling companion had said. Hope is indefatigable. Stuart certainly needed hope, the more the better. First of all, he was tied to the chair. His presence in it was far from voluntary, despite the previous week's quest to find the villa and its owner. Second of all, one of the owner's employees, a short, tough-looking man, was standing by a nearby table. The burly employee occasionally eyed Stuart with a smirk on his face, but his focus was on a large kitchen knife, which he was handling with a skill that both impressed and greatly worried Stuart. The tense atmosphere in the room suggested to Stuart that he might soon have a close-up experience with that knife. At the moment, though, the man was slowly slicing a pineapple, whose sweet smell wafted over to Stuart.

Stuart's head began to spin in the heat and he soon lost track of time. Eventually, another man entered the room, stepping in from the veranda, with a quick nod goodbye to someone who was just out of Stuart's sight. The man was tall and well built. He was smartly dressed in long trousers and a shirt, the sleeves of which he had rolled up above his elbows. It was a strange choice of attire given the climate, and it suggested the man had high status. The rough employee nodded in respect. Stuart tilted his head in contemplation. He got a sudden feeling that he had seen this man somewhere before.

Before Stuart could place him, the man took the few steps necessary to reach Stuart and struck him with impressive force. Stuart's head flew to one side and quickly bounced back. His whole body would have toppled over had it not been for the sturdy chair he was tied to, and his knuckles turned white as he clenched the wooden armrests.

The man waited a moment for Stuart to regain his senses.

"Would you like some pineapple?"

Stuart's head was still spinning, but he looked up at the man.

"What?" he mumbled.

"Pineapple?"

The man looked in the direction of the employee and gave a slight nod, calling for the plate with the pineapple slices to be brought over.

"Well," Stuart said, taking a deep breath. His mind was starting to defog. He found the question odd, but he had to buy some extra time before the henchman put the knife to another, bloodier, use. "Yes, thank you."

The employee slowly brought the plate over and handed it to his boss. He then retreated back to the table, placing his hand on the knife.

"The house belongs to my boss, Mr Gleeman," the man said, still standing over Stuart. He did not offer Stuart any of the pineapple slices, which did not matter much since Stuart's hands were still securely tied to the back of the chair. "But you know that, of course. What I'm interested in is whether your companions know where we are?"

Stuart's mind was clearing up. They know my name, he thought, but after the escapades of the previous week, he was not too surprised. The man slowly ate a slice of pineapple, looking intently at Stuart. Stuart was not sure how to proceed. He took another deep breath to clear his mind even further. The relatively simple favour he had been asked to do by the shadowy man in London had taken a real turn for the worse. What should have been a half-hour detour from a business meeting had become a matter of life and death. The past week had been a fast-paced nightmare of murder and more murder, leading to him being kidnapped by the criminal organisation he was chasing down.

"Well?" the man insisted, with a sterner tone. "Your companions?"

Stuart looked away and out over the valley. Despite the mountaintops disappearing into the heat haze, it truly looked like paradise. Then he noticed that the burly employee came over. In his hand was the knife.

"I am disappointed," the man said after another moment of silence. He subtly nodded his head at the door. With some effort, the employee slid the rolling door shut. Paradise disappeared. Stuart desperately needed a way out.

Chapter 1

"Contact, lieutenant!"

Lieutenant Rebecca Hayden was standing in quiet contemplation on the port bridge wing. She was looking out into the night, a sliver of sea shimmering in the moonlight. Out in the depth of the Caribbean Sea she was not expecting to see anything other than an inward contemplation of life. There was something insurmountably magical about sailing through the darkness, which allowed for a deep and meaningful connection with the universe.

The watch had so far been uneventful, with midnight more than three hours gone. She had mostly paced up and down the bridge of the HMS Atholl, her mind focused on the performance of the frigate. Finally, she had decided to let the eager but nervous new midshipman take the helm, and she had stepped outside, joyfully breathing in the cool night air.

The HMS Atholl was sailing southwards, having left Grand Cayman the previous evening. She was heading towards her patrol zone in the area north of Panama and Colombia, where she was relieving a US Coast Guard cutter, which was now heading back to Puerto Rico. They were currently some 160 nautical miles northeast of the San Andrés Islands, a Colombian archipelago east of Nicaragua. Captain Cranston, with his usual boundless optimism, had earlier attempted to deliver a motivational speech, describing the archipelago's descent from an English Puritan colony to being a pirate haven and then home to slave plantations, before becoming a beach paradise for tourists. His officers had dutifully nodded along, failing to see exactly what was meant to be motivational about that.

She turned around and saw a petty officer standing by the bridge door.

"Radar contact, ma'am," he said, giving a quick salute.

She followed him back onto the bridge, licking her lips and tasting the salty air as she went. It was her trick to stay awake. Inside, the still nervous midshipman was supervising the ship's controls. She let him be and continued further inside to the radar operator's station.

"Report."

The petty officer pointed to an erratic dot on the screen, which showed a map of the southern Caribbean along Panama and Colombia. The somewhat hyperactive dot was currently some 90 nautical miles to the south of the HMS Atholl.

"High-speed motor vessel, lieutenant. It's travelling, broadly, northbound, and at great speed, coming out from Colombia. However, its manoeuvering is bizarre, it's randomly zigzagging. It's suspicious."

"Agreed," the lieutenant said, her eyes tracking the dot on the screen as it made another sharp turn to starboard. "There are no other ships or aircraft around it? It's not being followed?"

"No, ma'am." He pointed to other dots on the screen. "There are several fishing boats out from Panama and Colombia, and a long line of container ships coming from the Canal, but they are far from the target."

"Is the skipper drunk?"

"Could be, ma'am," the petty officer said and chuckled. "Could have been drinking all evening before he set off."

"Right, track it. We'll head to intercept."

"Yes, ma'am."

Lieutenant Hayden walked back to the bridge and looked out at the vast darkness into which the ship was sailing. The magic of the emptiness was replaced with excitement. The behaviour of the motorboat was strange and in these waters it was worth investigating. The orders for their patrol was to search for smugglers coming out of Colombia and Panama, primarily carrying drugs north towards Mexico and the United States. How fortuitous it would be, she thought, if they could catch one on their very first day on station. She ordered a course change and an increase in speed, and soon the rugged old frigate was flying south across the calm Caribbean Sea.

**

Twelve hours earlier Manuel Lopez had driven his rusty old pickup-truck down a dirt track to an old wooden house, which was pleasantly situated by the Caribbean shoreline. It had been a long and arduous drive for Manuel and his two passengers. They had been on the road since early morning, having driven from the city of Medellín to the decrepit port town of Turbo.

Manuel had passed the time in silence, remembering all that had happened on that road over the course of his life; all his friends who had died in battles with guerrillas and paramilitary outfits, and everyone he himself had killed. He visited the vast graveyard housed in his memory every time he drove that road, each time as unpleasant as the one before. He had kept his wits about him, however, since the roads here were not permanently secured by the army, and there was every chance they would be attacked by someone. His passengers, two men much younger and athletic than him, had kept their hands on their guns, but thankfully the drive had been uneventful.

Once through Turbo, they had continued on a smaller dirt road out of town, which led through large banana fields. Eventually, he had turned onto a narrow side road, marked by a wooden post with a pineapple carving on it. Once through a narrow wooded area they had reached the compound, which was securely controlled by the cartel for which they worked. Here, they were far away from the potentially prying eyes of the military, who from time to time patrolled the country roads, or the brainless tourists who sometimes decided to go on an adventure in the areas around Turbo. Not all survived.

Manuel parked the car and slowly stepped out, his old bones protesting after the long drive. The two passengers seemed unaffected, however; they quickly jumped out and headed inside the house. Manuel instead stopped and gazed through the trees that lined the shore and out over the Caribbean. He could see a few fishing boats scattered about but none, thankfully, was anywhere close to the compound.

The afternoon was unbearably hot and Manuel was soaked in sweat. He shook his old t-shirt, trying to cool down, but it hardly helped. Sighing, he grabbed his bag from the back of the pickup and walked down towards the shore. Large trees overhanging the water obscured a wooden pier, against which was moored a sizeable motor yacht. A man with a machinegun stood on the pier and cheerfully greeted Manuel, who mechanically said hello before climbing onto the boat. There were already a few other men on board, stowing parcels of drugs into the hold, each securely wrapped in plastic to protect the valuable white substance inside from the elements.

"Manuel," one of the men said sombrely and embraced him. "I'm so sorry, I heard about…"

Manuel waved him off.

"Thank you, Victor," he said slowly and took a deep breath. His whole life flashed before him in an instant, and he knew he had to hold himself together to accomplish what he had set out to do. "I appreciate it," he added and forced a faint smile.

Victor nodded in understanding and released the embrace. He gestured around the cabin.

"You taking her across?"

"Yes, yes I am."

Manuel placed his bag on the driver's seat. He took the opportunity to quickly check the controls and he was happy that everything was in order. The two young men who had arrived with him now also stepped on board and headed downstairs to help stow the drugs.

"Mr Reyes says we have more than fifteen million American dollars down there," Victor said and grinned cheerfully. "You'll be careful, of course."

"Yes, of course," Manuel said.

Victor looked at him closely.

"Out there is a good place to think, it's you and the sea." Victor paused to let the message sink in, before looking down the staircase. He shook his head. "And those two idiots."

"Yes," Manuel said noncommittedly.

Victor patted him on the shoulder.

"How are your wife and daughter?"

"As you would expect," Manuel said.

"I understand."

They walked over to a table and sat down on the worn sofa. Manuel grabbed some charts and spread them out on the table.

"Right, I don't know if you were told, Mr Reyes has also heard that there is a patrol ship coming this way," Victor said and gestured vaguely at the charts. "Stay close to Panama, Costa Rica, Nicaragua, go between the mainland and San Andrés."

"I understand," Manuel said.

When the men had finished stowing the drugs they stepped ashore. Not long after, as the sun began to set and cooler winds came in from the sea, they started a fire, sat down around it, and ate heartily. Manuel shared stories of taking boats up to the United States during Pablo Escobar's days, and of the perils that had eventually made them reroute the smuggling routes to Mexico. The young men, who were sailing for the first time, listened in amazement, as Manuel, perhaps with some dramatic flair, spoke of untold riches in Miami, battling with Jamaican crime families, outrunning US Coast Guard ships, but their faces turned serious as he warned them of the viciousness of their new collaborators in the Mexican gangs. No trip was routine or without its risks.

Once darkness had fallen Manuel and the two others headed back onto the motorboat. Victor waved them off as Manuel slowly and quietly manoeuvred the boat away from the pier and out to sea. The first few hours passed quickly as they sped north. Soon the two men went below to sleep, leaving Manuel alone upstairs in the main cabin. It was a clear night and for a while he was mesmerised by the heavens above, the moon and the stars paving the way to eternity.

Manuel then focused his mind back to the present. Tragic events over the past weeks had forced him to reach a difficult decision. It was now time to put his plan into action. He turned the wheel hard to port, and soon thereafter hard to starboard, and for the next few hours he continued to zigzag northwards. He had heard at home in Medellín, as Victor had repeated, that a British frigate would be patrolling the area, and he desperately wanted to catch their attention.

**

A new day dawned. The HMS Atholl was racing south over the calm, blue sea, its decks now a hub of activity. Captain Cranston was sitting in his seat on the bridge, reviewing the information he had been provided. Two hours had passed since lieutenant Hayden had increased speed in response to the peculiar motorboat. It was now only a dozen nautical miles away, and the frigate was getting ready to intercept.

Captain Cranston had waited for dawn before starting the engagement process. The first step was to dispatch the Lynx helicopter to visually observe the motorboat and ideally get it to stop and surrender for boarding. The meteorological officer had reported good flying conditions. There were clear skies and only a light wind.

"Tell the helicopter to go," the captain ordered.

He walked out onto the bridge wing and looked aft along the ship. It was already a moderate temperature, and the captain allowed the gentle breeze to energise him. Soon he heard the unmistakable roar as the Lynx fired up its engines, and shortly afterwards the large helicopter hovered away from the deck. It quickly gained speed and was soon disappearing into the horizon.

The captain put his head through the bridge door.

"Can someone get lieutenant Hayden back to the bridge?"

"Yes, captain."

A seaman scurried away from the bridge.

"I'm sure she'll survive on two hours sleep," the captain said to no one in particular, stepping back to the railing.

After a while, lieutenant Astwood, the officer of the watch, appeared in the doorway and asked the captain to come back into the bridge. The Lynx had spotted the target and was reporting its sightings over the radio.

"Target is banking hard to port, it might be trying to avoid us," the Lynx observer reported over the radio. "Main hull approximately fifty or sixty feet, superstructure with a deck on its roof. It looks quite fancy."

"Not the most inconspicuous drug boat," lieutenant Astwood remarked.

"No, but I guess it will blend in when it reaches Miami or Cancún, or wherever it is going," the captain said.

The radio was silent for a few moments. Everyone waited patiently.

"Two men are coming out on deck," the Lynx observer continued. "Erm…yes, they are carrying automatic rifles! Go higher, go higher," the observer said to the pilot.

"Bingo," the captain said, keeping his eyes on the speakers. "Smugglers."

Suddenly they heard the unmistakable crackling of automatic gunfire coming through the radio.

"They're shooting, they're shooting," the Lynx observer said.

Lieutenant Astwood looked in shock at the captain.

"We're safe, we're safe," the Lynx operator said. "Maintaining a safe distance."

The captain shook his head in disbelief.

"These guys are serious. Sound the general alarm. Action stations, action stations."

As the alarm blared out across the ship, lieutenant

Hayden walked onto the bridge, her eyes red from an all too brief sleep.

"Good morning, lieutenant," the captain said. "You speak ten words in Spanish, so you'll lead the boarding party."

"Yes, sir," lieutenant Hayden said, pleased that knowing how to order a drink in Spanish qualified her for the task.

"The motorboat just fired at the helicopter, so special caution."

"Sir," lieutenant Hayden said, frowning. Shooting at the Lynx was a strange and desperate move. Despite the coming danger, she was pleased that her intuition about the motorboat had been correct. She turned around and headed off the bridge to prepare for the boarding. She rubbed her eyes to keep awake and out on deck took a few deep breaths of the rapidly warming morning air. She needed to be in top form for this.

It did not take long for the HMS Atholl to catch up with the motorboat. Thankfully it came to a stop once it realised that it could not outrun the warship. Lieutenant Hayden and a complement of heavily armed sailors boarded two Pacific 24 RIBs and set off. The HMS Atholl itself slowly moved in closer, the heavy machineguns along its deck trained on the target. The captain took position on the bridge wing, next to one of the machinegun crews, eyeing the motorboat through his binoculars. On the RIBs, the sailors had their automatic rifles trained on the target as well. The two men who had fired at the Lynx, still hovering above at a safe distance, had retreated inside. Lieutenant Hayden could not see any movement on board.

She gestured to the petty officer she had brought along, who actually spoke Spanish. It was a crucial skill to have when hunting Latin American drug smugglers.

"Crew of the motorboat, put down your weapons and come out on deck with your hands up," the petty officer shouted in Spanish through a megaphone. They waited for a few moments but nothing happened. "Come out on deck with your hands up!"

Suddenly, lieutenant Hayden saw movement inside the cabin.

**

Manuel had the whole night to think about what had happened, how his life had led up to it, and what the future would hold. He kept turning the boat every so often, ensuring it had an erratic pattern, but kept the general direction northwards. He would stay to the east of San Andrés, rather than going between the islands and the mainland as Victor had suggested. The first-timers down below would never know the difference.

Manuel sighed and pondered at the reason why he was trying to find the British frigate. It was undoubtedly the most difficult thing he had done in his life, at least voluntarily. After a lifetime of hard work, sometimes at the border between lawfulness and lawlessness, but mainly deep inside the criminal side, a line had now been crossed. Manuel had to take action.

Having grown up in the slums of Medellín, then one of the then most crime-ridden cities in the world, it had not surprised anyone that Manuel had become involved with the drug cartel. His parents, and his whole extended family for that matter, had been very poor. They had been running a little community store, selling anything and everything. It had been popular locally, but it had not provided much money; certainly not enough to feed and clothe Manuel and his siblings. Having grown up hungry, and often in tattered clothes, and without any real education or medicine, the first unsurprising event had been when, one day, Manuel's oldest brother had announced that he was leaving home to join the then newly formed FARC. Manuel had noticed how his parents had shown both concern and pride in his brother's decision. Concern because they knew how the government would respond to the FARC, but pride because not everyone in the impoverished community believed the organisation was criminal. Many saw it as fighting a righteous battle for the sake of the poor and downtrodden, those subjugated to nothingness in a society built by the rich for the rich.

His brother's decision had naturally had a deep influence on Manuel, but Manuel did not share his brother's innate sense of adventure. Manuel had not wanted to go to live and train in the Amazonian rainforest. Even small spiders annoyed him, and there was far worse than that in the Amazon. Manuel, however, had wanted to join the struggle, to do something to make a difference for his family. Gradually he had become involved in the now infamous Medellín Cartel. Manuel still carried fond memories of the first time he had met Pablo Escobar. Though he had mainly been working as a mechanic, servicing their vehicles and boats, he had shared a purpose with the Cartel: make some money and improve his community.

To Manuel's surprise, his parents had initially been outraged when he joined the Cartel (apparently it had been more offending to God than joining the FARC), but their indignation slowly lessened when Manuel started bringing home a weekly income that greatly surpassed what the store was generating. They had been able to buy new clothes, new furniture, and eventually even install a proper bathroom. Whilst his parents never fully accepted his involvement with the Cartel, when they died in the late 1980s, they had died happy and in a comfort they could barely have dreamt of in their youth.

Manuel had stayed in the rickety, wooden house after his parent's death. His younger sister had got a job as a housemaid to a wealthy family in Medellín and lived in a servant's bedroom. After their parent's death, she rarely returned to visit. After a few years, he learnt that his brother had been killed during a bomb raid by the Colombian Air Force. The dreams of equality, the end to poverty, and the redistribution of land and wealth, quickly evaporated. It was not going to happen.

All was not bad, however. One day, when driving a senior cartel member to a meeting in a different neighbourhood in Medellín, he had met a woman, whose name was Lucia. Manuel deeply admired her for her optimism, despite having grown up in a shackle made of corrugated steel, which flooded every time it rained. They had married and had a son, Jorge, and a daughter, Sara. It had been a time when he had felt complete and that, despite the dangers of his job, his life made sense.

The dismantling of the Cartel following Pablo Escobar's assassination led to a distressing time for Manuel. Whilst the senior members of the cartel and others who had been more directly involved in its violence were hunted down, Manuel took refuge in his home. However, the police raid he had dreaded day and night never came. Manuel soon realised that he was too unimportant for the authorities, and now that they were going after the Cali Cartel, they had bigger fish to fry.

Manuel had tried to build up a more law-abiding life. Gradually, however, through old friends and contacts, he began doing odd jobs for a newly emerging drug cartel, led by an elusive leader called the Hermit. It was one of thousands of criminal gangs that were emerging in the city as the new millennium dawned, but this one quickly gained power and importance, fuelled by the personal wealth and connections of its leader. Manuel did not know much about the Hermit. The leader sometimes stayed at a large estate south of Medellín, but apparently spent most of his time in Bogotá. It was said that he was ruthless to his enemies, but was incredibly generous to those who were loyal to him.

But very few seemed to know who he actually was. Indeed, even though everyone referred to the Hermit as a man, it was only a presumption. For all he knew, the Hermit could be anyone.

Manuel had started working as a mechanic for the cartel, servicing various vehicles and sometimes driving trucks back and forth to the cocaine production fields in the region near Panama. On occasion, as in the old days, he had also sailed the cartel's motorboat to Mexico. Recently, to Manuel's distress (he had begun to understand his parents' concerns), his son had become involved with the Hermit's cartel, mainly working as a supply driver. He was very grateful that he had managed to keep Lucia and Sara out of the organisation.

Everything had changed a few weeks ago. He remembered the phone call in excruciating detail. An old acquaintance, a colleague, if that is what they were, in the cartel had called and informed Manuel that his son had been killed.

It had thrown Manuel into a daze. For the first time in decades he returned to the church in which he had been married. It had looked much the same, but there was a new priest, who Manuel had a long conversation with. After that, Manuel had spent the days looking after his wife and daughter, but as the weeks went by he had mustered the strength and courage to ask around about the details of his son's shooting. The local police had not investigated, but that was to be expected. Manuel had learnt a bit from his old friends, who shared the information out of respect and time-honoured camaraderie.

A few days earlier Manuel had been lucky. He had been asked to cover for another cartel member who apparently was ill. Manuel's task was to drive a top lieutenant from the Hermit's country estate to an event in Medellín, and back later in the night. On the way back to the estate, he had overheard the lieutenant speaking on the phone. The lieutenant clearly had not known who Manuel was. The conversation had been a shock, and it was a minor miracle in itself that Manuel had managed to keep control of the car. He now knew what had happened to his son and why he had been killed. He had spent the whole night trying to figure out what to do, how to react, how to respond. When he was asked to run the motorboat up to Mexico again, with the very specific warning about the British frigate, he had decided on what to do.

**

Manuel's mind was rescued from its dark thoughts by one of the young men climbing up from below decks. Dawn was nearly upon them. Manuel sighed. He had not managed to find the frigate. He knew it was out there somewhere, but exactly where was a mystery. All he could hope for now was that they would be found during the day or the next night. With a simple greeting, he handed the controls to the young man, hoping that he had been properly instructed, and with a pervading sense of disappointment he headed down below to get some sleep.

His sleep was troubled and short. He awoke abruptly by loud banging. He sat up in his bunk, listening. A loud droning reverberated throughout the boat. He could feel the hull vibrating. The banging continued and he realised it was machinegun fire. He clambered out of bed as quickly as he could and raced up to the main cabin. Outside he saw the two young men standing on the foredeck, machineguns in their hands, looking up into the clear blue sky. He followed their line of sight and spotted a large helicopter hovering at some distance. The motorboat was still speeding forwards on its own, but there were no other ships in sight so Manuel let it be. He ran through the cabin, out the back and headed around to the foredeck.

"Stop, stop, stop," he yelled at the men, who seemed surprised at his command.

"It was right on top of us," one of them said, seemingly undisturbed at having shot at an unknown helicopter. "We had to get rid of it somehow." The man looked at his gun. "Is there a better way?"

"Now they're going to come after us with everything they have," Manuel said angrily. He watched the helicopter and tried to make out its markings. Even at this distance he could clearly read Royal Navy written on its body. "It's the British navy," he told the men, who began to look concerned.

Leaving the young men to worry on their own, he

turned around and headed back into the cabin. He closed his eyes and took a deep breath. He reminded himself that he had now, after all, accomplished what he had set out to do. He had been trying to grab the attention of the British frigate. What he had not accounted for were the trigger happy men he was sailing with. Now, it would be all that much harder to get the attention he needed from the frigate's officers. Would they listen to his story now? Would they be willing to help?

"What do we do now?"

The two men had come back inside the cabin and looked enquiringly at Manuel. They clearly assumed that he had some foolproof plan for saving them.

"That helicopter is not going to let us leave," Manuel said.

It was mostly true. Had he genuinely wanted to escape, it might have been possible to turn the motorboat around and outrun the frigate back to Colombian waters. They would be safe if they could make it to the remote dock they had set out from, but that would also entail slipping through Colombian naval patrols, who had no doubt been notified of their precise location by the British helicopter.

But, he did not want to escape, despite the risk that he would not be listened to.

"We're cornered," he said.

"Is there nothing we can do?"

The two men looked like they were starting to panic. To give them something to do, Manuel ordered them to start throwing the drugs overboard. He explained that they might be better off if there was no evidence of drugs on board when they were captured. The men nodded, but they all knew that after the shooting they would not be let off, drugs or no drugs. Manuel also knew that with the large quantity of drugs below there was no chance that they would have time to throw it all overboard before the frigate arrived. Still, it would keep the men occupied in the meantime.

Time seemed to move slowly. The two men ran up and

down throwing drugs into the sea. The helicopter nosied closer, observing their progress. The morning was heating up, and the men had to slow down, already drenched in sweat. During a water break, Manuel finally saw it. The long, grey frigate appeared on the horizon. His heartbeat sped up. Seeing the frigate made him appreciate the finality of his decision and the inherent dangers it posed, both to him as well as to his wife and daughter back in Medellín. He took a deep breath, and another, trying to stay focused and in control. He knew that he had to persevere. He had to respond to what had happened to his son.

The frigate was soon on top of them. Manuel turned the boat's engine off. They had barely thrown half of the drugs overboard. The three of them hunched down in the cabin as two RIBs were lowered from the frigate and raced across the water towards them. A voice filled the air, commanding them to come out on deck. Manuel hesitated, but he knew there was no alternative. As the command was repeated, he motioned the young men to follow him out on deck.

**

Cautiously, lieutenant Hayden climbed onto the motorboat. Her team of sailors quickly followed, pointing their automatic rifles at the three-man crew. They subdued the crew, tying their hands behind their backs. Lieutenant Hayden observed the process closely.

"We observed some strange manoeuvres this morning," she said, translated by the petty officer, after the men had been tied up and made to sit at the back of the motorboat. "We decided to make a routine inspection of your vessel, however, you proceeded to open fire on our helicopter."

She studied the crew. They looked tired and worn-out. One of them was much older, in his fifties if not sixties, and once she mentioned the shooting he had looked apologetic. The other two were much younger and their expressions seemed to waver between defiance and terror. She guessed that it was the young pair who had started shooting, probably without thinking or asking for the older man's permission.

"No one else on board, ma'am," a sailor said, stepping out from the cabin. "There is a lot of drugs below decks, ma'am. They didn't manage to throw everything overboard."

"That's great. Physical evidence." She turned to the crew and continued, addressing them now in a formulaic way. "You will be detained. You and the evidence will be returned to the Colombian authorities. They will decide whether to arrest and prosecute you." She turned back to the sailor. "We'll remove the crew to the Atholl whilst we secure the drugs and weapons."

The sailor took charge. The two younger men were lifted up first, escorted to the railings and helped into one of the RIBs. Whilst this was happening, the old man nudged his head, indicating that he wanted to speak to the lieutenant alone. Suspicious, but intrigued, she discreetly made a gesture and the petty officer walked the old man into the cabin, ready to translate the conversation.

"I manoeuvred deliberately," he said slowly.

Lieutenant Hayden furrowed her eyebrows.

"You wanted to be spotted?"

"Yes." The man looked down on the floor and took a deep breath. He seemed a bit unsure about how to continue. "I want to help you take down the cartel. I will tell you everything." He paused for a moment. "I hope in return that you can help my family."

Lieutenant Hayden frowned, a bit unsure of what to make of his proposition. She was a navy officer, after all, not a police officer. However, common sense told her it was unusual for a drug trafficker to turn on his superiors, and this intrigued her further.

"Why haven't you surrendered to the police in Colombia?"

The man snorted.

"I do not trust them. Besides, what I know will interest

you more than it will them." He paused again. Lieutenant Hayden raised her eyebrows, waiting impatiently. "An English prince will visit Colombia in a few weeks. My cartel is planning to assassinate him."

Chapter 2

The morning sun was finding its way past the edges of the drawn, black curtain, lighting up the bedroom. Tara Lawson started moving uneasily, stretching, and reached out for a person who was not there. She opened her eyes and looked around the room. Where was he? She sat up in the bed and listened. From another room she could hear a muffled voice talking animatedly. She smiled gently to herself. Her boyfriend was a busy man, even on a Sunday morning.

Tara got up and started stretching. She had not slept late since her lazy teenage years, followed by some lazy university years. The laziness had abruptly stopped when Tara one day had felt bound to do something with her life. She had decided to join the army. Knowing the inevitability of her being sent on an active tour in the war on terror or oil or liberty for the oppressed, her parents had not been too happy. Nonetheless, they had never seemed prouder than during her passing out parade as a newly commissioned second lieutenant.

Tara had spent a few years in a Military Intelligence unit, but her tour in Iraq was cut short after she got injured in an attack. Apart from a scar on her left leg, Tara had physically recovered, but had been discharged from the army. Still feeling a need to do something, Tara had joined SIS as a desk officer. She steadfastly refused to call it MI6, and at any rate, her family and friends all thought she worked at the Foreign Office. Yearning to get out into the world again, away from the grey dreariness of London and her counterproductively doting parents, as well as seeing an opportunity to brush up on her GCSE-level Spanish, Tara had managed to secure her current position at the embassy in Bogotá.

At the embassy she had the exalted title of Head of Security. In many embassies and consulates, this was a convenient title for the resident spy, but in countries such as Colombia there was also a practical and very real element to the job. British interests in Colombia had to be kept safe, especially from guerrillas, paramilitaries (though thankfully there were not many left of those), drug cartels, and run-of-the-mill crazies. Tara, receiving regular security and intelligence reports, was fully aware of how the guerrillas and cartels disliked the UK, given the UK government's continued political and military support of the Colombian government. The danger was very real, though thankfully the embassy building was not perceived as much of a target.

Having finished stretching, she rolled out her yoga mat and started with other exercises. Given her job, Tara needed to stay in shape. It was unlikely that she would ever have to go into the jungle to fight the FARC, but the risk could not be entirely discounted. The Ambassador liked taking trips on the weekends, in order to get out of the big city, which presented a headache-long list of security concerns. Thankfully, the Ambassador had stayed away from the Amazon.

A half-hour later she was done. Her boyfriend was still in the other room, talking animatedly, presumably on the phone. Tara knew to leave him alone, though she wondered what could possibly be so important early on a Sunday morning. She took a quick shower and then headed to the kitchen to prepare breakfast. With a glass of juice and proper English cereal, she headed out onto her balcony and settled down. From this position, she had a panoramic view over the city, which sprawled out across a wide plain, beneath the high peaks of the Andes. There was no view like it in London.

She started reading the daily news on her tablet. The past few months had consisted of only two headlines: the upcoming presidential election, with the big choices it entailed, and the fact that Colombia was going to the World Cup for the first time in sixteen years. More recently, the news had also been preoccupied with the Malaysian airplane that had somehow vanished over the

Indian Ocean.

Today there was another headline that caught her attention. An English Prince was visiting the city of Cartagena after Easter, something which had been well publicised. The newspaper reported that a firebrand presidential candidate, Senator Susana Reyes, had given a speech ferociously attacking the visit, saying the sitting President was kowtowing to Western imperialists and that this was a deep insult to hardworking Colombians. Tara chuckled to herself. It was not the first time she had heard from Senator Reyes, all the more so since she had announced she was seeking the presidency. Tara read on. The only other part of the article that caught her attention was a rebuttal from a charismatic congressman from Medellín, Fernando Escaso, who said he was eagerly awaiting the Prince's visit, calling it an opportunity to create stronger trade links with Europe. This would undoubtedly benefit Medellín, which had a rapidly growing business sector. The article finished by saying that neither the President nor the main Challenger had made any statement in response to Senator Reyes.

Having finished reading the news she opened the latest security and intelligence reports from London. They dealt with other matters that did not necessarily reach the newspapers. There was another update (saying there were no updates) on the investigation into the murder of a Home Office civil servant, James Westbury, who had been shot outside his London home a few weeks ago. The update included a reminder of the murder of a Spanish civil servant, gunned down alongside his fiancée in central Madrid just a week before Mr Westbury, and the need for all officials to take precautions. No need to remind me, Tara thought.

She then opened the Colombia-specific folder. There were no updates but simply reminders. The Prince was visiting the city of Cartagena in three weeks' time, on Easter Monday. His Highness would have a tour of the city followed by a banquet, which would be attended by the

President. This reminded Tara that Congressman Escaso, who sat on the Foreign Affairs Committee in Congress, had managed to invite himself to the banquet, no doubt to talk about organic farming with the Prince. Alongside promoting high-tech industries, the Congressman owned both coffee and banana plantations. The report continued by saying that the frigate HMS Atholl would officially visit Cartagena at the same time, with the mooted suggestion that the Prince and the President would tour it together.

The morning was quickly passing by. She was coming to the end of her reports when her boyfriend stepped out onto the balcony, smiling as he took in the views and the pleasant morning air. Unsurprisingly, his phone was in his hand.

"Good morning, my darling," he said and leaned in for a kiss. "I'm sorry for the phone calls, I hope I haven't disturbed you."

"Of course not," Tara said. She had met Julian about a year earlier when she had been out to dinner with a group of colleagues from the embassy. He was the owner of the restaurant, taller than most other men she had met in Colombia, and had a rugged handsomeness that suggested a life of adventure. "Is everything okay?"

Julian sighed and sat down. He shared some of his concerns, absentmindedly stroking Tara's naturally red hair, and she listened attentively. Julian had introduced her to his work early on in their relationship, and she had offered some insights from time to time. It was a welcomed distraction from her own work. Suddenly, her own phone started ringing.

"More problems for you," Julian said with a smile.

Tara quickly answered.

"Hiya Tara!"

It was the unmistakably chipper voice of Robert Hughes, the embassy's Deputy Head of Mission. He was a relatively young man for the position, which he had got following a meteoric rise in the diplomatic corps. Tara knew though that she was not the only one to find fault with his indefatigable sense of excitement.

"Good morning, Robert. What is it?"

"I need you to come down here right away."

Tara left a dismayed but supportive boyfriend and drove to the embassy. It was located in the northern parts of Bogotá, a nice and safe distance from the political targets in La Candelaria, the central area where the Congress and Presidential Palace were located. She lived conveniently close by, and had this been England, or many other countries, she would have walked, but security reasons suggested that driving might be better. Better safe than sorry was a winning motto.

She parked in the secure carpark and entered the embassy building. Robert, impeccably dressed as always, greeted her in the hallway.

"I've had a fascinating phone call from the Foreign Office," he said, beaming. He was clearly excited about it. "They want us to take a short trip."

"What is going on?"

"I'll explain on the way."

Robert handed over her official passport, which he must have retrieved from her office whilst waiting for her to arrive. They headed outside and into one of the embassy cars, chauffeured by someone they trusted.

"This morning, early, one of our warships in the Caribbean made a drug bust," Robert said as the car pulled out.

"The HMS Atholl?"

"Yes, that's the one. How did you…of course you knew. Well, they captured the crew. One of them," Robert started shuffling through some notes he pulled out of his briefcase, "a Manuel Lopez, from Medellín, had some interesting things to say. The captain of the Atholl says that Manuel has valuable information to provide, in return for safe haven in Britain." Robert built himself up so as to better reflect the gravity of the situation. "A matter of national security! We've been asked to go find out what he knows and how we can assist."

Tara looked at him quizzically.

"Go and find out? Where?"

Robert broke out his widest smile yet.

"We're going to the Atholl!"

"Oh, for fuck sake, Robert," she said and looked at him angrily. "That's all the way out in the Caribbean. Did you think I might have other things planned for a Sunday?"

Robert shook his head.

"Well, you know how it goes, Queen Elizabeth commands…"

"I bet she doesn't have to interview drug dealers though."

Robert huffed in exaggerated outrage.

"What were you doing, spending time with your boyfriend?"

"As it happens, yes," Tara said. "Not that it concerns you."

Robert had never met Tara's boyfriend, but he had heard some inevitable gossip in the diplomatic community. The boyfriend was some high-powered restauranteur and businessman, who was rumoured to have been involved in some shady deals with the wrong people.

"You can do better than him," he said. However, he had always trusted Tara, and she was the security chief, so he had to believe that she knew what she was doing.

"Aw, don't be jealous, Robert."

Tara sank back in the seat and sighed. Short notice trips were nothing new in this job, but it was not the Sunday she had been expecting. As the security chief, she sometimes got to meet with random people who came in off the street claiming to know something or just wanted something. It was usually attention. On the rare occasion, however, they actually had something useful to divulge. This had better be one of those occasions. If this Manuel Lopez, whoever he was, had convinced a Royal Navy captain and in turn the Foreign Office that he was useful, well, Tara guessed this was going to be worth her time.

**

"I really enjoy those little juice boxes Avianca gives you on the flight," Robert said cheerfully as they stepped off the plane in Cartagena. "It's comforting, reminds me of my youth, picnics in preschool and all that."

"I'm sure the airline will appreciate your feedback," Tara said testily.

It was early afternoon and Tara and Robert had arrived at Cartagena's airport. They left the arrivals hall and walked into a solid wall of heat. The blazing Caribbean sun was completely unlike the moderate climate in Bogotá, which was located two and a half kilometres up into the mountains.

"Good God," Robert muttered in agony.

They quickly found a taxi and jumped inside, eager to enjoy the air-conditioning. Robert psyched himself up to speak in Spanish.

"Naval Base Bolívar, please," he said slowly, accentuating every word, and ignored Tara's rolling eyes.

The driver nodded and set off. Robert turned to Tara, and his discomfort turned into gleeful anticipation.

"The Atholl's Lynx helicopter is waiting for us. Oh, I'm so excited!"

The thought of warships and military helicopters brought Tara's mind back to her days on duty in Iraq, but she quickly forced those memories away. That was a different life. She instead looked at the world passing by outside. The taxi navigated through a residential neighbourhood and eventually made it onto the main road which ran along the seafront. They sped past the impressive defensive walls of the Old City, and behind it, the cupolas and towers of the old colonial churches glistened in the sun. The modern neighbourhood of Bocagrande, built on a long and narrow peninsula, with its whitewashed high-rise residential buildings, lay ahead.

Nestled between the old and the new lay the naval base, its natural port protected by the peninsula. A medieval cannon, which looked like it had been raised from the sea, guarded the entrance to the base, which was overlooked by an old ship's radio mast and a fluttering Colombian flag. They paid the taxi driver and stepped out into the heat.

Robert explained to the sentries who they were, and after their ID cards and passports had been carefully checked, they were escorted onto the base by a young and sprightly Colombian navy lieutenant. A car was waiting for them, and they were quickly driven to a helicopter landing pad. A Royal Navy Lynx stood there, patiently waiting for their arrival.

"Thank you for your hospitality," Tara said to the lieutenant once they were walking up to the helicopter.

"We are always happy to assist," he said warmly, seemingly mesmerised by her flaming red hair. "And thank you for the two smugglers who are now in our custody."

Tara smiled as if she knew exactly what the lieutenant was talking about, but Robert had not mentioned anything about any drug smugglers being handed over to the Colombians. Surely those two would mention that a third crewman had stayed on the frigate? This would raise awkward questions with the Colombian authorities later on.

Hoping to avoid such questions at this point, she quickly hopped on board the Lynx. Its pilots were already in place and the engine fired up immediately. They soon rose above the base, Robert eagerly looking at the various warships with childlike enthusiasm, and then they set off, out over the open sea. Tara saw a large cruise ship inbound for port alongside numerous smaller pleasure crafts, but soon the Caribbean was empty, and the sea and sky merged in varying shades of blue.

An hour later the pilot indicated that they had reached the HMS Atholl. Tara and Robert tried to look ahead through the cockpit windows, and eventually they spotted the sleek, grey hull of the frigate. Soon thereafter the Lynx touched down on the landing deck and they quickly jumped out.

"Welcome aboard," a lieutenant said. She led them off the flight deck. "I'm Rebecca Hayden. I hope you had a good trip over?"

"Definitely," Robert said enthusiastically.

"I'll escort you to our prisoner".

"Thank you," Tara said.

They headed inside the ship. The lieutenant expertly navigated through the corridors. Robert was soon lost but Tara paid careful attention to every turn they made. It was an old habit. Soon they found themselves outside a closed door, guarded by two armed sailors. They saluted the lieutenant as she arrived.

"He has one hell of a story to tell," lieutenant Hayden said. "But it's very credible. And unsettling. Good luck."

**

Tara and Robert stepped into a room, which looked like it was ordinarily used for storage. A table and some chairs had been arranged in the middle. The only occupant was Manuel Lopez, sitting on the opposite side of the table.

Tara scrutinised him closely. He seemed to be somewhere in his fifties, though the toils of life had added several years. His clothes were old and torn. He seemed collected, a bit apprehensive perhaps, but not nervous or frightened. Tara got the feeling that he was here voluntarily, but that he had spent some time convincing himself of the need to come. She had seen the same on the tour with Military Intelligence in Iraq; someone who due to circumstances felt compelled to give information to the other side.

"Good afternoon, Manuel," Tara said in Spanish and sat down.

Manuel leant forward, but kept his eyes on the table. His face turned pensive. For the last time, he was convincing himself that talking was the right thing to do. He then looked up at Tara, and similarly took in her appearance, a tall, slender, attractive woman in her early thirties, with striking red hair which he had never seen before, well dressed, and a strong posture which suggested a life in uniform. Her face was expressionless, and her eyes bore into his. They did not seem to blink.

Manuel knew what he had to do. He took a deep breath.

"You must promise, please, not to hand me over to the Colombian authorities," he said.

Tara and Robert exchanged glances. It was a difficult promise to make since it depended on what he could tell them, but there was no point in worrying him about that. Tara nodded vaguely to get him to start talking.

"I have a job as a mechanic," Manuel began. "I used to have a proper mechanic's job, but I work now for a drug cartel in Medellín. I drive and service their cars and trucks, and sometimes I take the motorboat with their drugs, up to Mexico."

Tara gestured for him to pause. She asked Robert for a notepad, which he provided from his briefcase, and she started taking down some notes. Whilst some Colombian cartels were only pretending at greatness, others were not to be underestimated. Information was always valuable.

She then asked Manuel to continue. He explained that the cartel smuggled drugs on the motorboat, as well as through the commercial ports in both the Caribbean and the Pacific, shipping to the US as well as to Europe. Manuel said that his son, Jorge, had also become involved in the cartel. In particular, he had been transporting shipments of drugs from the cocoa fields to the commercial ports.

"Which cartel is this?" Tara asked.

"The Hermit," Manuel said.

Tara's eyebrows involuntarily shot up.

"You know them?" Robert asked in English.

"Yes...yes, I have a file on them." She turned to Manuel. "Do you know the leader?"

Manuel looked worried.

"I know of him," he said.

"His name?"

Manuel shook his face.

"He calls himself the Hermit."

Tara tapped her pen on the notepad.

"Do you know his name?"

Manuel paused and Tara bored her eyes into him. It was up to him to be cooperative, but she understood that it could be difficult for a cartel member to divulge such information about their organisation. In many ways, it was their family.

"I don't know his name. I have never met him. I have never communicated with him directly. It is always through the lieutenants."

"All right." Tara relented and decided to proceed on the basis that Manuel was telling the truth. Her instinct told her that he was. "Go on."

Manuel started to explain what had led him to seek out the frigate and surrender himself. A few weeks ago his son, Jorge, had been told about a serious plot that was being hatched by the cartel. Jorge was meant to play a very important role. He had suddenly got cold feet and explained that he wanted out. However, no one left the cartel. The boy had been shot and killed.

"I'm very sorry," Tara said. From her perspective though this was a commonplace event and she was getting anxious to find out why the British had anything to do with it.

Manuel had choked up at the memory of his son. He sat in silence for a few moments before he collected himself. He explained that he had started asking around his friends and associates for information about what had happened to Jorge. Finally, a few days ago, he had been asked to chauffeur a cartel lieutenant and he had overheard a conversation the lieutenant had had on his phone.

"I have learnt two important things," Manuel said. "I will share the details but I want your help first."

Robert had said that Manuel wanted sanctuary in Britain. It was certainly something that could be arranged, but only if he provided genuine information.

"Tell me briefly what it is, and I will consider it," Tara said.

Manuel paused and then nodded.

"The cartel is expanding into Europe and it has a contact in London."

Tara and Robert looked at each other, now paying close attention.

"And the second thing?"

"This is what is linked to my son. The cartel knows about the Prince's visit."

Tara frowned.

"So does all of Colombia, Manuel. It has been widely announced."

"I know. The cartel also knows that this warship will visit Cartagena with the Prince."

Tara shook her head.

"That's also been announced, Manuel."

"Yes, I understand that." He paused again. "The cartel is planning an assassination. They are going to attack the Prince, and I think also the warship."

Tara tapped her pen on the notepad again, studying Manuel. Now that he had started sharing his story and had time to breathe, he seemed far more relaxed. By all accounts he was telling the truth, but she had to question whether he had invented this story in order to claim asylum. It sounded a bit convoluted.

Robert, on the other hand, was taking deep breaths whilst his mind sorted out the seriousness of the situation. The diplomatic and political meltdown that would follow if the Prince was the subject of an assassination attempt, whether successful or not, in a foreign country was really too big to speak of.

"All right," Tara said. "If this is true we should be able to help you out. Do you know the name of this contact that the cartel has in London?"

"Yes."

"Do you know any details about the planned attack on

the Prince?"

"Yes."

Tara paused for a second.

"Tell us about what you want in return for sharing this information."

Manuel took a deep breath. This was his big ask, for him, his wife and daughter. Their ticket to a better life. This was his chance to leave his old life behind and create a physical distance between himself and the nightmarish memories that haunted him in his home. It was his chance to, alongside his family, go to a country where, at least in his mind, equality was a reality and not just a distant dream fought over in the jungle.

"It's not really about me, it is about my family. My wife, Lucia, and my daughter, Sara. I want them to be safe, which they won't be if the cartel knows I am sharing information."

"You want asylum for your family?" Robert asked.

Manuel nodded slowly.

"Okay."

Robert gave Tara a nudge and they stepped out into the corridor. They walked a few steps away from the guards to speak in private.

"His request is predictable enough," Tara said quietly.

"Yes," Robert said. He paused for a moment, reviewing the information. "What are the odds that he took a guess that the frigate will visit Colombia?"

"Our warships visit from time to time," Tara explained. "We have regular anti-drug patrols in the Caribbean and sometimes they put in to the naval base in Cartagena."

"So there is a chance this is just him taking a punt? Making up an extravagant story in order to claim asylum for him and his family?"

Tara nodded.

"Yes. I mean, an assassination attempt? That is a big claim!" Her mind went over what she had learnt about the man so far. "He's obviously poor and works as some low-level functionary in the cartel. No doubt expendable, in their eyes. I doubt he knows much about international politics. It's quite a big gamble for him if he just made this up."

"I agree," Robert said. "Well, there is no problem making those arrangements for him and his family if this checks out. I say we get some more details, see how much he really knows about things."

They headed back into the room. Manuel looked up, a mix of fear and expectation in his eyes. Robert took the lead, speaking in his slow but steady Spanish.

"Manuel, we want to help you, and your family. But we will need information. What is the name of this man in London?"

"I honestly don't know his name."

Robert rolled his eyes and Tara's heart sank. Maybe this was not as promising as they had thought.

"You just told us that you did."

Manuel gestured apologetically with his hands.

"When I learnt that the cartel had killed my son, I decided to get more information, for leverage. I got a camera from my brother-in-law. You know, a digital camera. A few days ago I went to the Hermit's estate…" Manuel paused, fear flickering in his eyes as he recalled the event. "No one pays any attention to me, just being the mechanic. The Hermit was out, none of the lieutenants were in the house, and I went into his office. I took photographs of a book. It has details of payments made, including to one person described as being in the British government."

Robert allowed himself to be cautiously optimistic. Tara was tapping her pen again.

"So there is photographic evidence of who the cartel is paying off?" Robert asked.

"Yes, sir."

"And…do you have it?"

Manuel shook his head.

"I left the camera with my wife and daughter, in Medellín."

Robert took a deep breath to quell his annoyance.

"I understand," Tara said.

The man's ploy was indeed understandable. This was his way of ensuring that his wife and daughter would be helped.

"So right now we only have your word for it. Is there anything you have heard about this British official?" Robert pressed.

"No, I just assume that this person has valuable information which he sells to the cartel."

Robert turned again to Tara and spoke softly in English.

"So, the allegation is that a British government official has leaked information to a Colombian drug cartel, perhaps details about the Prince's visit that they can use to assassinate him. Alarming, if true, but I'm sceptical. Isn't it more likely that the cartel got their information from some corrupt official in Cartagena? What possible motive would someone in London have to leak information to a Colombian cartel?"

Tara had to agree, racking her mind for an answer.

"A corrupt local official seems more plausible, I agree. But this seems credible, we have to entertain it." She paused again to think. "The source might have family connections or friends from Colombia. Or they might be on a moral crusade; I know there were, are, plenty of MPs unhappy we give military aid to Colombia. The Colombian army hardly has an unblemished record. I think it is plausible for some government official to have motive."

Robert sighed, realising that Tara was right.

"And we know the cartels are trying to expand into Europe," Tara continued after some further thinking. "This might just be a case of good old-fashioned bribery where money trumps political or national allegiance."

"Fine," Robert accepted. He turned to Manuel and again spoke in his slow and controlled Spanish. "Why does the cartel have a contact in London, in the British government?"

"They want to keep the smuggling routes open and safe to use," Manuel replied.

"How does the man help?"

"I don't know."

Robert sighed.

"What else does the cartel do in Europe?"

Manuel replied as a matter of fact.

"They are seeking contacts and power. They killed a government official in London and also one in Madrid, whose girlfriend also died."

Tara now got more curious about what Manuel had to offer. She had read about both murders in her intelligence reports, but there had been no suggestion of a Colombian link to them.

"Are you saying that those murders were committed by the Hermit cartel?"

"Yes," Manuel answered, realising that he had got their attention. He looked at them pleadingly. "Please, I will tell you all when I know my family will be safe. They have the camera with the evidence. I've said enough, you know I'm not lying. You know I have information."

Robert and Tara closely scrutinised Manuel in silence for a while.

"There are no signs of deception, no signs he is making this up, and he has some details. It is certainly credible," Robert said in English.

"I agree," Tara said. She looked at Manuel. "We believe you. We will help you."

"Thank you so very much," Manuel said happily. "Thank you."

Robert noticed that his heart had sped up and his palms were sweaty. The gravity of the situation was sinking in. For once he was not overseeing visa applications or helping hapless British tourists who had lost their passports in a nightclub. He was in the middle of deep political intrigue and he was proud of how he was handling the questioning.

"Please wait here for a little while," Robert concluded.

He stepped outside the room again, followed by Tara. "What's the plan?"

"I'll have to speak to SIS," Tara said, and Robert's eyes lit up. She returned a look clarifying that he would not be involved with that. She sighed and thought things through. "Well, I guess we need to arrange for someone to go to Medellín to get his family out, and we need to get him out of here somehow." She smiled. "Let's go to work."

Chapter 3

Tara was sitting in the captain's office aboard the HMS Atholl, writing an email on her secure tablet. Robert knocked on the door and stepped inside, carrying coffee from the ship's mess. He handed a mug to Tara and looked with excitement at the tablet.

"So that email goes to some faceless spook in London?" Robert asked.

Tara chuckled.

"Yes, it does Robert. But I know the face."

"Will London grant asylum?"

Tara placed the tablet on the captain's table.

"Yes, I spoke to…you know. It will all be approved." She chuckled again. "Trust me, they get very motivated when there's a credible threat to the Prince. What we have to arrange now is travel documents for Manuel and his family, since they don't have passports." She paused and adopted a more serious tone. "It is our view that we should wait to provide them with proper passports, rather than potentially raise problems with embassy-issued emergency travel documents. But I wonder if there is some way we can get that camera in advance."

"You don't trust the immigration officers here?"

Tara shook her head.

"I don't trust anyone. The cartel knows that Manuel is here, so I want a smooth exit for the family."

"It will take a while to sort out the passports for them. Is it safe for them to wait? Especially if the cartel actually does have a contact in the British government."

Tara sighed.

"Well exactly," she said. "They might not be any safer just by going to Britain. Or anywhere else, for that matter. Manuel was taking drugs up to Mexico, so they clearly have contacts there, and probably in the US as well. And they killed that civil servant in Madrid, and his fiancée. Frankly, they might be safest staying at their home, whilst we get the passports sorted."

"Yeah, I guess you're right." Robert drank some of his coffee, and nervously eyed the photo of the Queen, which was hanging on the wall. "It will be difficult to arrange the Prince's visit with this threat hanging over us. Especially if we can't trust our own people, if one of them really is an informant for the cartel."

"It's a nightmare. We need to get that camera."

Tara finished her email and sent it off. They then left the captain's office and made their way back to the holding room. Manuel was still sitting behind the table. He did not seem to have moved in the hour since Tara and Robert had left him, though someone had provided him with coffee and a sandwich. They sat down and Tara explained that they would help him out.

"Thank you," Manuel said. He took a deep breath and his face became one of contentment as he finally managed to relax. "You know, we all had such high hopes when we started this life of crime. But it's all fallen apart. Now they have killed my son, just because he didn't want to kill a foreign prince." He shook his head slowly and scoffed. "I had to leave that place. Most importantly, I have to save my wife and daughter from this."

Tara could not stop herself from feeling empathetic. She knew full well that sometimes joining a criminal organisation was the only way to ensure some form of income and structure to life. Any hope for a good life was, however, generally overtaken by a constant fear, both from within the organisation and also from the law. The Colombian authorities were not known for being lenient with drug traffickers.

"Do you speak any English?"

"No," Manuel said.

Tara smiled. He would survive somehow.

"Where can we find your wife and daughter? We need to give them their travel documents."

Tara could detect fear in his eyes every time his wife and daughter were mentioned.

"I told them to stay with my wife's brother. He works in a small shop in the centre of Medellín, and you can meet them there. Give me a time and a place, I can call him at the office phone, and he will ensure that the meeting goes well."

"We can't meet them at his home?"

Manuel shook his head.

"No, it's not a good neighbourhood. For an outsider." He leant in again. "I'm afraid the cartel might be watching them. But there is nothing suspicious about them going to my brother-in-law's shop."

"Okay," Tara said. "Do you have photographs of them?"

He handed over a crumpled old photograph showing a woman in her fifties and a younger woman, who was maybe twenty. They were sitting together on a sofa in a nondescript room.

"Thank you," Tara said. "Can your brother-in-law take your wife and daughter to the embassy in Bogotá?"

Manuel shook his head again.

"No, no, that is much too dangerous. If they go on a bus to leave Medellín, I'm sure someone will stop them." He lowered his head. "I put them in terrible danger, coming here. But I had to. It was the only way."

"Don't worry, Manuel," Tara said. "We'll arrange a time, meet them at your brother-in-law's shop, hand over passports and plane tickets, and escort them to the airport. Everything will be all right."

"Thank you," Manuel said again.

"It's going to take a while to put the documents together, Manuel."

Manuel nodded slowly, but Tara could see the fear in his eyes.

"Don't worry, Manuel, it will all be fine," she said, trying to sound supportive. "It might just take a few days."

They agreed that an embassy official would arrive with all the travel documents at the brother-in-law's shop at midday on Friday, and if the documents had not been sorted out in time, the official would return at the same time the following Friday. It was good to have a backup date agreed. Manuel nodded in agreement.

"The cartel will know that you have been detained, but that's normal, isn't it? Just make sure your family keeps a low profile. No one needs to know you are helping us."

"Widows and children often get a lot of financial support," Manuel said. He chuckled in disbelief. "We get better social security from the cartel than from the state. I'm worried, of course, because I'm here." He paused. "But I have to help you."

"We appreciate it. Look, we'll tell the Colombians that you resisted arrest and got injured, and we are keeping you on the ship for treatment. The cartel shouldn't suspect anything."

Manuel smiled.

"Thank you".

"When will you call your brother-in-law?"

"I can call him tomorrow when he is at work."

"Good. You have all the information to pass on." Tara smiled encouragingly. "We must head back to Bogotá now. I don't know how long you'll have to stay on board here, but we'll find a way of getting you to the UK. All right?"

"Thank you for your help," he said. He looked around the small storage room. "This is a nice ship. I can stay here a while."

**

William Cooth was waiting patiently. The secretary guarding the private office behind the heavy door was working on her computer, and intermittently shuffling through the piles of paper and lever arches that covered her desk. She occasionally shot a smile at Cooth, which he reciprocated out of instinct, not emotion. Suddenly, having no doubt received some inaudible notification, she stood up and invited Cooth to head through into the grand office.

"Mr William Cooth, sir," she announced to the man within.

Cooth stepped inside and gave her a final smile. She quickly stepped out and closed the door behind her.

"Good morning, Mr Foreign Secretary," Cooth said.

The Foreign Secretary came out from behind his desk, a big smile beaming across his face.

"William," he said in his broad Yorkshire accent, stretching out his hand. "How nice to see you."

Cooth shook his hand and they walked over to a large conference table that occupied one quadrant of the spacious office.

"So, you asked for an urgent meeting. What's going on in Latin America?"

Cooth reflected on his exalted title. It did say 'Latin America' on his office door. It was his job to oversee any and all intelligence operations in that part of the world, united as it was by history, culture, language, and a dangerous affinity for home-grown forms of communist, socialist and nationalist governments.

He recounted to the Foreign Secretary what had transpired during the previous day on board the HMS Atholl. The Foreign Secretary stroked his bald head, carefully absorbing the information as Cooth related it. He could not prevent a look of deep concern spreading across his face. There was a moment of silence after Cooth had finished.

"To me it sounds rather fantastical," the Foreign Secretary said eventually, having weighed up the possibilities. "A Colombian cartel going around executing civil servants, planning to assassinate His Highness and attack the frigate. Is this likely to be true?"

"I trust my people on the ground," Cooth replied diplomatically. "They spoke to Manuel Lopez at length yesterday. And fundamentally, sir, the allegations are plausible, if rather extravagant. The situation is this, as you know. The drug market is worth a considerable amount of money, billions of pounds annually, and many of the cartels are quite wealthy. Buying corrupt officials in that part of the world is nothing new. From their perspective, it surely makes sense to try to replicate that process in Europe, in order to facilitate the drug shipments."

"A fair point, I guess," the Foreign Secretary said.

"It is very plausible that the murder of James Westbury and the Spanish customs official, Carlos Muñoz I think his name was, and his fiancée, is the cartel sending a message. Cooperate, don't stand in our way. And I have to say, a successful attack on the Prince would be a triumph for the cartels, all of them, and it would not surprise me if one of the cartels is mad enough to go through with it. This is all a bit of a problem for us."

The Foreign Secretary listened attentively, still stroking his head. Yet another weight had fallen on his shoulders. This was one problem too many in a world full of trouble.

"Usually when we meet you entertain me with the latest craziness the Argentinians have come up with," the Foreign Secretary said. "Like putting maps of the Falklands on their public transport." He walked over and stood by the window, looking every bit the paragon of a pensive politician. "This, however, is the bad kind of crazy."

"I appreciate you must be very busy with Syria and Iraq, and that airplane they somehow can't find. But if the drug cartels are going to turn militant, and threaten to attack our warships and kill our people, we have to start paying attention. And here we have the promise of a camera with photographic evidence of those corrupt officials, including, allegedly, one of our own."

"Yes," the Foreign Secretary agreed. He sighed to himself and nodded. "I will liaise with the Home Secretary, but we'll arrange the documents. It's a bit of a gamble, but if this informant is the real deal, he can come in useful."

"Yes. Thank you, sir."

"Well, keep me informed," the Foreign Secretary said. "I hope you can get the camera and the evidence so you can deal with this cartel. We need to stop them in their tracks. I would hate to have to cancel the Prince's visit. It would be a diplomatic nightmare."

"We'll get the answers, sir."

**

"How dare you, sir! How dare you kidnap one of our citizens?"

The British Ambassador to Colombia was desperately trying not to laugh at the bizarre scene unfolding in front of him. The news had quickly broken that the HMS Atholl had captured a drug boat, but that only two of the three crew members had been returned to the Colombian authorities for prosecution. The firebrand Senator Reyes had taken this as a personal affront and had spent the whole week in front of the news cameras, saying this was proof of how the imperialist West mocked the Colombians. Ultimately, the Senator had demanded a meeting with the Ambassador, which despite the absence of cameras had quickly devolved into a tirade of abuse. Robert and Tara were both in the room, standing behind the Ambassador, also watching in disbelief.

"Madam Senator, if I may interject," the Ambassador said pleadingly, but to no avail.

"This gentleman must be returned to Colombia immediately! Only the Colombian authorities can prosecute him for any alleged crime, which may or may not have taken place. What do you have to say? Speak!"

"Madam Senator, as we have said in public already, Mr Lopez suffered a suspected heart attack when the boat was boarded. It was quicker to fly him to Grand Cayman for treatment. He has not been kidnapped."

This statement, a well-rehearsed cover that Tara had thought of on the way back from the Atholl, and which had been repeated throughout the week, did not go down well with the Senator.

"An English hospital? Don't you trust Colombian

doctors? Do you think Colombian doctors would set this man free?"

"I fully trust Colombian doctors, Madam Senator. It was just faster to get Mr Lopez to the Caymans. As you know, we have spoken to your Justice Department. Only the two men returned to Colombia resisted the arrest by shooting at our helicopter, and given Mr Lopez's heart condition the Justice Department has decided not to prosecute him. He is a free man! No one has been kidnapped."

The Senator huffed a bit further but eventually left, no doubt to launch another tirade to the first news crew she came across.

"How tiresome! What do the polls say?" the Ambassador asked.

"She'll be lucky to get ten percent of the vote," Robert said. "Hopefully we'll have fewer speeches after the election."

"We'll have to put up with her at the Prince's dinner reception first," Tara pointed out. "She insisted on attending. No doubt to report back on Imperialist decadence afterwards."

The Ambassador sighed heavily.

"Why is she coming?"

"Well, she is from Cartagena, sir, but more importantly, she's the senior senator on the Intelligence Committee in Congress," Tara said. "She knows how the Colombian intelligence community cooperates with us, and the Americans. Thankfully she also understands the need for secrecy, but she has a part in Anglo-Colombian relations."

"Good grief!" the Ambassador said. "Please tell me she is seated far away from the Prince."

"Yes, she is," Tara assured him. "Ultimately, I think she is padding for the reception."

"Excellent," the Ambassador said. "Right, what's next?"

"Congressman Escaso wishes to see you as well, sir," Robert said.

The Ambassador's whole body seemed to deflate.

"Oh, I'm not in the mood for another bollocking."

"No, sir, the Congressman is here to suck up," Robert said, trying to sound positive. "He wants a better seat at the Prince's reception."

"Why the hell is he coming?"

"He's the senior congressman on the Foreign Affairs committee, sir," Tara explained. "He has played a big role in organising the Prince's visit."

"Oh yes, right, of course. Why didn't I remember that? Send him in."

"And he likes organic farming, sir," Tara quickly added as Robert walked over to the door.

Robert let the Congressman in. He was in his early forties and looked sharp as a tack. His dark suit was clearly tailor made, and he exuded both wealth and confidence.

"I hope that Senator Reyes did not offend you," he said as he shook hands with the Ambassador.

"Not at all."

"I hear not even her own family is voting for her, so don't pay her any attention. I, on the other hand, want to say thank you, on behalf of the whole Colombian nation, for your heroic efforts in capturing these drug smugglers."

"How kind of you."

"They are the enemies of peace and progress. They must be stopped."

"Then we are on the same page," the Ambassador said.

"I also wish to say how excited we are for the Prince's visit after Easter. It is now just over two weeks away."

"And I want to say thank you for all your work in organising the visit," the Ambassador said, grateful that Tara had reminded him.

"Thank you. Mr Ambassador, I just wanted to rebuke anything that Senator Reyes had to say. There is so much that we can discuss in terms of cooperation. My city, Medellín, has so much to offer…"

"Mr Escaso, your support is welcomed, it is much

appreciated," the Ambassador said quickly, cutting him off. "And Medellín is wonderful, I've been there many times. Let me just say, we can only discuss foreign policy with your Foreign Minister, and I have no influence over any seating arrangements, if you know what I mean."

"Ah…"

"His Highness looks forward to visiting Cartagena. I am sure he has a few minutes to spare to talk about your organic farming, a matter which I know is close to his heart."

"You are too kind."

"And I look forward to our continued warm relationship."

"Thank you, Mr Ambassador. Erhm, I understand we are attending the same business conference tomorrow, in Cali."

"Oh, right?"

"I hope we can have a friendly talk. There is so much that we can achieve. Do you know, a British company is signing on to lead a major renovation of a hydroelectric power plant in Medellín?"

"I didn't know that."

"So much to discuss."

"I'm sure we can find a few minutes," the Ambassador said.

He quickly stood up, ending the conversation. The Congressman shook his hands again and smiled warmly as he walked out of the office.

"Well, one of them hates us and the other one loves us. Is that enough for today?"

"Yes, sir," Robert said.

Robert and Tara bid the Ambassador goodnight and retreated to Robert's office, which was next door. Neither of them looked particularly optimistic.

"Any news on the passports?" Robert asked.

"None," Tara said. "We'll be lucky if they arrive tonight. We so need them for tomorrow."

"And what are you going to do about the Ambassador's

trip?"

"I'm thinking," Tara said.

**

The next day was Friday. Tara stomped angrily into the embassy early in the morning, having spent the night coming up with a new plan. She was briefing a low-ranking embassy official who she had decided was going to fly to Medellín to meet with Manuel's family. She threw her bag into a corner, cursed a few times whilst banging on her desk, and finally threw herself into her chair. Bureaucracy had once again reared its ugly head.

The official picked for the task was called Molly Reed. Tara had gleaned from her file that she was just twenty-four and an alleged prodigy out of Oxford, who had joined the diplomatic service right out of university. It must have been a fun wakeup call when her first overseas posting turned out to be Bogotá.

It was still early when Molly walked into the room. Tara had only really interacted with her once before, a few months earlier on Molly's first day, when Tara had given her the mandatory security briefing. Be careful when you are out and about, do not walk down dark alleys, always carry a few banknotes to give to a robber (just in case, never fight back because they will have a weapon and they will kill you). Tara had done the briefing countless times for new staff; to her, it sounded trite but she had also noted a distinct lack of worldly common sense amongst some of her co-workers. Thankfully there had not been any major incidents. At least not yet.

Tara quickly sized up Molly. She was young and looked it. She had unfortunate blonde hair and looked more gringo than most. It was hardly ideal for a covert transaction. Instinctively Tara started having doubts about her plan. Well, her backup plan.

On Monday, Manuel had spoken to his brother-in-law from the frigate and had relayed all the information. Tara had also scanned the picture Manuel had given her and sent it through to London. However, the previous evening she had been informed that the passports had not been finished. Apparently, it had taken longer than expected to edit the picture into acceptable passport photos. Tara had yelled angrily on the phone about the government's lack of photoshopping skills, but that, of course, had not changed anything.

Her boss at SIS, William Cooth, had suggested that Tara go to Medellín anyway, tell Manuel's family the news, and assure them that the travel documents would arrive the following Friday. If possible, secure the camera, but Tara knew that the family would not go for that. It was also an opportunity to ensure that the family was safe, something which Tara had worried about every day.

However, to her further annoyance, the Ambassador had insisted on attending a business conference in Cali, which he had committed to months earlier. Tara, of course, had to accompany him to provide security. This had led to her last-minute backup plan, approved by Robert, to send Molly to Medellín. Robert felt that he was rather too important in standing to play the messenger, but did agree to take a few minutes out of his day to berate London for the delayed documents.

"You're on Avianca's 9.05 to Medellín," Tara told Molly. It was just six o'clock at the moment, so time was not of the essence. Tara scrutinised Molly's clothes. "No formal dress, Molly. Shorts, or a skirt, and a top. You will have to blend in a bit more. By which I mean, bluntly, look poorer, like someone who is not worth robbing."

Molly nodded. Tara continued by filling her in on what she had to do. Fly to Medellín. Take a taxi to the city centre. Tara suggested going to Berrío Park metro station, which was close to the address Manuel had provided. They looked closely at an online map of downtown Medellín, and Molly identified which streets to take from the metro station. Once at the address, ascertain the safety of Manuel's wife and daughter. Tara showed Molly the photograph, so she knew who to look for. Explain that the passports had not arrived yet.

"If they don't feel safe, buy them bus tickets and come with them back to Bogotá and take them here to the embassy," Tara said. "I know we're not a hotel, but Robert and I agree it's probably for the best. Get them out of harm's way. If they don't want to, remind them that the passports will be delivered same time next Friday. If so, you just fly back here, job's done."

"Sounds good," Molly said.

"This is not dangerous", Tara said reassuringly; after all these years she was an expert liar. "It is a simple meet, greet, exchange info, and leave."

"I understand," Molly said. She seemed calm and collected on the outside, but Tara could detect nervousness, perhaps even a hint of fear, in her eyes.

"Go home and change, and then head off. Please call me with regular updates." Tara rummaged around her desk and handed an envelope to Molly. "Here's your plane ticket to Medellín."

"Thank you," Molly said. She smiled weakly and left the office.

Tara put the Medellín matter out of her head. She found her briefing notes for the trip to Cali and started reading.

**

Later, Molly arrived at Bogotá's El Dorado airport, looking like most young tourists. She was wearing shorts, a flappy t-shirt which casually advertised something British, which Congressman Escaso would surely love, and a small handbag. She went through security and into the domestic terminal's waiting room. It was very busy, and not seeing a free seat, she sat down against the wall, waiting for her gate to be called.

Molly had joined the diplomatic service out of an interest in politics, world events, but also with a desire to have an adventure, to be able to visit, explore, and live in fascinating new countries. Today, however, leaning against a wall in the airport terminal, she was starting to question the need for adventure. Was it the case for everyone, she wondered, that the allure of adventure was overtaken by anxiety once it actually began? She was not sure what she would encounter in Medellín. Would she find the address? Would she find the family? Would she be safe? All the horror stories she had heard about Colombia, which had festered in the back of her mind, started creeping to the forefront.

Suddenly her gate was called. She passed through the ticket check, walked down a long, canopied walkway, went through an opening marked with her gate number, and found the airplane. In line with the other passengers, who seemed to be an eclectic mix of rich and less rich, families and businesspeople, and a few obvious tourists, she slowly climbed the steps and found her seat on the plane. Once airborne, she looked out the window, trying to take her mind off her task, and instead attempted to put every little landmark to memory. The flight attendants served little juice boxes, which provided some welcomed morning energy. Before she knew it, the plane touched down in Medellín.

Molly's anxiety was growing. It was not clear to her exactly what she was nervous about; she was not doing anything dangerous or difficult, and she spoke the language, more or less. Perhaps it was the uncertainty of the coming events, or perhaps it was some strange, undefinable premonition emanating from her subconscious.

Once off the plane, it only took a few minutes to get out of the terminal. She found a taxi that would take her into Medellín. The driver explained that it was a quick drive, in a literal sense: the distance was quite great but the taxi drove at breakneck speed. The roads were good but wound their way up and down the rolling countryside. The airport was located on one of the high plains of the Andes, some fifteen hundred metres above sea-level; the Andes grew higher in the south towards Bogotá and gradually lower in the north towards the Caribbean, but the Antioquia region in the middle consisted of spacious and sometimes surprisingly flat highlands.

The taxi driver was passionately engaged in a soliloquy on the upcoming World Cup and why Colombia was guaranteed to win. Molly had not been able to avoid the football fervour which had gripped the country over the past few months. She noticed a number of old-fashioned football cards scattered on the front passenger seat, displaying photos of the players on the national team. Molly had never fully engaged in the sport, though she had accompanied her father and various boyfriends to some games. She listened to the driver's detailed assessment in an effort to pass the time. It took her mind off her task.

"Are you a tourist?" the taxi driver asked as they reached a more built-up area, perhaps realising that the white, blonde, young woman in his back seat did not know or care about Colombian football.

"No, I have a job in Bogotá," Molly answered vaguely, as Tara had instructed during her induction many months ago.

"First time in Medellín?" the driver asked, content with the answer.

"Yes. I am excited to see it."

"You are going to love the view now."

The taxi was approaching open sky. It was a precipice. The road crossed the edge and dropped down into an enormous valley, a deep bowl in the rolling highlands. Filling almost the entire valley, from its bottom so far down it was barely visible and sprawling up the sides, and stretching as far as the eyes could see, was the city of Medellín. Molly could not help but be awestruck.

The traffic got heavier as they got to the bottom of the valley and soon they were proceeding at an urban crawl. Cars were honking their horns all around them. Eventually, they made it out onto the main motorway that ran through the valley, from north to south across the city. The centre, with its small collection of skyscrapers, came closer. To her left, Molly noticed the river and the tracks to the metro, which she had learnt was the pride of Medellín's infrastructure.

Finally, an hour or so since leaving the airport, they arrived at Berrío Park metro station. Molly thanked the driver for the interesting conversation and stepped out. She was standing on a busy street, lined by tall and occasionally glamourous-looking office buildings. Flying above her, following the street and almost entirely blocking out the sun, were the tracks of the metro. She noticed several staircases running up to the station itself. The street was crowded with people, some, clearly businesspeople, were hurrying around, and others were progressing more calmly on shopping trips. Turning around to get her bearings she noticed an endless variety of shops and entrances to various shopping malls. The city continued to impress her.

She walked to a corner, where the sun found its way through the interstice between the top of the building and the tracks. She reminded herself of the directions Tara had provided and looked around, orientating herself, and saw where she had to go. She had less than half an hour to the meeting, and not knowing exactly how far it was, she set off at a quick pace. She walked down the road, past a few streets, and at the third one she turned left.

**

William Cooth sat in his office, having returned from a meeting with C, the Foreign Secretary, and the Home Secretary, and thought about what had transpired. His Friday had started well. Many of his colleagues had been excited about the Grand National. The newspapers were still providing detailed coverage of the missing airplane. He was pleased that that was not his responsibility. Nor was Crimea, or the rest of Ukraine, or Syria, or the wider Middle East. Latin America, thankfully, was relatively peaceful, except for the demonstrations that were ongoing in Caracas, which Cooth monitored daily. Venezuela was going bankrupt, which was not an altogether surprising event in that part of the world. Even Friday afternoon had been relatively uneventful, other than the moping of colleagues who had lost money on the horses. He had even managed to leave the office before he got the game-changing phone call.

It had been Tara Lawson. There had been an unfortunate development. The young official sent to Medellín, Molly Reed, had not checked in and was not answering her phone. Tara had heard from contacts in the Colombian National Police of an incident involving a foreign tourist near to where the meeting was to take place. The police report had not been positive. In short, Molly Reed was gone. Unless further contact was made, she had to be presumed killed. The call had ended on that note.

Cooth had immediately raced back to the office and arranged to see the head of SIS, the chief, C. It had been a worried meeting. It was not the first time that a government official had disappeared overseas. Given the wider context, however, it was agreed to have a ministerial meeting on Saturday morning.

The Home Secretary had been distraught. She had not been happy to see a civil servant murdered in London, and the seriousness of the threat posed by the cartels was starting to sink in. She was already fighting organised crime, disorganised crime, and extremism in its many forms. This was just one new problem, but the immense pressure was starting to get too much. The Foreign Secretary had been mostly angry but partly reasonably reflective. To him, the world was falling apart at a rapidly increasing speed, and there was seemingly nothing that could be done to stop it.

C had taken the lead in the meeting.

"There are a number of immediate concerns," he had said. "The first is to identify the whereabouts of Molly Reed. The second question, which may well be answered by the first, is ascertaining whether this was a random street crime or whether this is connected to the Hermit cartel. Thirdly, we have to ascertain the whereabouts and involvement of the informant's family."

"We are trying to get all the information we can from the police," Cooth continued. "However, they did not make any real headway yesterday, and with the time difference it is still night time there now."

"What's your instinctive answer?" asked the Foreign Secretary.

"Random street crime," Cooth said immediately.

"Why the hell was that young girl out there alone?" the Home Secretary asked angrily. It was a question Cooth had asked himself as well.

"The embassy security team had to accompany the ambassador to Cali," he said, knowing that it did not really answer the question. "I guess from an operational standpoint, sometimes a single person attracts less attention. And there was no known threat associated with this visit."

"And what the hell was the Ambassador doing in Cali?" the Home Secretary fumed. "What has that place ever given the world?"

"Salsa dancing," the Foreign Secretary offered, but cowered in his seat from the icy glance the Home Secretary shot him.

"What we need, sir," C said slowly, addressing the Foreign Secretary, but casting nervous glances at the Home Secretary, "is instructions on how to proceed. A second date for handing over the passports has been prearranged and is this coming Friday. On the assumption that what transpired yesterday was a random attack, we are of course interested in proceeding in order to obtain the information on this camera. It is still the easiest way to ensure that this informant continues to cooperate willingly with us."

"Has he been told about this?" the Foreign Secretary asked.

"No, sir."

"Should he?"

"No, sir," C said. "For all he knows, his family is safe. It is best to keep it that way until we know anything for certain."

The Foreign Secretary nodded slowly. The Home Secretary did not seem to agree, but she did not say anything.

"Who would you send next Friday?" the Foreign Secretary asked.

"We would, of course, make an operative decision on that point, sir."

The Foreign Secretary looked lost in thought. He leaned back in his upholstered chair, sighing, and let his mind wander.

"On the assumption that this was not a random street crime, how did the cartel know when we would arrive to meet the informant's family?" he asked after a while.

"We have been investigating this, sir," C explained. "Given that the informant suggested that the cartel has a collaborator in our government, we have asked GCHQ to monitor past and present communications to see if there is a Colombian link. Nothing has come up, as of yet. Of course, we can't be sure there actually is a collaborator. The more likely situation is that the cartel has been monitoring the family. They must have stepped in when Ms Reed arrived."

"That raises the question of whether we should send someone else next Friday."

"Yes, sir. But the promise of this photographic evidence strongly suggests that we should send someone."

"Why can't we ask the Colombian authorities to go in and secure the place?" the Home Secretary asked.

Cooth and C glanced at each other nervously.

"This is photographic evidence of who the cartel is paying off, for support and information," Cooth said. "The problem is that we don't know who to trust."

The Foreign Secretary returned to his pensive mode.

"Given what has transpired," he said, "I guess a second

operative would be safer, because he or she would go in with their eyes open, expecting trouble. And, perhaps he would have some backup?"

"Yes, sir."

Back in his office, Cooth was thinking about next Friday's drop-off. He was twiddling his thumbs, waiting for this mind to magically come up with a solution. He went through his messages, of which there were many, but none from Colombia. He guessed that Tara would be catching up on sleep at this hour.

He thought through various scenarios. If this was a random street attack, where was Molly? Muggers usually did not hide bodies. They did sometimes kill, though. But there was no body. It pointed to something more planned. If the cartel knew that Molly was coming, what did that mean for the informant's family? In that case, does the cartel know about the second date? The Foreign Secretary was right, sending a second operative was risky, but in a way safer. Sending Tara was not the best option; as the security chief, the cartel might know her face. With her red hair, she also stood out more than most. This time she would have to attend as backup, though, in case things went wrong. Who could he send to Medellín? Who would not stand out? His mind raced through ideas. Suddenly he remembered something, and his mind formed a cunning plan. He smiled.

He knew who to send.

Chapter 4

Stuart Gleeman woke up with a start. His heart was beating fast and he felt lightheaded. Panicking at his dizziness, he shot out of bed and gradually got blood back to his head. He took a few deep breaths and his heart slowed down. He had had a nightmare, a vivid and unexplainable dream where vicious eagles, with glowing red eyes, had been chasing him through an inhospitable jungle. He rubbed his eyes and looked around the dark bedroom, checking for dangerous animals. His constitution was not made for what was to come. It was Tuesday morning. Tomorrow he was going to Colombia.

Satisfied that he was alone he laid back down in his bed. He tried to rationalise his nightmare, the details of which were thankfully fading from consciousness. He had always been more of a book adventurer. He had never been very outgoing in life and had gradually come to accept his introverted nature, even though certain parts of his life, such as university, had been a challenge for someone with such solitary desires. Books, films and TV were his windows to the world, and they had always been more than satisfactory.

Stuart had made it through university and had come out with a law degree. He had decided to pursue a career as a solicitor. It was perhaps more people-focused than he would have wanted, but he had successfully pushed through the psychological barriers and had managed to embrace his colleagues and clients.

Once he had overcome his struggle with people, the next task had been deciding what to specialise in. Commercial law had seemed too much of a rat race and did not suit his character. Criminal law had seemed too frightening, real estate too tedious, family law too maudlin and human rights too overexciting. Stuart had no interest in fighting for causes. By chance, he had come upon environmental law, in which he had found his calling.

The law firm he had joined five years earlier consisted of an eclectic bunch, from those Stuart called tree-huggers, fighting every lost cause, to the money-chasers, who worked with big businesses to defeat the tree-huggers. Stuart found himself at an equilibrium between the two: a non-money-chasing non-activist environmental lawyer. Somehow, caring neither for the environment nor money had made him very successful. In his melancholy moments, which were many, he marvelled at his special status of being the ultimate Anti-Don Quixote, a successful, uncommitted crusader.

Stuart looked at his clock. It was too early to get up, but after his nightmare, he was not sure he would get any more sleep. He looked over at the other side of the bed, but it was empty. It was not surprising, it usually was, but for the past few months, he had had a girlfriend. He had just gotten used to reaching for her as he woke up when she had left. Her leaving was still a sore subject.

Her name had been Kate. He had met her at one of his firm's parties, which were social evenings designed to attract more business. Kate had come as a friend of one of the tree-huggers, and she and Stuart had become engrossed in a long-lasting debate about the immorality of multinational companies exploiting the environment. Stuart had feigned a position on the matter just to keep the debate going. Their relationship had slowly blossomed from there, or so Stuart had thought. She had said from the start that she often had to go away for long periods of time with the environmental organisation that she worked for. A while ago she had gone to southern Argentina, somewhere in the remote Patagonia region, in order to map penguin migrations. The non-committed non-environmentalist in Stuart had sighed inwardly and smiled outwardly. However, soon after, she had ended their relationship with an email. She had met someone else out in the wilderness. Thankfully, his own imminent trip to Colombia had allowed him to focus his mind away from Kate.

He looked at his empty suitcase which stood by the

wardrobe. Stuart had never done much travelling. He had gone to France a couple of times with his parents, and once even ventured to Italy. The thought that he now had to fly to some unknown place across the Atlantic caused a great deal of distress. He sighed and reflected on his misfortune. Why him? Reflecting on life was one of Stuart's few passions. If you can't reflect on it, it didn't really happen, that was his motto.

The trip had not been Stuart's idea. It came about after one of his clients, a company dealing in hydroelectric engineering, had successfully put in a bid to overhaul a hydroelectric power plant near some city called Medellín. The project leader had invited Stuart to come along to the meeting in Medellín where the contract was to be signed. The client wanted to use Stuart's key asset: Stuart spoke a bit of Spanish. The client had for some reason assumed this meant Stuart had travelled widely in the Spanish-speaking world, and out of fear of losing the client, Stuart had not corrected him.

Stuart had regularly reflected on that moment. If only he had said that negotiating the contract with the Colombian lawyer on video-conferencing had been sufficient for him. Perhaps he could have pleaded with the client to let him stay in England? But no, he had said nothing and then his boss had felt that the trip was good for the firm. A chance to expand globally.

Every time the trip had crossed his mind he had felt trepidation. For the first time, he was venturing into the great unknown. Based on everything he had ever heard about Colombia, which did not amount to much, he was certain that he was going into some version of jungle hell. Of course, the fact that the Colombian lawyer, a fast-talking but altogether charming young lady, that he had dealt with had had video-conferencing facilities, a suit much more expensive than his, and represented a hydroelectric power plant should have told him he was not going anywhere near a dangerous and uninhabited jungle. Despite his enthusiasm for personal reflection, he had not ventured that far into logic.

Accepting that he would not get any more sleep, he shuffled himself into the living room and turned on the TV to watch the morning news. His heart nearly catapulted out of his body as he realised the news report was about Colombia. What were the odds?

"Senator and presidential candidate, Susanna Reyes, strongly criticised the impending visit to Colombia by the Prince and his wife, the Duchess. The senator called the visit a display of Western imperialism, which Colombians had fought hard to overthrow during their war of independence against Spain, and therefore was, as the senator put it, 'an insult to all Colombians'. Their Royal Highnesses are visiting the Colombian city of Cartagena in just under two weeks' time, on Easter Monday, where they will tour the city and attend a banquet hosted by the Colombian President."

This was the first time that Stuart had heard about this. He made a mental note of it, since it might be a useful conversation starter at the inevitable post-contract signing dinner.

"The British Foreign Secretary, speaking from his Yorkshire farm, stated that the Prince's visit was an important symbol of Anglo-Colombian relations, and provided a platform for bilateral discussions on important issues such as trade, combating organised crime, as well as being an opportunity to highlight the British government's firm support for the Colombians' desire to secure peace with the FARC rebels."

Stuart cringed. Drug smugglers in the jungle. That was about the sum of his knowledge of Colombia.

"The Colombian President, who is fighting a tough re-election campaign, similarly reiterated his support for the Prince's visit, saying it highlighted Colombia's high standing in the world, and an affirmation of the country's commitment to combatting drug crimes, as well as pursuing peace from its long-running civil war with several guerrilla groups, of which the FARC remains the most formidable. The main Challenger to the presidency also stated his support for the visit, saying that whatever domestic disagreements he had with the President, including on how to deal with the FARC, he saw the Prince's visit as an opportunity to strengthen Colombia's international reputation."

Stuart nodded to himself. He did not know anything about a civil war, but made a mental note to find out more. The armchair traveller had to become a real explorer. He was about to reflect on this further when the next headline made his head spin even faster.

"Australian and Malaysian authorities continue the search for the missing Malaysian airliner, expanding their search pattern over the south Indian Ocean. MH340 mysteriously vanished on what was meant to be a routine flight from Kuala Lumpur to Beijing, exactly one month ago on the 8th of March."

Stuart quickly turned the TV off. He did not need to know anything more about that. He was stressed enough as it was with his impending trans-Atlantic flight. Instead, he reflected on the day's tasks. He had to go to his office and collect the paperwork that he needed for the trip. Additionally, his boss had asked for yet another meeting to discuss something of great importance. They had already had so many meetings about the Medellín trip that Stuart was struggling to see what could possibly be left to discuss. Nonetheless, it would be nice to say goodbye.

Stuart also needed some time to mentally prepare himself for the least attractive part of the trip. At a certain point in the process, his client had insisted that they get a second legal opinion from a top barrister. There was nothing strange about that request, but Stuart's heart had sunk when he learnt that the barrister in question was the most obnoxious, if still highly effective, lawyer in London. Roderic Geoffrey Moylan-Roth.

Stuart shuddered. Even the name betrayed the insufferable poshness of the man. Stuart had suffered through the meetings that Roderic had attended, but last week Stuart had learnt that the barrister was also coming to Colombia. He did not know why, but maybe the client wanted a demonstration of legal force. There was no way that Roderic was going to charm the Colombians. If anything, Stuart could only hope that the Colombians would not cancel the deal once they encountered Roderic. It was a nightmare without compare. Well, demonic eagles might be worse, but at least those could be escaped by waking up.

Stuart somewhat apprehensively decided to read the morning news on his computer, waiting for a more sociable hour before he could head into the office, hoping the news on the computer was better than the TV news. It was not. He read a few articles on the continuing investigations into the murders of James Westbury and the Spanish civil servant and his fiancée in Madrid, but there were apparently no leads in either of the cases. Turning his laptop off, he spent the next hour reflecting on life and death, before deciding it was time to head off.

Despite the wait, it was barely seven in the morning as Stuart stepped out onto the street, with his old, battered, but trusty briefcase in his hand. It was a chilly morning. He shuddered and pulled his coat close around him. Perhaps, he thought to himself as he took the first few steps down the street, jungle hell was an improvement on this drab London weather, no matter how many drug dealers there were in there.

Stuart set off at a good pace, heading for the nearby Tube station. He lived on a quiet residential street, which seemed to be empty at the moment. He could hear the morning traffic in the distance, out on the main road.

He had only taken a few steps when he got the feeling that there was someone behind him. In London, this was not unusual, even on this street, but for some reason, Stuart felt that this was different. He tried to discretely look behind him, and sure enough, there was a man in a dark jacket some ten or fifteen steps behind. Instinctively, Stuart picked up the pace. He was not sure where the man had come from, as he had not seen anyone when he walked out the door.

Walking quickly, he reflected on the local violence. It had been a Tuesday morning when Stuart had first read about the murder of James Westbury. Most murders made headline news, and this one especially so since the victim was a civil servant. The information was that James Westbury had been gunned down just outside his flat in Marylebone, which had felt close enough to Stuart, even though it was a few neighbourhoods away. Speculation was rife given the earlier murder of the Spanish civil servant in Madrid. Stuart, however, had not read much beyond the headlines. It had been the day of his first meeting with the client who was taking him to Colombia and his mind had been elsewhere.

Stuart rounded the corner and entered the main street. There were quite a few people walking around, together with a steady flow of traffic. Without reacting Stuart sped past the homeless man asking for change, trying to reach the Tube station as quickly as he could. He looked back again, seeing the man in the dark jacket rounding the corner, still following him at an equal pace. Stuart tried to speed up again.

Suddenly, a well-dressed man in a suit came out of a local supermarket and stopped right in front of Stuart.

"Pardon me," the man in the suit said politely, but then took a quick step back, spreading out his arms, preventing Stuart from walking on.

"I don't have time," Stuart said mechanically.

He tried to push through, assuming that the man was representing some charity and was asking for money. His mind was still on the man with the dark jacket behind him.

"You are Stuart Gleeman, am I correct?"

Stuart stopped and stared at the man in the suit.

"Yes," he said hesitantly, unsure of what was going on.

The man in the suit gestured towards a car which was parked nearby.

"We would like to have a word with you, sir," the man

said, still with a soft, polite tone, suggesting an impeccable education. It disarmed Stuart for a second, but alarm set upon him again when the man with the dark jacket walked up.

"Who are you?" Stuart asked, with a noticeable hint of panic.

People kept hurrying past, heading for the Tube station clearly visible just down the street. They paid no attention to the three men.

"You may call me Henry," the man in the suit said. "You have nothing to worry about, sir. Our boss would like to have a word. We'll be sure to have you at your office in good time."

The man in the dark jacket opened the car's back door, and Henry, if that truly was his name, made a firm gesture for Stuart to get in. It was clear to Stuart that he had no alternative. Slowly, with a great sense of anxiety, he got into the car. It was an expensive car, and the back seat was very comfortable. It helped him to calm down somewhat. The man in the dark jacket jumped into the driver's seat whilst Henry sat down in the front passenger seat. They pulled out and joined the London traffic.

Stuart soon realised that they were heading towards Victoria. Ideas were rolling through his mind; he had been picked up by the police (but they had not shown any police IDs), the government wanted to hire him for legal advice and had forgotten all social skills (but then the government already had a lot of lawyers), he was being taken to the Colombian embassy, for something...

The car came to a stop. Henry opened Stuart's door and led him to a large office building. Stuart's fear evaporated. Now he was only confused. He was being led into the passport office.

**

I have never heard of the passport office kidnapping people, Stuart thought as he was being shown into a small room. Then again, the common view was that the Home Secretary was crazy, and maybe her sanity had finally snapped?

Henry indicated to Stuart to sit down, and then he left, carefully closing the door behind him. Stuart could not hear a lock turn, but he guessed that Henry and the other man were standing guard outside.

He found himself in an archetypally bland interview room. There was an old plastic table, the kind which must have looked rickety even in the shop, and some chairs. Stuart pulled one out and sat down, ensuring that he had a clear view of the door. The walls had various notices about passports and warnings about the perils of foreign travel: diseases, crimes, corrupt governments, and everything in between. They did nothing to calm Stuart. However, his legal mind was catching up and began formulating various protests about whatever was going on, and possible ways to sue whoever was behind it. He had long marvelled at how law school had corrupted his thinking: everything was now about ways to sue people he did not like.

It was quite a while before anything happened. It was still early in the morning, so there were no regular staff around. If Henry and the other man were standing guard, they were doing so in silence. Eventually, Stuart picked up voices coming from further down the corridor, muffled through the door. His body tensed up, ready and waiting for something, anything, to happen.

Finally, the door opened and a middle-aged man walked in. He was a bit taller than average and wore a dark suit. He had brown, wispy hair, and he seemed tired and worried, as if stressed by bad events and not having slept properly for a long time. Stuart did not detect anything immediately hostile in his appearance or demeanour. On the contrary, the man seemed pleased to meet Stuart. This put Stuart off the strong opening protest he had formulated in his mind.

"Thank you for coming in, Mr Gleeman," the man said whilst pulling up a chair, pretending to be oblivious to

Stuart's forced presence. Despite the stress marks he spoke slowly and calmly. He had an incongruous rucksack with him, which he placed on the chair next to his.

"What's the meaning of this?" Stuart demanded, but it did not come out as forceful as he had wanted it. He was still perplexed by the man's troubled appearance, not to mention the old rucksack which surely no self-respecting suit would carry. "Who are you?"

"William Cooth," the man answered calmly. He began looking through his rucksack and pulled out a bundle of papers. "Now, as a lawyer, you are of course familiar with the Official Secrets Act," Cooth continued in the same calm, monotonous tone.

Stuart did not know what to make of this. It was the most peculiar situation he had ever faced. At least he did know the Official Secrets Act, which anyone learning state secrets had to sign. The typical state secret was how much the government paid for paperclips, but Stuart had a sense that whatever secrets this man held, they were more dangerous than that.

"Yes," Stuart answered hesitantly.

Cooth pushed the document across the table and placed a pen on top of it.

"I would be obliged," Cooth said.

Stuart picked up the pen but his hand hovered above the document. He was sure that no good could come from this. He did not want to know secrets, not even the cost of paperclips. Cooth was sitting still, but his distress was clearly visible. Something was going on, and curiosity got the upper hand. Stuart signed the document.

"I am a friend, of sorts, of Roderic Geoffrey Moylan-Roth," Cooth said after collecting the documents and returning them to the rucksack. Stuart rolled his eyes, immediately regretting getting involved. "He does not know you are here, however, nor should he find out." Stuart nodded but felt confused. "That said, I have spoken, in brief, to your boss. He has volunteered your services."

"Really?" Stuart said, surprised. Services! He cursed

his own curiosity.

"You are free to say no, of course," Cooth continued, managing to very clearly convey that Stuart was not actually free to say no.

"Of course," Stuart said, cursing his curiosity again

"You are going to Colombia tomorrow," Cooth said.

It was an interesting revelation, the first piece of the puzzle, and Stuart's legal mind kicked into high gear. It wanted some answers.

"Mr Cooth, who do you work for?"

Cooth hesitated for a moment. Stuart kept silent, waiting for an answer.

"I signed the Act," he added after a while.

"The Foreign Office," Cooth said slowly.

Stuart again tried to keep silent to press Cooth into revealing more. However, Stuart realised he was dealing with a professional, albeit a distressed one.

"That doesn't tell me much," Stuart said, again having to break the silence.

"You are working with a hydroelectric power plant in Medellín," Cooth said, ignoring Stuart's remark.

"Yes, in a manner of speaking," Stuart said. His client was, after all, overhauling a power plant in Medellín. He looked questioningly at Cooth. "And what are you doing in Colombia?" he asked, trying to get some more information. There had to be a reason why he had been taken to this meeting, and that reason gave him a slight upper hand.

"We are delivering a package," Cooth said cryptically. "Or more precisely, you will be."

Stuart took a moment to think.

"Who do you work for?" he asked again. "Delivering packages is surely why we pay for an embassy?"

"It's a bit more time sensitive," Cooth said, which did not answer the question. Stuart did not let up.

"Who do you work for?"

Cooth sat in silence for a moment, wondering how to proceed. His hand moved over the rucksack and the signed

Official Secrets Act within.

"It is for SIS," he said after a while.

"What?"

Cooth hesitated again.

"MI6. The secret intelligence service."

Stuart took a deep breath. He had not seen that coming, though maybe he should have.

"And you're delivering a package?"

Cooth nodded. Stuart relaxed. If this was the truth, it seemed relatively straightforward. It would not require any James Bond antics.

"What kind of package?" Stuart asked after a moment of reflection. His legal mind was chiding him for relaxing: smuggling unknown packages through Colombian customs was probably a bad idea. It was time to ask some questions.

Cooth looked inside his rucksack and pulled out a small, padded envelope. He threw it on the table, perhaps to indicate that it was harmless. Stuart carefully picked it up. It was difficult to tell through the padding but it seemed to contain some documents, including something with a hard cover.

"What is it?"

Stuart thought that he could see Cooth smirking.

"Not quite the master spy yet," Cooth said. "You must work on that before you leave."

Stuart kept feeling the envelope. Suddenly it dawned on him. He was in the passport office, after all.

"Why me?" Stuart asked, still thinking this was something the local embassy could be dealing with. He had not managed to wrap his head around it. There had to be a good reason why he had been pulled in.

"You are going to Medellín," Cooth said, returning to the calm, matter-of-fact voice.

"Yes, but aren't there some, erm…"

"Spies?" Cooth suggested.

"Spies in Medellín who can do it?"

Cooth again hesitated for a second before answering.

Stuart changed his mind, thinking that Cooth was perhaps not a master spy either. Probably stuck at a desk job.

"When I learnt that you were visiting I felt that this was easier," Cooth said vaguely, an answer without meaning. Without probing too deeply, Stuart assumed that the answer meant budget cuts. The age of austerity probably affected spy agencies too.

"But I am not properly qualified," Stuart said.

"Such as lawyer's answer," Cooth said, the mischievous smirk returning. "Anyone can deliver a package."

He turned again to the old rucksack and pulled out another, small envelope. "The time and place for the delivery of the package are written in here. Present the package to the woman and her daughter. Escort them to a taxi, send them to the airport. There is money inside. They should have a camera on them, make sure they have it. There are plane tickets inside so they can fly to Bogotá. They will be met at the airport there."

"Sounds simple enough," Stuart said. "Give them the envelope, put them in a taxi."

"Make sure they have the camera," Cooth repeated.

"And I can promise them that someone is waiting at the airport?"

"Yes, in Bogotá," Cooth said.

Stuart frowned.

"And our mutual friend, Roderic Geoffrey Moylan-Roth, why didn't you ask him?"

Cooth scoffed.

"He's hardly subtle in appearance. If we need to infiltrate 18th century Vienna, he's our man."

Stuart nodded in agreement. Cooth had become visibly more relaxed now that Stuart had indicated he would do it. He had to press a final time: "And why can't the embassy deliver the package?"

"The package is in London, the delivery address is in Medellín, and the embassy is in Bogotá. You, Mr Gleeman, happen to be in the two important cities."

"That's not really an answer," Stuart protested.

"You are a legitimate visitor to Medellín," Cooth said.

He zipped the rucksack close, to indicate that the meeting was over.

"What does that mean?" Stuart asked, with more than a hint of serious concern. It had been a very cryptic answer. Why did it matter that he was a legitimate visitor? Who in Medellín had cause to be concerned whether he was a legitimate visitor? Why did this man not want to send an embassy employee, or one of his own operatives, into Medellín?

Cooth stood up and moved towards the door.

"The situation is this, Mr Gleeman. You speak Spanish, Moylan-Roth doesn't. You have cause to be in Medellín, the embassy staff doesn't. The embassy staff are overworked, and you are a gratuitous courier. There is nothing more to it than that. Her Majesty's Government thanks you for your service."

With that, Cooth left, leaving Stuart to wonder at exactly what had happened. Henry immediately stepped in and indicated that Stuart should follow him. Stuart placed the package and the letter in his briefcase and followed Henry out of the room. They returned to the car and Stuart was driven to his office, his head spinning.

Chapter 5

It was a crisp morning but Stuart did not feel cold. At this point, he was not really feeling anything. His mind was too preoccupied as he walked the short distance from the taxi into the terminal hall at Heathrow. He was only rolling a single bag to take as hand luggage, containing the padded envelope, which had been preying on his mind since he had received it almost twenty-four hours earlier.

It was very early in the morning and the gargantuan terminal hall was almost empty. The vastness made Stuart stop in his tracks. He had a feeling, a premonition, that something bad was about to happen. He shuddered and forced himself to keep walking towards the check-in desks, which seemed an impossible distance away.

Stuart eventually found a manned check-in desk, where he hoped to get the boarding passes for each of the three legs to Medellín. First up was a six am flight to Madrid. It had necessitated a very early start at home, which Stuart had planned to face with an early bedtime. However, sleep had eluded him. Most of the night had been spent turning over the day's events in his mind. For the first time, he had cursed his enthusiasm for personal reflection.

The man in the dark suit calling himself Henry had driven him to the firm. Stuart went to his desk and for once was pleased with the open plan layout. His colleagues' curious eyes stopped him from taking out the envelope. It remained, like a bad omen, inside his old briefcase. Like the infamous Ring, Stuart felt an overpowering call to examine it further, but forced himself to put up a mental block.

He had not spent long reviewing the legal documents he needed to bring with him before the partner, William Fomes, called Stuart into his office. Stuart walked in with some trepidation, bringing the briefcase with him.

"I wanted to have this meeting because of a cryptic phone call I got yesterday," Fomes said.

Stuart sat down in the chair in front of Fomes' large desk.

"It was someone from the Foreign Office," Fomes continued. "An acquaintance of that barrister you are working with, Mr Disastrously Posh. They said they would meet with you this morning."

Stuart nodded.

"Yes, we had a…meeting."

"Excellent," Fomes said. He looked inquiringly at Stuart, no doubt eager to learn what Stuart was getting up to. Stuart, mindful of the Official Secrets Act he had signed, just sat in silence. "I told the man that you would be more than happy to help out the Foreign Office," Fomes continued. He raised his eyebrows again, trying to coax some information out of Stuart, but Stuart remained silent. "I trust your judgement, and I hope that helping the government could be good for the firm in the long run."

"Absolutely," Stuart said, to say something. He was not going to reveal any information. "I am happy to help."

"Excellent, yes, Queen and Country and all that," Fomes said airily. Stuart did not reply. Did people still believe in that? "So, moving on, are you all set for the trip?" Fomes leaned forward across his desk with a serious face, to ask a serious question. "Are you mentally prepared for a week with Roderic Geoffrey Moylan-Roth?"

Stuart nodded slowly. He was as ready as he would ever be.

His boss had given him a Shakira album as a parting gift. Stuart had gone home early to pack. The packing was slow, as now, alone at home, Stuart had time to think. The event had been so surreal that Stuart would have thought he had dreamt it, that it had been a continuation of his demonic eagle nightmare, had it not been for the padded envelope lying on the bed next to his suitcase. The reality was slowly sinking in, and now Stuart had to plan out what he would do on Friday.

Stuart started thinking about what he would do, where he would go, what he would say, what could happen. The most difficult aspect was that on Friday at noon he would have to somehow get out of the official events that his clients would be bringing him to. He would have to plan the Friday carefully so he had an hour to spare. Early lunch, perhaps, but one that he ate alone.

Having packed, he spent some time watching old Top Gear episodes, simply to distract his mind. He then listened to Shakira's upbeat Latin tunes, but the jovial mood they put him in was short lived. For the rest of the evening, whilst finishing off the packing, Stuart's mind kept rerunning the events of the day and conjuring up dark ideas of things that might happen.

Stuart only managed a few hours of sleep before the alarm went off at three am. Feeling oddly alert, running on adrenaline no doubt, he got ready and went down to his pre-booked taxi. He had carefully looked up and down his street, but there were no shadowy men around this time. The taxi driver had helped him with the luggage, and they had set off for Heathrow.

"Where are you flying to?"

Stuart returned to the present. An elderly lady with a big smile was manning the check-in desk. She was looking up at Stuart.

"Far away," he said, rummaging around for his passport. "Madrid, Bogotá, Medellín".

"Oh, how exciting," the lady exclaimed, without in any way betraying whether or not she knew where those places were. Stuart had a sense she had said that many times before, but it felt genuine. "Doing anything fun?"

Stuart did not know how to reply. He had never liked chatty people, least of all in this situation. His mind was involuntarily drawn to the envelope.

"Business," he made himself say, which was sufficiently vague.

The lady handed over the boarding cards. Having thanked her and said goodbye, Stuart made his way towards the security checkpoint. It was almost empty, which unfortunately seemed to motivate the security officer.

"Laptops, tablets?"

Stuart put his tablet into the tray.

"Is this your bag?"

"Yes."

"You packed it yourself?"

"Yes."

Stuart had prepared himself for the next question. It had been late at night, as sleep was finally coming upon him, when his mind had realised that he might be asked this question. He had jolted back awake, pushing sleep back another hour.

"Have you been asked to carrying something for another person?"

Stuart smiled, almost involuntarily.

"No."

He spoke confidently, calling on all his legal training and experience. The officer looked at him for a second, but then pushed the bag and the tray with the tablet down the belt. He motioned for Stuart to walk through the scanner. Stuart felt relieved. He had made it. He unexpectedly felt excitement coursing through his body. He had successfully carried out his first James Bond antic. Then he sighed and wondered how many laws he had broken with that single lie.

There were a few more people inside the terminal, and shops were gradually opening up. The hubbub of daily life helped to calm Stuart down. He felt safe. That the envelope had passed through security suggested to Stuart that he was in fact only carrying a passport and nothing strange or illegal. The idea of dropping it off to a woman and her daughter suddenly felt like a minor task and something he could easily manage. Passing security seemed like a threshold, it has dissipated his concerns and fears and returned him to the lawyerly calm, focus and dedication that he normally had. Why ever had he worried?

He ordered tea at a shop close to his gate and sat down

at a table. It was not long before he spotted a gentleman in a three-piece white, linen suit effortlessly striding up to him.

"Mr Gleeman, how do you do."

Roderic Geoffrey Moylan-Roth helped himself to a seat, placing his leather briefcase on the floor next to him. His appearance was polished to the last detail; his suit fit perfectly, he was shaved to perfection, and not a strand of his brown hair was out of place. He smiled gently but did not convey any emotion beyond pure professionalism.

"Good morning," Stuart said.

Having anticipated the hot weather at the final destination, Stuart was only wearing a shirt, his sleeves unbuttoned, ready to be rolled up, but the barrister's polished appearance suddenly made him feel naked.

"Do you always fly in a three-piece suit?" Stuart asked.

"Of course," Roderic said sharply, with an air of superiority.

Stuart sighed to himself, not sure how to respond.

"Well, this is a splendidly good show," Roderic said, ignoring Stuart's obvious despair. "I'm rather excited, if I may say so."

"I worry a bit about the heat," Stuart said.

He had never been able to have a proper conversation with Roderic, and mostly just said things to pass the time. True to form, Roderic frowned almost imperceptibly, undoubtedly thinking that Stuart was uncultured, uneducated and all-around unimpressive.

"An acquaintance of mine phoned the other day, asking about you. Wanted to know if you were trustworthy to advise the government on something or other."

Stuart gulped. He had hoped to avoid this conversation.

"What did you tell him?" Stuart asked nervously.

"I said surely the government can find more experienced lawyers to get advice from."

"Of course you did."

Stuart remembered what Cooth had said when Stuart had asked him about Roderic. Roderic would only be good for infiltrating 18th century Vienna. Clearly, Roderic's putdown had been enough to convince Cooth that Stuart was good enough for the task.

"Yes," Roderic said. "You told me you didn't even go to a real university."

"It was very real, thank you, even if it wasn't Oxford," Stuart said. "Anyway, your friend did call."

Roderic frowned.

"Ah, well, government work," he said disparagingly, but Stuart thought he could detect a hint of jealousy. Surely Roderic knew that his friend worked in the Foreign Office and that the work was of some excitement. "Will you do it?"

Stuart realised that he had already said too much. He should have kept silent after the insult.

"We will speak when I come back," Stuart said, with a certain amount of truth, as he assumed he would indeed speak to Cooth once he returned from Medellín.

"Excellent," Roderic said. He looked around, thinking of something else to say. "So, last time we spoke you had some sort of girlfriend. Sad to leave her behind for this trip?"

Stuart felt a pain shoot through his body.

"We broke up very recently," he said.

"Ah, yes, well, I'm sure that she can find someone better," Roderic said, but seemed to give an uncharacteristically supportive smile.

"She did," Stuart said slowly. "She was on a research trip to Argentina, studying penguins."

"Well, there's your answer, Mr Gleeman. No way that you can compete against that Latin passion."

Stuart took a deep breath. The email that Kate had sent had included some details of the biologist she had met. He was not sure why he was revealing this to Roderic, but it felt cathartic to tell someone.

"Actually, she met a biologist from Germany."

"Good God man," Roderic spat out. "You lost your girlfriend to a German scientist? You bring shame to your country, sir!"

Stuart sighed.

"Your support means a lot to me," he said slowly.

He was spared from further insults by the announcement that the gate had opened for boarding for business class travellers. Roderic stood up and straightened his suit.

"Are you in business?" Stuart asked.

"Of course."

Stuart sighed again. Roderic looked at him inquisitively.

"I'm in economy," Stuart explained.

"Why?"

"The client didn't offer anything else."

Roderic gave him another strange look.

"You didn't insist on business class?"

"I didn't know I could."

Roderic sighed and picked up his briefcase.

"How very uncouth of you." He scoffed. "You don't insist on business class and you lose your girlfriend to a German scientist. Are you sure you're a real lawyer?"

With that, Roderic walked away, heading confidently towards the gate. Stuart shook his head but was pleased he had, more or less, survived his first encounter with Roderic. He guessed there would be many more to come.

Eventually, economy class boarded. Roderic did not look up from his seat as Stuart shuffled past him down the aisle inside the airplane. Stuart had a window seat at the far back and was pleased to discover that the seat next to him was going to be empty. Now that he was on board he realised that for a trip this long he really should have insisted on a business class ticket. Well, he thought as the plane left the gate, there was no point worrying about that now. It also spared him from having to travel next to Roderic.

His suitcase was in the overhead compartment, the envelope safely tucked away inside. Stuart kept glancing up from his seat, but thankfully it was a clear morning and once the plane was airborne the view from his window attracted all of his attention. He saw the English Channel, filled with ships, and the sky in which other planes were crisscrossing, heading for unknown destinations. He could clearly make out a jumbo-jet with Lufthansa markings, no doubt an incoming redeye from somewhere in the US. Stuart continued looking out as the plane flew across France, above the majestic Pyrenees and finally over the distinctive green-beige fields of northern Spain. On landing at Barajas, Stuart noticed a white cross carved into a nearby hillside, which made him chuckle gently. Spain is a different place.

As was typical, or so he thought despite his limited flying experience, the arrival gate was furthest out in the long terminal building. It was an annoyingly lengthy walk to the centre of the building, where Stuart realised he would have to go through another security checkpoint in order to transfer to the departure lounge. His mind immediately returned to the envelope and the worry returned. Roderic was nowhere to be seen, and Stuart guessed he must have already passed through. Given his fears about the envelope, he was quite pleased to be alone.

There was a bit of a queue to get past security, but although the security officers were in no way lax, Stuart quickly got through without any troubles. Again, passing through this threshold cheered Stuart up. As he headed down into the departure lounge he even smiled to himself and thought that he was slowly getting the hang of this spy thing.

Stuart spent the next few hours pacing around the departure lounge waiting to board the flight to Bogotá. Roderic was still nowhere to be seen, and Stuart guessed he was relaxing in some first class lounge somewhere. Shortly before boarding, he headed off towards the departure gate. He sighed when he realised it was furthest out the long terminal building, just opposite from where the London flight had parked. Typical.

The gate next to Bogotá was boarding for Caracas, and Stuart could not help but feel relieved that he was not going there. The city was full of violent protests, or so the news had told him, and apparently Venezuela had run out of loo rolls. Colombia suddenly felt like the epitome of civilisation. Up ahead he spotted Roderic, who again boarded as a business class passenger. Stuart sighed, annoyed that he was now facing a 10-hour flight in the cheap seats. It was going to be a long flight.

**

Between being annoyed at other passengers for blocking the aisle, Stuart marvelled at the size of the plane. The people furthest down the aisle seemed tiny. It was amazing that this palace could fly. He gave Roderic a nod, but again Roderic ignored him. Maybe he had been serious when he accused Stuart of not being a real lawyer.

Stuart finally spotted his row. A man dressed in black was sitting in the window seat. He seemed to be around Stuart's age, in his early thirties, of medium build, with a bronzed Mediterranean complexion and a quickly receding hairline. He was wearing black trousers, a black shirt, and a distinct white collar. Stuart was stunned. He would have to spend the next ten hours sitting next to a priest.

He sighed, but thought that between this and Roderic, the priest was the lesser of two evils. Indeed, anyone would surely be the lesser of two evils compared to Roderic. As he edged closer, Stuart saw that the priest was mumbling to himself, and he was clutching something tightly in his left hand.

"I'm afraid this is me," Stuart said in Spanish, pleased he would finally get the chance to practice it a bit.

The priest looked up and chuckled.

"You must be British."

Stuart wrinkled his forehead as he took his seat. He burrowed himself into the seat and reached for the seatbelt.

"You apologised for sitting down in your own seat. Only the British do that."

Stuart smiled involuntarily. That was fair enough. He saw that the priest was clutching a rosary. He should not have been surprised that a Spanish priest was Catholic.

"I'm sorry if I interrupted your prayers," Stuart said, realising too late he had apologised again. He was too British for his own good.

"God knows even if we don't speak," the priest explained, brushing off the apology in a theological manner.

"Praying for a safe journey?"

It was subtle, but the priest looked taken aback, as if he had missed the obvious. Stuart was pleased his legal mind was still switched on, despite what Roderic might think of him.

"No, yes, for strength." The priest unfurled the rosary. "Let's say one for a pleasant trip."

"Oh," Stuart said, wondering what a priest needed strength for. "No, I'm not religious, but you go ahead."

The priest chuckled again.

"I'm Antonio," he said, awkwardly angling around to reach out his right hand.

"I'm Stuart."

They shook hands as the flight crew announced that the boarding was completed. The plane rolled away from the gate, and they settled into their seats as the safety announcement was played. Thinking about the bizarre disappearance of the Malaysian airplane a month earlier, Stuart felt compelled to pay close attention. He got the sense that Antonio was doing the same.

Once the safety announcement was over, the screen in the seatback switched to a live feed from a camera placed on the plane's tailfin. Stuart saw the plane taxiing towards the runway. It was an exciting perspective to watch the take-off from. However, very quickly the screen froze, and then started jumping around as if the signal from the camera had failed.

"Are you sure your prayer worked?" Stuart asked, meaning it as a joke, but he realised too late that it sounded un-Britishly confrontational.

Antonio seemed undisturbed.

"Eh, Spanish planes," he remarked with a smile and a wave of his hands. That did nothing to alleviate Stuart's concerns. Antonio looked over at Stuart's concerned face and chuckled heartily. "Relax, my friend," he said, "all will be well."

The picture was still jumping around, perhaps an ominous sign of the uncertainties ahead, as the plane thundered down the Barajas runway and rose into the midday air. Safely up, Stuart relaxed and tried to make himself comfortable. He had a long flight ahead of him.

**

"Look," Antonio said.

Stuart had been half-engrossed watching some TV-shows on the in-flight entertainment and half-obsessing about his envelope. He now shook himself back into reality and removed his earphones.

"The beauty of the Caribbean," Antonio explained and pointed outside.

Stuart leaned over and looked out the window. He was greeted by a magnificent vista, reminiscent of pictures he had seen on the TV. He saw a clear blue sea, dotted with lush, green islands. Small ships and boats were crisscrossing between them. Below, close to one of the larger islands, was a cruise ship, which seemed sizable even from the plane's altitude.

"It's wonderful," Sturt said, reluctantly settling back into his seat. On his screen, he pulled up the in-flight map. It suggested that the large island below was St Lucia.

"Have you ever visited?"

"No," Stuart said. "I'm not much of a traveller. This is by far the furthest from Britain I have ever been."

"Your Spanish is very good," Antonio remarked.

Stuart nodded and reflected on an earlier part of his life.

"Yes, the family that lived next to mine when I was growing up were from Spain. I learnt a bit from playing with their children and such, when I was young. I've managed to keep it alive."

"That's excellent," Antonio said. "It helps to expand your horizons." He looked out the window again, taking in the scenery. "This will be the furthest I've travelled as well. It's very exciting. Are you travelling for work?"

"Yes, definitely," Stuart said, indicating that he would never venture this far away from home on his own accord. "You?"

Antonio was silent for a moment. Stuart noted a sadness in his eyes, a sadness and a resolve. Screw Roderic, his legal brain was still working.

"A pilgrimage, of sort," Antonio said sombrely.

"Is that a priest's holiday?" Stuart asked, trying to lighten the suddenly darkened mood. Antonio chuckled but did not respond. Stuart kicked himself for his insensitivity. British jokes never worked abroad.

"What's your business?" Antonio asked after a moment.

"I'm a lawyer," Stuart said. "I'm helping a client sign an agreement."

Antonio seemed to cheer up.

"A lawyer," he exclaimed. "So am I!"

Stuart was taken aback.

"Really?" he asked. He had never heard of a priest being a lawyer before.

"Yes, I was a lawyer in Madrid for a while," Antonio said, still sounding cheerful. "When I became a priest I thought I would be working in a church, you know, with the people, but they made me a lawyer in the bishop's office. So, my job didn't change much." He laughed again, shaking his head. "But I do enjoy it."

"What made you become a priest?" Stuart asked.

His inquisitorial, legal mind was definitely up and running. He looked at Antonio with a soft smile to soften the blow of the direct, personal question. The sadness returned to Antonio's face, and Stuart chided himself for probing into the personal. Being abroad was clearly impacting on his Britishness. Rule number one, never be personal.

"A woman," Antonio said quietly. Stuart barely heard him over the droning of the plane's engines. Through the window, in the distance, Stuart saw the seemingly endless coastline of South America. The New World, so called. Antonio, breaking out of his melancholy, looked out as well and managed to smile. "Venezuela," he said. They looked at the map. It seemed they would be flying in over Caracas.

"How does a woman turn you into a priest?"

Antonio chuckled again, through the pain visible in his eyes. Stuart again reprimanded himself. When would his inquisitive mind turn itself off?

Antonio closed his eyes and thought back to a fateful day. It had been many years earlier. He had just qualified as a lawyer and started his first job. An acquaintance from university had invited him to a get-together in a small tapas bar, somewhere near the Palace. He had just got a new job and wanted to celebrate. Antonio was not sure why he had been invited, because the two of them had never been close. He had had no real intention of going. During the day he decided that he would text the acquaintance to say that he was stuck in the office. This would be a small, white lie, which would keep everyone happy. However, as evening came something persuaded Antonio to go. At the time, he did not know what it was that had persuaded him, but he later came to believe most firmly that it had been the voice of an angel. Nothing else could explain the consequences of him going to that little, unknown bar.

Antonio greeted the acquaintance. They spoke briefly and Antonio congratulated him on his new job. It was well-deserved, Antonio had said, earnestly hoping that this really was the case. After this he sat at the bar, with a glass of wine, having a few conversations with new people. Having finished the glass he got up to leave. This was when she had walked in.

At once, Antonio saw no one but her. She was the light

of the room, and everyone and everything else disappeared entirely from view. She had the most radiant smile, glowing blue eyes, and long cascading blonde hair. Had he not heard her laugh as she greeted the acquaintance, Antonio might well have thought her to be an apparition. But no, she was real, a living goddess.

And the angel was still at work, because the acquaintance led her over to Antonio.

"This is my friend, Daniela," he said. Antonio took hold of her hand, smiling. "And this is my other friend, Antonio."

"Hello," Daniela said. This was all she had to say. Looking back now, many years later, he thought that it sounded too much like a fairy-tale, something unrealistic, but it had happened. He had fallen for her, completely, and unconditionally. It had been a whirlwind descent into true love at first sight. They had talked and laughed all night, a night which ended with a deep and meaningful kiss.

The angel, however, had not been an angel of love. Rather, it was an angel sent to show Antonio that his path in life was meant to be different from the one he was currently on. The day after, Antonio called Daniela. They talked on the phone for a while, but when Antonio asked her out she firmly said no. Despite the obvious connection, Antonio was not the man for her.

It had been earth-shattering. His whole life caved in on him. Happiness was extinguished, and life lost all meaning and purpose. Confusing and alarming his family and friends, he decided to leave his job, which he had spent so many years at law school to obtain. He had spent weeks at home in quiet contemplation. The angel slowly guided his mind to his grandmother and the joys he had shared with her, which had regularly involved visiting her local church. Having walked through his personal wilderness, he began to be drawn towards a new goal in life, with a different kind of love and happiness. So it came to pass that he, Antonio Posada Velasquez, entered the seminary to be ordained a priest.

"It was love at first sight," Antonio said to Stuart. He had to try to explain it somehow, which was difficult because the night did not always make sense to him. He had tried to understand it religiously, which some days had him convinced that it had been God's plan, and some days had him in complete doubt. One instructor at the seminary had suggested that life was not always meant to be understood, as long as it was lived to the full in pursuit of what was good. Antonio had struggled to accept the absence of understanding, but with time he had immersed himself into living for each day. "Well, love at first sight for me at least. I asked her out, but she said no. I was..." Antonio sighed. "I was lost."

Stuart did not doubt the priest's sincerity. To him though it was an odd story. One woman, one meeting? Antonio seemed to read his mind.

"It was an intense encounter," Antonio said. "I remember her eyes, her smile." He chuckled again. "It was a feeling I have only experienced that one time. The rejection made me lose my sense of self. I left the law firm and...well, here I am."

"I'm very sorry," Stuart said.

He was not sure how to respond. It seemed, to him, a tragic story, of someone giving up their life for someone they did not even know. How much can one learn about another person in a single meeting? He thought back to his first meeting with Kate. Yes, it had affected him. Yes, he had felt an attraction. But if she had said no to another date it would not have affected Stuart much, if at all. He would have carried on with his life. He looked at Antonio, who still had that sadness in his eyes. There was something unsettling about his account. What if his lightning bolt experience had been that elusive true love? Stuart clearly had not experienced it with Kate. Would he ever, he thought?

"Don't be sorry," Antonio said. "I am happy."

Stuart smiled sympathetically.

"So, becoming a priest, you got over the heartbreak?"

"I did, yes," Antonio said.

"And, does Daniela know you became a priest?"

"Yes," Antonio answered slowly. "Yes…she knows."

Their conversation paused. Antonio looked out the window again, lost in thought. The plane, its engines still droning in a constant rhythm, was passing over Caracas. Beyond it Stuart saw a great, flat plain, stretching to the horizon. The Venezuelan interior. Stuart leant back and closed his eyes. His thoughts about Kate and true love had affected him, and he suddenly felt tired. It had already been a long day since he had woken up, worried about the envelope and airport security, and his morning skirmish with Roderic.

He must have dozed off, because suddenly he woke up to an alarming sight.

"What's that?" he exclaimed groggily.

Antonio was startled. He too looked out of the window but did not see anything worth being concerned about.

"What do you mean?"

Stuart did not know what to make of it. Outside the window, he saw a massive snow-capped mountain.

"Mountains," he said with a hint of panic.

Antonio looked confused.

"Yes, the Andes. Magnificent, are they not?"

"But Colombia…where is the rainforest?"

It took a second for Antonio to figure out why Stuart had panicked, and then he started laughing.

"We are a long way from the Amazon, my friend," he said heartily. "Is this all you know about Colombia?"

"I thought…," Stuart started before trailing off. He realised he did not know anything. Kate, in one of their last conversations, had told him to read a bit about Colombia, but Stuart had been so worked up about the inevitable jungle hell that he had refused to. That had possibly been a mistake.

Antonio was still laughing.

"Tell me, did you just pack for a tropical rainforest? If you're staying in Bogotá you'll find yourself rather cold."

"No," Stuart said. "I am going to Medellín. I just packed for warmth."

Antonio again lit up.

"Ah, Medellín, so am I. A coincidence. It's up in the mountains, you know. But it's warm, I'm sure your packing will be fine."

Antonio chuckled again. Stuart kept looking out the window, amazed at his own stupidity and naivety.

A short while later the plane landed in Bogotá. Stuart had made it across the Atlantic. Disembarking, followed by the still laughing priest, he should have felt proud of his achievement, but his mind again wandered to the infernal envelope.

Chapter 6

They caught up with Roderic whilst heading for the immigration checkpoint. He gave Stuart a bemused look as Stuart introduced him to Antonio.

"Ah, padre," Roderic said in in his posh English. "Muchos pleasure to meet you and all that."

Stuart stared at him in disbelief but Antonio took it in his stride.

"The pleasure is mine," Antonio said in English, with only the faintest trace of an accent.

"Enjoyed your flight back with the masses?"

"Can't complain," Stuart said.

They got through immigration in an awkward silence, as Antonio tried to make some polite remarks. Stuart more successfully avoided speaking to Roderic, who bid them farewell in the baggage hall.

"I'm spending a couple of nights in Bogotá," he said. "I have some other business to attend. I will see you on Friday, Mr Gleeman. Padre."

With that, he walked off. Stuart smiled, relieved that he had been unexpectedly released from spending the next few days with his obnoxious colleague. Instead, he followed Antonio as they set off to find their domestic connection to Medellín. Eventually, they found a shuttle bus that took them to the domestic departure hall. Out on the tarmac, heading for the bus, he took a good look around and saw the high-rise buildings of central Bogotá in the far distance, overshadowed by the tall mountain peaks. He shivered slightly. It was a lot colder than he had expected. Once at the departure hall, they found some seats and settled in, since they had some time before the flight.

"So, what's this pilgrimage you are going on?"

Antonio chuckled.

"No, it's not really a pilgrimage," he said. "I am spending Easter with an old friend of mine, who's a priest in Medellín. He has a church in the city."

"That sounds nice," Stuart said.

"It will be," Antonio said. "I'll get to do real parish work, for a change. Finally out of the bishop's office."

Stuart's smiled supportively before looking around to take in his surroundings. Darkness was slowly falling outside the big windows and the mountains were disappearing from view. A plane was boarding with passengers clearly dressed for a cold climate followed by another plane boarded by passengers dressed for the beach. Stuart kicked himself again for not reading up on the country. This was going to be a difficult trip.

**

The flight to Medellín was mercifully short. Stuart dozed off again, and on landing, a cheerful Antonio told him he had missed out on a complimentary juice box. Fruit is healthy, Antonio said as they stepped off the plane. It was a quick affair for Antonio to collect his checked luggage and then they left the terminal building. It was a pleasantly chilly evening and Stuart almost felt at home. They found a taxi and agreed to share it into the city.

"I have a hotel somewhere downtown," Stuart said, pulling some paperwork from his bag.

"Are you staying in El Poblado? Most of the hotels are there."

"Erhm, yes, thereabouts," Stuart said looking at the map on the hotel booking printout. He turned to Antonio. "How do you know this, you said it was your first time?"

"I read up," Antonio said calmly.

The taxi set off, speeding out of the airport. It was completely dark outside and Stuart could not see much beyond what the street lights illuminated. They were clearly out on a country road, racing through a rolling landscape. It was quiet, with hardly any traffic, but Stuart felt very uncomfortable at the speed the car was driving at.

"Ah, Spain and England are good teams," the driver

exclaimed after they had explained where they were from. Unsurprisingly, he had caught on to their accents.

"Spain certainly is," Stuart said self-effacingly. Everyone in England knew the England team was not very good, though of course no one would ever admit that. "I overheard some people at the airport, is Colombia playing this year?"

"We most certainly are," the driver said enthusiastically, turning around to reveal a massive grin. Stuart looked in horror at the road ahead, which was thankfully empty. "First time in sixteen years! We are all very excited. When Colombia is playing my boss has given everyone the afternoon off. He said that no one will want a taxi during the game."

"Your boss is probably right," Stuart said non-committedly.

He was not sure if he had ever watched a complete football match in his life. All he had seen were the ups and downs of newspaper headlines whenever the England team went to a competition.

"First we must survive the presidential elections," the driver said after he had paid his way through a tollbooth and carefully added the sum to the meter. "It's a big mess."

"I understand it is quite a turning point," Antonio said. Stuart had a look of confusion on his face. "It is about how to deal with the guerrillas," Antonio explained. "The incumbent wants to continue his peace negotiations and the opponent wants to return to a hard line military strategy to wipe them out."

"Peace negotiations seem like a good option," Stuart said.

"It's very important," the driver said but commented no further.

"I agree," Antonio said. "As a priest. But peace negotiations have been tried many times before and I understand it has always been more charade than anything serious."

The driver did not say anything. Antonio gave Stuart a telling smile: leave the subject alone. Stuart put it out of his mind, it was yet another world problem that did not affect him. He looked out the front window and realised that the road was heading towards complete darkness. It was a ridge.

"This is Medellín," the driver said as they crossed over.

Stuart saw before him a sea of white light. It was a massive city cradled inside a deep valley. Once the initial shock wore off he was impressed. This was as far from jungle hell as he could imagine.

Stuart's ears popped as they drove down to the bottom of the valley, and he had to yawn to clear them up. They finally joined a large motorway that was heading towards what appeared to be the centre of the city, consisting of a handful of lit-up skyscrapers. The taxi soon turned off and navigated some smaller roads. Stuart eventually found himself outside his hotel. It was a perfectly nice, modern high-rise building. It relaxed him a great deal. He was going to survive this trip. Antonio scribbled something on a note and handed it to Stuart.

"I am staying at the Church of Santa Teresa. Here is the address and phone number. If you are free one day or evening, give me a call. Best of luck with your work."

"Thank you. I definitely will," Stuart said. He knew English people never meant it when they gave such an invitation, but he had a guess the Spanish were different. He stepped out, paid the driver for the journey so far, and watched the taxi drive off.

Chapter 7

Incense was slowly filling the spacious, redbrick cathedral. It was burning into Antonio's eyes. He rubbed them hard, trying, hoping, to suppress his headache. His mind was somewhat soothed by the organ, gently playing a piece he was not familiar with. He looked around and noticed that the cathedral was packed, with people even crowding in the aisles. The entrance procession had begun and a long line of priests in white copes and colourfully embroidered stoles snaked their way through the multitude towards the altar.

Antonio had woken up early, having had his sleep plagued by the same nightmare he had had for the past few weeks. His lassitude was not helped by the jetlag or the energy he had expended yesterday keeping a polite and civil disposition with the Englishman. Despite his tiredness, he had not been able to go back to sleep. He had laid restless in bed for a while, but eventually gave up and got up. He had diligently, if mechanically, said his morning prayers before tiptoeing down to the friary kitchen.

The parish church of Santa Teresa Ávila was located just north of the city centre. It was managed by a community of Carmelite friars, who lived in an adjacent house, connected to the church through an inner courtyard. The parish priest and leader of the community was Father Juan, who Antonio had met during his seminary studies in Spain. Juan had visited Spain for three months, and they had quickly struck up a friendship. With Juan were a small group of Carmelite priests and novitiates, who served clerical roles in the local hospitals and hospices. The community had enthusiastically welcomed Antonio the previous evening and had offered him a sumptuous dinner, after which Antonio had retired early.

The city had still laid in darkness as Antonio prepared a sandwich for breakfast, which he had eaten in the courtyard. He had taken a deep breath and had been somewhat refreshed by the cool morning air. He had smiled. The nightmare aside, now that he had arrived in Medellín he felt content. He was resolute in his reason for coming, his personal pilgrimage.

Later in the morning, Juan had taken Antonio to the cathedral. It was located in the heart of Medellín, at the north side of Bolívar Park. On arriving, Antonio had not seen anyone in the park other than a group of vagrants, some of whom he clearly recognised as being far gone under the influence of some drug or another. The cathedral had been more energetic, as priests from all over the diocese were gathering for the annual Chrism Mass, which was celebrated by the Archbishop himself. The cathedral was surrounded by armed military police, there first and foremost to protect the Archbishop. Because of the senior clergy's vocal opposition to the many guerrilla groups and drug cartels, the Archbishop had a constant target on his back.

In the sacristy, a spirited caretaker, pleased to welcome an international guest to the cathedral, had shown him around and had pointed out various portraits of previous archbishops that hung on the walls. Enthusiastically, and with deep pride, he had waxed lyrically about the one who had become cardinal and had even died in Rome. Rome, the Eternal City. Antonio had listened patiently, knowing that it was likely that the impoverished caretaker had never left the city. To have got to see Rome must have been an achievement beyond compare.

Antonio rubbed his eyes again. Any energy he had got from the morning air was quickly draining away in the hot, incense-filled cathedral. Unarmed military police in dress uniform were lined up in front of the sanctuary and scattered throughout the nave. He saw Juan, dressed in the brown habit of the Carmelite order, walk in the procession, kiss the altar, and then ungracefully shuffle through the crowd of priests to sit down next to Antonio.

"You should have joined in," he said.

"I'll leave it to the locals," Antonio said.

Juan looked around and leaned in to whisper, so that no one else could hear him.

"So, are you ready to start?"

Antonio did not answer immediately. He was rubbing his temples, still trying to suppress the headache. The Archbishop, looking every bit as an animated gold bar, dressed as he was in a gold cope, a gold embroidered stole, and wearing a gold mitre, walked up to the altar, bringing the procession to a close.

"Today we pray," Antonio said, his eyes heavy. "Let's start tomorrow."

"Very good," Juan said, offering a sympathetic smile. "Just know that I am with you, to the very end."

"Thank you."

Up by the altar, the Archbishop turned to face the congregants and raised his arm for the blessing.

**

Stuart woke up after sleeping surprisingly well. He sat up in his bed and on seeing his unpacked bag, he felt a painful jolt in his stomach as he remembered the envelope. He realised though that somehow he had avoided thinking about it since landing in Medellín the previous night. He got up and pulled open the curtains, looking out over the city, which last night he had only seen as a sea of light.

Now, from the comfort of his tenth floor room, it turned out he could not see much anyway, as directly opposite was another high-rise building. Turning to his right, he could see a large and busy motorway, beyond which lay railway tracks. A metro train was pulling out of a nearby station. He could see the city stretching out to both his right and left, with high-rise buildings nestled on the high slopes of the valley. It was very different from London.

The hotel room though looked like all other hotel rooms. There was a bed, two nightstands, a small round table with a single chair, a work desk with another chair, and a wardrobe. Stuart sank down in the chair by the small round table and thought back to his great accomplishments the previous day. He had successfully smuggled an envelope into a country notorious for smuggling things out.

He wanted to pat himself on the back, but stopped when he realised that he still did not know why he had done it. Some mysterious man from the government had asked him to. Now that he was here he realised that it was all a bit too fantastical. He got a sudden burning desire to open the envelope, but he stopped himself as soon as he had stood up from the chair. Cooth had just about told him that it was a couple of passports and plane tickets. For a mother and her daughter. Why was the government interested in them, Stuart wondered?

He walked over to the suitcase and began unpacking, hanging up his now crumpled linen suits. He found the envelope, still tucked away amongst his clothes. He wondered what to do with it. The meeting was tomorrow at noon. He contemplated putting it in the hotel room safe, but for some reason he did not trust hotel room safes. In the end, he put it back in his bag, hidden amongst his underwear. It was unlikely that any nosey housekeepers would look there.

Stuart put his tablet and work documents on the desk and sat down to read through them. Again. He knew everything inside and out, but it was still a good distraction from the envelope. His client was signing a deal with a power company to overhaul a nearby hydroelectric power plant. Now that he was here, he realised that in none of the photographs of the plant and its surroundings that his client had included in the paperwork were there any signs of a jungle. It was a gentle, rolling landscape, with a lot of really normal-looking trees. It could have been the English West Country, for all he knew. He laughed at his own stupidity. All that worrying for nothing.

Today, Stuart was meeting the Colombian lawyer for

lunch. Her name was Carolina Rojas and she worked for the power company. It sounded rather unglamorous but he was excited to meet her. For the past months, they had had email contact and the occasional videoconference call whilst negotiating the agreement and writing the actual contract that was about to be signed by the corporate suits. Stuart had got a positive feeling from their conversations and he was sure they would get along. The other day she had sent him an email, inviting him to a non-work lunch, so they could meet in person and she could show him the city. He had accepted immediately.

Just before midday Stuart took the lift down to reception and stepped outside. It was warm, but not overbearingly so. On checking in the night before he had asked for directions, which he had got along with a map. He set off towards the metro station at a brisk pace, but quickly had to slow down as he started to sweat. Eventually, he crossed a walkway over the motorway and entered the station. He was pleasantly surprised by the train that soon arrived, which he thought put the old, screeching London Underground carriages to shame. It was only a short journey to Berrío Park station, where Stuart stepped off.

Using the map he successfully navigated down a series of streets, passing a square which he took to be the optimistically named park from which the station took its name, a small church, a narrow street next to the church where traders were selling an alarming amount of pornography, and eventually ended up on a busy pedestrian road that, according to the map, ran through the city centre. It was crowded, so Stuart had to take the map's authority for it. Carolina had said to meet underneath the imposing Coltejer Building, the city's tallest skyscraper. It was not hard to miss.

When he arrived he saw a strikingly beautiful young woman wave at him and quickly walk over. She had a positive energy about her which the videoconferencing call had not managed to convey. A zeal for life, something which the introverted Stuart could not fully comprehend. She was quite short, compared to Stuart, but had long, flowing brown hair, and a radiant smile.

Stuart took a deep breath; this was his time to be suave and sophisticated.

"Mr Gleeman," she said, eagerly shaking his hand.

"Yes, hello," Stuart said, who despite trying to be suave was a bit taken aback by her charms.

"It is so exciting to meet you in person," she said, beaming.

"You too," Stuart said, smiling apprehensively. He had not mentally prepared himself for the onslaught of such an exuberant woman.

"Right, let's go to lunch," she declared.

She led the way down the pedestrian road to a restaurant, hosted in a building which was designed in old, Spanish, colonial style. Stuart was sure it was not actually that old. They climbed a staircase to the open seating area and grabbed a table by the wooden handrail that overlooked the street. A cool breeze was sweeping in, which relaxed Stuart.

"This is nice," he said.

He looked down on the pedestrians walking up and down the street, heading in and out of shops and restaurants. It all looked very, well, normal.

"Yes," Carolina said, still smiling broadly. "I hope you like beans."

Stuart was not a massive fan.

"Yes, yes, definitely," he said. "Is that common?"

"It's popular. I'll order for you."

Stuart had no idea what he would get for lunch. Just as he had never been much of a traveller, he had never been much of a culinary explorer either. However, he knew that it was polite to accept local recommendations. As they waited for their food, Carolina asked about Stuart's trip and he started telling her about his flights.

"Fourteen hours with a priest? I wouldn't want that," Carolina said, laughing.

"We had some interesting conversations," Stuart said. "He didn't seem like a zealous crazy person. In fact, he is a lawyer."

Carolina smiled but did not comment any further. Instead, their drinks were delivered.

"Pineapple juice, it's very good," Carolina said.

They toasted each other.

"So, what do you think about Colombia?"

Stuart took an extra big gulp of juice. He had to answer this politely and diplomatically.

"I really like what I have seen so far," he said, truthfully. "I didn't know about all these mountains, though."

"Oh, right," Carolina replied. She might have realised that Stuart had been expecting the guerrilla-infested jungles that it seemed most foreigners associated Colombia with.

"It is really beautiful," Stuart said. "The landscape around London is quite boring," he added in an appropriately self-deprecating manner.

"I've always wanted to see London," Carolina said, smiling again.

"I hope you do."

Stuart smiled back. He was very taken with Carolina. He remembered that he had queried Antonio falling in love at first sight. That was not happening here, but he felt a positive energy coursing through his body. He forced himself to look down at the street for a moment. He was far from home, and the last thing he needed was positive energy from a woman. He was pleased that they were interrupted by the arrival of their food, which turned out to be a rather tasty green bean stew with a fried egg mashed in.

Their conversation slowly moved towards work, but this turned out to be a short discussion. The work had already been finished. The two companies were having a small signing ceremony on Friday afternoon, followed by a dinner. Stuart knew that he was only here to beef up his client's entourage, and perhaps to be on hand in case something unexpected and unforeseen turned up. The trip was, in reality, more of a holiday, which would have pleased anyone who enjoyed travelling. To Stuart, the trip had originally been more of a waste of time. Now that he had met Carolina, however, he started to change his mind.

"We'll have dessert somewhere else," Carolina announced forcefully as a waiter cleared away their plates. "You like dessert."

It was not a question but Stuart agreed with the statement.

"Definitely."

They left the restaurant and back on ground level started walking down the street.

"I'll show you the city centre," Carolina said without any obvious enthusiasm. She was craning her head looking up and down the street.

"That would be nice," Stuart said politely. "If you have time." He was British enough to know never to bother other people, but he also thought that it would be useful to have some time on his own to find the address where he was dropping of the envelope tomorrow.

She looked at him and the big smile returned.

"Of course. I just don't like walking around here. It is not always safe."

Stuart's senses woke up and took a closer look at their surroundings. The road and the side streets were crowded with people. It was loud, with hawkers peddling their wares every few steps. Stuart noticed that some of the tacky-looking stores had employees walking around shouting into microphones, trying to lure in customers with good deals. Most stores also had armed security guards, and Stuart did not know what he thought about that.

The afternoon heat was coming in, and Stuart wiped his forehead. After a while, they reached the end of the pedestrian road. Ahead, over a crossroad, was a pleasant-looking park. Stuart tried to cross the road but Carolina hesitated.

"Oh, I guess I should show you the cathedral," she said and crossed over.

The park was full of people, but Stuart noticed that most of them looked like they were homeless and destitute.

"There are only homeless and crazy drug addicts here," Carolina said, a bit dismissively, staying close to Stuart. "I never visit. It must have been many years since last time."

Stuart kept a close eye on the people around him. Thankfully they all seemed docile, indeed, the only ones who paid him any notice all looked at him with surprise and interest. He relaxed. They circled around a large fountain and sat down on the steps in front of the imposing redbrick cathedral. The sun was beaming down and Stuart felt a tingling on his neck. Sunburn was inevitable.

"This is not the Colombia that you should be seeing," Carolina said apologetically.

"Don't worry," Stuart said. "Every place has its problems, and I have been very impressed with everything". He arched around and looked at the cathedral behind him. "This looks nice."

"You're too kind," Carolina said smiling. "There are still a lot of problems here, with guerrillas, drugs and violence." She seemed to be scanning the people in the park. "But it is not all bad."

"I learnt that there is some sort of peace process in place."

"With the FARC? Yes, but that's nonsense. You can't negotiate with criminals. You have to beat them, like the previous president almost did. This current one is weak, he's just letting the criminals get away with everything. We have elections in a few weeks, and I really hope he doesn't get re-elected. That would be disastrous. The Challenger wants to cancel the negotiations and send the army back in."

Stuart listened patiently. Instinctively he thought that surely a negotiated peace was better than perpetuating a war against whoever these guerrillas were, but it wasn't his country. It wasn't his reality.

"I can understand that," he said vaguely.

"Oh, don't worry about our politics," she said warmly. She stood up. "Shall we go?"

Stuart stood up as well. He looked at the closed doors of the cathedral.

"Can we go inside?" he asked. It felt like a normal tourist thing.

Carolina snorted.

"No, it's always closed. Not much help to these poor people, eh?"

"No," Stuart said.

"Let's get that dessert."

They walked back through the park.

**

Tara was sitting on her balcony, relaxing in the late afternoon. Her boyfriend had bought some fresh pineapples, which he had expertly sliced for her. She ate a slice every so often, reflecting on the juxtaposition of this tranquillity with the violence which was still engulfing many parts of the country. When she had first taken up the position as head of security at the embassy, Tara had engrossed herself in the British government's background notes on Colombia and its security situation.

She had discovered that it was an armed struggle the origin of which was shrouded in obscurity and deeply conflicting opinions. What there was agreement on was that the struggle had been, and might still be, centred on ownership of land. Wealthy landowners had exploited the poor, illiterate farmers who had worked on it. This hardly seemed unique to Colombia, but then Latin America did seem to prefer a more violent approach to conflict-resolution.

The country had been embroiled in civil wars ever since its independence from Spain in 1819. Like the rest of

Latin America, the struggles had intensified in the 1930s, though Colombia had escaped with only one, brief military dictatorship. The conflict had led to most of the country being ungoverned, and the divide between the ruling oligarchy trying to, or pretending to, rule from Bogotá and the excluded farmers had continued to grow. From the 1960s, inspired by communist ideals and seeking an armed overthrow of the oligarchy, various guerrilla groups, most famously the FARC, had been formed. The government's war on the guerrillas had been less than successful, and eventually many industrialists and landowners formed their own private armies, ostensibly to protect their interests from the guerrillas. In the armed struggle between the guerrillas, the paramilitaries, and the army, the resulting climate of lawlessness had afforded the opportunity for drug cartels to spring up, independent from the FARC, which nonetheless remained one of the largest suppliers of cocaine.

The conflict between the four groupings was brought under some sort of control at the start of the 21st century, but the struggle was far from over. Decades of conflict had led to millions being displaced, who had moved into slums in the bigger cities. Some of those were virtually independent communities, where criminal gangs often ruled. It was a perpetuation of lawlessness, which merely seemed to have moved from the remote countryside now occupied by the army into the slums of the cities.

Controversies had arisen over successive governments' unofficial support of the violent paramilitary groups, and accusations of human rights abuses came in rapid succession. It raised many questions about the propriety of diplomatic relationships with the Colombian government. Even if some sort of peace could be negotiated, people from all sides still had to be held to account for past transgressions. That was going to open many scars, and Tara believed that that was an excuse for all sides to simply continue the fighting. With the conflict still going on, each side could carry on blaming the others. Tara had also got the impression from many wealthy people that they were strongly opposed to any negotiated peace because they could not accept having to forgive the guerrillas for the deaths, kidnappings for ransoms and other terrors the guerrillas had imposed over the decades. Many in the guerrillas seemed to have the same thought regarding the oppression caused by the wealthy's paramilitary groups. Unless something changed, the country seemed doomed to perpetual violence.

Tara sighed as she looked out over Bogotá. It felt senseless. At least she was relatively safe at home, since the building was surrounded by a barbed-wire fence and armed security guards. Though she was used to living with security from her days in the army, it had been somewhat of an adjustment to also live under guard at home.

She ate another slice of refreshing pineapple. Julian was on his phone again, arguing loudly with someone about late deliveries. Tara was used to it. She had enjoyed discussing the Colombian situation with him. He came from a poor community in the north, close to the Caribbean coast, and his father had been involved in the FARC. Julian had managed to get out and make it to Bogotá where he had started a very different, and far more profitable, life.

Tara had her tablet on the table. It contained her classified report for the handover in Medellín tomorrow. She knew the details off by heart, but had spent most of the day rereading them. Circumstances had put her in a difficult position. Tara knew she was meant to go to Medellín to protect that English lawyer who had been asked to undertake the handover, but the Ambassador had announced a new schedule at the last minute.

She was not sure what to feel about it, but the Ambassador had, many months earlier, found himself a mistress in the Caribbean city of Barranquilla. She put it down to what she and Robert called Shakira fever. As the dutiful security officer, she travelled with him every time he flew up there. Julian only laughed at it, saying the powerful would always get away with things like that. Tara had a feeling he was more revolutionary than he would let on. At any rate, she could not go to Medellín.

Robert had thought the Ambassador's last minute trip to his mistress, despite knowing about Friday's handover in Medellín, had something to do with the fact that he had spent last evening having dinner with an old friend of his, a barrister from London called Roderic Geoffrey Moylan-Roth. Tara had shuddered at the name. I'd want a vacation after meeting a name like that, she had thought to herself. After a long discussion, they had agreed that Robert would go to Medellín in Tara's place, to supervise the handover.

Robert had been somewhat reluctant to go, given Molly's disappearance last Friday. There had been no news about what had happened to her and the police had no leads. Not even Senator Reyes had had anything to say about it. Congressman Escaso had come to the embassy again, offering his sincere sympathies and apologies, expressing outrage that something so vile could happen in his hometown. He had promised to put pressure on the police to investigate extra carefully, but nothing had come of it. Molly was gone.

Tara had told Robert to be vigilant. She was worried about Manuel's family but hoped that they were safe. There had been no suggestion in the news that anyone matching their description had been killed. She sighed and ate the last slice of pineapple. She was sure that everything would be all right.

Chapter 8

It was Friday morning and Robert was annoyed. Really annoyed. The Ambassador had taken an early morning flight to Barranquilla to spend the day, and probably the weekend too, relaxing with his mistress. After the stress of dealing with the disappearance of Molly Reed, the obnoxiousness of that visiting barrister, planning for the Prince's visit, and the almost constant onslaught of Senator Reyes, Robert accepted that the Ambassador was entitled to a day off. That was not the problem.

The problem was that Robert should have been in Bogotá, as acting ambassador. Now, it was true that that title, which Robert might have bestowed upon himself, did not really mean anything, but he liked it when the boss left for a day or two, and he could strut around the embassy with an inflated sense of his own importance. Today, however, he had been denied the luxury.

He was on his way to Medellín to provide backup to this English lawyer, Stuart Gleeman. He had to ensure that the handover of the passports to Manuel's family went off without trouble. Molly's disappearance the Friday before had really shaken him. Though he knew of the dangers in this country, until that point they had been mainly academic. None of the embassy staff had actually been involved in any trouble.

He also felt ill at ease about the plan. Tara had insisted that it was best to send in someone who was not connected to the embassy. If the cartel was behind Molly's disappearance, they might not react to an outsider. Robert would supervise, indeed, he might even be a decoy in case the cartel were on the lookout. He trusted Tara, absolutely, but he did not like the idea of putting an outsider at risk.

He had spent the week worrying about Manuel's family but hoped that they were safe, hiding out somewhere with the brother-in-law. All they had to do now was come to the brother-in-law's shop to get the passports. They would then be taken to the airport and flown out, first to Bogotá, and then on to London, where he hoped that they would be safely reunited with Manuel.

Robert's mood was not improved, quite the opposite, by the travel companion imposed on him. Yesterday, as on Wednesday night, the Ambassador had been hosting that barrister. They had apparently met at university, doing who-knows-what between pretending to study. The barrister had spent some time in the embassy and had been introduced to Robert. Robert quickly realised that the friend was an insufferable fool, and the Ambassador's sudden trip to his mistress suggested that he felt more or less the same. Nonetheless, the Ambassador had suggested that they travel together to Medellín.

"I say, you don't have an embassy car?" Roderic asked.

"No," Robert said sharply and headed for a taxi. He could have arranged for a private hire car in Medellín, but he was willing to forego that to see the barrister suffer in a taxi.

"I must speak to the Ambassador," Roderic said.

They drove into Medellín in a frosty silence. Robert did not feel compelled to say anything or in any way look after the Ambassador's supposed friend. They enjoyed the view of the city from the top of the valley with the briefest of smiles. There was heavy traffic on the way down, which included small mopeds whizzing around at alarming speeds. The driver seemed utterly unfazed by everything the road was throwing at him.

"Are you here to look for that employee you lost last Friday?" Roderic asked as they came to a standstill at the bottom of the valley. He seemed unperturbed by Molly's disappearance.

"In a manner of speaking," Robert said testily. He did not like the barrister's tone.

"Ah," Roderic said with a smile. "Do you want my assistance? I'm sure you would benefit from it."

Robert shot him an angry look.

"No, I do not want your assistance. This is official

business."

"It never hurts to have a lawyer with you."

Robert did not respond. Roderic smiled superciliously, which made Robert's blood boil, but the barrister kept silent. They continued on at an agonisingly slow pace in an even frostier silence. Eventually, they reached Roderic's hotel, but he did not immediately step out.

"I don't know any details," Roderic said quietly. The smile had mysteriously disappeared. "I know that you have asked Mr Gleeman for help, and I guess that this has something to do with it. Not that Mr Gleeman would ever admit that. But I'm sure an extra intelligent head would not go amiss. I was at Oxford, after all," he added with a chuckle.

Robert sighed to himself. Of course the barrister knew what was going on, he should have guessed as much. It was not clear if Roderic wanted to help because he cared about his colleague or because he thought his colleague was not up for the job, but either way, Robert had to agree that the annoying barrister could come in useful. Perhaps, if they ran into trouble, the cartel would capture Roderic and Robert could make his escape.

"Yes, of course," he said slowly. "You can come with."

"Let me leave my luggage."

Roderic disappeared inside the hotel with his suitcases. Robert waited patiently in the taxi, whilst the driver was entertaining himself by singing along to some upbeat Latin tunes. The clock was ticking closer to midday. He really needed to be downtown. He took a deep breath and built up the confidence to speak Spanish.

"How long will it take to get to Berrío Park station?" he asked the driver with his slow, staccato pronunciation.

"Not long."

Of course not, Robert thought. What else would a taxi driver say? Thankfully, shortly thereafter Roderic walked out of the hotel. Robert was banging on the seat in frustration, but the barrister did not seem to be in any rush.

"Don't stress," the driver said cheerfully, still moving

along to his music. "You from the US? They are always stressed in the US."

"Yes, I just need to get to Berrío Park station as fast as possible."

Roderic entered the car, and the driver set off, thankfully at a quick pace.

"They gave me a rather nice room," Roderic said. "Somewhere near the top. I have a nice view."

"I'm so happy for you," Robert said snarkily.

"Did you go to Oxford?"

"What? No, Cambridge."

"Ah, that explains your tedious need to panic." Roderic smiled again. "All will be well in the end. I think that's Oxford's motto."

Robert scoffed and turned to stubbornly look out the window. The car was now inching forward in heavy traffic, and he felt the need to bang on something again, but using all the energy he could muster, he managed to stay still and in control. The clock was unstoppably nearing midday. He could not bear to think that something might happen to Stuart Gleeman whilst he was stuck in a taxi somewhere, unable to help. This was a really bad situation.

Finally, they reached the station. Robert quickly jumped out and tried to get his bearings, whilst Roderic exited with more grace.

"This way," Robert said.

It was already a few minutes past midday. Robert walked quickly, panic building up inside him. He could not afford for this to go wrong. He had to make sure that the lawyer and Manuel's family were safe. With the unperturbed barrister in tow, he soon reached the side street where Manuel's brother-in-law had his jewellery shop and started to walk down it.

He immediately sensed that something was amiss. A large number of people were hurrying in the opposite direction. Robert edged his way through, wondering what was going on. He kept on walking, but suddenly he spotted something which made him stop in his tracks.

A large number of police cars were parked erratically outside a building some fifty metres down the street. They were blocking the street, causing a backlog of other cars, and seemingly all of the drivers had started hitting their horns impatiently. The few remaining people around the police were hurriedly walking away.

"That doesn't look too promising," Roderic said calmly.

"Oh, this is bad," Robert agreed.

They kept on walking forwards, more slowly now. He was not sure whether the police were outside the building that they were heading for, but his senses told him they were.

As it turned out, they were not.

Robert reached the address that he had written in his notes, but the police cars were still slightly further down the street. Numerous police officers were standing around them, but none seemed to care about the two Englishmen. Keeping a close eye on the police, Robert opened the door and walked inside.

"So, Mr Gleeman is meant to be here?"

For the first time, Robert heard a trace of emotion in Roderic's voice. The barrister was possibly a bit concerned.

"Yes. He is meeting some, erm, persons of interest."

Robert looked around. They were in a long corridor, with a staircase on the left and a few lifts to the right. On the wall was a building directory, which Robert walked up to and studied. He realised that the units in the building housed small businesses, by all accounts covering a wide range of areas. A few were jewellers, and he found the one he was looking for.

"I'm just meant to supervise, nothing more, but we have to go and find him."

"Lead the way," Roderic said.

They took the lift, which was the slowest Robert had ever experienced, to the fifth floor. Once there they stepped out into another whitewashed corridor. They quickly made their way down, looking for the right door. He noticed that they were all heavy-duty metal security doors. It was not clear exactly what business was carried out behind them, but it made sense if they stocked expensive jewellery.

"It's somewhat empty," Roderic remarked. Again, his voice betrayed the slightest hint of concern.

"A bit eerie," Robert said. He wondered how Molly must have felt last Friday, coming to this place on her own. He tried to shake off his worry. After all, she had had no reason to be concerned. The only reason he was afraid was because of what had happened to her. What had happened to her? Why had Tara let her go on her own?

"Is this it?"

Roderic was pointing to another metal security door. It had 5-13 painted on it.

"Yes," Robert said.

The door was slightly ajar. Robert did not know what to make of it. It was out of place, but perhaps Mr Gleeman was inside. He looked around but the corridor was still empty. Slowly he pulled the heavy door open and stepped into what looked like an entrance hall. It was also empty. Robert stepped up to the business counter and tried to look around inside.

"Hello," he said.

Roderic came in behind him and stepped around the counter. There was no response, and Robert quickly followed him. There was a door into a back-room, which turned out to be a workshop. It, in turn, had doors to rooms on both sides. The workshop was empty as well. It had tables and counters which were filled with various implements and knickknacks, clearly the tools of the jewellery trade.

"Empty," Roderic said.

"What is going on?" Robert pondered out loud. His heart was starting to race now. Something was clearly amiss.

He went to the door on the left hand side and looked into the next room. It was a small kitchen. There were dirty dishes on the counter and a half-eaten meal on the table. Robert felt a growing sense of unease. Slowly he walked over to the other side of the workshop. He looked into the side room.

It was a sparsely furnished office, with a desk, some chairs, and a few filing cabinets along the wall. The window shades were down and the room was dark. As Robert turned to leave he noticed two odd, red splotches on the wall. He had made it back out into the workshop before his mind caught up. Those red splotches were out of place.

Slowly, confused, he walked back into the inner office. Roderic followed him, a curious look on his face. Robert saw that the red splotches were creating trails along the wall as they trickled downwards. He found a light switch next to the door. In the bright light, there was no mistaking what the red fluid was.

"I say, there's an awful lot of blood in here," Roderic remarked calmly.

Robert looked angrily at the barrister and then apprehensively took another step into the office. He peered behind the desk and his heart jolted. Roderic stepped forwards and also looked behind the desk.

"I say."

There were two bodies lying on the floor, an old man and an old woman. Their skin was wrinkled, their clothes old and dirty. Blood was pooling around the bodies. Robert took a few deep breaths, trying to think, but his mind was spinning.

"I do think the police are here for this," Roderic said calmly. "We should make a quick exit." He made a point of looking around a final time. "Mr Gleeman is clearly not here."

As they stepped back into the workshop, they could hear voices coming from the corridor and the unmistakable crackling of a police radio. Robert shuddered. There was no other way out. They were trapped inside, with the two bloody corpses.

**

Stuart woke up with a start. He had had a nightmare of his girlfriend Kate yelling at him, accusing him of betrayal. He looked over to his left and saw Carolina fast asleep. Clearly, his subconscious had had a valid point. He did not have much practice at this, but various TV shows had taught him to make a discreet exit. That felt like a good plan. He swung out of bed as quietly as he could and took a few steps across the room. He then stopped, his mind having realised a few important points.

First, Kate was no longer his girlfriend. She had left him. There was no way that he could have betrayed her. Secondly, he could not surreptitiously leave Carolina, because he was spending the whole afternoon with her at the contract signing. Leaving would make it awkward. Thirdly, and perhaps most importantly, he was in his own hotel room. There was nowhere to go even if he wanted to leave.

Unsure about what to do, he stood absolutely still. Memories of the previous night came back, but his mind and eyes quickly wandered to the infernal envelope, still hidden inside his bag.

After they had left the cathedral, Carolina had led him to her car and she had driven them back to El Poblado. Stuart had seen his hotel from the road but Carolina had headed a short distance uphill. It was a world away from the crowds, noise and squalor of the city centre. The area was nice, calm, quiet, and above all quirky. The streets were lined by trees, providing a welcomed shade from the afternoon sun, and flanked by colourful two-story buildings, housing cafés, boutique shops, and small hotels. As they walked down the pavement, Stuart had for the first time noticed a few young backpackers, and had heard a variety of languages, including a distinctly loud couple from the US. It felt homely, apart from the heat, and Stuart had managed to completely relax. He had even started to enjoy being in a foreign land.

They had gone to a small café and spent a few hours talking about this and that. They had talked with an ease that he had never felt with Kate. He had had passionate moments with Kate, but he had often felt that they were two very different people. Kate must have felt the same, which would explain why she had succumbed to the charms of that German biologist. Stuart had certainly never felt the kind of passion that the priest Antonio had described. Stuart had still not been able to make any sense of that. Even now, standing awkwardly in his own hotel room, he could not imagine giving up his entire life for Carolina.

He looked at her, still sleeping soundly. Was there something wrong with his emotions, he wondered? Did he have the capacity to feel so strongly about anything? He sighed, realising that he had never really been passionate about anything. That realisation pained him. Maybe it was a character flaw, one which would prevent him from having any meaningful relationship. He sighed again. This was not the right time to sort out his life.

"I know the perfect place for dinner," Carolina had said as darkness had started to fall over the city last night.

"Excellent," Stuart had said.

She had driven them further out from the city centre. They parked near a cluster of cargo containers, which had been left close to the main road. The industrial feel of the place had confused Stuart.

"They have a restaurant inside the containers," Carolina had explained. "The best burgers in Medellín."

The dinner had definitely lived up to that epitaph. They had sat outdoors, on a deck placed on top of the containers, enjoying the cool evening air. Sturt realised that his memory of the meal was hazy, but he could see flashes of smiles, laughs, and cheeky touches. Where on earth had he discovered that charm?

"Do you want to come for a drink at my place?"

His memory of this question was crystal clear. He had frozen for a moment as the cursed envelope had flashed in his mind.

"My hotel is quite close," he had said, but only because his mind had told him that he had to get back to check on the envelope. After all, he had not seen it all day, and the hotel cleaners must have been in his room. Who knows who else might have been in there?

"Of course," Carolina had replied with a smile.

Now, the morning after, he realised what that smile had meant. Somehow he had managed to get a woman to his room without really meaning to. Typical, this night of all nights.

In the dark, Stuart edged forwards, trying not to make a single sound, and found his bag. This was the first time he thought about how loud the zipper was, but very slowly he got the bag opened. He rummaged around inside and thankfully found the envelope where he had left it, wrapped up inside his underwear. Leaving it in place, he realised that his main challenge now was getting rid of Carolina without raising any suspicions. She could not be around when he went to deliver that bloody envelope. But he was not sure on the best way of getting rid of her.

He edged over to the window and carefully peeked behind the thick curtain. Outside it was getting light. The digital clock on the TV told him that it was barely six am, but the main road into the city centre was already busy. Realising that he did not have any options, he slowly returned to the bed. He lay there, with his eyes wide open, staring at the ceiling. It was very bland. He went through different reasons he could give Carolina to get her to leave, so that he would be alone at midday. It had to be something believable, something that would not raise any questions.

"Hello."

Stuart looked over. Carolina was awake. She stirred and stretched.

"Good morning," Stuart said and could not help but smile.

"I should get going," Carolina said and started to get out of the bed.

Well, that was easy, he thought to himself. Why had he worried so much?

Having got out of bed, Carolina turned around and looked at Stuart with a broad grin. Her whole body was lit up by the weak morning light coming through behind the heavy curtain. Stuart was struck by her beauty, which he had failed to consciously acknowledge yesterday. The envelope must have really weighed on his mind.

"Yes, yes, of course," Stuart said.

He sat up on the bed, unsure whether it was appropriate to watch her get dressed. Instead, he started scanning every corner of the room.

"I'll see you this afternoon at the meeting."

"Yes, absolutely, of course."

She laughed.

"You are very happy this morning," she said playfully.

"Yes, yes," was all Stuart could say and he realised that he was blushing.

She hurried around the bed and gave him a kiss.

"And we will continue this after dinner."

It was not a question. Stuart smiled back and nodded.

In an instance, she was gone. Locking the door behind her, Stuart did a little dance to himself. He then went to take a shower. He stood in the shower for a long time, once again reconstructing what had happened yesterday and then he went over his old relationship with Kate. He really was not sure about what to do with his emotions. At least half an hour had passed before Stuart's mind finally returned to the present. That pestilent envelope. He only had a few hours to prepare for his task.

Stuart studied the map he had got of the city centre, trying to find the address. The streets were laid out in a grid system, albeit a sometimes wobbly system. The streets and cross-streets were consecutively numbered, which made finding his destination quite easy. He would once again take the metro to Berrío Park and the address was a relatively short walk from there.

He twiddled his thumbs for a few hours before he decided it was time. He would finally be free from that awful envelope. He could then go to the contract signing with peace of mind and thereafter spend an enjoyable weekend with Carolina, before heading home to London. That sounded nice.

**

It was almost half past eleven when Stuart arrived at Berrío Park metro station. Despite the heat he was wearing his suit jacket, with the envelope safely tucked away inside the inner pocket. In order to be nimble and ready for anything, he had left his briefcase with his work documents in the hotel room. He was certain there would be enough time after delivering the envelope to go back to the hotel and retrieve the documents before the contract signing.

He made his way down to street level, where he took out his map and tried to orientate himself. He remembered where he had walked yesterday and soon figured out where to go now. Down the main road for a short bit, as yesterday, but then turn left instead of right.

His anxiety level rose with every step that he took. He was not sure why. Strictly speaking, all he was meant to do was meet someone and hand over an envelope. And yes, make sure the lady and her daughter got into a taxi and went to the airport. And yes, make sure they remembered their camera. There was really no skill involved.

Stuart realised that his nerves were caused by the mysterious cloak-and-dagger routine of William Cooth and his lackeys in London. Why did they have to kidnap him off the street? They could have just called and asked nicely. There were also too many unanswered questions, which his legal mind kept asking. Why had he been requested to do this? Why not anyone else, such as someone from the embassy? Cooth had not given a satisfactory answer.

Stuart stopped and looked around, but he could not see anything strange. There was no one following him, no one looking at him, no cars or motorcycles behaving oddly. All he could see was a normal, cosmopolitan city; heavy traffic, with delivery trucks, taxis, cars, and some cyclists; businesspeople walking fast in business clothes; shoppers walking leisurely in more heat-appropriate clothes. He took a deep breath to steady his nerves. Cooth's cloak-and-dagger routine had probably instilled in him a flight of fancy, an idea that he was James Bond on a mission, but in reality, he was just a postman. No offence to postmen.

He walked on, feeling better, and soon found his side-street. It was much calmer than the main road, with just the occasional car heading past him. He saw all sorts of shops; small convenience stores, a clothes shop, and a shop selling carpets. It was just normal city life.

The building he was looking for was not too far down the street. It was not yet midday, so he waited outside the entrance, using the opportunity to properly investigate the street. A handful of men carried a heavy, rolled-up carpet out of the carpet shop and flung it onto a pickup truck. After a while, an old lady left the building and hurried down the street. The pickup truck drove off, spewing black exhaust smoke. A moment later, a group of men, one of them in a suit, also left the building and headed up towards the main road. There were a few people walking up and down the street, nipping in and out of the shops. There was absolutely nothing out of the ordinary. Either he was awful at surveillance or there really was nothing to worry about.

Just before midday, he headed inside. To his surprise, it looked like a block of flats, not a place for shops, but there was a business directory hanging on the wall. The business he had been told to go to was on the fifth floor. He took the lift up, wondering what he would say when he arrived. Probably just hello, I have a package for you. Keep it nice and simple. The main problem might be getting the women to leave. What if they did not want to? Convinced that that was his main concern, he stepped off on the fifth floor and started looking for the right door.

5-13.

What a lucky number, he thought to himself. The door was made from metal, and he really had to apply himself to get it opened. This was not the time to be self-conscious about not going to the gym, he told himself. Inside the door was a small room, which had a business counter at the far end.

"Hello," he said loudly as he stepped in.

He could not hear anything. He now started realising that something was amiss. He had not seen anyone else inside the building, and the whole floor was absolutely silent. His heart started speeding up.

"Hello," he said again.

He walked across the room and stopped at the counter. Behind it was a door, but it was closed. He took out his phone and confirmed that it was indeed midday. It was the right day, right time and the right place. He now realised that Cooth had not told him anything about what would happen if the intended recipients were not around. There was only one thing for it. He had to trespass behind the counter and go through the back door. James Bond style.

The door was unlocked and led to a workshop. He could see various precious stones lying on the worktops. That did not seem right. Surely a jeweller would lock up his stones? He slowly walked across the workshop, trying to really see. See what was going on here, or what had happened. Tools and precious stones were scattered about. A chair had fallen over in the back corner. It was not much, but any decent lawyer could weave at least a handful of different stories out of it. Most of them would include some sort of struggle and perhaps a quick exit.

He checked one of the side doors. A kitchen, with half-eaten food. The 'someone making a speedy exit' story was looking more plausible. He walked across and looked inside the other side door. It was an inner office. His heart almost stopped at what he saw.

"Bad, bad, bad, bad, bad," he heard himself saying over and over until his heart finally started to slow down. He took a cautious step inside. "Oh dear," he mumbled as he looked behind the desk. He repeated it many times as he looked at the two dead bodies, the expanding pool of blood, and the numerous streaks of blood adorning the otherwise bare walls. "Oh, this is not good," he concluded, a bit lawyerly and matter-of-factly.

Stuart tried to study the bodies more closely. One man and one woman, both old. He had been told that he was looking for a mother and her daughter. The old woman could certainly be the mother, but then where was the daughter? He carefully moved around the inner office, looking for a third body, but there was none. He quickly looked around the workshop and the kitchen again, but no third body. The daughter was not here.

Suddenly he heard muffled voices coming from far down the corridor. It took barely a second for him to decide to make his own quick exit. He got out into the corridor and pushed the metal door shut, but he did not have time to close it fully. He ran down the corridor in the opposite direction to the lifts, as silently as he could.

He knew that he had to get out of the building as quickly as possible. He was not proud of it, but he just had to get out and leave this be. He could not get involved in some Colombian double-murder investigation. Cooth could hardly be angry at him for failing to deliver the envelope in these circumstances.

To his luck, he found the stairs. He opened the door and stepped into the stairwell. Thankfully it was empty and eerily silent. He quickly ran down the stairs and soon reached the ground floor, but stopped at the door which led into the lobby. He had to be careful. Stuart tried to listen through the door. The lobby was quiet. Realising that he could not stay in the stairwell all day, he took a chance and opened the door. The lobby was empty. He stepped out and quietly walked towards the front door.

He stopped at the front door, panic setting in. The street outside was crammed with police officers. Where had they come from? Had the voices on the fifth floor been police officers, responding to a call about the murders? He stepped away from the front door and headed further back into the building. How had the police arrived so quickly? He had not been upstairs for that long, and he had not seen anything when he had been waiting outside on the street. He kept heading down the corridor. A tall, white, pale Englishman. Someone must have seen him loitering outside the building, waiting for midday. The police would have his description in no time. They would be looking for him. Panic was really setting in.

He walked on, passing yet more heavy steel doors. Finally, through some windows, he could see a courtyard, and eventually he found a door that led into it. Stuart quickly crossed the courtyard and found a door into the building on the other side. It had a similar corridor, but in this building the businesses were open, selling all manner of knickknacks. There was a steady flow of customers and Stuart could calmly walk through, pretending he was there on legitimate business. He got a few curious glances, probably because he was a tall, white, and pale Englishman, but no one challenged his presence. He stepped out into the street and looked around for any police officers. Thankfully there were none in sight.

He walked very slowly up towards the main road, where he would find taxis and Berrío Park station. He could get out of here. He took deep breaths and somehow started to calm down. His mind was trying to make sense of the situation. Who were the victims? Who had killed them? Why had the police arrived so quickly after he entered? Had he just been extremely unlucky or had someone wanted the police to arrive at the same time he had?

Stuart's mind could not come up with any answers. He did not have any information to go on. All he knew was that he was meant to have delivered an envelope and sent two women to the airport. So, who were these women? Why did the British government want them to leave Medellín? So many questions.

Back on the main road, he decided to take a taxi to the hotel. The metro was too public and there might be police officers on the lookout at the station. He found a taxi and it was soon manoeuvring its way through the busy traffic. Stuart tried to make himself as small as possible in his seat and he did not look out the window. His mind was retracing the same questions. What was going on?

Suddenly, in a split second of clarity, he realised that he did have a clue on which to get started. He still had that infernal envelope in his pocket. How could he have forgotten about it? Feeling utterly stupid he reached for it but then stopped himself. Not here, inside some taxi. He would have to wait until he was somewhere safe, where he would not be disturbed.

As they got closer to the hotel, Stuart tensed up again. What would await him there? The police? The killer? MI6?

Sure enough, when the taxi had almost reached the hotel, he could see a group of police cars parked outside. This was his worst nightmare. They were clearly there to look for him.

"Just stop here," Sturt said to the driver.

The driver must have seen the police cars as well and might have understood why Stuart suddenly did not want to go to the hotel, but he did not say anything. He stopped the car, let Stuart out and quickly drove away. Stuart stood still on the pavement, looking down the street. He could see police officers entering the hotel and a few others were taking up position outside the front entrance. He saw a young couple walk up to the hotel and were inspected by the police before they were let in. He took a deep breath, once again trying to calm down.

He needed a plan.

Chapter 9

"I say, this is a ghastly police station."

Roderic was unceremoniously led into the large detention room by two heavily armed police officers, who carefully locked the metal door behind him. He quickly walked over to Robert, who was seated on an empty bench. He looked around with a clear sense of disgust. The room, made out of concrete and filled with old metal benches, was otherwise rather full. There were some stereotypically heavily muscled men in tattoos, who were casting curious looks at the two white men in suits, and a spectrum of others, who to varying degrees seemed conked out on drugs.

"Don't worry," Robert said, trying his best to sound optimistic. "I showed them my diplomatic papers, so I'm sure we'll be out very soon."

Roderic sat down on the bench. Robert leaned in close to him, eager to know what had transpired during Roderic's interrogation.

"What did they ask you?"

"Oh, standard questions. Who I am, why I'm here, why we were at the workshop with the two dead bodies."

"What did you say?"

"The truth," Roderic said. "I'm a highly respected lawyer from London, and I certainly did not kill anyone."

"Highly respected," Robert mumbled to himself.

Roderic leaned in even closer.

"I say, though, there is something strange going on here. I don't speak Spanish, because what's the point, so the officers let their guard down a bit in the interview room. They left some documents on the table and there was quite a big file on you."

"What?"

"Yes," Roderic said. "It had your name, picture, and everything."

Robert thought for a second.

"Well, I did show them my diplomatic papers."

"Yes, but we haven't been here an hour yet! That file didn't look like something they just printed off at the last second."

Robert took a deep breath, wondering what all this meant. Why would there be a file on him?

"Well, I'm the embassy Deputy Head of Mission," he said after a moment. "Of course the Colombians have a file on me."

Roderic nodded.

"I accept that you're senior enough to warrant your own file. Which will be held in some government office in Bogotá, not some local police station in Medellín. Trust me, I'm a lawyer. There's something strange afoot here."

Robert sighed. At the moment he could not make sense of this. Had the Medellín police been expecting him? Possibly, since they had been on site even before he and Roderic had arrived. How had they known that he was coming, rather than, say, Tara, as had been the original plan? Once he got out of here there were some serious questions to ask. He was not yet sure who he would ask them to, but he would figure that out as well.

"Do you think Mr Gleeman killed those people?"

Robert shook his head, annoyed at having his thoughts interrupted.

"No, of course not. He, we, have been set up."

Roderic's eyes lit up in excitement.

"So, you know who's behind this?"

"Yes, I have a good guess." Robert started whispering. "It's most likely a drug cartel that we are investigating."

"Ah, marvellous, so tell that to the police and we'll be out of here."

Robert sighed.

"I can't do that. For all I know half the police officers here are on the cartel payroll. Maybe that's why they have my file, I don't know."

"Ah, well, that is a problem."

"Yes, it is. When they asked why you are here, did you

tell them about Mr Gleeman?"

"Yes, of course."

Robert looked over in a flash of anger.

"Why?"

"I just said he's in the city, as my colleague."

Robert sighed heavily. Had he not been in a police station he would have punched the barrister.

"So now they'll be out there looking for him! And he has the… he has sensitive information that he was meant to hand over to the deceased." He could feel the anger rising in him. "I guess street smarts is not something they teach at Oxford?"

**

Stuart started walking away from the hotel, his panic growing. What was happening to him? He quickly turned a few corners to get out of sight from the police. He realised that he had to get away from this neighbourhood, in case the police began some sort of search. But where would he go?

His first reaction was to call Carolina and explain the situation. However, Stuart hesitated. He was not sure how to relate to Carolina at the moment. It had only been a few hours since she had left his hotel room with a cheeky smile on her face. Calling now to tell her that he was implicated in a double murder would probably not go down too well. That said, a local lawyer would definitely come in handy.

Still walking, he fished out his phone from his pocket, ready to make the call. He then found himself faced with a problem. He had never called her before and only had her number written down somewhere in his work documents, which were still in his hotel room. He could take a taxi to her office building but he realised that might be dangerous. By now, surely, the police would have searched his hotel room and figured out why he was here. That probably meant that they would stake out Carolina's office, waiting for him there. He had never hidden from the police before but he was quickly starting to appreciate how difficult it could be.

He needed a different plan. He had to go somewhere the police would not be looking for him. He stopped for a second and looked at the smiling face of a Congressman Fernando Escaso, whose poster was asking for votes in the upcoming election. Stuart shook his head in frustration, but he did remember who he had first discussed the Colombian election with. Yes, that was the answer.

He sped up and soon found a busier street. Nearby he saw a couple of taxis, parked close to a small art museum. Stuart walked up to the museum entrance, pretended that he was just coming out, and from there stepped up to the nearest taxi.

"I don't have the exact address," Stuart told the driver as he climbed inside, "but I'd like to go to the church of Santa Teresa."

"Right away, sir," the taxi driver said cheerfully. He turned around and grinned at Stuart, before setting off. "Are you a tourist?"

"Yes," Stuart said vaguely, trying to keep his anxiety at bay.

"Excellent, sir," the driver said, still grinning. "Where are you from?"

"England," Stuart said automatically, before realising that giving away too many personal details might not be a good idea.

"Ah, yes, I follow Manchester United," the driver said and laughed. "Football, yes."

"That's great," Stuart said non-committedly.

"You must be very excited for the World Cup?"

"Absolutely," Stuart lied, trying to make himself sound normal and therefore more forgettable.

"Me too," the driver said. "Oh, and the Queen. My wife loves her."

"Good," Stuart said, struggling to make conversation. "They are very popular."

"You know the English Prince is visiting Colombia in a

few days, just after Easter? My wife really wants to go to Cartagena to see him and his wife. I don't know if I can get off work," the driver added more sombrely.

"I heard about the visit on the news," Stuart said. "I'm sure it's a great experience to get to see them." Stuart was very sure it was actually not a nice experience, but he had to avoid saying anything controversial.

The taxi made its way onto a main thoroughfare, which followed the Medellín River, and once again Stuart was heading back in the direction of the city centre. Thankfully the driver had stopped talking, and Stuart sank back in his seat, feeling exhausted. What was he going to do? There was no way he could go to the contract signing. He was sure that the police would be there. Of course, if he did go there he would hopefully be able to see Carolina and get some legal help.

However, in the safety of the taxi, his legal mind was beginning to catch up. Something strange was going on. On top of that, he did not have the greatest faith in the Colombian criminal justice system. To be honest, Stuart did not even know if they had one. No, his best option right now was to seek guidance from the priest, Antonio. Stuart felt better about his decision as he recalled that Antonio was a lawyer too. It was a small world.

The thoroughfare continued along the Medellín River, which divided the city into two halves. The road was beautifully lined with tall trees and, in the verdant tranquillity, Stuart managed to calm down. In the distance, he could see the skyscraper under which he had met Carolina yesterday and the other high-rise buildings in the city centre. The taxi carried on, leaving the centre behind. After a while, the taxi turned off the motorway and onto the smaller city streets. The street headed ever so slightly uphill and, just before reaching a hospital, the taxi turned into another main road.

In the distance Stuart saw a large church, looming over its neighbouring buildings. The taxi arrived at the rear of the church and turned up a narrow side street. It took them up to another main road. The driver had to pass through the intersection and pulled up on the other side of the main road.

"Sorry, couldn't stop there," the driver said.

Stuart paid, said his thanks and stepped out. Standing in the shade of a large tree, he looked across the road at the church. It was definitely an imposing building. It was built out of yellow-white stones, and the façade was lined with red details. The front of the church had a single, tall tower. On the top of the tower was an impressively large statue of the Virgin Mary, which looked out of all proportion to the church itself. To the rear of the church was a much smaller dome.

The road itself was lined with mainly two-story buildings, housing shops of various types. There were a lot of people walking around, but no one seemed to be going anywhere with any sense of purpose. A few people were sitting around outside a corner shop drinking coffee. It was a slow and casual pace of life and Stuart realised that in his suit he would stand out even more than he had in the city centre.

He crossed the road and saw a food cart a few metres down, which made him feel very hungry. However, this was not the time to stop for food. He looked up at the church again. Over the main door was a bas-relief of Jesus, who was carrying his cross. For the first time, Stuart could understand the power of the story, the ultimate sacrifice for others. The envelope was still burning in his pocket. Whoever the two victims were, they had clearly died for something. He felt a strong desire to get justice.

To think, only a few days ago his greatest fear had been leaving his home to go abroad. Looking up, he felt his fear of wrongful imprisonment slowly fading away. For once, in his rather dull, mediocre and introverted life, it was time to step up.

Unfortunately, that might prove difficult, as the door to the church was firmly closed. Worse still, a group of menacing-looking young men were sitting on the front steps. They had been eyeing him curiously and he heard some remarks about his suit. He dug deep to look confident and in control, the first test for his newfound passion, but in reality, he was still afraid.

Well, the taxi was gone. There was nothing to do but go forwards.

"Hello, do you know where the priest lives?" he asked as nicely but resolutely as he could. They were either going to be friendly or not.

"They live in the back, doctor," one of the men answered. "Just go around the corner." The man pointed down the side street the taxi had just driven up.

"Thank you very much," Stuart said and tried to smile politely. "I'm not a doctor," he added.

"Yes, sir," the man said, grinning broadly.

He immediately forgot about the young men as he turned the corner and walked down the side of the church. The whole wall was painted in the same white-yellow colour, with red details around the windows and edges, which gave the church a particular sparkle amongst the otherwise concrete-grey and redbrick buildings around it. It took a minute to walk the whole length of the church, and once out on the other road, he saw that the church was attached at its rear to a two-story redbrick building.

The front door had a door with a large cross nailed onto it, so he was sure he was in the right place. At this point he stopped himself, remembering that Antonio had given him a note with the church's address and phone number. The police would definitely find that note amongst his papers in the hotel room. He wondered whether it was best to walk away, but realised that he had no options. If the police came searching for him, then there was nothing he could do about it. He would have to take his chances with the Colombian criminal justice system.

He stepped up to the door and knocked on it a few times. After a while, it was opened by a young man dressed in a very distinctive brown habit. He seemed rather taken aback by Stuart. Clearly, they did not get many tall and pale visitors from England.

"Good afternoon, sir," he said politely but inquisitively.

"Good afternoon. I'm Stuart Gleeman, I am a…a friend of Father Antonio. I was hoping to see him now."

Stuart tried to speak firmly but he could not hide his stress and anxiety. The young man was sizing Stuart up. After a second, he stepped aside and gestured Stuart inside.

"Come in, doctor," he said kindly.

"I'm not a doctor," Stuart said, trying to sound polite.

"Of course, sir." The man was smiling. "It's a general term of respect in Colombia."

"Oh," Stuart said. "Oh, yes, right, thank you. Erm, is Father Antonio here?"

"I'm afraid not. He is with Father Juan, our prior, and they have gone out for a few hours."

Stuart took a deep breath. That was not what he wanted to hear. The young man could clearly sense Stuart's agitation.

"I will give them a call, sir."

They were standing in a small entrance hall. There was a door to the left which led into a small parlour. The young man went inside and Stuart saw him reach for an old landline phone. Stuart waited patiently, contemplating his continued bad luck. It was true that he knew nothing about what priests actually did on a daily basis, but he had assumed that Antonio would be at the church. This was a great disappointment. He kept taking deep breaths to stay in control but what he really wanted to do was shout, scream, yell, and panic. Maybe he would get an opportunity later.

"Sir, Father Antonio is on the phone."

The young man had reappeared in the parlour door. He motioned Stuart inside and showed him to the phone. The parlour was a small and simple room with an old sofa, some chairs and a small coffee table. Stuart grabbed the phone.

"Hello, Antonio."

"Hello, Stuart," he heard the excited voice of Antonio exclaim. "It is so very good to hear from you. I'm sorry that I'm not there at the moment to meet you. Are you free today?"

"Yes," Stuart said, his worries clearly coming through in his tone of voice. "Yes, Antonio, something has happened and I need your help, right away."

"Colombia, eh," Antonio said, having picked up on Stuart's panicked voice. "It's not just coffee and chocolate. Yes, I am in a park above the city, up in the mountains. You should come and join us up here. It's calm, serene, and has plenty of fresh air."

"Right, yes, sounds good," Stuart agreed.

He was sure that the further away from the city centre he went the better. Also, fresh air did sound quite appealing. Anything to get the image of the dead bodies out of his mind. He really needed a place to think things through. He had so many questions and with his newfound desire for answers, a walk in the park sounded great. Antonio gave him the directions. Stuart thanked him and said he would see them soon.

The young man, who introduced himself as James, volunteered to walk Stuart down to the nearby metro station. James explained that there was no harm in having a companion, especially when dressed in an expensive suit. He did not want to speak ill of his parishioners, but there had been a few incidents over the years, and realism before idealism.

"Are you a priest?" Stuart asked as James led them back up the side street towards the front of the church.

"Not yet," James said. "I'm still training. I have at least two or three more years to go."

"That's a long time to study," Stuart said.

At the front of the church, they turned onto the main road. Stuart was constantly casting careful glances around him but, although a few people were eyeing him curiously, he did not feel afraid. He realised that there was probably nothing wrong at all with the neighbourhood. Most importantly, though, there was not a police officer in sight.

"There is a lot to learn," James remarked pensively.

"Why did you become a priest? If you don't mind me asking, it is a personal question."

James waved the apology away.

"It is a simple but complicated story, like so many stories are. I come from, well, not so far away from here. It is a poor neighbourhood and many of my friends got involved in crime and drugs. Some died, very young. I felt predestined for that life. No one in my family ever went to church but one day I met a priest. He was an old man. We knew about him in the neighbourhood, he was respected. I only met him once and he asked me about my dreams. A simple but powerful question. I felt for the first time that perhaps I did have a choice in life. Perhaps the path I was on was not preordained. I thought about that question for a long time, coming up with an answer. After a few years I went to a church and here I am now."

Stuart did not know what to say. His mind was too preoccupied to think it through, but he did feel for what James must have gone through.

"I'm glad you got a choice."

It was a general and vague reply that nonetheless sounded very profound. It is a trick every lawyer needs to know, no matter how stressful a situation might be.

"Yes, having a choice means a lot in life," James said.

Once they had reached the metro station, James reiterated the directions to the park, and with a strong handshake, they parted ways. Stuart hopped on a northbound train. He felt calmer with every passing minute, as the train rattled on, further and further away from the city centre. The buildings outside the train windows were getting smaller and shabbier. The poverty level was going up. This gave Stuart some pause for concern, as it might not be the safest of places to travel through, but neither Antonio nor James had said anything. Besides, these looked like neighbourhoods where the police might not have complete control or access. If he wanted to get away, this was probably the best place to be.

As instructed, he stepped off at Acevedo station and followed the signs to the cable car. He queued up with a large number of locals, many of whom seemed to be returning from shopping trips. Once again he was on the receiving end of many curious, but always polite, looks. Eventually, he was ushered into a carriage, together with a handful of other passengers. The doors closed and they set off.

Stuart's curiosity took over, somehow suppressing his worries. The carriage passed over the Medellín River and then flew above the houses and roads of the local neighbourhoods. It was a sea of red, as almost every building was made out of bricks. The cable car climbed higher and higher up the eastern side of the valley and the neighbourhoods below became increasingly poor. The carriage slowed down at a couple of stations, where some of the other passengers stepped off.

At a station called Santo Domingo, everyone stepped off. At the very last second Stuart realised that this was the end of the ride, as the carriage was circling around to go back down. He jumped out, keenly aware that this was not some country park outside the city. There was an open plaza and a road, surrounded by buildings of varying quality and upkeep. Looking around he saw that he was nowhere near the top of the valley, and following signs for the Park, he found another cable car, which continued further upwards. In this carriage there were no locals. He was all alone.

As the car climbed higher up the slope the neighbourhoods became even poorer. Eventually, any semblance of city planning wore off. The only buildings left at the highest level of the valley were a haphazard collection of wooden shackles, some with corrugated steel roofs, others simply protected by tarpaulins. The devastating poverty was curiously juxtaposed with the beauty beyond. Looking up, Stuart could see the entire Medellín valley, with the city spreading out far to the south. The skyscrapers in the city centre were barely visible through the heat haze, and from what he could see they looked tiny. The unbelievable vista, unlike anything he had ever seen before, calmed him down.

When the carriage came to the very top, Stuart prepared to step off. However, as the carriage crossed over the precipice he was in for a surprise. The cable lines seemed to continue on indefinitely down a narrow gap cut through a thick forest. Stuart tried to see further into the distance, but could not make out anything but trees. He sank back into the seat and resigned himself to a bizarre journey, slowly flying through the dense forest.

**

After a bizarrely long journey, the cable car finally arrived at Arví Park. The station was set in a large clearing in the forest and stood alongside a collection of other wooden buildings. Stuart left the station and walked out onto the plaza, which was busy with visitors. The buildings housed various food stands and information points, and the dazzling aromas of fried meat made him even hungrier. Walking around, he quickly spotted Antonio and his friend, both dressed in priest's black.

"Hello, Stuart," Antonio said cheerfully, reaching out his hand. "It is so nice to see you again. This is my friend, Father Juan."

Stuart shook hands with Juan. It might have been the black clothes and the distinctive collar, but Stuart thought that they looked very much alike. They must both have been in their early thirties and sported youthful and energetic looks. Stuart remembered the haunted look Antonio had had on the flight over, and he felt that he could again see hints of it hiding behind Antonio's smile. But perhaps he was just projecting his own anxieties.

"It's very nice to meet you, Stuart," Juan said. "I want to say, I hope you like Colombia, but erm…" He trailed off, inviting Stuart to explain the predicament that had led him up here.

"It's very nice," Stuart said, speaking honestly. Everything until midday had been great. "But yes, something has happened, and I didn't know who else to turn to. I'm sorry to disturb you, of course."

"We are happy to help," Juan said.

"Indeed," Antonio chimed in. "We were going to get some obleas to eat, please join us. It will make things better."

"Yes, thank you," Stuart said. "I'm rather hungry, I haven't eaten all day."

Juan led the way over to one of the food stands and ordered the obleas. Stuart looked on with hungry eyes. He saw that they were large, round and thin wafers, on which the stallholder was spreading a smooth caramel paste.

"Do you also want strawberries and cream?" Juan asked.

"Of course he does, he's English," Antonio interjected cheerfully.

Obleas in hand, the trio started walking away from the main area. Juan explained briefly that Arví Park was a large nature preserve laid out on the high plain to the east of the city. They were following a road which ran steeply downhill, passing a few more food stands. Juan bought a few bottles of Colombiana, an orange soft drink, before they turned into a deserted path leading through the forest. With some sugar in him, and having enjoyed some refreshing sips of Colombiana, which tasted very Scottish, he felt calm and relaxed. There were certainly no police officers looking for him out here.

"So, Stuart, tell us what has happened," Antonio enquired. "You sounded very distressed on the phone earlier."

Continuing their walk through the forest, joined only by a cacophony of birds, Stuart decided to tell them the whole story, starting with his mysterious meeting with William Cooth. Antonio and Juan listened patiently, showing no surprise or disbelief when Stuart explained how he had found the dead bodies in the jewellery shop, other than dutifully making the sign of the cross.

By the time Stuart finished, they had reached a wooden building set in a clearing by a large lake. They went to a bench and sat down, looking out over the water. Stuart mostly saw green trees around him, but spotted some flowers blossoming in blue, red, and yellow. The lake allowed for a light breeze to come through, which cooled Stuart down. The air was fresh, which was a welcomed change from the city.

"This is a very serious situation," Juan said. "Do you still have this envelope? Can we see it?"

It was time. Stuart reached into his pocket and pulled out the envelope. He opened it very carefully, and pulled out two passports, details of flight reservations and a small wad of Colombian bank notes. The passports were British and were made out to a woman and her daughter. Juan asked for the passports and inspected them carefully, a curious look on his face.

"This older woman, is she the one who was killed?"

Stuart took the passport. Studying it thoroughly he noticed that there was something slightly odd about the photo, as if it had been digitally altered. Thinking back to the murder scene, his heartbeat sped up. He had not looked at the bodies very closely, and they had both been lying on their stomachs, their heads turned out, so he had only seen the faces in profile. The dead woman could be the woman in the photo, but he was not certain.

"It's possible," he concluded.

Juan gave Antonio a strange look, the first of many, but Stuart thought nothing of it.

"I am very certain I know who that is," Juan said.

"What? Really?" Stuart looked at him, surprised.

Juan took the passport and looked at it again. He then glanced at Antonio, who seemed to nod almost imperceptibly. Stuart was still too caught up in his anxiety to notice.

"You see, a few weeks ago a man came to the church.

It turned out he had got married there, many years ago, long before me or my brothers took over running the church. He showed me a picture of his family. It was him, his wife, his daughter, and his son. This, I am sure, is the wife." Juan took another close look at the second passport. "Yes, I am sure this is the daughter."

Juan stopped for a moment, still engrossed in the two passports. Stuart eyed him impatiently, eager to hear more.

"The man was called Manuel. He explained that he was involved in one of the local drug cartels. Recently, his son had been murdered and Manuel found out that the cartel was responsible. The son had been disloyal, somehow, and Manuel had a crisis of conscience. He turned against the cartel, uncovered some secret information, and sought guidance from me."

"What did you tell him?" Stuart asked.

"Well, he said he was not comfortable going to the authorities here. He spoke about going to the British embassy in Bogotá, because the information would, somehow, be useful to them. You know, this is why I made the link when I saw the British passports. I am not sure what Manuel did, because I have not heard from him since he left the church."

"If Britain is handing out passports to his family I guess he did go to the embassy," Stuart said.

"Then why didn't he bring his wife and daughter with him?" Antonio asked.

"He must have spoken to the British somehow," Juan said. He suddenly drummed his legs with a big smile. "You know, a few days later, I thought nothing of this until now, it said in the news that a cartel boat was captured by a British frigate outside Cartagena. Maybe Manuel was on board?"

"Perhaps," Stuart said, his legal mind working again. "Seems a bit fortuitous that he would be captured by a British warship just days after speaking to a priest about it."

"Yes," Juan said. "But clearly the purpose of this

handoff was getting his family out of Colombia in exchange for Manuel's information about the cartel."

"So the cartel killed the wife? Then, who was the old man? Where is the daughter?"

Stuart thought back to the most terrifying part. How had the police got there so fast? How had they known at which hotel he was staying? He asked this out loud. Juan sighed and a worried look came upon his face. He stirred nervously on the bench and looked around. A few visitors were walking around up by the house, but they were well out of earshot.

"We should keep walking," Juan said nonetheless.

They set off down another path, once again heading through the forest. The lake was visible in the distance through the trees. The path was deserted, so they could speak freely.

"Ah, the cartels and the authorities and all the rest," Juan said airily. "It's a big mess, I can tell you that. Do you know anything about it?"

"No," Stuart said. "Oh, there's peace negotiations with the FARC, and the current president wants to continue them, but his opponent in the upcoming election wants to end them and go back to military action. I learnt that much."

"That is a part of it, in a nutshell," Juan said. "I think this was a fragmented country right from the start, when it became independent from Spain. Many would say, I think correctly, that Bogotá has been ruled, for the most part, by a powerful oligarchy, albeit one that waged civil war against itself for the first hundred years. However, the oligarchy has never had much control over the rural areas, not even in the other towns and cities around the country."

They kept walking down the path, which was now rising upwards as the terrain became hillier. Whilst birds were still singing all around, there were no other people in sight.

"All these areas around the country have been controlled by various vested interests, usually landowners and other wealthy individuals. The workers have never been treated very well. Now, militant communism maybe started in Russia, but it spread around the world, including Colombia, and communist guerrilla groups formed to, as they put it, fight for rights for the workers. Key was always land reform and giving farmers the right to the land they worked. These guerrillas started off with a reasonable amount of support, but they eventually turned more militant and violent. They attacked the landowners, kidnapped them for ransom, and killed them. There was continuous violence for a very long time."

Juan paused and stopped. They had reached a fork in the path, and Juan turned to the right.

"In Britain, I guess such things would be handled by the police, or maybe even the army?"

"The police, yes," Stuart said.

"Yes, and it works, because the government has control over the country. In a benign way, I'm sure. But here, as I said, the government never had much control outside Bogotá. So these landowners and businessmen, the wealthy, formed their own protection groups. Well-armed paramilitary outfits. The paramilitaries became violent and dangerous. Soon they started to indiscriminately kill anyone they thought was undesirable to society, not just the guerrillas. They were 'cleansing' the country."

Juan shook his head.

"Anyway, you can imagine, in this lawlessness, criminal gangs, growing and selling drugs, had almost free-reign. At the same time, the guerrillas and the paras could do the same to finance their work. Now, the former president offered an amnesty to the paras, in return for them disbanding. That was ten years ago, they are not too much of a problem now. The guerrillas have also been decimated by the army and the old, large drug cartels have also fallen. Escobar, and all that. Which, I guess, is all a good thing. But the problem is this. There are a lot of disbanded paras and guerrillas, and no plan for what to do with them. Many have no formal education, they live in poverty, and they have no job prospects. Perhaps understandably, not saying it is inevitable, but many have returned to a life of crime. So there are new drug cartels springing up all over the place. People are still killed or just disappear far too often. The other problem is this. It seems the army and the paras were often working very closely together and there have been plenty of human rights accusations against the government."

"That's rather worrying," Stuart agreed.

In the distance, they could see another large building, housing what looked like a restaurant. There were a few people around the building, but the path was still empty. They walked on but slowed down.

"I don't know much about this cartel that Manuel was involved with," Juan said. "However, there is the possibility that it consists of former paras who have friends in the police."

"So Manuel speaks to the authorities, the cartel kill his wife, and arrange for their friends in the police to arrest me?"

"Yes," Juan agreed. "Generally, a lot of people don't trust the police. There is every chance that some police officers are working with the cartel. Their speed in arriving at your hotel would suggest that." He paused. "If this is cartel business, you do not want to be involved. You really don't. Do you have your passport? Can you get out of the country fast?"

"No," Stuart said. "It's in the hotel room."

"That is bad news," Juan said, and Antonio nodded sombrely.

"What about your colleague?" Antonio asked.

Stuart had completely forgotten about Roderic. He took out his phone to check for messages from him, or Carolina, or his clients, but there was no reception.

"They will wonder where I am," Stuart said.

"You shouldn't contact any of them," Juan said. "Don't get anyone else involved." He sighed but then started chuckling. "This is not what I expected when Antonio said you had a problem."

"I'm really sorry to have involved you," Stuart said. Reflecting on everything Juan had just told him, he realised that he had likely put Juan and Antonio in serious danger.

"Think nothing of it," Juan said.

"Indeed," Antonio said. "I think that Stuart should come with us back to the church. There are a lot of questions that need answering before we make another move."

"Agreed," Juan said. "Yes, as a priest I sometimes have to move in interesting places. I have some contacts that we can speak to." He suddenly looked at them gravely. "I'm very worried about Manuel's daughter. If she isn't dead, the cartel might have taken her."

Stuart took a deep breath. This was a really bad situation. They turned around and started the long walk back to the cable car station.

Chapter 10

There was a rapid knock on the front door.

Stuart, Antonio, Juan, together with James and Father Pedro, who was another Carmelite priest, were sitting around the dining room table in the friary. As the first knocks rattled in, they all looked up at each other. The trio had been tense ever since their return from Arví Park and the dinner had been very quiet. James and Pedro, unaware of what had passed, ate in a more upbeat contemplative silence. Antonio and Juan had quietly been reviewing their new predicament. Stuart had only managed to feel awkward and out of place, and consequently had kept silent.

They had returned from Arví Park without incident. At the cable car station, Stuart had regained a signal for his phone and a long line of texts had quickly appeared. Several were from his clients, asking where he was. They got increasingly angry, but the last one informed him that the contract had been signed. Another simply read "Status?", and was from an unknown Colombian number. Stuart had assumed that it was someone from the embassy, wondering what had happened.

"Don't send any replies," Juan had advised him. "We must keep a low profile."

That had been easier said than done, as several other visitors to the Park had asked for blessings from the two priests. Stuart had managed to chuckle a bit as he watched them signing crosses with their hands as quickly as was spiritually possible, all the time moving towards the station. Finally, they had got through and had ridden the long way back down to Acevedo metro station, and returned to the friary from there. It had been a lot later than Stuart realised when they got back. Dinner had been prepared, and Stuart had eaten heartily, since the oblea had been his only food all day, and it had not sustained him for very long.

More knocks rattled in from the front door. Juan asked James to go and answer the door, with the clear but unexplained instruction not to let anyone in, unless it was a real emergency.

"We often get parishioners calling, seeking spiritual advice," Juan explained.

Stuart, however, could sense that Juan was worried. Stuart feared it was the police, that they had tracked him down using the note that Antonio had given him. Or maybe someone had thought that he did not belong in this neighbourhood and had called it in. If it was the police, he was trapped. As he had accepted earlier, he would have to surrender and deal with the consequences later.

Down the hallway, they could suddenly hear an argumentative female voice. The trio looked at each other in surprise, but Father Pedro just sighed to himself and kept eating. He had probably joined the priesthood to get away from argumentative women. Not too long later James walked back into the kitchen, followed by Carolina.

Stuart was stunned. How had she found him here? She let out a loud shriek of relief as she saw Stuart. She ran up to him with a big smile and tightly embraced him.

"I have been so worried," she said. "Oh God, what has happened? Why are you here? You missed the whole afternoon, your clients were angry…"

She trailed off and looked around the room. James had sat back down, Juan and Antonio were smiling at her, guessing at who she was, and Father Pedro was still eating, seemingly oblivious to what was happening.

"Well," Stuart began hesitantly but he did not know what to say. The images of the dead bodies, which had haunted him all afternoon, were replaced by more exciting flashes from the previous night, which did not help the situation.

"I'm so glad you're all right, that nothing has happened," she said, realising that he was not going to say anything more. She looked down at the priests again, clearly wondering what had in fact happened.

"Perhaps we should speak in private," Juan said.

With a small, almost imperceptible gesture of his hand, he dismissed James and Pedro, who left without objection, carrying their half-eaten plates.

"I'm Father Juan and this is Father Antonio."

"Ah, the Spanish priest," Carolina exclaimed.

Juan and Antonio now looked closely at Stuart, who slowly sank back down into his chair. It felt like a scolding look and he now wished he had not told Carolina anything about anything yesterday.

"Yes," Juan said after a moment. "Can I ask, does anyone know you are here?"

"No," Carolina said curtly and folded her arms. "Why?"

"That's good."

Juan tried to smile appreciatively and indicated for her to sit down, which she did. She discreetly grabbed Stuart's hand under the table, squeezing it tightly. Stuart did not say anything, still wondering if the priests were upset with him for telling Carolina about Antonio. There was silence for a while. Juan was motionless, Antonio had started swirling his wine glass around, and Stuart and Carolina kept holding hands.

"So," Juan opened slowly, looking at Carolina but hoping that Stuart would chime in. "I have a guess, but who are you?"

"I'm sorry," Stuart said. "This is Carolina, the lawyer I am working with."

"Excellent," Juan said.

There was another moment of awkward silence. Finally, noticing that Stuart did not feel comfortable speaking, Juan continued. He spoke slowly and carefully, choosing his words with a practised delicacy that Stuart's legal mind could appreciate.

"I didn't mean to worry you, Carolina, it's just that we have a small problem. Stuart has been, wrongly, of course, implicated in... a minor crime. Antonio and I are helping him out."

"Crime," Carolina blurted out, thrusting her hands into the air, causing Stuart's arm to drop into his chair. "What crime?"

Juan looked at Stuart, indicating that he was reluctant to tell another person's story.

"Stuart?"

Stuart sighed and summoned some strength. For the second time, he told the story of what had happened to him. He simplified the story by saying that he was dropping off a parcel for a business associate in England. He did not want to place any more burden than necessary on Carolina, having realised that he had probably put the two priests in danger. Juan and Antonio nodded along, both listening attentively even though they had heard the story just a few hours before. Neither of them made any gesture to indicate surprise at the details that Stuart left out. Perhaps they understood why he chose to do so.

"Oh, Mother of God," Carolina again blurted out, putting her hands over her mouth, as Stuart explained how he had come across the two dead bodies inside the jeweller's office. Juan and Antonio again dutifully made the sign of the cross.

There was another moment of silence as Stuart finished his story.

"I have a lot to figure out," Stuart said reflectively. "I could not come to the meeting this afternoon, and I asked Antonio and Juan for assistance."

"So, is this why your colleague didn't show up either?" Carolina asked.

Stuart furrowed his eyebrows.

"He didn't show up," Carolina explained. "Your clients were beside themselves with anger that neither of their lawyers had shown up, which was funny at the time, but…not now. I can't remember his name, it's weird, but is he also involved in this?"

"I don't know," Stuart said, in shock. "I haven't seen or heard from him since I, well we, left him at the airport in Bogotá. Antonio was there."

"Roderic, wasn't it?" Antonio said. "Yes, he was very English. Very, erhm, distinctive." He turned to Carolina. "You're saying he's also missing?"

"I don't know," Carolina said, having pulled out her phone. "He wasn't there. I'll just quickly check the news."

Juan was about to speak when Carolina put her hand up.

"I haven't checked the news all day, clearly you haven't either. It says here that two Englishmen have been arrested for murder. Double murder, in the city centre."

"That's not good," Juan said.

"Two?" Stuart asked. "Who? How many Englishmen are there is this city?"

"Oh, this is not good," Carolina continued as she kept scrolling through the news report. "They are searching for a third Englishman. It says more details about the suspect will follow shortly."

The room fell silent.

"Stuart must leave immediately," Antonio said firmly. "We'll drive him to the airport and fly him out on the first flight, before anyone has the chance to get his details to the airport police."

"Yes," Juan said. "The cartel was probably hoping that you would be arrested at the scene, like these other two were, but now you're just a loose end. The cartels do not like that. We have to get you out. I'm sure there's a night flight to somewhere."

Carolina started pressing away on her phone.

"I don't have my passport," Stuart said. "I told you in the Park."

They all looked at him.

"Oh, yes," Juan said and sighed.

"There's a flight at eleven to New York," Carolina said.

"Still need my passport."

Carolina patted him gently on his leg.

"Maybe one of us can get the passport for you," she said. "The police aren't looking for us, nor is any cartel."

"Do you think that you can do that?"

"Yes," Juan said. He took a deep breath. "To be honest, it's not certain that they're actually looking for you. The police might have just arrived at the murder scene at the same time as you by coincidence and they might have been at the hotel looking for your colleague."

"I guess," Stuart said, allowing himself to feel a bit of optimism. Maybe they had been there looking for Roderic?

"I think I have an idea," Antonio interjected enthusiastically, putting his wine glass back on the table. "Yes, I can pretend that a hotel guest has called for a priest, and gain access that way. The police might be watching, for whoever they are looking for, outside, but surely not in the corridor. I can use your key and collect some of your things. The passport, at least."

"That could work," Juan said, nodding.

Carolina snorted.

"That sounds utterly stupid," she said dismissively. "Who asks for a priest these days?"

Stuart opened his mouth but could not think of anything to say. He was sensing some hostility between Carolina and the two priests, which he could not quite understand or explain, and given how they had helped him it made him uncomfortable. The priests did not say anything to acknowledge the enmity but instead retreated into a contemplative silence.

"It's worth a try," Juan said after a moment, but less sure of himself.

"Fine," Carolina said brusquely. "I'll drive."

No one argued with her.

**

They stepped out onto the street, and Stuart breathed in the cold night air. The atmosphere inside the kitchen had become tense, but the freshness outside woke him up. For a brief moment, he felt fine. Not happy, not sad, but just fine. After this day, that was the best feeling he could imagine.

He reflected for a second on the many questions that he had. Who was the unknown dead man? Why had Manuel's wife been killed? Where was his daughter? How was Roderic caught up in this? None of this made any sense. Even though his tired mind could muster some curiosity, the thought of somehow getting his passport and getting on a flight out of Colombia was appealing. At least that would mean that he would be safe. He would not be wrongfully arrested for murder nor would any cartel consider him a loose end.

Carolina had parked just outside the friary. The priests climbed into the back of the car, and Stuart joined Carolina in the front. She revved the engine impatiently and then shot down the street. Out on the highway through the city they encountered some traffic, but the evening rush hour was winding down, and they quickly made their way to the hotel.

The hotel was situated at the north end of a large square, in the middle of which stood the ruins of an old industrial-looking building. Textile industries, all gone now, Carolina explained. Stuart had noticed them the day before when he had walked to the metro station for the first time. He had thought that it was a strange ornament to have in a public square. The was another tall building to the south, smaller buildings to the east, and the western side opened up to the main road and the metro tracks beyond it.

Carolina parked on the south side of the square. The hotel entrance was hidden on the other side of the ruins. The whole park had an eerie silence and darkness to it, and there was no movement, other than the lights of the cars out on the main road.

"Right then, Father, off you go," Carolina said dismissively as she turned off the engine.

No one reacted to her hostile tone. Stuart handed his room key to Antonio and explained how to get there. The priests then left the car. Antonio set off with a confident stride, and Juan followed more slowly, stopping in front of the ruin. Antonio disappeared from sight as he walked around the ruin and up to the hotel entrance.

Stuart turned over and looked at Carolina.

"You don't seem to like them very much," he said.

She scoffed but kept looking up ahead at the black silhouette of Juan, who was standing motionlessly by the ruin.

"Priests? No, definitely not. They're just self-centred and self-serving. I can't understand why you asked them for help. You should have come straight to me."

"I didn't want to trouble you," Stuart said slowly. He did not know what to make of her hostility but this did not seem like the time to press the matter.

"Were you embarrassed after last night?"

"No," Stuart protested, a bit too quickly.

Carolina shot him an angry stare.

"Why then?" she spat out. "You are being implicated in a fucking murder, and instead of going to a lawyer you go to a priest. Stupid!"

Stuart was taken aback and tried to make himself smaller in his seat. He looked out of the front window, avoiding her gaze, but all he saw was Juan, still waiting by the ruin.

"Look, priests like them only have one agenda," Carolina said after a moment, speaking more softly. "They want to put themselves into a position of political power and influence, and protect rich, conservative businessmen from any opposition, be it the guerrillas or anything else, through any means." She paused for a moment. "You know, when the businessmen arranged paramilitary death squads, many priests supported them. Just with words, but still. Said it was acceptable to kill communists, since they reject God anyway."

"Really?" Stuart said, a bit sceptical.

"Yes, the old president put an end to most of these paramilitary outfits, but it was only ten years ago." She scoffed. "Guerrilla group this, paramilitary group that, and those people doing God knows what in the middle of it, benefitting only themselves in the process."

"Surely it can't have been all priests?" Stuart said. "Anyway, Juan is not old enough to have been a priest ten years ago, and Antonio is Spanish. He has no agenda here."

"Don't be naïve. It's about the institution, not the individuals. It had an agenda then, and it's slow to forget. I wouldn't trust a word they're saying."

"I," Stuart started but faltered. Carolina gave him another cold look. "But they have really supported me today."

"Exactly," Carolina exclaimed. "One priest you met on a flight, and one you've never met before, just suddenly agree to help a complete stranger who's been implicated in a murder and God knows what else. Who does that? Trust me, they are up to something."

"But…you're also helping me," Stuart said before realising the implications of the statement. Unsurprisingly, Carolina gave him yet another ice cold look.

"Yes, but we've been working together for months, you're not a stranger to me. Besides, I'm a lawyer, I understand cartels, setups and police corruption."

"I really do appreciate it," Stuart said quickly, trying to defrost the situation. He smiled at her, in vain, and then looked over at Juan again, who was still waiting by the ruin. "So, what do you want to do about the priests?"

Carolina sighed and shook her head.

"Let's see if he can get your passport first. If they can, we get you out tonight, and everything will be fine. I can try to find out what's going on with the murder and the missing daughter."

"Will I really be able to get through airport security?"

Carolina dismissed his concern with a small wave.

"I'd be surprised if the city police have bothered to speak to anyone else about you, let alone the airport police." She chuckled in disbelief. "You know, I once saw some drug addicts fighting each other on the street, and two policemen just looked on for a while before walking off. I'd be more worried about the real murderers who are trying to set you up, who might not like that you are still free, and to avoid them you better leave."

Stuart was about the respond when Antonio finally reappeared around the ruin, joined up with Juan, and headed over to the car. They were walking briskly, and Stuart could sense that things had not gone well. Antonio had a harried look on his face as they got back into the car.

"Go, go," Antonio said.

Carolina drove off without hesitation or argument, quickly heading away from the hotel.

"What happened?" Stuart asked.

Antonio sighed.

"There were quite a few police officers around the lobby, and there were two of them patrolling the corridor outside your room. They are far more interested in you than I had thought. They asked me what I was doing and I told them I was there to see a guest who had asked for a priest. I tried to strike up a friendly conversation, you know, colleagues working the night shift. They said they were waiting for the guest in your room. The bad news is that they've removed all your belongings, taken it to the police station. There is no way that we can get your passport."

"Damn," Stuart said. He turned around and looked at Antonio. "I'm glad you made it out all right."

"Oh, yes," Antonio said. "I had to pretend that I was on the wrong floor, and went back to the lift. No questions were asked, so I think we're okay."

Carolina pulled up outside a dark building. Stuart recognised it from earlier in the day, because Congressman Escaso was still smiling on the wall. That felt like a lifetime ago.

"How did this happen?" Stuart asked. The day's events did not add up. "The police were at the jewellery shop moments after I arrived. It's like they were expecting me to be there. I was lucky to get away. I spent, what, fifteen minutes in a taxi, and the police were already at my hotel.

That's impossible!"

"Not impossible," Juan said. "You were set up to take the fall for this. Someone bears you ill will, Stuart."

Stuart groaned, his head spinning. What was going on?

"So, we really need new travel documents for Stuart," Carolina said. "Right away."

"Yes, I agree," Juan said. He sighed and resigned himself to reality. "But it's late, we'll arrange that tomorrow."

"You know where to get a false passport?" Carolina asked incredulously.

"Of course. I'm a priest. Do you?"

"Yes! I'm a lawyer."

"Excellent," Stuart interjected, trying to prevent a spat between them. "Tomorrow sounds good. I could do with some sleep."

"I'll drive you back to your church," Carolina said, addressing the priests. "Stuart can stay at my place tonight. It's guarded, he'll be perfectly safe."

"Thank you," Stuart said.

Juan and Antonio remained silent.

Chapter 11

Stuart spent the night tossing and turning in bed.

Carolina had a nice and spacious flat, almost on the top floor of a high-rise building, nestled high up on the eastern slope of the valley. When they arrived last night Stuart could not help but be impressed by the panoramic views over the city, lit up in the darkness of the night.

"You can sleep in my bed," Carolina had said with a cheeky smile.

Stuart had instead opted to take a seat out on the balcony. It was a cold and crispy night, but Stuart's mind seemed immune from the climate and kept working in overdrive. Carolina, sensing his need to reflect, had left him in peace.

When Stuart finally had started shivering he realised that it was time to call it a day. He had tiptoed into the bedroom, thinking that Carolina would have been sleeping, but she had startled him when he sat down on the bed.

"Finished thinking?" she had asked, a voice coming out of the darkness.

"Yes," Stuart had said.

She had crawled up behind him and placed her arms around him.

"You know," she had said, and kissed him on his cheek, "despite what you might think, I've never been with an outlaw before."

"I wasn't thinking that," Stuart had said awkwardly, accepting, with the slightest tinge of disappointment, that he did not have a romantic bone in his body.

Carolina had smiled and leaned in to kiss him again.

Despite everything, Stuart had had a scattered sleep, and he felt exhausted when he woke up. The sun was up and the bedroom was brightly lit. He heard some clattering from the kitchen, suggesting that Carolina was up making breakfast. He rubbed his eyes, trying to find some scraps of energy. He knew that he would not get any more sleep, despite his heavy head, and he slowly pulled himself out of bed. To his dismay, he realised that he had no fresh clothes, since apparently all of his possessions were in a Colombian police station.

Reluctantly, he pulled on yesterday's clothes. He then walked down the short hallway and into the small kitchen, where he found Carolina supervising an elderly and somewhat rotund woman, who was wearing an apron.

"Good morning," Carolina said as he stepped in. "You stink," she added cheerfully.

"I know," Stuart said quietly.

He looked at the old woman, who was busy frying some eggs, but who had completely ignored him. Maybe she did not approve of overnight guests in smelly clothes.

"Don't mind Flora," Carolina said. "She's my very own wonder woman."

"Ha," Flora exclaimed, placing the fried eggs on a plate. She then proceeded to pour a large glass of orange juice and handed it to Stuart with a stern look on her face.

"Good morning," Stuart said.

He took the juice and drank it quickly.

"Let's eat on the balcony," Carolina said.

She led the way outside and Stuart followed her. He could not decide whether he preferred the day view or the night view. They were both awe-inspiring. They say down at the table and Flora came out carrying a tray with more juice, the eggs and a fried sausage.

"You are English, yes," Flora said as she put the sausage in front of Stuart.

"You're too kind," Stuart said, not knowing what else to say in response to a solitary sausage, which, to be fair, did look quite succulent. It was probably what he needed in his sleep-deprived state.

Flora headed back inside and disappeared into the kitchen.

"She's lovely," Carolina said. "She's been with me for ages."

"Yes," Stuart said noncommittedly. He sensed that the

housekeeper was not entirely happy with him. Maybe she did not like having to cook for two.

"What a day," Carolina said with an odd cheerfulness.

"Yes," Stuart said again. He took a bite of his sausage, cheering up. It tasted well. "Worst day of my life," he added.

He ate the sausage, feeling a bit better with every bite, but the sun was starting to burn, and he squirmed in his day-old clothes. They were really uncomfortable now.

"We must get you some clothes," Carolina said, casting a scrutinising eye over Stuart's dishevelled attire. "After breakfast, we'll go to the mall and buy you some things."

They were interrupted by the buzzing of the intercom. Carolina immediately tensed up and rushed inside. Stuart stood up and waited by the balcony door. Flora had answered the intercom, and after nodding a bit she turned around, covering the phone.

"Police, ma'am."

Stuart and Carolina exchanged panicked looks.

"They're here for me, aren't they?" Stuart said. He then looked at Flora, realising he had said too much. He opened his mouth to speak but Carolina cut him off.

"We don't know that. I'm the lawyer working with you, they probably just have some questions for me. I can handle it." She paused. "Flora, hide him in the washroom."

Flora sighed, but without questioning why she was hiding a stranger from the police, she led Stuart through the kitchen and into a small room behind it. In the room was a washing machine and some cleaning equipment. She told him to stand still and then closed the door behind him. It felt like this was not the first time the old housekeeper had hidden someone in a cupboard.

Stuart lent up against the door and listened carefully. He could hear Flora moving around in the kitchen and then a knock on the front door.

"Good morning."

It was a man's voice, just about audible through the door. Stuart heard Carolina invite the policeman in. Now for the big question. Did they know that Stuart was here? He held his breath.

"We understand you have been in contact with one Stuart Gleeman," the officer said, horribly mispronouncing the English name. "We are looking for him."

"Yes," Carolina said, unperturbed. "The English lawyer. I had lunch with him on Thursday, then yesterday he didn't show up to our meeting. I saw the news, you think he killed someone."

Stuart wanted to jump up and down in joy but managed to restrain himself. The police did not seem to know that he was here. They were just looking for information. Whilst quietly celebrating, he had missed some of the conversation outside. He leaned up against the door again.

"You did not report him missing yesterday," the policeman pointed out.

"No. His clients asked me if I had seen him, I said no. I assumed that they would try to find him."

There was silence for a moment, and Stuart strained himself to hear what was happening.

"So you are here alone?" the policeman asked.

"Yes."

"But there is breakfast for two out here."

The policeman was further away, clearly by the balcony door. Stuart's heart sped up. The breakfast, still on the table. Evidence of a guest.

"Yes?" Carolina asked.

"You're sure Stuart Gleeman is not here?"

Despite everything, Stuart could not stop himself wincing at the mispronunciation.

"I had breakfast with my housekeeper."

"With your housekeeper?" the policeman asked, in disbelief.

"You don't?" Carolina queried, sounding stern.

Stuart's heart was still beating fast. The policeman was suspicious. He was obviously going to search the flat. Stuart knew that he was going to be found. He looked around the washroom for an escape, but there was none, not even a small window. He was absolutely trapped in here. Instinctively he picked up a mop and held it tightly in both hands. It was the only weapon in the room. Maybe he could push past the policeman and make a run for it. Get back to the church somehow?

He heard footsteps. Coming closer.

The door opened, and Stuart thrust the mop forwards. Someone grabbed it and pushed back, and Stuart tumbled over, falling onto his back.

"Ha," Flora scoffed. "Big, brave man."

Chuckling, she walked out of view. Carolina appeared in the doorway.

"Why are you on the floor?"

"Erm, hiding," Stuart suggested, feeling a bit ashamed.

Carolina helped him up and they walked back into the living room. Stuart sank down on the sofa, enveloped in lassitude. Flora handed him a refilled glass of juice. He drank it quickly, and soon he had managed to get his nerves under control.

"They don't know where you are," Carolina said chipperly.

"Are you sure?" Stuart asked. "He sounded very suspicious about the breakfast."

Carolina sat down on the other sofa.

"I made him think I ate with Flora. Don't worry about that."

"Have you ever eaten breakfast with Flora?"

"No."

Stuart sighed.

"Don't worry," Carolina repeated. "I know how to handle local police officers." She quickly stood up and clapped her hands together. "Come on. We have to go shopping!"

**

"What do you think happened to her?"

They were in Carolina's car, heading for a shopping

mall. Stuart was still uncomfortably wriggling around in yesterday's clothes.

"Manuel's daughter? No body, so I guess she was kidnapped."

"What for?" Stuart asked. "If Manuel is really with the British. Who's going to pay?"

Carolina scoffed.

"I think you answered your own question. They kidnapped her to stop him from talking. But who knows, maybe she has a wealthy relative."

"Are kidnappings common here?"

"No one's going to kidnap you," Carolina said, somewhat evasively, and gave him a smile.

They had a few hours before they were due to meet up with the priests. The previous night, when dropping off Juan and Antonio at the church, they had agreed to meet on Saturday afternoon. Because Holy Week was upon them, the priests had asked for some time to make various preparations. They had invited Stuart and Carolina to morning mass, but Carolina had quickly declined and sped off before Stuart had had the chance to say goodnight.

"This is what I mean," she had said angrily, as the church had disappeared in the car's rear view mirror. "They're weird! First they offer to help a stranger, but now they can't, because they have to sort out their church dresses. Fucking useless."

Stuart had not responded.

Having navigated the steep hillside roads, they eventually arrived at a large shopping mall. They parked in the basement, took the escalator up, and spent a good half-hour getting Stuart some new clothes. They then braved a camera store and got Stuart some passport photos, which he might need later on. Whilst a few people glanced at Stuart's tall frame, no one seemed at all worried that he was a killer on the loose. However, walking around looking at cameras caused Stuart some unease. He felt like there was something he had forgotten, something important.

"This is a refreshing new look," Carolina said after they had got the photos, eyeing Stuart in his new khaki-coloured chinos and sky-blue polo shirt. She had left Stuart's suit at the dry cleaners, for lack of a better way to dispose of it. "Very casual, elegant, handsome."

Stuart blushed.

They walked around the mall, Stuart carrying numerous bags, which were starting to weigh on him. To be on the safe side, he had bought enough clothes to last a few days. The mall was slowly filling up but was so spacious that Stuart hardly noticed. He looked over his shoulder a few times but shook his head at his own paranoia.

As it was approaching lunch time, Carolina took him to another burger place, El Corral, which looked like a local chain. Stuart suddenly realised how little he had eaten over the past few days and how hungry he now felt.

They ordered, and whilst Stuart was wolfing down a burger, Carolina looked at him closely, the cogs in her mind working as fast as they could.

"Now, tell me Stuart, who asked you to drop off that package?"

"What?" Stuart asked, startled.

"You said you were dropping off a package to Manuel's wife and daughter. Obviously, this has nothing to do with our legal work. So, who was it?"

Stuart sighed. He had hoped to keep Carolina out of it, but he knew that she was too perceptive not to figure out the gaps in the story he had told her last night. After protecting him from the police this morning, she definitely deserved to know everything.

"Okay," he said. "In London, just before I left, I was stopped in the street and taken, much against my will, to a meeting. It was with a man who said he was from the British Foreign Office, who asked me to deliver this package and send the two women to the airport."

Stuart still had the envelope on him. He had transferred it from his suit into his chinos before Carolina had left the suit at the dry cleaners. He looked around carefully, as he had not shaken the paranoid feelings he had had since arriving, but the only people he saw were happy shoppers. Some luxury cars were being displayed not too far away, and they had attracted a small crowd. He reached for the envelope and handed it to Carolina.

"Two passports and plane tickets," Carolina said, examining them carefully.

"Yes. It was Juan who identified them as Manuel's wife and daughter."

Carolina continued to inspect the passports, looking closely at each page in turn.

"I assume Manuel is someone the British authorities want to give, well, asylum or something," Stuart continued, trying to fill the gaps that remained. "His wife and daughter were offered the same protection, and I was handing over the documents."

"It is interesting," Carolina said. "What happens to you now? What will you say to that man in London?"

Stuart had not had time to think about what he would say to William Cooth once he returned to London. If he returned to London. His mind could not displace the fear of being arrested and wrongfully sent to prison. He had been standing over the bodies! Any prosecutor would be successful in convicting him of murder.

"I've been thinking," Carolina said before he had replied. "Last night, we must all have been in shock. Not thinking clearly. Isn't the best option right now for me to drive you up to Bogotá? I know it takes ten hours, but still, and get you to the British embassy? You'll be safe there whilst all of this is being sorted out."

"That's one idea, but the risk is I'll just end up like Julian Assange," Stuart said. "I don't want to live in an embassy for the rest of my life."

"I'm sure you won't."

Stuart shook his head, once again replaying his visit to the murder scene.

"I was seen," he said, remembering the old lady and the group of men exiting the building. Were one of them responsible? "My fingerprints are there. No, I should get out of the country."

"You really think that priest knows how to get a fake passport? They're Carmelites, you know, Juan and his friends, in their brown habits. They spend their days praying to the Virgin Mother. Are you sure you want to trust your life with them?"

"For all your dislike of them you sure know a lot," Stuart said.

"Sunday school."

Stuart smiled.

"I was dragged to that once as well. But we mostly drew pictures with crayons."

"I was taught by a nun who I think covers for the Devil when he goes on holiday."

"My teacher was Mrs Bigglesworth, the deacon's mother. She brought biscuits."

"I can tell this was not a Catholic church!"

Stuart shook his head.

"No, but if what you're saying is true, then maybe Catholic priests are the ones to ask for help."

"Maybe," Carolina said reluctantly. She took out her phone. "I wonder if Colombia has an extradition treaty with England. No point getting you out if you'll just be sent right back."

Stuart finished his meal in silence as Carolina was typing away. Her facial expression grew more and more concerned, which fuelled Stuart's fear. He started looking around again, feeling the paranoia starting to overwhelm his mind. He could swear some people looked familiar.

"I'm reading a news article published today. It says that an English lawyer is being sought for a double murder committed downtown yesterday morning. Okay, we know this. And why do they always quote Senator Reyes and her outrageous statements? But I'm confused about this next bit. It says that you're also wanted in connection with the disappearance last Friday of an English embassy official."

Stuart's mouth dropped open. He stared dumbly at

Carolina, at a loss for words.

"I wasn't here last Friday."

"Molly Reed, an embassy official in her mid-twenties, was visiting Medellín for the weekend when she was reported missing by the British embassy. New leads suggest that she was visiting the English lawyer in question, who…was her lover?"

Carolina looked up at Stuart, who was in utter shock.

"What? I don't know what to say," he stuttered. "I don't know who that is. I've never heard of her. I …wasn't here last Friday!"

"I know," Carolina said, sounding genuinely concerned. "I don't understand this at all. I can't remember seeing anything about this in the news last week, which is strange."

Stuart took some deep breaths, trying to stave off the feeling that the world was caving in on him. It was becoming clear that there was much more at play here than simply handing over some passports. Using the media, someone was constructing a whole new narrative. Some pieces of the puzzle were starting to fall into place, however. He had pressed Cooth on why he had to deliver the envelope, not an embassy official. Clearly, an embassy official had tried to do so, a week before. She had obviously fared worse than him, because at least he was free.

Carolina handed over her phone.

"There's a photo of Molly Reed."

Stuart looked at it carefully, but he was certain that he had never seen her before. His mind, however, shifted gear. The camera store. He had taken passport photos before lunch. A photo of Molly Reed. Cameras.

"I have screwed up," he said slowly.

"What?"

"Yesterday, I must have been so shocked that I forgot. I was instructed to hand over the envelope and to make sure that the women had a camera with them. The camera is obviously important. My guess is that it contains evidence of some sort."

Carolina sighed heavily.

"Well, that's interesting," she said. "You didn't see a camera in the room?"

"No," Stuart said, looking around again. It was becoming more and more difficult to contain his jitters. "Look, I know this will sound crazy, but we have to go back."

"What?"

"We have to go back and find the camera. It's important."

"We can't do that," Carolina said. "It's a murder scene. And surely the police removed it as evidence."

"Why? To them, it surely has nothing to do with the murders? They will have removed the bodies, collected fingerprints, strands of hair, and whatever else they do on CSI, but why a camera?"

Carolina shook her head.

"This is insane," she said.

"We have to go and check," Stuart pressed.

"Did you not hear me? We can't go back there. It's too dangerous."

"We'll be careful," Stuart said. "We have to try."

**

They drove down the steep valley roads, towards the city centre. There was not much time left before they were due to meet with Juan and Antonio. Carolina was driving as fast as the traffic allowed, generously using her horn to get ahead. Stuart was fidgeting with his hands, trying to come up with a plan.

"Are you quite all right?" Carolina asked, as she was navigating the smaller streets in the city centre. "You got almost obsessed before."

"Yes," Stuart said. "We need to at least look and see if the camera is there. If people have died and been kidnapped for whatever is on it, we have to try."

Carolina parked by the side of the street. It seemed

familiar to Stuart and he realised that the building he had escaped from was just a short walk away. Carolina turned to face him.

"This is beyond stupid," she said. "There are locals who might recognise you and the police might still be guarding the scene. Or worse, the cartel might be, if you're a loose end to them."

"It'll be all right," Stuart said and stepped out of the car. "This is the first truly exciting thing I've ever done in my life. I have a feeling it'll be okay."

"That doesn't make any sense!"

It was hot out on the street, unprotected as it was from the glare of the midday sun. The street was busy, with a steady flow of both cars and people, most of whom were carrying shopping bags. In his short-sleeved polo, Stuart was feeling much fresher than in the suit he had worn yesterday. He led the way to the building and they stepped into the hallway. Stuart nervously looked at the armed security guard, who he had not seen yesterday. He felt his heartbeat speed up. Carolina, however, walked right past the guard, and before he knew it, Stuart had followed her.

As yesterday, the units in the building were open for business, but none of the customers paid much attention to Stuart. They crossed over the courtyard and into the second building. Stuart took a deep breath. Gruesome images flashed through his mind. He knew what was waiting for him on the fifth floor.

Unlike yesterday, the units on the ground floor were open for business, and the hallway was bustling with customers. They crowded into a lift with a number of shoppers. Carolina pushed past Stuart and pressed the sixth-floor button. The lift stopped at every floor on the way up, except the fifth. No one, apparently, went to the fifth.

"The stairs?" Carolina said quietly once they had stepped off on the sixth floor.

"Huh?"

"Where's the staircase?"

Cautiously, Stuart led the way down the corridor and found the door leading to the stairs. When he was sure that no one was looking, he opened the door and headed into the stairwell. It transpired that there was no need for secrecy. He could hear plenty of people talking and footsteps above and below. Carolina led the way down.

"Just wait here for a second," she said at the fifth-floor door.

She walked through, leaving Stuart standing in the stairwell. The noises from above turned out to be a group of middle-aged ladies, who now appeared on the stairs, making their way down. He tried to make himself look inconspicuous but realised that was impossible when just loitering, so without worrying about what lay beyond, he opened the door and entered the fifth floor.

It was dark and quiet.

He made his way down the corridor, towards 5-13, wondering where Carolina had gone to. She could not have gotten far. He peaked around a corner and saw that there was no one in front of 5-13. It felt like there was no one at all on the whole floor. He tiptoed over to the heavy door, which, like yesterday, stood ajar. He carefully pushed it open and stepped inside.

"Good God!" Carolina exclaimed, clutching at her chest. "You gave me a heart attack."

"I'm sorry," Stuart said. "There were people on the stairs."

"So? Why couldn't you just play on your phone like everyone else? I was checking to see if there was anyone here."

"It feels empty," Stuart said.

He walked over to the counter, remembering exactly the steps he had taken yesterday. Taking a deep breath, he stepped into the workshop and led the way into the inner office. Images of the dead bodies flashed before his eyes and he had to steady himself against the doorframe.

"Are you okay?" Carolina asked. She put her hand on his shoulder as comfort.

"Yes."

Stuart continued into the office. He carefully looked behind the desk, but the bodies had been removed. The bloodstains, however, were still there, covering the floor and the back wall. Some blood had also splattered across the desk. Focus, Stuart said to himself. He was here for a camera.

His mind was distracted though by Carolina, who was taking off her top.

"What are you doing?" he asked, feeling a mild sense of panic. "It's a crime scene, keep your clothes on."

"Fingerprints," she said calmly. "I'm not leaving mine here."

Smiling, and with her top in her hand, she started poking around the room. Stuart turned back to the desk and decided that since he was already wanted by the police there was no need to worry about leaving fingerprints. He leant down and looked through all of the drawers, but there was no camera. He looked through the filing cabinets, but still without any luck. He looked questioningly over at Carolina but she shook her head.

Not giving up, Stuart headed back into the workshop and carefully started going through it. Carolina walked through to the small kitchen. However, rummaging through the drawers in the workshop revealed nothing except tools of the jewellery trade.

"This certainly looks like a camera."

He turned around and saw Carolina beaming in the doorway to the kitchen. In her hand, she held a small digital camera.

"It was hidden inside a cereal box."

"Wonderful," Stuart said and took the camera. He wanted to check if it had any photos, but he suddenly felt an overwhelming urge to leave. "Put your top on, please," he said and headed towards the door.

**

Once they were safely back in the car, Carolina started flicking through the photos on the camera's small screen.

"They seem to be photos of documents, but I can't make out what's going on." She kept flicking through the photos. "Oh, here are some of an office. Not the murder scene, I don't know where this is."

She handed the camera to Stuart. The office looked exquisite. There were some trees outside a window, but there was nothing which provided any hints about where the office was. The documents in the other pictures seemed to be handwritten, but Stuart could not make any sense of them.

"Hopefully Cooth can decipher them," Stuart said. Almost subconsciously he reached for his phone. "I have that text message. It's a Colombian number, so I guess it's someone from the embassy. It just asked my status. Juan told me not to reply, but maybe I should let them know that I have the camera and that I'll give it to them if they help me."

"Told you those priests are strange," Carolina said. "Well, as I said, I think you should go to the embassy now. Send them a text and we can arrange to get you to Bogotá."

"You think? Should we ask Juan and Antonio first?"

Carolina shook her head and pulled out of the parking spot.

"We really don't need a blessing, you know," she said testily.

Stuart started writing a text, agonising over what words to use. After a long while, with many angry stares from Carolina, he sent it off.

Not soon after they arrived at the church. The neighbourhood was much the same as yesterday, with numerous locals walking around or sitting outside the corner shops, enjoying the afternoon. Stuart wearily stepped out of the car, constantly checking his phone to see if there had been a reply. Nothing yet.

Carolina knocked on the friary door. It was James who

opened.

"Welcome back," he said and motioned them inside. "Juan and Antonio are in the church."

James led the way into a small courtyard, in which was scattered a plastic table, some chairs, and a small outdoor grill. On the other side was a door, leading into the church. The church had a cool interior, but with its whitewashed walls, it was bright and energetic. The altar was inside a spacious vault. On the wall above it hung a large crucifix. Further up, above a series of stained glass windows, a gilded image of the Virgin Mary had been painted onto the wall. She was wearing a white dress, wore a large crown on her head, and seemed to be smiling, but Stuart could not be sure.

Juan and Antonio were standing by the altar. Stuart did not want to interrupt whatever they were doing and instead sat down at the end of a pew. Carolina quietly sat down in the pew behind him, and James left and returned to the house.

Stuart, who had only ever been to a church for a wedding, found it a great place in which to reflect. He closed his eyes and slowly replayed everything that had happened since he had met Cooth, trying to make sense of it. However, that turned out to be a struggle. There were still so many unanswered questions and missing links.

After a while, he was interrupted by a presence. He looked up and saw Antonio beaming down on him.

"Welcome," Antonio said quietly. "Sorry to interrupt if you were praying."

"Not at all," Stuart said and indicated to Antonio to sit down. "I was just reflecting… on it all."

"As was I," Antonio said and turned to greet Carolina. "How are you?"

She smiled weakly but did not say anything. Stuart ran through what they had done, from remembering the camera, to visiting the murder scene, to sending the text message. Whilst telling the story, Juan came over. The priests listened patiently and did not seem alarmed that

Stuart had texted the unknown person.

"Maybe it's for the best if you go to the embassy," Antonio said.

"Can I see the camera?" Juan asked.

Stuart handed it over, and Juan slowly flicked through the photos.

"Can I copy these to my computer?" he asked after a while. "I want to make sense of what happened to Manuel, and what this is all about."

"Of course," Stuart said.

Juan headed off. The others slowly followed but ended up in the kitchen. As they were chatting, Stuart's phone pinged.

"This is it," Stuart said.

He read the message. It asked him to meet a contact at Medellín's bus terminal at eight o'clock that evening. He would be escorted to the embassy from there. The text ended by reminding him to bring the camera.

"With any luck, that's the end of my adventure," Stuart said.

"Careful what you wish for," Antonio said.

**

There was a really tense atmosphere in the room. Robert was fuming. Roderic was calmly looking the part of a classic Bond villain. Tara was thinking about how to diffuse the situation.

It was Saturday afternoon and they were sitting in her office at the embassy in Bogotá. Tara and the Ambassador had flown back to Bogotá earlier that morning, after learning that Robert and Roderic had been arrested on suspicion of murder. After lengthy discussions with numerous Colombian officials, Robert had been released, thanks to his diplomatic immunity, and after even more discussions, the officials had agreed to release Roderic as well. They had taken the first flight available back to Bogotá.

"What happened?" Tara dared ask after a while.

"Oh, just a spot of bad luck," Roderic said but was interrupted by a knock on the door.

"Ms Lawson, the Ambassador wants a word," the Ambassador's secretary said, leaning in from the door.

"Just a minute, please," Tara said.

The secretary was about to speak, but she quickly scurried away after Robert shot her an angry look. Tara remained in her seat, eager to hear what had happened.

"The hell with bad luck, we walked into a bloody ambush," Robert said angrily once the door had been shut. "It was a murder scene, two dead bodies, and the police were there in seconds. There's no bad luck involved. The whole thing was timed perfectly. The cartel was waiting for us."

They sat in silence for a moment, contemplating the implications. Roderic went to fetch a water bottle from the mini fridge that Tara had in her office. Tara was responding to some messages on her phone. Robert took the chance to review everything again. He had tried to make sense of it all and had gone through everything over and over since they had been arrested yesterday. Manuel's family had clearly been in danger ever since Manuel had agreed to share his secrets. But Manuel seemed to have thought that his wife and daughter would be safe with the wife's brother. They had agreed the two dates for handing over the documents, but how could the cartel have known about this? Manuel knew, the brother-in-law, wife and daughter knew, Tara knew, and of course, he himself knew. Tara's SIS contact in London knew.

How had the cartel known? Had Manuel played a game? Had he wanted his family gone? It seemed unlikely. Further, Manuel could not have contacted the cartel. He had spoken to his brother-in-law once, supervised by the naval officers, but he had been living on the warship ever since. Was someone in the family responsible? Perhaps the daughter was a cartel member and had passed the word on to her superiors? Something spoke against that though.

Manuel surely would have known if his daughter was involved with the cartel. Robert could not explain the feeling, but he was sure that the daughter had been taken, same as Molly Reed. It suggested that the cartel might have forced the information out of the family.

There was one very troubling thought that had haunted him all day. Even though Manuel had seemed fine with it, it was Tara who had insisted that the family should stay in Medellín, rather than allowing the family to live in the embassy. The Ambassador went to Cali last Friday, and Tara had insisted on going with him. It was her idea to send Molly Reed instead. Had Tara known what was going to happen? To Robert, there had not been any pressing need for Tara to accompany the Ambassador. He had attended a conference, which was heavily guarded, as many politicians and high-level business leaders had been present. It was the same story yesterday. The Ambassador had offered to travel solo to Barranquilla, but Tara had insisted on going with him. Why could she not have gone there after first going to Medellín? Again, had she known something?

Another thing that worried Robert, and had done so for much longer than just the previous day, was Tara's boyfriend. He had only seen the boyfriend once, waiting on the street outside, standing next to a ridiculously expensive car. He had heard rumours around the diplomatic community that the boyfriend was involved in this or that shady deal. That was perhaps not too surprising for a local businessman, but still. Robert had to admit that he had not given this gossip too much thought, not least because Tara had been very successful at her job. There had never been any issues. But it was Tara who did the security checks for the embassy, and who would know what checks she did on her own boyfriend? Was it possible that this boyfriend was involved in the cartel or had dealings with it?

The thing that worried Robert the most was the file. He had not seen it himself, but Roderic had been very clear.

The police had had a file on Robert, which included a photo of him. The fact that the police had had the file right after their arrest was troubling. It was as if they were expecting him. But there was no way they could have known that Robert would be at a murder scene. Was there? He had known that he would be present since the night before, but he had not told anyone. There was only one other person who knew that he would be there. She was sitting on the other side of the table, sending texts.

Robert tried to shrug it off. No, the most likely answer was that the cartel had forced the information out of Manuel's family. They must have spoken to the family immediately after Manuel lost their boat. It had been all over the news that Manuel had been taken the Cayman Islands, officially for medical treatment. But that did not explain the file. Was it possible, just possible, that Tara, through her boyfriend, was, in fact, the source? It was a scary thought, but there was something to it. There were just too many questions about her behaviour over the last two weeks. And with the Prince's visit less than ten days away, Robert could not afford to take any chances.

"How do you think the cartel knew we were coming?" Robert asked, looking at Tara. He spoke gently, trying not to sound accusatory. "And what happened to Stuart Gleeman?"

"We have no news about Mr Gleeman, other than that he is being sought by the police," Tara said. "I've told them he's innocent, but they're still looking. I don't know how the police found out about him."

"That's on me," Roderic said casually. "Or rather, I told the police that he was in Medellín with me, as my colleague. I did not say that he was at the murder scene, because I did not see him there."

"Marvellous," Tara said and rolled her eyes.

"The cartel must have found out somehow," Robert pressed. "For all the cartel knew, Manuel was receiving medical treatment. Why would the cartel interrogate his family?"

"I don't know," Tara said. "These are ruthless people. Fake heart attack story or not, maybe they blamed Manuel, and took it out on his family? They cracked under pressure?"

Robert tilted his head. It made sense. But if the cartel was this ruthless, why had Tara acted the way that she did? Why had she not insisted that the family come straight to Bogotá to live under the embassy's protection? Had she misunderstood the situation? No, she was too good for that. Had she wanted all this to happen? That did not make much sense, but then nothing made much sense right now. He looked at her carefully, asking himself, what was she up to? Was she behind this somehow?

She met his gaze.

"We'll figure this out, Robert," she said.

**

Stuart and Carolina were roped into cutting tree branches for the rest of the afternoon. Juan gave clear instructions that they had to be cut into small, manageable pieces. Antonio explained that they were handed out to people on Palm Sunday, in a re-enactment of Jesus's final entry into Jerusalem before his crucifixion. It made no sense to Stuart, but he found it a nice distraction, or would have if Carolina had not spent the whole afternoon huffing. Once evening arrived they had a quick dinner before gathering in the lounge.

"Please call when you get to the embassy," Antonio said. "I hope that everything will be all right now."

"I will," Stuart said. He felt very melancholic about having to say goodbye. "Hopefully I can clear my name soon."

"We'll try to help," Juan said. "We'll start looking at the photos right away."

Stuart and Carolina headed outside. Juan and Antonio stood in the doorway, watching them leave. Once the car was out of sight they walked over to Juan's office. It was a small room, crammed with books, files and folders, as well as a computer standing on a desk in the corner. Juan sat down by the computer and pulled up the photos, which he had transferred from the camera. Antonio carried a chair over from the kitchen and sat down next to him.

"That's a nice office," Antonio said, as they were looking through the photos. "Does the outside tell you anything?"

"Not really," Juan said, zooming in the photo. "It's mainly trees." He kept clicking through the photos. "Well, now, this is interesting."

They had come across a photo of a large notebook, which had been placed on the desk inside the office. The next photo was of a page inside the notebook. They looked at it for some time, studying the notes and numbers.

"Ah," Juan said triumphantly. "I think this is an old-fashioned ledger. Look at these numbers here. They are payments." He pointed to the letters at the start of the line. "See, this surely means 'Mr N'. Yes? It's the initial of the last name. Then it says POL. Then this is obviously a street name, and MED must be for Medellín. And the numbers are how much money is being paid out. P/M I guess means per month."

"I can see the logic," Antonio said. "So, what's POL?"

"Not sure," Juan said.

He pulled up his web browser and typed in the address, assuming that it was for Medellín. He whistled when the result came up.

"That's a police station," he said. "So POL is police." He opened a map online. "Alarmingly that police station is not too far away from here."

"That's frightening," Antonio said. "I'm guessing we won't find out who Mr N is?"

"No, and there'll probably be more than one Mr N at the station. Let's move on to the next line."

The next person in the ledger was a Mr W, JOR.

"The address suggests a newspaper office down in Manizales," Juan said. "It's a large town, south of here."

"This evidence is really explosive," Antonio said. He sounded genuinely scared.

"Oh yes, this will get us killed, for sure."

They exchanged nervous glances but kept going through the names.

"But why would any of this interest the British?" Antonio asked after they had gone through a handful more police officers, another journalist, and some local businessmen.

"I don't really know," Juan said. "Manuel, when he came to see me, told me that the cartel was behind a murder in London, a government official." Juan put his hand on Antonio's shoulder. "And the Madrid murders." He smiled comfortingly. "But beyond that, he was a bit vague. He said the cartel was planning an attack, and his son had been killed after he tried to back out. I'm not sure why the British would go to all this trouble just to prove that the cartel was behind the London murder."

Antonio took a deep breath before he spoke.

"Yes, it is a lot of effort." He paused for a moment. "What do you think the cartel is planning to attack?"

"I don't know," Juan said. He thought for a moment. "No, they wouldn't, would they?"

"What?"

"You know that British Prince is visiting Cartagena, on Easter Monday. Nine days from now. Do you think the cartel is crazy enough to attack him?"

Antonio shook his head in disbelief.

"I can see the British authorities being interested in that."

"Yes."

They returned to the photos and kept going through the various names. It was faster now that they had cracked the codes for the different professions.

"Why do you think they have the addresses listed in here?" Antonio asked.

"I think it's a threat. The cartel is saying to these people that they know where they work, undoubtedly where they live. There is no escape."

"That's nice." Antonio pointed to the screen. "EMB. What's that job?"

"Don't know," Juan said. "That's a Bogotá address."

He typed the address into the search engine.

"Holy Mary, Mother of God," they both exclaimed as the result came up, and quickly made the sign of the cross.

"Stuart," Antonio said urgently. "Isn't he in danger now?"

"Oh, yes," Juan said. "Stuart and Carolina are in grave danger." He flicked back to the photo and read the whole line carefully.

"Let's go," Antonio said, already by the door. "We have to go warn him."

"Yes," Juan said, taking a final look at the photo. "Well, Ms L, at the British Embassy. We are definitely going to find you!"

Chapter 12

The bus terminal occupied a large building to the west of the river, on the opposite bank across from Stuart's old hotel in El Poblado. As Carolina pulled up to park, Stuart spotted a small airport situated just behind the terminal. It did not seem to be very active. Since they had a few minutes to spare, they remained sitting in the car. Stuart was twiddling with his phone, anxiously counting down the minutes.

"Listen to this," Carolina suddenly said, reading something on her phone. "The news says that the two Englishmen arrested yesterday have been released without charge. They are named as, well, Roderic Moylan-Roth, who we know, and Robert Hughes, a diplomat at the British embassy." She looked over. "Do you know him?"

"No, I don't," Stuart said. "But I'm glad they have both been released. Hopefully, that might mean I'm off the hook as well."

"Yes," Carolina said, reading on. "No, says here the police are still seeking Stuart Gleeman, a lawyer from London."

Stuart's heart sank. He was still a wanted man. They stepped out of the car and Stuart anxiously looked around. Darkness had descended, but in the distance, he could make out the contours of the valley against the night sky, the city lights glistening up the slopes. The evening air was cool and pleasant, a major difference from the burning heat of the day. He was worried that there would be police officers looking for him here. He also tried to spot the person he was meant to be meeting. Might it be this Robert Hughes, or even Roderic? However, the only people he saw were locals heading to and from the terminal.

They walked inside and found themselves in a large open space, which could only be described as busy. People were hurrying around, heading to and from their buses, or just sitting around waiting, engaged in animated conversations. Along the walls were counters for the ticket offices, one each for the very large number of different bus companies. Signs pointed towards the bus gates in the distance. Posters hung on the walls, advertising different destinations, various events, as well as many of the candidates for the upcoming election. Congressman Escaso was still smiling on his poster but the President looked more serious in his.

Stuart looked around but could not figure out where he was meant to go. All he noticed were the many security guards walking around, all with guns in their holsters. Thankfully, at the moment at least, they were paying him no attention. The good news was that there were no police officers in sight.

"Where are you meeting this person?" Carolina asked.

Stuart could sense that she was nervous. So was he. Going to the embassy in Bogotá seemed to be the safest option, but it was a long way there. It was encouraging that Roderic and Robert Hughes, whoever he was, had been released, but the news report was clear. The police were still looking for him. At any moment he might be spotted by someone. However, the conspicuous absence of police officers at the bus terminal suggested that they were not too bothered about finding him. Reflecting on that made him even more nervous. Surely this place should have been crawling with police?

"I don't know," he said. "The text didn't say."

"Let's just walk around," Carolina suggested.

They slowly made their way along one side of the large terminal, past ticket counters and bus gates. The passengers, hurrying back and forth, did not seem to either notice or care about the wanted man walking amongst them.

"Which one is the bus to Bogotá?" Stuart asked.

"A lot of them go there," Carolina answered. "That will not help us find whoever you are meant to meet."

Many minutes later they had circled the entire station and were back at the main entrance. It was now well past eight o'clock. Stuart was getting very anxious. Where was the person from the embassy? Was it Robert? Would Roderic also be here? What a nightmare that would be. They were taking another lap around the station, Stuart frantically looking around for anyone who looked like they could be from the embassy.

"Let's cross here," Carolina suddenly said with a surprising sense of urgency.

Instead of continuing around the perimeter, she quickly started walking across the centre of the great hall, skirting around waiting passengers.

"What's going on?" Stuart asked, struggling to keep up with her.

"There were three men behind us. I got a weird feeling."

Back by the main entrance, Stuart turned around to see who Carolina was referring to. In the distance were indeed three men, walking quickly across the main hall, and Stuart got an instinctive feeling that he had seen them before. They were plainly dressed but with their menacing faces, they did not look like weekend bus travellers. When they saw that Stuart had noticed them they stopped. One of them quickly put his phone into his pocket. They were not far away and there were only a handful of other passengers between them. The men started walking again, more briskly this time, and Stuart saw that they were reaching for something inside their jackets. The objects they pulled out were unmistakable.

"Run!" Carolina said and tugged on his shirt as she darted for the exit.

**

They ran out the main entrance, heading for Carolina's car. Travellers and taxi drivers gave them confused looks, wondering what was going on.

It was lucky that they had managed to park so close to the entrance. Stuart jumped into the passenger seat and

Carolina quickly pulled out.

"What the hell was that?" Stuart said, panting after the sprint.

Carolina was gunning it through the parking lot, heading for the exit.

"Three guys with guns, looking for you? They must be the real murderers."

Stuart dared take his eyes off the road and looked at Carolina.

"You mean they were cartel soldiers?"

"Yes."

Carolina made it out to the main road and drove as fast as she could, slaloming between the other cars. Stuart pressed his hands against the dashboard to stay put, his knuckles turning white, holding on for dear life. His mind was racing, trying to catch up to this new reality. How had three cartel soldiers managed to find him? He remembered his paranoid feeling earlier at the mall. Had he been followed the whole time?

Eventually, he dared to look at the road behind them. To his horror, he saw a yellow SUV chasing after them, similarly skirting around the traffic. It was desperately trying to catch up with them.

"I think they took a taxi," he said.

"What?"

"We're being chased by a really big taxi. I guess they stole it."

"Fuck."

Carolina suddenly veered across the central reservation and drove into another, small street, and sped up, carefully avoiding the numerous parked cars. Stuart, still looking behind, saw that the taxi had also jumped the central reservation and was still following them. Carolina turned into another street, even smaller, and slowed down.

"What are you doing?" Stuart asked anxiously. "Speed up."

"Don't you know anything about car chases?" Carolina asked, sounding surprisingly calm, as she turned once again, narrowly avoiding a parked pickup truck. "A high-speed chase always ends with a crash. The better choice is erratic driving and hope that you eventually lose them."

"What? Is this what they teach in Colombian driving schools?"

"Should be," Carolina said.

After a few more erratic turns, with Stuart fumbling around despite his attempts to keep upright, he saw that they were back out on the main road and were zooming past the bus station. In a split second, as they passed by, Stuart could see that there was a commotion around the taxi stand, probably where the three men had commandeered the taxi a few minutes earlier.

Carolina raced on and then turned left into another street, which thankfully was empty, and sped up. They flew past redbrick and whitewashed buildings, which all looked tired and worn down. Electricity wires were crisscrossing in the air above them. The rundown state of the neighbourhood only made Stuart more anxious.

At an intersection with many oddly green-painted buildings, Carolina swerved left, throwing Stuart into the side window, and managed only by a hair's breadth to avoid all the parked cars.

"This is why you don't drive too fast," she explained calmly as Stuart was recovering from his head thrashing about.

Many turns later, as they were driving down a narrow yet pleasingly tree-lined road, a black SUV suddenly pulled out of a side street and came to a halt in the middle of the road. Carolina hit the brakes and Stuart flew forwards, his seat belt painfully holding him back. Swearing loudly, Carolina tried to turn the car around, but the road was too narrow. The only option was another narrow side street, not much more than an alley, which was in front of the black SUV. Carolina turned into it but it had been a trap. The taxi was racing up the narrow alley from the other end and came to a screeching halt about halfway down. She was about to reverse out when the black SUV pulled in and blocked the rear end of the alley.

Carolina was swearing loudly as the three men, two from the taxi and one from the SUV, quickly walked up towards their car. They all carried guns, which they casually aimed at the front window.

"Get out of the car!" one of the men yelled and for added effect kicked the front bumper.

"Not much to it," Carolina said, having very quickly calmed down.

Slowly they stepped out of the car.

The street consisted of opposite rows of two-story residential houses, some of which were nicely painted in bright colours. Stuart could sense various eyes peeking down on him from behind curtains, but there was no other movement in the street. His heart was already racing from the car chase, so the three armed men did not faze him any further. He kept his hands in the air to indicate that he would not cause any trouble.

Trying to remain in control of his fear, he studied the three men carefully and again got the feeling that he had seen them before. He replayed the events of the past days before it struck him. These were the men who had left the murder scene yesterday whilst Stuart had been waiting outside, counting down the minutes to midday. However, yesterday they had been with a fourth man, who Stuart remembered had been comparatively well-dressed. That was clearly their boss. However, the boss was not with them now.

Looking behind the two men coming from the taxi, Stuart could make out movement inside the car. The terrified taxi driver was climbing out of the back seat, slid into the driver's seat, and aggressively reversed back down the street. The two cartel soldiers turned around with their guns but did not shoot. The taxi was already too far down the street and gunfire would only alert anyone in the neighbourhood who was not already spying on them.

"Stand against the car," the man who had spoken earlier said. He was clearly in control. The other two had their guns trained on Stuart and Carolina. The leader pointed at Stuart. "You, the camera."

During the commotion with the escaping taxi, Stuart's mind had had time to catch up, but he was not ready for that demand. He involuntarily furrowed his eyebrows. How did the cartel soldiers know about the camera? Even if they had been following him, and seen him and Carolina go back to the jewellery shop earlier, they could not have known that Carolina had found a camera. However, the answers would have to come later. Now, all he could hope for was that the cartel soldiers would leave if he handed it over, though that did not seem very likely.

He slowly reached into his trouser pocket and pulled out the camera. He showed it to the leader and held it out. The leader, still pointing his gun at Stuart, stepped forward and snatched it, before carefully putting it away in his pocket. He then motioned for Stuart to move along, and Stuart slowly stepped sideways around the front of the car and stopped next to Carolina. The two henchmen from the taxi followed him around at a safe distance.

"I don't know who you are," the leader said, now pointing at Carolina, "but you're both coming with us." With his head, he motioned over towards the black SUV, still standing idly further down the street.

Slowly, Stuart and Carolina started walking towards the SUV. Two of the cartel soldiers had retreated and were now standing by its bonnet, guns in hand. Stuart could feel the leader close behind him.

"We already have two wonderful hostages," the leader remarked with a disturbing amount of pleasure. "You will make two perfect additions. Especially you, Mr Gleeman."

Stuart stopped in surprise and turned around.

"You know my name?"

"Yes," the leader said, smiling. "Ah, you were meant to be captured by the police yesterday, but now we think you'll make a better hostage than fall guy."

Stuart took a deep breath. So he had been set up. He knew the police had arrived too quickly. But he could not understand how the cartel soldiers knew his name or that he had the camera.

"The boss has big plans," the leader continued. "But first he wants a lot of money for you and your government colleague." The man motioned for Stuart to keep walking. "And if the boss doesn't get paid, he's going to turn you into an Easter sacrifice."

The man laughed sinisterly. Stuart took a deep breath. He was fairly sure he knew what an Easter sacrifice meant. And there was no resurrection for mortals like him. The man had said they had two other hostages, including one from the government. That could only mean Molly Reed. So, even though the newspaper alleged that Stuart had killed her, she was clearly alive. For now. The other hostage hopefully meant Manuel's daughter. This was, after all, good news. She was alive. Again, for now.

They had just reached the SUV when a gunshot rang out.

Stuart and Carolina instinctively ducked in front of the car, and Stuart thought he could hear one of its windows falling apart. The three cartel soldiers hunched down, their guns trained on the road beyond, searching for the shooter.

Another gunshot rang out, closer this time.

Stuart became a bit fuzzy about the details. The three cartel soldiers were still crouching by the SUV, looking for the shooter. They did not pay much attention to Stuart and Carolina. He felt her drag him along, running back towards her car. It was the fastest he had ever run. He could hear shouting behind him and the sound of more guns being fired. His heart nearly stopped as Carolina's rear view mirror exploded right in front of him, but through some unseen power, Stuart managed to jump into the passenger seat unscathed. The key was still in the ignition and in a split second Carolina had the car racing down the street. Stuart crouched in the seat, his heart pounding like it never had before. He felt the car shudder as it was hit by another shot.

Then it was over.

Carolina turned a tight corner and came out onto a bigger road, where she gunned it. After flying through a few more turns, they were out on another main thoroughfare. Stuart slowly regained his senses and looked back to see if the SUV was chasing them, but he could not see it. There were plenty of cars, buses and trucks, most of whom angrily honked their horns at Carolina's insane driving, but they were not being chased. Moments later they crossed the Medellín River, with the high rise buildings in El Poblado providing a guiding and welcoming light. Without saying anything, they once again got onto the highway and headed through the city centre towards the church of Santa Teresa.

Somehow, they had escaped.

**

Carolina parked on the side street next to the church. Stuart wearily stepped out and leant against the car. Carolina walked around the looked at the rear view mirror, which was badly damaged. Without hesitating, she gave it a vicious kick, and it fell off completely. She picked it up and threw it in the trunk.

"I don't need the mechanic to see a bullet hole," she said casually.

"Is there any other damage?" Stuart asked. "I felt the car rattle, like it had been hit."

They looked around but could not find anything. It was possible that the rattling had been caused by a pothole. Satisfied, they left the car and headed to the friary. Again it was James who opened the door and he seemed surprised to see them.

"You are back," he said as he let them in. "I thought you had gone to Bogotá."

"Slight change of plan," Stuart said and invited himself into the front parlour.

"Father Juan and Father Antonio left a while after you," James said. "I don't know where they went." He looked at his guests closely. "Are you all right? You seem shaken."

"We're fine," Carolina said and sat down on the sofa. "Call Juan and ask where he is."

"Of course," James said and headed off.

Stuart sat down on the sofa next to Carolina and leant back, closing his eyes. He felt Carolina curl up next to him. Soon, he fell asleep. All of his adrenaline had vanished in a second. He did not know for how long he was asleep but he woke up to hushed voices. He looked around and saw Juan and Antonio speaking to James in the entrance hall. He carefully slid out, leaving Carolina asleep on the sofa, and walked over to them.

"Are you all right?" Antonio asked.

Stuart nodded slowly.

"Come," Juan said. "We should speak in private. Should we wake Carolina?"

"Let her sleep," Stuart said. "I'll tell you what happened."

Juan led the way through the friary and over to the church. They walked across the sanctuary, through a door, and up a narrow spiral staircase. It led out onto one of the balconies which ran the length of the nave. They sat down on the front pew and looked down into the church. It was an eerie feeling, as it lay in almost complete darkness, with only a few rays of light coming in from the streetlights outside. There were also a few prayer candles burning on both sides of the altar and they were causing the nearby statues of the saints to cast unearthly shadows, dancing on the walls.

"I like coming here to think," Juan said softly, his voice echoing through the church. He turned to Stuart. "I'm glad you're safe. What happened?"

Stuart quickly explained what had happened, starting with the news that Roderic and Robert Hughes had been released. Juan nodded along as Stuart recounted the gunshots fired in the narrow street and how Carolina had ensured their escape.

"I can explain that," Juan said.

Juan described the explosive details that he and Antonio had found in the photos. Stuart listened, utterly aghast, as Juan explained that one person on the list worked at the British embassy.

"So, when I texted that person earlier, the message actually went to the cartel?"

"Yes, I'm sure of it, through this Ms L. That's how those cartel soldiers knew where to find you."

"I can't believe it," Stuart said and sighed heavily. It completely cut off any hope of escaping this nightmare through the embassy. "So, who did the shooting?"

"Ah," Juan exclaimed, more cheerfully. "That was our guardian angel."

"Do angels have guns?"

Juan smiled.

"This one does. Her name is Silvia."

"Who's she?"

"She runs a little café down the street. You see, many years ago, long before the Carmelites took up residence here, the church was burgled. Silvia's husband, who is dead now, offered his protective services. It was a different time, the church was more vulnerable to being attacked then. A lot of priests, bishops even, have been murdered in Latin America for political reasons. As I said, her husband died many moons ago, but she still checks up on us."

"You make it sound like she's rather old," Stuart said.

"Oh, yes," Juan said. "But she's very good with a gun. Anyway, we all drove down to the bus terminal, and there was a big commotion at the taxi rank. Then we saw your car being chased by a taxi. So we chased after. Luckily we found you and Silvia fired some shots off."

"Wow," Stuart said and chuckled lightly, thinking of a gun slinging grandmother. "What happened to the three men?"

Juan chuckled too.

"She's not to be messed with. Yes, they left after you drove off, looking quite angry. There were sirens closing in, police I guess, so they didn't stop too long to search for us, thankfully."

"Wow," Stuart said again, amazed. "I didn't know that priests could get involved in gunfights."

"You'd be amazed," Juan said.

They sat in silence for a moment, gathering their thoughts. The engine noise from a passing truck reverberated through the dark church.

"So, the embassy is compromised," Stuart said. "I won't be safe there. And the cartel has two kidnap victims, who they'll execute in a week if they don't get a ransom. And we think the cartel is planning to attack the English Prince who's visiting Cartagena in a few days' time. And now they want to kidnap or kill me!"

They sat in silence again for a while. Stuart looked out into the darkness.

"So what do we do now?" he asked.

Chapter 13

"I have a plan," Juan announced confidently.

They were back in the friary kitchen. Carolina, bleary eyed, had woken up and had joined them.

"So, never mind the police chasing Stuart, now the cartel is too. He's a loose end, he knows too much."

Stuart gulped.

"Don't lose hope," Antonio said.

"Yes," Juan continued. "It is clear that Stuart can't go to the British embassy. That is out of the question. We're back to our first plan, where we get Stuart a fake passport."

Stuart nodded.

"It's a good thing I took those photos earlier," he said slowly.

"Yes. Now, through my work with, erm, my parishioners, I know someone we can ask for help. He owes me a favour." Juan looked at Carolina, who looked more like she belonged to a country club than in an inner-city church. "I don't think these people will want to help a bunch of lawyers. I suggest that Carolina stays here whilst we go off to see my contact."

"Really?" Carolina said, annoyed.

"Yes," Juan said unapologetically. "But it would be genuinely helpful if you could spend that time going through the photos, with a lawyer's eyes."

Carolina sighed but did not object.

"Now," Juan said, turning to Stuart. "To make you more inconspicuous, since Carolina got you some rather fancy clothes…"

"You're welcome."

"…I think, Stuart, you should change and dress like a priest."

Carolina snorted in laughter.

"Is that the best idea?" Stuart asked, unconvinced. It did not sound very inconspicuous.

"Yes," Juan said, sounding very certain. "People notice priests, sure, but they don't see them."

"I agree," Antonio said. "It's like a uniform. People see the uniform, not the person within."

"I'm not sure you have anything that fits," Stuart said, looking down at his tall and gangly body.

Juan smiled.

"Yes, we do actually, which is why I suggested the idea. You see, last year a German Carmelite friar visited, but he had a slight luggage mishap, so we had to get him some clothes. He was about your size. He left the clothes behind, in case they were ever needed again."

"Really?" Carolina asked derisively. "A German priest came here? Why?"

"His passion is German church organs. The organ in the Cathedral is from Germany, and he came to listen to it."

Carolina sighed heavily, rolling her eyes.

"Okay," Stuart interjected before she could say anything else. "Let's just focus. We get me a fake passport, and thank you for cashing in your favour. What then?"

"We get you back to London," Juan said.

Stuart took a moment to reflect. The memory of the bas-relief of Jesus carrying the cross, on the front of the church, flashed in his mind, and he remembered the feeling he had had yesterday. He discounted it as a religious experience, it was certainly not that, but he had felt a real desire for answers and justice. He still wanted that, even more so now that he had learnt that the cartel had two hostages, which they were likely to kill. Though he had lived a life loathing adventure, the thought of flying back to London did not feel right.

"I'm not sure," he said slowly. He looked at Juan. "You said, hearing it from Manuel, that the cartel killed that civil servant in London. I'm not sure I'm safe there either."

"True," Juan said.

"So I'm tangled up in this, and I've dragged you all

into it, which I'm really sorry for, but I feel like I should stay and see this through."

"See this through? You mean try to rescue the hostages and stop the cartel attacking the Prince?"

Juan looked at him quizzically, but it did not seem like he was opposed to the idea.

"Yes," Stuart said. He looked around the room. "Is that something we can do?"

"You mean bring down a drug cartel?" Carolina asked. "No, we can't do that."

"Maybe we can try," Juan said pensively. He thought for a moment. "We need to gather more information about them and plan a move."

Carolina scoffed in disbelief.

"Are you serious?"

"Yes," Stuart said. "There are two lives on the line. And the Prince, if he gets attacked, and who knows how many bystanders. And as I see it, we can't just hand over the photos to the authorities. Not yet anyway, because we don't know who to trust. Surely we have to do something?"

"Yes, we do," Antonio said. "I agree, we have to try."

"Excellent!" Juan exclaimed. "Well, it's almost eleven, and Saturday night is just getting started. Stuart, let me show you your new wardrobe."

**

A while later Stuart returned to the kitchen, dressed in black trousers, a black shirt with priest collar, and to guard against the cold night, a traditional black cassock on top. Around his neck hung a small golden cross. Carolina started clapping.

"It is a fantastic look," she said cheerfully. "Take care now, I wish I could come with you."

"I'll be all right," Stuart said.

Juan tried to smile apologetically, looking at Carolina.

"You know as well as I do, these are dangerous

neighbourhoods," he said softly. "A rich lady like you can't just walk around in there, it's too dangerous, and we already have two dead bodies." He gestured around at all of them. "We don't need four more."

"I know," Carolina said, for the first time sounding like she agreed with the priest. "Don't worry, I'll look at the photos and see what I can make of them."

Stuart, however, was starting to feel anxious.

"How bad are these neighbourhoods?"

Juan looked at him.

"Well, not everyone likes priests, especially the ones who have loyalties to the cartels or the guerrillas that the church criticises, but it's unlikely that they'll harm us."

"Unlikely?"

"Unlikely. Many are religious. It's nearly impossible to get them to come to church, but, yes, it's a religious society. Being a priest is like having an all-access pass. Even if they don't like you, they'll leave you alone, and that's exactly what we want."

"I can see the logic," Carolina admitted, having previously snorted at the idea.

"And if we're murdered the Church might make us saints, so, there's one form of immortality," Juan added.

Carolina burst out laughing, breaking the earlier tension. Juan showed her to his office and left her by the computer. The trio then stepped out onto the street, Juan in his brown Carmelite habit, and Antonio and Stuart in their black cassocks. They turned the corner and walked up the side street until they reached an old Renault, which had clearly seen better days.

They set off, heading up the eastern slope of the Medellín valley. Juan expertly navigated through the gradually narrowing roads. Stuart anxiously looked out the window, seeing the buildings become smaller and increasingly dilapidated. Soon he felt that this was a million miles even from the run down council estates he had seen in England. He was hoping that the fear of violence and the stories he had heard were a lot worse than the reality. Of course, he could not see beyond the closed doors, but what he did see were people relaxing and enjoying their Saturday night. Poverty, of course, did not mean the absence of community. Nonetheless, he struggled to relax.

After a while, Juan pulled over on a street which was lined with small industrial buildings. Some were clearly automotive shops as old cars were languishing outside. A group of young men were sitting around a plastic table outside one of the workshops. Their jovial conversation quickly dried up as Juan parked and turned off the engine. The fear inside Stuart was slowly taking over.

"Relax, Stuart," Juan said. "This won't work if you fall apart."

Stuart nodded and took a deep breath. The priests stepped out of the car and Stuart slowly followed after them. Up here the night air was really cold and Stuart instinctively tried to pull his cassock closer around him. The neighbourhood was calm but from various points he could hear distant conversations and music playing. The city illuminated the valley below them, like a sea of light, and as Stuart listened he could hear the droning of the city's nightlife filling the air.

As he walked around the car he saw that the group of young men had stood up and adopted defensive postures, lining up in front of their workshop.

"What's going on?" one of them said, pulling back his jacket to reveal a gun. However, the group struggled to maintain their macho postures once they realised that they were facing three priests, which helped Stuart to stave off his panic.

"Good evening," Juan said unperturbed, walking up to the men. "We are here to see Mauricio. I am Father Juan, a friend of his."

The young men whispered to each other. They undoubtedly knew how to handle the local customers and no doubt their many criminal opponents, but they had clearly never faced a trio of priests. Had he not been nearly frightened to death, Stuart would have seen the absurdness of the situation.

"Wait here, Father," the man said uncertainly. He headed inside the workshop through a narrow door. Juan, Antonio and Stuart congregated at their car, smiling politely, whilst the remainder of the young men tried to figure out what to do.

"They'll kill a person in a second, if they have cause," Juan whispered, "but I have always found that the bigger the criminal the deeper the religious conviction. They have a tormented soul and, I think, the frequent reminder of mortality makes them stay in touch with the deeper questions."

"I don't think that I've seen that in English criminals," Stuart managed to say.

"Catholics, huh?" Juan said and laughed, before looking at Stuart more seriously. "You need to calm down. Everything's going to be fine. Okay, we are meeting Mauricio, who is involved in, erm, things. Don't ask any questions, yes?"

"Don't worry," Stuart said. "I will see nothing and hear nothing."

"Like I said, I know Mauricio. Everything's going to be fine."

After a couple of minutes, the young man emerged from the workshop.

"Follow me," he said, and quickly added, "Father."

They went inside and navigated their way between a few cars which were ostensibly in for repair, but Stuart got the feeling that they might all have been stolen. The young man showed them into a small and dingy office, with a desk, chair, and window covered by steel bars. A crucifix hung on the back wall. Sitting behind the desk was another young man, dressed in jeans and a t-shirt, counting stacks of money. Having realised he was not going to be killed, Stuart had managed to calm down sufficiently to appreciate what a bad stereotype this scene was. He guessed that the wads of cash had come out especially for the occasion because there was an open safe in the corner.

"Father!" Mauricio exclaimed as they walked in, leaving his money on the desk and stood up to embrace Juan. "It's so good to see you."

"Likewise," Juan said, returning the embrace.

Mauricio sent the young man out of the room and Stuart watched him head back outside. Mauricio returned to his chair, where he made a point of returning the stacks of money into the safe.

"You come here in the middle of the night, Father, so I guess it's not a social call," he said when he was almost done.

"I'm afraid not, Mauricio," Juan said. He pointed to Stuart. "My good friend here finds himself in need of some travel documents."

"Ah!" Mauricio exclaimed and closed the safe. He cast an examining eye on Stuart, who smiled gently in return. Stuart did not feel comfortable being scrutinised by an unknown criminal, but a few more deep breaths allowed him to retain control of himself.

"If the gringo has lost his passport, why can't he go to his embassy?" Mauricio asked after finishing the visual inspection. Not even the clerical outfit could hide his paleness, if anything, Stuart realised that the black clothes accentuated it. He was not sure if Mauricio's question was some sort of test and he did not know what to say.

"He's in a delicate situation," Juan said calmly. "I would consider it a personal favour."

Mauricio hesitated and once again looked closely at Stuart. He was probably wondering whether Stuart was a real priest, and what was really going on, but eventually he nodded. Even the criminal probably thought it best not to ask too many questions.

"I'm already indebted to you, Father," he said.

Stuart's legal mind, which managed to make an appearance now that he had slightly calmed down, did not know what to make of this information. Juan had said that Mauricio owed him a favour, but it was not clear why a low-level criminal owed a favour to a priest.

"I'm very grateful," Juan said.

Mauricio examined Stuart again.

"So, what do you want, gringo?"

"I'm British," Stuart said slowly.

"Ah!" Mauricio exclaimed again. "A lot of you Englishmen in the news recently."

"Yes, that's right," Stuart said but stopped there.

Juan and Antonio twitched nervously but Mauricio did not seem to notice. Instead, he shook his head in his professional capacity.

"No, I don't think so," he said. "No EU stuff. That's very attractive but too complicated."

"How about a US passport?" Juan asked.

"No, no, no!" Mauricio said loudly, waving his hands. "No, that's too common, customs officials look at them too carefully." He paused for a moment and scrutinised Stuart one last time. "No, you'll be Canadian."

"Oh," Stuart said, dejected. "Really?"

"Yes," Mauricio said, smiling. "No one cares about them. When do you need it?"

"As soon as possible," Juan said and motioned for Stuart to hand over the passport photo. "Can you have it tomorrow?"

"I'll see what I can do," Mauricio said with a positive tone.

Juan took that to be the end of the meeting. They all thanked Mauricio profusely and agreed to meet up the following day. They then filed out of the office and returned to the car, making a point of politely saying thanks to the young men outside, who had returned to animatedly discussing the upcoming World Cup.

"That was a very positive outcome," Juan said as they were driving back down the valley towards the city centre.

"My first meeting with a real criminal," Stuart confessed, sinking back into his seat. "I survived it!"

The two priests laughed.

"Let's hope you survive the whole night," Juan said. "I

have another friend who we should meet. He works, indirectly, for the cartel!"

**

"What?"

Stuart was shocked by this revelation.

"Yes," Juan said calmly. "I should explain. His name is Guillermo and he's an old friend of my father's. He's getting on in age now, but he works as a security guard for an accountant. That accountant sometimes does work for the crime bosses around here."

Juan paused for a moment as he navigated through some busier intersections at the bottom of the valley.

"After Manuel came to see me, a few weeks ago, I went and asked Guillermo if his boss, the accountant, works for Manuel's cartel. He said yes, sometimes. So I think Guillermo is a good person to talk to if we want some more information about the cartel."

Stuart was amazed.

"You could have mentioned this earlier!"

"Yes, but I didn't know until just this evening that you wanted to take on the cartel," Juan said unapologetically. "Nor did we know about the hostages until today. As you said, now that we know about this, we have to do something about it, and I'm glad you're with us."

"You were going to do something even if I had decided to go back to England?"

"Of course." Juan quickly glanced around to the backseat. "Does that change your mind? We can still put you on a plane as soon as we get your passport."

"No," Stuart said. "No, I'll stay."

Juan made it down to the bottom of the valley and joined up with the thoroughfare which ran alongside the river. It was almost empty, so Juan could drive fast, heading further and further north. Soon they had left the city almost entirely behind them. Thereafter they left the main road and carried on down increasingly winding country roads, which soon turned into dirt paths, crossing over the rolling slopes at the north end of the Medellín Valley.

Having driven for some ten minutes down a bumpy path, Juan pulled over and turned off the engine. They stepped out into the cold night. Stuart quickly looked around. Ominously, a thunderstorm was raging in the distance, and the lightning strikes illuminated the contours of the surrounding hilltops. He saw a few dirt roads leading in different directions, lined by homes which could only be described as shacks. Some were built out of wood, a lot of which looked old and rotten, and others were constructed out of corrugated steel. The road was lit up by the occasional streetlight, but the houses were dark and silent. A stench of waste and garbage permeated the air. Stuart's heart was pounding again and he leant back onto the car.

"I can't believe people would live here," he said weakly.

"You have to live somewhere," Juan said softly.

He started walking down one of the paths, joined by Antonio. Stuart forced himself to follow after them, all the while looking around with a feeling of utter disbelief.

"As a priest, how do you help these people?" Stuart asked.

"Those who have nothing?" Juan asked. "That is a difficult one. You tell them Jesus was born in the same conditions, poor and oppressed by a powerful oligarchy in Jerusalem. Substitute Bogotá and you have the same story. You use the narrative. The story says that even against all the odds, there is always hope."

"Does that work, talking about Jesus?"

"For some. Some find hope elsewhere. Sadly, some only find it in crime. If you have nothing, and the cartel offers you financial security and stability for you and your family, why would you say no?"

"Because it's a crime?" Stuart offered.

Juan and Antonio laughed.

"You reveal your privileged background," Juan said. "But don't worry, Antonio did the same when I first met him. If you can't find any other prospects in life, you don't think of it as a crime, you see it as a way to save your family. You know Pablo Escobar, probably the biggest drug baron in the world in his days, provided so much for the poor in this region. There is no real welfare state and the Church cannot provide financial stability to all, so how are we to stop those with nothing from joining the cartels?"

"So what can you do?"

Juan again gestured at the homes around him.

"We give as much spiritual assistance as we can. Give people some dignity, a sense of life and purpose, ideally away from crime."

"I must confess," Stuart said, "I never saw the church as much more than people ranting against gays and abortion."

Juan laughed and gave him a knowing look.

"Yes, I know, it's sad. We should definitely be nicer to our fellow humans," he said. "But then, those are big debates for the cardinals in Rome. I have more pressing issues. I deal with the people who live here, too many have no electricity, no running water. You can imagine I have little time for what the cardinals in Rome have to say."

"Yes," Stuart agreed.

They kept walking. Out here the night was really cold and Stuart wrapped his cassock tight around him. They heard the occasional vehicle in the distance and some dogs were barking up ahead. The loudest noise was the continuous chirping of the insects that, although out of sight, seemed to be everywhere.

Finally, Juan stopped outside a house. It was small, built of wood, with an old corrugated steel roof. Around the side, Stuart saw a small wooden shed, which was covered by a tarpaulin. Inside, he could see what looked like a metal still, and he wondered if the man they were meeting was in the business of brewing his own alcohol.

Juan saw that Stuart looked unconvinced by their endeavour.

"He might live in a shack but he is rather perspicacious about these things," Juan said. "He will have answers, I'm sure."

Juan knocked on the door. After a while, they heard footsteps and the door was opened by an old man, taller than most, but skinny to the bones.

"It's the middle of the fucking night...oh, it's you, Father." The old man looked a bit taken aback by his midnight visitors. He looked around at Antonio and Stuart. "A bit late, but good to see you."

"Hello, Guillermo," Juan said and stepped up to embrace the man. "I'm sorry for the late hour, I hope we didn't wake you." He turned to Antonio and Stuart. "This is my friend, Guillermo Adler. As I said, he knew my father, many years ago."

Antonio and Stuart were introduced and then Guillermo led the way inside. Stuart followed last. At the door, he was met with a pungent smell that wrinkled his nose, but he forced himself to walk on, trying not to breathe too much.

Once inside, he looked around, unsure of what to expect. It was a scrimy place. There was a single room with a dirty wooden floor. A light bulb hung from the ceiling, casting a weak light around. They walked over to one corner, which had a threadbare sofa and a small table. The three of them crammed into the sofa, whilst Guillermo pulled up a rickety chair from the other side of the room, which had a small counter and some kitchen appliances.

"It is a pleasure to meet friends of Juan," Guillermo said. "Can I offer you a drink?"

"Thank you," Juan said politely.

Guillermo slowly shuffled back over to the kitchen corner and returned with a glass bottle and four glasses. The bottle had a handwritten label reading Aguardiente. Stuart had been correct; this was homemade alcohol. He baulked at the uncleanliness of the glasses and the dangers of homemade drink but realised he had no option. Guillermo poured generously with an unsteady hand and then passed the glasses around. Stuart managed to accept it with a sincere-sounding thank you.

"This is a Colombian must have," Guillermo said and sank down into the chair. "Salud."

Stuart felt a sharp burning sensation running down his throat but managed to suppress an impolite coughing fit. Guillermo smiled, undoubtedly proud of his creation.

"So, Stuart, do you like Colombia?"

Despite his age and frailty, Guillermo had strong and piercing eyes, which now looked intently at Stuart.

"It's very nice," Stuart managed to say.

"Are you looking forward to the World Cup?"

"I'll definitely watch Colombia play," Stuart answered, smiling. If I am alive by then, he added to himself.

"Excellent! So, what brings you here tonight?" Guillermo asked, looking at Juan.

Juan recounted the events of the past few days as quickly as he could. Guillermo closely scrutinised Stuart as Juan spoke of the murders and the aftermath, but he seemed to accept Stuart's innocence in the matter.

"You know people," Juan concluded, without any hint of accusation, "and we are seeking some information."

Guillermo sat still for a while, thinking. A loud cicada suddenly pierced the silence, making Stuart jump in his seat. Guillermo chuckled.

"It has been a long time since Juan here was a boy," he said, speaking loudly to be heard over the cicada, which sounded as forceful as a bullhorn. He waited for it to stop before continuing.

Guillermo explained that he and Juan's father had been farmers in a small community on the plains east of Medellín. The landowners had not been particularly friendly to their tenants. Violent disputes had often broken out between the various families, which had culminated some fifteen years ago when the town mayor's son had been killed. Juan nodded solemnly and said that whilst he had never been friends with the mayor's son, they had been of similar age. The murder had shocked Juan. It had made him more aware of the treacherous reality of the community he was growing up in.

Everything changed after the murder. Rumours started flying around, stating that the mayor, together with some fellow landowners and businessmen, were bringing in a death squad as retaliation. The farmers and workers in the town had dismissed this as ridiculous, but a few weeks later the death squad arrived. Guillermo was delivering produce to a small shop when two large cars pulled up at the town square and some ten men in military-style clothing stepped out. They were openly brandishing their weapons. The mayor greeted them and they all went inside the town hall.

It had not taken long before the whole community had heard the news. Some people were brave enough to walk around the square, trying to find out what was going on, but the armed men stayed inside the town hall. Guillermo did not know exactly what happened next, but the following day two farmers, who were known communist sympathisers, were gunned down. Their corpses were left outside their homes, for every passer-by to see. This was just the start of the terror.

"They came and went for the next couple of years," Juan said. "Everyone was terrified of the mayor and his friends, and they used that fear. They demanded money, they destroyed our crops and our tools so we couldn't work and earn, and when we couldn't pay they took anything else we had."

Guillermo continued, explaining that a few of the farmers and local workers had tried to fight back. Others left to join the guerrillas but many instead packed up and left for the relative anonymity of the large cities.

"Of course, I was one of them," Guillermo said and gestured around his shack. "It's hard to believe I once had a decent house and a plot of farmland. My wife and I came here with nothing and I had to build this with scrap materials. I've managed to do it up over the years. Sadly my wife died a few years ago. I pray that she is in a better place. And brave young Juan, it was his first funeral. As a priest, I mean."

"Yes," Juan said.

He and Guillermo looked at each other in silence.

"Yes, we went to many funerals back home," Guillermo said after a while. "Juan's father was one of them."

"It was just a memorial," Juan whispered, and despite the weak light inside Stuart could see tears forming in his eyes.

"The death squad didn't always leave the corpses on display," Guillermo explained. "Some people just disappeared. They're dead, there's no doubt about that, but where their bodies are is known to God alone."

There was a prolonged silence in the room. Stuart's heart was beating fast, in complete disbelief. In his legal career, he had met the occasional criminal, but this was human atrocity on a whole different level. He began to understand how Juan could take the murder of Manuel's family, and the kidnappings, in his stride, and why he had been so willing to help out. Stuart glanced over at Antonio. Carolina might have had a point. It was not clear why he was so willing to help out.

"I'm just glad you got out of there alive," Guillermo said to Juan. "I'm not sure why you became a priest, though, grateful as I am that you buried my wife." Guillermo turned to the others. "The local priest out there was a complete nutter. Everyone knew he was sharing the mayor's prostitutes and he kept saying that the death squad was God's answer to communism."

Juan started laughing, wiping tears out of his eyes.

"He was crazy," Juan said. "From what I heard, when the paramilitary amnesty law came in in 2005, the bishop finally dared to fire him, but I don't know what he is doing now."

"Burning in hell, I hope," Guillermo said seriously.

"But then, I guess, so should I. I had no money, no prospects, and I knew some people who were running drugs."

Guillermo paused. The direction his life had taken was clear.

"I don't know too much, I'm afraid, but I'll tell you what I know," he said. "But first, I should confess my sins to you, Father."

"Yes," Juan said.

Guillermo nodded in thanks.

Juan turned to Stuart and Antonio and asked them to wait outside. Stuart headed outside as quickly as he could, trying to escape the smell inside. Just outside the door, he tried to take a deep breath, but there was a putrid stench outside as well, which almost made him gag.

"Someone doesn't have sanitation," Antonio remarked, trying to sound cheerful. "Let's stretch our legs, see if we can find some fresh air."

They started walking further up the dirt path. The insects were still humming away and a few cicadas, some near and some far, screeched from time to time. The distant night sky was still lit up by the occasional lightning strike but the thunderstorm seemed to be moving away. It was even colder now and Stuart wrapped his cassock tight. The streetlights became fewer and fewer as they walked on. In their weak glow, Stuart could see the occasional bat fluttering past, before disappearing into the darkness.

"What was the amnesty law that Juan mentioned?" Stuart asked once they had walked for a few minutes.

"Oh, as I understand it, the paramilitaries got amnesty if they surrendered their weapons and resolved to get legal jobs," Antonio explained. "Given all the terror they had caused it was controversial, but it brought an end to most of it. It is much the same situation now with the President negotiating with the FARC. Some see it as the only way to bring an end to the violence, some see it as surrendering to criminals and terrorists."

"I can see why people are so worked up about the

election," Stuart said. "Do you negotiate with the enemy or continue the war?"

"It is difficult to be an outsider looking in," Antonio remarked, "but they have been fighting almost constantly for decades, so maybe a negotiated outcome is worth it."

"I would agree with that," Stuart said. "Though it's hard to comprehend the horrors that Guillermo and Juan lived through."

"Yes, but the question is whether you want to perpetuate the violence, or at some point bring it to an end, even if that doesn't bring justice to everyone. I couldn't possibly tell you what the right answer is."

The distance between the houses was gradually increasing as they reached the far end of the path. Beyond them, the hills rolled on. They could hear families talking in some of the houses but the others were quiet. It was very late at night and most people would probably be asleep.

"This is not what I expected," Stuart said, looking at the buildings around him.

"What did you expect?"

"I don't know. Gangs, people dealing drugs, a lot of weapons. That I would be dead by now."

Antonio smiled.

"Your prejudices are getting in the way. Being poor doesn't make you a criminal."

"I know," Stuart said.

He stopped and looked out into the darkness that lay beyond.

"And not all Colombians are drug dealers."

"I know."

"But then, some are," Antonio added gravely. "I'm sorry you've ended up in the middle of something. Juan understands these problems. You've just heard, he has lived through them. He'll get you out."

"I'm so grateful for your help. I'm…I'm grateful that you're helping a stranger. I know we spent a few hours on an airplane together but I'm still a stranger to you."

"Don't worry," Antonio said. "God says never to turn a stranger away. We're happy to help."

Stuart smiled. He never knew what to say when someone brought God into the discussion.

"I…"

Stuart was cut off by the unmistakable sound of gunshots going off somewhere behind them. They quickly turned around and squinted into the darkness, but could not see anything.

"Let's go," Antonio said and started running back towards Guillermo's house. Stuart followed closely behind him, running crouched down to make himself as small as possible.

A few more gunshots rang out. Stuart could see what he thought was muzzle flashes in the distance. In a panic, he threw himself to the ground and landed in agony on the gravel. A number of people were emerging from nearby houses, all shouting enquiries to each other, adding to the noise of the night. After a moment, Stuart slowly pulled himself up.

"Hey, Father, what's going on?" he heard a man ask.

Stuart turned around and saw an old, rotund man in boxers and a t-shirt. The man had a gun in his hand but looked genuinely surprised to see a priest just outside his shack. The gun was obviously for protection, this man was not the shooter.

"I don't know," Stuart replied. "Someone's shooting."

He realised that Antonio had kept running towards Guillermo's house, so he simply said goodbye to the confused old man and started running again.

"But, Father," he heard the man shout behind him, but Stuart did not stop.

Further down he saw Antonio crouching behind a small shack, which stood next to Guillermo's house. Stuart crouched down next to him. He could hear voices inside Guillermo's house but he did not recognise them. Antonio put his finger to his mouth and they waited in silence. Stuart still heard people shouting from the various properties around them but he did not see anyone out on the path. They were clearly smart enough to stay close to home.

Suddenly, three men emerged from Guillermo's house, carrying assault rifles. They stopped outside, looking around. Antonio and Stuart held their breath. Finally, the three men walked away down the dirt path.

Stuart and Antonio looked at each other, panic stricken. All sounds and sights disappeared. All Stuart experienced was continuous nothingness. He did not know how long he sat there but he was suddenly pulled back to reality by Antonio patting him on the back.

"Come," Antonio whispered.

Carefully, with his joints aching, he stood up and looked out onto the path. It was empty. The three men had disappeared into the night. The neighbours had stopped yelling and the night was silent again, save for the insects. Hesitantly they walked up to Guillermo's house. Antonio, for good measure, made the sign of the cross, then opened the front door and walked inside. Stuart followed him.

The lightbulb inside had been turned off. However, in the darkness, they could see Guillermo lying dead on the floor. A small pool of blood was forming around his chest. Stuart gasped and leaned against the wall. It was yet another dead body but this was different. He had known Guillermo for less than half an hour but he had so intimately shared in his life story.

"Juan is not here," Antonio said, again pulling Stuart back into reality. Stuart looked around but there was no sign of Juan. "Shit!"

"I…I…," Stuart stuttered but could not say anything. He could not even react to Antonio swearing. Slowly, though, he managed to step out of the house.

It was silent outside. Not even the cicadas were screeching.

Stuart suddenly felt a hand on his shoulder and he jumped shrieking into the air.

"I'm sorry," Juan said.

Stuart turned around and saw that it truly was Juan. Antonio came rushing out of the house, alerted by Stuart's scream, and on seeing Juan embraced him.

"What happened?" Antonio asked, still affectionately holding Juan's shoulders.

"Guillermo and I were talking when there was a knock on the door. When he saw who it was he told me to run out the back, which I did. I heard gunfire and I hid. They obviously saw me, because one of them came out back searching for me. He shot at me but I managed to run away. Thankfully they didn't chase after me." Juan looked at Guillermo's house and bowed his head. "He is dead, of course." It was a statement, not a question.

"I'm really sorry," Antonio said.

Stuart, still in shock, said nothing.

"I have to say goodbye to my friend now," Juan said calmly. He walked up to the door and hesitated on the threshold. He turned around. "But I know now who's behind this."

Chapter 14

"I can't believe it."

Carolina grunted loudly as she was forcing her car up the steep road, bobbing her head to urge it on. The engine protested loudly but slowly they made it further and further up the valley. It was early on Sunday morning and thankfully there was only light traffic.

Stuart did not respond. His mind was still a whirlwind, as it had been since Friday. He had witnessed another murder, this time more personal, but at least Juan had managed to obtain some information. It had been a very quiet ride from Guillermo's house back to the friary. Once back, Antonio had explained what had happened to Carolina, who had again fallen asleep on the sofa in the living room. She had had a terrified, pale-faced look as she absorbed the events and their implications.

"So those three men are following us?" she had asked shakily. "Are they the same men who pursued us from the bus terminal?"

"Yes, I'm sure they are," Stuart had said. "They must have been highly motivated after they failed to kidnap us."

Juan had then filled them in on what Guillermo had told him before the cartel soldiers turned up. A few years earlier he had lost his job and through old contacts had become involved in a small but efficient new drug cartel. "The cartel that Manuel worked for?" Stuart had asked. "Yes," Juan had confirmed. Guillermo had been employed as a security guard at a small accountancy practice, consisting of one accountant and his secretary/secret-girlfriend. Amongst legitimate clients, the firm also handled the cartel's money, or at least some of it. By overhearing various conversations the accountant had had on his phone, Guillermo had managed to learn that the boss was referred to as the Hermit, but no name was ever mentioned. A few weeks back, the accountant had been in a state of absolute panic. He had been shouting on the phone that the cartel could not be expanding into Europe by shooting government employees. Juan confirmed that this was consistent with what Manuel had said when he had come to the church.

A while later, all hell had broken loose. Word had got around that there was an informant in the cartel. Guillermo, the accountant, and the secretary had all been questioned by some muscular idiots but had been cleared of suspicion. The previous week, the accountant had confided to Guillermo that the cartel bosses actually knew who the real informant was, but they had questioned everyone to see if anyone else was involved.

The real informant was of course Manuel.

"I guess Ms L at the Embassy told the cartel about Manuel?" Stuart had suggested.

"That would stand to reason," Juan had said. "And even if not, they had just killed his son, so they were probably not too surprised that it was Manuel."

They had stood in silence for a moment.

"So, what about the dead bodies in the jewellery store?" Carolina had asked.

Guillermo had said that the cartel had quickly moved in on the family. He had been unsure about the details, but the cartel must have found out about the handoffs, where Manuel's wife and daughter would get the travel documents to go to Britain. The deceased are Manuel's wife and her brother. They had kidnapped Molly Reed the Friday before, probably for ransom, and the plan was to pin the murders on Stuart when he arrived.

"Obviously that didn't happen," Juan had concluded. "We did not get any further than that. Right now, Stuart, you really are just a loose end for the cartel."

"Yes, I've been called worse," Stuart had said quietly, but he had become even more aware of the mortal danger he was in.

"So what about Manuel's daughter?" Carolina had asked. "From what those cartel soldiers said, she and Molly Reed are still alive, somewhere."

"Yes, we have to assume that," Juan had said. "But I don't know where the cartel is based. It can be here in Medellín, it can be anywhere. With that list of informants we have, we can presume it's in Colombia, but let's be honest, it can be Ecuador, Bolivia, Peru, Venezuela." He had paused. "I must think about who I can ask."

"Well, it would help if you knew more people who worked for the cartel," Carolina had said, somewhat sarcastically. She had been as surprised as Stuart that Juan had not told them about Guillermo earlier.

"What did you make of the list?" Juan had asked her instead.

"I couldn't make sense of it all," she had said. "Without an employee roster for those places, it doesn't tell you much. The British Embassy will not tell you who works there, other than the Ambassador, and it's not him because, erhm, he's a man."

"So we still don't know who we can trust."

Juan's statement had brought the night to a close. It had already been the early hours of Sunday morning, and once again Stuart had had a brief and troubled sleep in Carolina's flat.

The road finally levelled out at the top of the valley and the engine got a chance to calm down. Stuart could see that they were driving in the general direction of the airport. It was a beautiful day and even though it was only midmorning the heat was rising fast. Stuart ensured that the air-conditioning was blasting cold air right at him. Today he was back in some of the new clothes he had bought yesterday, which felt a bit more comfortable than the cassock.

"I can't believe it," Carolina repeated, speaking mostly to herself.

At an intersection inside a small community, Carolina turned right, but Stuart saw the signs for the airport pointed to the left. He had no idea where they were going.

"And do you see now why I don't like priests?"

Stuart looked at her, surprised.

"No," he said nervously. He did not want another angry conversation with her about priests.

"You're wrongly accused of murder, their friend is dead, and two poor women have been kidnapped. And do they help you? No! They take the whole day off to celebrate Palm Sunday. It's unbelievable."

"They said it was a very important day," Stuart said defensively, not really knowing what he was defending.

"Yes, yes," Carolina muttered. "Anyway, whilst we wait for them to hand out those tree branches, which we made by the way, we might as well leave the city. Too much death all of a sudden. I think some fresh air will do us good and it will help us formulate a plan."

"Yes, I guess," Stuart said slowly. "Where are we going?"

"El Retiro, a small town not too far south from here. My uncle lives there, we'll have lunch with him."

Stuart grimaced on the inside. Lunch with some uncle was the last thing he wanted to do, but perhaps, on reflection, it would be a nice distraction. He looked out the window. They were passing through a pleasantly rolling landscape, with elevations of varying heights and shades of green filling the horizon. The countryside was mostly empty, though he spotted the occasional farmstead and from time to time they passed through a small village.

After about an hour they pulled up in a small town, which was built on a hill. Carolina parked at its base, in the shade of a large ceiba tree, and they stepped out of the car. Stuart immediately started to feel uncomfortable in the heat but he managed to smile, happy to be in such a serene location. The horrors of the past two days somehow faded away. He put on his new Panama hat and they set off on foot.

The centre of the town, at the top of the hill, was marked by a church, sporting three white towers, which rose above the surrounding buildings. These were two-story, whitewashed colonial houses, each with beautifully carved and painted wooden doors, window frames and balconies, fronted by the occasional palm tree. The town as a whole was framed by green hills, which were visible above the rooftops.

"My uncle has a furniture repair shop here," Carolina explained. "Though he used to be the mayor of a nearby village."

"That sounds cool," Stuart said noncommittedly.

A light breeze tempered the rising heat but Stuart could feel sweat developing under his Panama hat. When they arrived at the base of the main street, which led up the hill in a straight line, he saw a furniture repair shop, but it looked small and decrepit.

"Is this it?" he asked.

"No," Carolina said and resolutely kept on walking.

Only a few steps up the road Stuart spotted another furniture repair shop, though this one was much larger, and had a brightly painted sign above the front door. It felt more suitable for a former mayor, Stuart thought to himself. He stopped in front of it but Carolina kept walking.

"That's not the one," she said.

Stuart was confused.

"So, how many furniture repair shops are there in this town?"

"A lot," Carolina said.

Suddenly feeling a bit uncertain about reality, Stuart followed after her.

Further up the road, about halfway to the main square, they caught up with a large crowd of people, who were walking in procession behind a number of life-sized statues, which stood on colourfully decorated platforms that were raised high into the air. Most people were carrying small branches in their hands. The chanting of various hymns filled the air.

"Palm Sunday," Carolina remarked.

"I still don't really know what it is," Stuart said, but observed the procession with interest.

"It symbolises Jesus's final entry into Jerusalem before

he was crucified on Good Friday. It is the start of Easter."

"Oh," Stuart said, trying to recollect anything he knew about Jesus. Apart from the dying on the cross thing, it was not much. He looked at Carolina, who was also observing it all with a smile on her face. "I thought you didn't like religion?"

Her smile was replaced by a cold look.

"I said I didn't like priests. That's different."

"Right," Stuart said, again feeling like he was lost at sea. He found it difficult to make any sense of Carolina. The image so far was a wealthy anti-establishment lawyer who was apparently religiously anti-clerical. Those were too many contradictions for his tired mind to untangle.

The long procession, which probably constituted most of the town's inhabitants, eventually reached the main square. The crowd was lining up in front of an altar, which had been built on a platform in front of the large church. Behind the altar stood a priest, adorned in deep red garments. Stuart thought of Juan and Antonio, who would now be doing the same thing, though in a very different neighbourhood.

"Let's go inside the church," Carolina said.

She began moving through the growing crowd, with Stuart following closely behind. The statues had been placed on the ground in front of the altar, and the community was crowding around them. A band, sitting on the altar platform, was playing a hymn, which the crowd was singing along to.

The inside of the church was also whitewashed. The pews were crammed with people, sitting in private prayer. Stuart and Carolina walked up the side aisle to the sanctuary, which was adorned in gold. Stuart could not discern whether it was real or just painted, but of the random things he had learnt about the country, he knew that Colombia was a major producer of gold. Stuart thought that it was oddly grand for a parish church in a small countryside town, not least the gold and red velvet chair that was obviously where the priest would sit.

"This is what I mean," Carolina said when they had exited. "A golden throne for the man who apparently cares for the poor."

"It did look odd," Stuart said but did not discuss the issue any further. Though strange, it had looked very striking.

They went over to the left side of the square. From here Stuart could observe the events. The band was playing a new hymn, which everyone was singing along to. The statues had been picked up again and were being carried around the square, with a large group of people joining their progress. Stuart could not make any sense of what was actually going on but assumed that someone surely had a plan.

"Right, I've texted my uncle, he'll come and meet us soon."

They waited in silence. Stuart took the chance to reflect, trying to process the events of the past two days. However, he was struggling. It was hot and loud and his mind was tried. It was becoming too much for someone who had never been so far from home.

After a while, an elderly and corpulent man walked up to them. He was dressed casually, wearing shorts, a polo shirt and sandals. The man walked with confidence, not surprisingly for a former mayor, but he had an altogether cheerful disposition. He beamed at Carolina when he saw her.

"Hello, my dear," he said and embraced her. He then looked over at Stuart and stretched out his hand with a big smile. "It's always a pleasure to meet friends of my favourite niece."

Stuart shook his hand.

"It's nice to meet you," he said.

"This is Paulo Gomez," Carolina said. "My uncle."

Paulo smiled warmly.

"So, Stuart, what do you think about Colombia?"

Stuart flinched. Everyone kept asking him this and the answer was becoming more and more complicated.

"It's...yes," Stuart said and forced a smile, trying to avoid giving an answer.

"Excited about the World Cup?"

"Absolutely," Stuart said with confidence, now that he had had plenty of practice.

Stuart took Paulo's broad grin to mean that he was pleased with the answer. He wiped some sweat from his forehead.

"Right, let's go have lunch."

With that, Paulo turned around and set off, with Carolina and Stuart following close behind. Paulo led them to the other side of the square, across from the church, which housed a couple of busy restaurants. Knowing exactly what he wanted, Paulo sat down at a table outside one of the restaurants. To Stuart, this was a man who seemed not only confident but acted like he was the boss in town. Perhaps, as a former mayor, he was stuck with old habits.

"Now, Stuart, Carolina told me that you are in some trouble," Paulo said after they had ordered some beers to drink. Stuart nodded slowly. Paulo smiled knowingly and made a sweeping gesture out across the square, where the priest was now saying mass. "Plaza Bolívar. Named after the man who liberated the country from the Spanish. Oh, those were the days."

Carolina shook her head.

"We're not here for a history lesson, uncle."

Paulo gave her a disapproving look.

"Yes, it is, we need to know the origins of all this nonsense."

"Fine," Carolina said. "The origin is that this country was cursed from the beginning. If you're going to liberate a country, make sure you do it alone, and whip all your followers into shape."

"What happened?" Stuart asked. A sip of the cold beer had woken him up and his mind was now, finally, telling him that it was time to take a deeper interest in the situation he had been thrown into.

"You know it was a Spanish colony," Carolina started. "It was liberated by two leaders, who had different visions. The second one, Santander, even ended up trying to assassinate Bolívar! Ha! What kind of independence movement it that? Their followers fought civil wars, or cold, political wars, for a very long time. Maybe they still are. And no one gave a damn about the rural poor, so of course, we got those infernal communist guerrillas. So the rich formed paramilitary groups, who with government and Church support, or at least blind eye, went crazy and started killing everyone. What a mess, eh? As I said, cursed from the very start."

"Yes, Stuart, it is a mess," Paulo said. "We got rid of the large drug cartels, and I doubt Escobar could repeat his success in today's climate, but the problem hasn't been solved." He sat up straight. "We're at a crossroads, Stuart, with this election," he continued in a more thunderous voice. "This weak president, who is negotiating with every criminal he can find, is creating a climate that supports and encourages crime. No wonder you are being chased by these cartel soldiers. If they kill some white foreigner it's a big publicity coup for them. We need the Challenger to win the election. That way we can go back to bombing all these criminals and get rid of them completely."

"I can see where you're coming from," Stuart said, mainly out of politeness rather than conviction. It might have been his liberal education, but a negotiated outcome felt like the best way forward. The only other option seemed to be further fighting, which is a vicious cycle so difficult to break.

"I took a very hard line when I was mayor," Paulo explained. "I could expatiate on this, but let me just say, I tolerated no nonsense in my village." He nodded vigorously. "The government in Bogotá does not reach every corner in this country, which is what allows these criminals to breed, but we definitely had a government in my village."

Paulo seemed very proud of whatever he had achieved.

Stuart, however, wondered what exactly strong government meant in this context. He remembered the story that Guillermo and Juan had told last night, of the mayor of their town calling in his own paramilitary group to violently and lethally enforce his will. Despite his cheerful disposition, Stuart got the sense that Paulo was not the kind of person to take no for an answer, and in the right context, he could probably have led his own paramilitary group. Perhaps the changes that had come with the paramilitary amnesty law is what had led Paulo to move to El Retiro. Owning a furniture repair store did not exactly seem to be what this man had wanted out of life.

However, their lunch was served, and nothing more was said on the subject. Paulo instead talked about the World Cup and Stuart listened out of politeness. After lunch, Paulo invited them to his home, which he described as a flat above his shop. Stuart asked why there were so many furniture repair shops in such a small town but Paulo did not provide much of an answer. It was just the way of the world that so many craftsmen had congregated here, he said.

They left the restaurant without paying. Paulo gave the waiter a knowing nod which was knowingly reciprocated. They headed down a wide road which ran parallel to the main street that Stuart and Carolina had walked up on earlier, together with the procession. The road was nearly deserted, as most the town was still congregating up on the main square. It had the same two-story buildings, whitewashed, but the doors, windows and the wooden balconies were all painted in pale, minty green. The tranquillity had a calming effect on Stuart who now felt oddly energetic.

"We have trouble," Paulo suddenly said with a sense of urgency.

He led them into a narrow alleyway, which passed through to the main street.

"What's going on?" Stuart asked, confused at the sudden change of tone.

"There were three men behind us," Paulo said. "I got a weird feeling."

"Three men," Stuart asked and turned around. Indeed, he saw three men rounding the corner into the alleyway. He recognised them immediately. Before he had time to wonder how they had managed to find him again, he simply yelled, "Run!"

Chapter 15

Tara was feeling queasy and had spent a good half hour in one of the embassy's bathrooms. Finally, straightening her attire, she stepped out and headed back towards her office. Most Sundays the embassy was quiet and peaceful, but today, having just received the most horrific news, it was abuzz with activity. She was walking slowly, feeling her head spinning, and had almost returned to her office when she was intercepted by the Ambassador's secretary. The secretary was ashen-faced and her eyes were bright red from prolonged crying. Without saying anything, she embraced Tara and held on tight.

"I can't believe this is happening," she said.

Tara unsuccessfully tried to wriggle out of the embrace.

"I know," Tara said and used her hands to get the secretary of her.

"He was so sweet."

"I know," Tara repeated. "How are you holding up?"

The secretary started breathing hard and had to steady herself against the wall.

"It's just too unbelievable. First darling Molly goes missing and now...," she almost choked before she could say it, "Robert is dead. Murdered!"

"Come," Tara said. "Let's get you some tea."

Tara gently guided the secretary down the hall to one of the kitchenettes and sat her down on a chair. Tara then poured her some tea.

"It's going to be all right," Tara said as she handed the mug over. "You know I have many contacts in the police. I'll find out who's responsible."

"I know you will."

"How is the Ambassador?"

The secretary looked up with her eyes wide open.

"Oh, that's why I came to see you. The Ambassador wants to see you. Oh, I'm sorry, I should have told you right away."

"Don't worry about it," Tara said. "Will you be all right if I leave you here?"

"Oh, yes, Tara, I'll be fine. Thanks for looking out for me, you're so sweet."

"I'll check on you later."

Tara headed out. She took the lift to the top floor and walked down to the Ambassador's office. It was a spacious but uninspiring room. The walls were covered almost entirely by bookcases housing official reports and manuals. The windows simply overlooked the street below and offered no view except of the office block on the other side of the road. The only feminine touch was the official photo of the Queen, which hung on the wall behind the desk, and that photo was mandatory. It was rumoured that the Ambassador kept a picture of his wife in one of the desk drawers, but no one had ever seen it and the wife steadfastly refused to come and visit, so if it did exist, the Ambassador had never had a reason to display it.

Today, the Ambassador sat sunken in his chair, staring into the air. He looked beaten and his appearance unsettled Tara. She had never seen him in this state before.

"Good afternoon, sir," she said as she walked in.

The Ambassador was startled and took a second to realise that she was there. He composed himself and sat up.

"Come in, Tara, have a seat."

Tara slowly took a seat.

"My condolences, sir. I know you were friends with Roderic Moylan-Roth and Robert was a good friend to us all."

"Yes, Robert was an amazing diplomat and a great person, and Roderic, yes, he was a bastard, but he did not deserve to get killed out here." The Ambassador paused and looked Tara in the eyes. She held his gaze. "Why did they die?"

Tara thought back to the previous evening. They had been sitting in her office, Robert and Roderic, asking about how the cartel could have known that they were coming to the jewellery store. They knew that they had been set up. It had not made any sense to them that the police had been there within a minute. To her, that was a dangerous allegation. Once again, Robert had alluded to her boyfriend. He had done so a few times before over the past year, but she had brushed it off as misguided jealousy.

Now, she had started to wonder. How much did Robert really know about her boyfriend, what he did and who he worked for? Had he figured it out? That it was her who had told her boyfriend about Manuel, about his family hiding out in Medellín, about Molly Reed, about Stuart Gleeman being asked to deliver the passports, and about Robert going there to supervise the handoff. She had had no idea that Roderic would go as well, that had come as a surprise to her. In that moment, in her office, with Robert's insistent questioning, she had known that she had to do something.

"I don't know what happened to them," Tara said to the Ambassador. "Their bodies were found in La Candelaria. It's not a safe area at night, you know that."

"What were they doing down there? Drinking to celebrate their release from prison?"

Last night, in her office, her immediate decision was to smile, divert attention away from the issue. Not many people knew about the handover time and location, Robert was well aware of that, and he would keep asking questions, which was a problem for her. So, in the short term, keep him occupied with something else. In particular, keep Roderic around so that Robert remained distracted.

She had suggested that they go downtown to have dinner and drinks, yes, to celebrate them being released. She told them that it would do them good to get their minds off their overnight incarceration. They had left the embassy and taken a taxi down to Plaza Bolívar. She had led them to a bar that she knew very well. Robert had come along without any hesitation. Good, she had thought. For now, at least, he still had some trust in her.

"That is a likely suggestion, sir," Tara said to the Ambassador. "There are plenty of bars and nightclubs down there."

"I guess that's what I would do if I had spent a night in a Colombian jail," the Ambassador said. "Do you have any word yet from the police about who is responsible?"

At the bar, Tara had slipped away and called her boyfriend. She had told him about her fears that Robert was on to her. He had agreed with her. Something had to be done.

It was her boyfriend who had suggested a permanent solution to the problem and Tara had agreed. It was the safest option, and although the murder rate in the area was quite low these days, bad things did happen. Her boyfriend had suggested that she lead them to a made up location in a rundown area, further away from Plaza Bolívar. He had asked for an hour to prepare.

It had been a tense meal, as Tara had focused on keeping calm. She drew on all her training and experience from the military intelligence unit she had served with back in the Middle East. She had undoubtedly been successful, since a bit over an hour later Robert and Roderic had willingly followed her when she had suggested another bar they could celebrate in.

They had walked up the old colonial streets, past the Colombian Foreign Office from where Simon Bolívar had escaped his would-be assassins, and further up along the old, colourful two-story houses. The three of them had felt like ghosts of centuries past. The mountains loomed like massive shadows in the distance, an ominous marker of where they were heading. Thankfully, having had a poor night's sleep in prison and having just had drinks for dinner, both Robert and Roderic seemed to struggle in the thin mountain air. Tara was unaffected. Undaunted, she walked on, and deliberately sped up to make them more tired.

Robert had started wondering about their destination just before she made the final turn into a narrow street. It was dark, with only a few patches weakly illuminated by some sparsely spread-out streetlights. The last thing she said to them was not to worry.

The rest happened very quickly and it was only thanks to her training that Tara managed to see the action. Two shadows jumped out and approached Robert and Roderic from behind, quickly putting their left hands over their target's mouth, and then efficiently pierced a knife into their chests. The bodies had then been dragged into a narrow walkway between two buildings, where they had been covered with a tarpaulin and some refuse bags.

Tara's boyfriend had emerged from the shadows and embraced her. Together they had reiterated that this was for the best. After all, this was nothing more than two foreigners who had walked into the wrong neighbourhood. Yes, an embassy official would make the headlines, but the premise stood. They were easy targets who were in the wrong place at the wrong time. Her boyfriend had ensured that his henchmen cleared the site and he then had taken Tara home. On the balcony, overlooking the city, they had toasted their success with champagne. The boss, the Hermit, would surely be pleased.

"I have spoken to the police," Tara said to the Ambassador. "Unfortunately, they have no information." She paused. "As I said, and as you know, it's not the safest of neighbourhoods. I don't know why Robert opted to go there."

"No, it's strange," the Ambassador said. He sighed, sat back up in his seat and shuffled around for a memo. "Now, Tara, I have some more bad news for you. I spoke earlier with the Foreign Secretary and then the Head of the Diplomatic Service."

Tara twitched slightly as she had a hunch of where this conversation was heading.

"We're in an impossible situation," the Ambassador continued. "Molly has disappeared, feared dead. Now Robert is dead. This lawyer, Stuart Gleeman, publically accused of murder, and he's missing. This whole thing you have going on in Medellín has gone completely pear-shaped."

"I know, sir," Tara said. "I really regret everything that has happened."

"Yes, well, let me get straight to it. You have been recalled, Tara. Immediately. There is too much at stake with the Prince's visit."

Tara's heart sank. She had been fearing this moment for a long time and even more so for the past few weeks. It was not altogether surprising. This operation with the Hermit's cartel had come too close to home and she had allowed it to become too messy. Probably, from the moment since she had sent Molly into the clutches of the cartel, she had known that this would come to a drastic end.

It had all started that day when Manuel Lopez was captured by the HMS Atholl. She could not believe her misfortune when he told his story and revealed who he worked for. It was luck, pure and simple, that she had never met him before. If she had been alone, she would have invented some story and somehow ensured that Manuel was taken care of. But Robert had been there.

There was nothing she could have done, other than scramble to come up with a plan. Keep Manuel's family in Medellín, far away from the embassy, and it would be taken care off. It was probably already at this point that Robert started wondering whether something was wrong. Why could the family not hide in the embassy? Robert and Tara could have gone straight to Medellín to collect them.

She thought she had managed to smooth that over. Yes, the really messy bit had come when the Ambassador had insisted on going to that business conference in Cali. He offered to go alone but she had insisted on going with him. Robert was probably concerned about that as well, because Tara could easily have gone to Medellín, just as the Ambassador had said. But she had insisted it was her duty to protect the Ambassador.

Her boyfriend had come up with the idea of sending

another embassy employee, whom the cartel could kidnap for ransom. Tara had suggested it. Robert had been unsure but Tara had insisted it would work. Finally, Robert had relented. He probably regretted that. She sighed to herself. She knew she should never have gone along with her boyfriend's plan. She should have known that this would all spiral out of control.

"I understand, sir," she said to the Ambassador, biding her time.

Now she would have to come up with something to save herself. She knew that the cartel's plan had been to issue a ransom for Molly Reed and Manuel's daughter after Stuart Gleeman had been arrested, but Stuart had not been arrested. He was still at large and had managed to evade the cartel, twice last night. She knew the cartel would ask for the ransom in the next few days, or maybe after Easter when the Prince was visiting. One was never entirely sure with the Hermit.

After that, she would have to make some serious life decisions. Importantly, would the cartel allow her to leave? Could she become their person in London? Or would she leave her job and stay here in Colombia?

In the meantime, she would have to try to keep her job.

"I know this is a terrible situation, sir," she said, trying to sound humbled, "and I do understand why you think I should be replaced, but I beg you to reconsider. I know people here, I have contacts, and you don't create that kind of network overnight."

"True," the Ambassador said, but without conviction. "But then, you were new once. Look, London is nervous about the Prince's visit. Nothing can go wrong. The idea that the Prince would be assassinated, even just attacked, on foreign soil is unthinkable. It cannot happen."

Tara decided to step it up a bit.

"Yes, sir, I understand, but I must say that it is a bit unfair to replace me. Bad things happen, sir, no matter what country you are in. Short of assigning a bodyguard to everyone who works here, I don't know what else I could have done."

The Ambassador sighed.

"I understand what you're saying, Tara. Look, you can take it up with your boss in person. The Foreign Office told me that, erm, a William Cooth is coming out here in person this week, to oversee the preparation for the Prince's visit."

"What?" Tara said and twitched again at the mention of her boss's name. "Cooth is coming here?"

"Yes," the Ambassador said. He looked at her closely. "Is that a problem?"

"Not at all," Tara said quickly. "No, I look forward to seeing him again. It's been a while. I'll speak to him about my job."

She stood up and headed back to the door.

"I'm sorry it has come to this," the Ambassador said, clearly not believing that she would be successful. "We had a few good years together."

"Yes, sir," Tara said, her hand on the door handle. "I'm sorry too."

Chapter 16

They ran as fast as they could.

Back out on the main street, they sprinted up to the main square and tried to escape through the crowd. The band was still playing and the square was as busy as it had been all day. Stuart kept looking over his shoulder, trying to spot the cartel soldiers, but all he managed to do was lose sight of Carolina and Paulo. He stopped, in panic. Where had they gone?

Suddenly he felt a hand grab his and pulled hard. It was Carolina. She seemed to have taken the mad dash through the afternoon heat in her stride, but her eyes betrayed the fear she was feeling.

Staying together, they kept pushing through the crowd. They reached Paulo at the other end of the square, next to the church, and he was panting heavily. He was not a fast runner but from here he expertly led them through the small streets and alleyways. Stuart was by now drenched in sweat and was also breathing heavily but, finally, Paulo dragged him into a narrow alleyway and up to a closed door.

"Through here," Paulo said and ushered them inside. He followed and carefully closed the door.

Having been in the bright sunlight, it took Stuart's eyes a few moments to adjust to the darkness within. Finally, he realised that they were inside a workshop. A wide range of furniture was crammed into every corner of the room, in varying degrees of disrepair. Paulo had clearly led them to his shop.

"You spoke of the devil and you have led him here," Paulo muttered as he ushered them through the room. Stuart felt a pang of guilt but this was not the time to worry about that. He made his way across to the other side of the room, where he found a door, which led through to an old wooden staircase. "Quickly now," Paulo commanded as they heard voices outside and they all ran up the stairs.

On the first floor, Stuart found a small living room, a kitchen, a bathroom, and a small bedroom placed around a narrow landing. Just as outside, the walls were whitewashed, and all rooms were accessed through old, heavy wooden doors.

Paulo headed into his bedroom without saying another word. Stuart remained by the staircase, unsure of what to do. They were being chased by the cartel soldiers, who once again had managed to find him. He could not understand how they had done that. And once again, he had put other people in danger. Paulo seemed angry, outraged, and justifiably so. Stuart wanted to bang his head against the wall but restrained himself. He made himself focus and listened for any noises coming from downstairs. At the moment he could not hear anything.

Carolina put her hand on his shoulder and motioned for him to sit down on the floor.

"You look like death," she said affectionately. "Take a deep breath. I'll go get a glass of water for you."

Carolina walked into the kitchen as Paulo returned from his bedroom. He had a grave look on his face. In one hand he was carrying a rifle and in the other hand he held a gun. He handed the gun to Stuart, who hesitated before slowly reaching out and taking hold of it. It was cold and surprisingly heavy.

"Really?" Carolina asked angrily as she returned with a glass of water and saw the weapons. Stuart took the glass with his free hand and gulped down the water so fast that his throat hurt. He coughed and put the glass down on the floor.

"Yes," Paulo said and at that moment they heard loud banging on the door downstairs. He noticed that Stuart was eyeing the gun with a blank look on his face. "You have used a gun before, right?" he asked incredulously. His face betrayed what he was thinking. What type of man hasn't used a gun?

"No," Stuart said quietly.

The banging downstairs got louder. Paulo shook his head in disbelief, but he leant down and pointed at the safety catch.

"Make sure the safety is off, aim, and shoot. Remember you only have fifteen bullets. It's not like in the movies."

With that, Paulo grabbed hold of his rifle and slowly began walking back down the stairs. There was a crash in the distance as the front door to the workshop was forced open. They could hear the three men walk inside. Panicking, Stuart pulled himself up and stood at the top of the staircase. He held the gun in his right hand, well aware that the safety was off. Carolina slowly headed back towards the kitchen door, which overlooked the staircase. Paulo had stopped halfway down with his rifle ready to shoot.

They could hear the three cartel soldiers making their way through the workshop. In only a second they would appear through the doorway at the bottom of the stairs. Stuart's heart was speeding up even more and his hands were sweating so much that he could feel the gun starting to slip away. His eyes focused on the doorway and everything else started to disappear from sight.

Any second now.

There was silence. Stuart managed to tear his eyes off the doorway and he gave Carolina a confused look. What was going on? Carolina carefully leaned over the railing and looked down into the stairwell. Paulo took a step further down and the wooden board creaked alarmingly loudly.

"Follow me," he whispered to Stuart.

That was the last thing that Stuart wanted to do, but hesitantly he took a few steps down the staircase. Eventually, he had followed Paulo all the way down to the door which led through to the workshop. Paulo leaned up against it and listened, his eyes closed. He then slowly shook his head. There was nothing to be heard from inside the workshop. The uncertainty was scaring Stuart far more than the loud banging of the three men breaking in. He was struggling to stay in control and his right arm was starting to ache from the weight of the gun.

Moving slowly, Paulo put his hand on the handle, stepped behind the door and cowered. He motioned for Stuart to take a few steps back up the staircase and then he quickly flung the door open. Stuart tensed up, waiting for someone to run through the door, but nothing happened. The workshop was still quiet. Stuart took a few steps back down, keeping close to the wall to stay out of sight, and Paulo, still crouching, peeked around the doorframe into the workshop. Again he looked back at Stuart and shook his head.

Had the three men left?

Stuart slowly walked down the last step and stopped at the bottom. Somehow he plucked up the courage, from where he did not know, and slowly peeked out behind the door frame. Across the workshop, he could see the front entrance, used by customers coming in from the street, and to his left the light coming from the side entrance that they had used earlier. In the room itself, he could only see furniture.

There was suddenly a deafening bang.

Stuart instinctively jumped backwards and fell over onto the staircase. His ears were ringing and he lost all his other senses as his mind turned to black. Paulo, still crouching, rearranged himself to aim the rifle out into the workshop. From the top of the staircase, Carolina gave out a scream.

"They're shooting, Stuart," Paulo remarked calmly as Stuart slowly pulled himself back into reality.

His ears still ringing, Stuart managed to sit back up and shuffled over to the wall. He could hear faint movement coming from inside the workshop. He saw Paulo readying to fire the rifle and he screwed up his face to brace against the inevitable loud bang. He saw Paulo looking, aiming, and then he took the shot. Stuart felt his whole body shake from the explosion.

As his senses returned, quicker this time, he could hear

more movement inside the workshop. In the corner of his eye, he saw a shadow move, flickering through the room. He was terrified of shooting, fearing the noise and the pain from the recoil, but some sort of instinct took over. He aimed the gun through the doorframe, closed his eyes, and hesitantly pulled the trigger. The recoil violently pushed his arm back, pulling his muscles into agony, and his head again rattled from the sound.

"Ay, ay, Stuart," Paulo remarked with a look of exasperation. "You have to look where you shoot!" He rearranged himself to find a better angle from which to fire his rifle. "And try not to hit the furniture," he added, "I have to repair that."

"Sorry," Stuart heard himself say but his mind was still recovering from the bangs.

"Hold the gun with both hands and shoot when you breathe out."

They waited in silence for a few moments, listening intently but heard nothing. The three men had stopped moving and Stuart had no idea of where they were hiding.

"Get out of my house!" Paulo shouted.

The only response was a few more gunshots. Paulo quickly shuffled backwards and used the door as a shield. It was made from heavy wood and could possibly absorb a variety of small-arms fire. Stuart put his hand against the wall to stop himself from spinning. They were now thankfully in a stalemate and with each passing second, he felt himself getting back in control. As he pushed himself up onto the next step, he felt his phone in his pocket.

"Should we call the police?" he asked, thinking it might be an easy way to get rid of the three men.

"No, no," Paulo quickly said. "The only one who will be arrested is you. And probably Carolina for helping you."

Stuart left his phone in peace, realising that Paulo was right.

"Is there another way out of here?"

"No. Unless you want to jump from the upstairs

window?"

He looked up and saw Carolina, still leaning over the railing, smiling back down. It made him feel better. The idea of jumping out a window did not appeal to him but maybe it was better than staying trapped at the bottom of the staircase.

"What's happening?" Carolina whispered. "And do you have a third gun?"

"There are no other guns," Paulo replied. "Just stay out of the way."

Stuart summoned the courage to have another peek into the workshop. He inched forward and the room slowly crept into view. He could see two of the men, or rather bits of their heads, crouching in the far distance, near the front door. They were leaning in, whispering to each other. He could not see the third man.

Again, an instinct, emerging from somewhere deep within, took over. He repositioned himself a few steps back from the doorframe, raised the gun and aimed at the two men. He took a deep breath to steady himself and on breathing out he pulled the trigger twice in quick succession. He could see that the two men tumbled over behind the furniture, but he did not know if he had hit them.

Slowly realising the implications of what he had done, Stuart took a few steps backwards and sat down on the stairs. He took some deep breaths to retake control of his swirling emotions, pounding head and aching arms.

"Are you okay?" Paulo asked.

"Yes," Stuart said. Despite everything, he realised he was more in control now than just a few moments ago.

"Good. I like that you're not wasting bullets."

Paulo edged around the door and looked into the workshop. He could see some movement and brought up his rifle and fired one shot. Stuart quickly shook off the bang and he returned to standing next to the doorframe. He saw more movement near the front door, and despite the imminent danger, he felt relieved that he had not killed anyone. Instinctively, and with much greater ease this time, he fired another two shots in that direction.

The next thing he heard was a loud cry of pain, followed by numerous gunshots and various profanities. Shrapnel of wood flew out from the door and the doorframe as the bullets landed. Again, Stuart jumped backwards.

Paulo fired his rifle.

The close hits had brought back his panic, and whilst trying to take control of his breathing, Stuart could hear movement out in the workshop. He could also hear moaning and some groans of exasperations. Then there was some shuffling. He peeked out again and saw the three men heading out the front door, two of them supporting the third man in the middle. Stuart fired a shot, deliberately aiming high, which spurred the men to hurry out.

"They're out," Stuart reported. "One of them is wounded."

"I could hear that," Paulo said. "Good shooting. But they will not be gone for long and we must leave right away." He looked up the staircase. "Carolina, let's go, now! Hurry!"

Carolina came scurrying down the staircase carrying two large kitchen knives. She had a harrowed look on her face but smiled when she saw that they were both safe.

"That's my girl," Paulo said proudly as he saw the knives. "They're better than guns in close quarter fighting. Not many people know this."

They headed into the workshop, keeping vigilant eyes on the two doors, but there was no one in sight. Carolina touched some of the bullet holes in the furniture, which betrayed the violence that had occurred.

"This will require a lot of work," Paulo said sombrely. "But that's for another day. You two must go back to Medellín. Find a safe place to hide."

"We'll go back to the friary and figure something out," Carolina said. "What about you, uncle?"

"I have a place to stay," Paulo said but did not expand

further.

As they reached the front door Stuart spotted some bloodstains on the floor. He pointed it out to Paulo.

"Yes, you hit one of them," Paulo said. He smiled encouragingly at Stuart and tapped him on his back. "You're going to be okay."

Carolina put her arm around Stuart's shoulders and smiled as well.

"It's all right," she whispered into his ear.

They stopped by the front door and looked up and down the street through the windows. It was empty. It appeared that the whole town was still celebrating down at the main square. Importantly, there was no trace of the three cartel soldiers. Stuart wondered how badly hurt they had been to have called off their attack. Walking away did not seem to tally with what brutal henchmen were supposed to do. Then again, all his knowledge was based on fiction.

Paulo opened the front door and stepped out onto the street. He carefully looked around but did not see anyone. Satisfied that it was safe, he motioned for Stuart and Carolina to come out. They moved quickly downhill until they got back to the road where Carolina had parked her car. It was still there, standing safely under the ceiba tree.

"Keep the gun, Stuart," Paulo said. "I fear you may have further need for it. Make sure you get some more ammunition."

"Thank you."

Stuart jumped into the car. Despite the shade of the tree, it was unbelievably hot inside. Carolina embraced her uncle, whispered something which Stuart could not make out, and then climbed into the driver's seat. Paulo walked off and quickly disappeared down a side street.

"Don't worry about him," Carolina said as she pulled the car out. "He'll be fine, he's been through a lot worse than this."

"Good," Stuart said. He looked over at her. Through the fear and panic, she seemed only a shadow of the

energetic and determined self she had been this morning.
"Are you all right?"

"Yes," she said.

Stuart leaned back in his seat. At least she still had her mental strength, he thought. That was what they needed most now. Carolina sped down the road, eager to get away as quickly as she could.

"Where the hell did they come from?" Carolina asked once the town was safely behind them. The traffic picked up out on the country road but Stuart could not see anything suspicious about the other vehicles. His fear was that they were being followed but there really were no cars tailing them.

"I have no idea," he said. "At the bus station it made sense, this person at the embassy must have tipped them off. But at Guillermo's house last night, I don't know. It was in the middle of the night, in a completely dark and secluded area. And now this. If they're following us, I don't understand how."

"I know," Carolina said. "It's strange. We were in town for over an hour before they attacked us. If they were just following us, why didn't they attack right away?"

"I have no idea," he said again.

He really did not have a clue. However, exasperation got the better off him, and feeling a momentary relief from fear, he leant back in his seat and closed his eyes. His ears were still ringing and he replayed the shooting in his mind. He did not feel as bad about wounding the man as he thought he should feel. Why did he not feel worse about what he had done? With this strange feeling of guilt in his mind, Stuart drifted off to sleep, as Carolina sped back towards Medellín, unaware of the danger ahead.

Chapter 17

Carolina drove on adrenaline alone. She pressed onwards at a breakneck speed that invited the occasional angry honk from the cars that she flew past. The afternoon was drawing to a close as Carolina finally parked the car on the side street, next to the church of Santa Teresa. Having turned off the engine, she closed her eyes and took a deep breath. The events of the day had deeply shocked her and she realised that it was dumb luck that she had managed to drive back to the city without a scratch. It was dumb luck that she was still alive.

Stuart was fast asleep in the passenger seat. His mind was completely frazzled from the past few days, not least from the shootout in the workshop. After a while, Carolina opened her eyes and looked at him. She saw him as he was, inexperienced in life, of sorts, shy, and withdrawn, but at the same time possessing a remarkable degree of courage. She was amazed that he had managed to stay sane, having witnessed several murders and having a constant target on his back. She was amazed that she had managed to stay sane as well.

Whilst she was wondering about how to get the strength to carry on, the car was rapidly warming up from the afternoon heat. She stirred uncomfortably in her seat, her clothes sticking to her body, and she reached out and shook Stuart awake. He groaned, yawned, rubbed his eyes, and looked around to orientate himself.

"We made it back," she said, desperately trying to sound calm and controlled. She smiled at him encouragingly and then stepped out of the car.

"This is just too much," Stuart said tiredly as he too stepped out onto the pavement.

He stretched with another loud groan and then looked around. However, there was nothing suspicious to be seen. They did not seem to have been followed out of El Retiro and they were not being watched here at the church. How did these killers keep finding them?

"Just stay calm," Carolina said, addressing herself as much as she addressed him. She too scanned the street but everything looked normal. The people closest by were some wrinkled old ladies sitting in plastic chairs outside a café, drinking coffee, but it seemed unlikely that they would be spies for the cartel. Carolina made herself look at them again. No, they were just old friends drinking coffee. "Let's go inside."

They walked down to the main road at the back of the church and knocked on the friary door. They waited in an uneasy silence, continuously glancing up and down the street for what seemed like an unbearably long time before James opened the door and let them in. Stuart thought that James was eyeing them suspiciously and he entered with a bad feeling. Where was this sudden hostility coming from? That notwithstanding, the calm atmosphere inside the friary was a welcomed relief. They both went into the living room and collapsed onto the sofas.

James was still casting unkind glances at them but he then offered to bring them something to drink and disappeared off to the kitchen. Stuart was too tired to wonder what was going on with James. He closed his eyes again, leaning back on the sofa. However, it was not long before James returned with a carafe of juice and, perceptively, a bottle of aguardiente.

"You look like you are in shock," James said quietly, pouring generous helpings of the spirit and handed them over.

Stuart quickly threw back his drink and his body shook awake as the spirit burnt him from within. He smiled at James in thanks but it was unreciprocated. He could not understand the cold reception that James was giving them. He remembered that James came from a calamitous background and should be able to understand their predicament better than most.

"Drink," James said and refilled Stuart's glass. He then pulled out a smartphone. "I'll go and give Father Juan a call. He and Father Antonio are out with our parishioners."

"Thank you," Stuart said.

James left the room with the phone to his ear.

"He's having a bad day," Carolina remarked.

"Oh, you noticed that too? I'm glad I'm not imaging it."

"It can't be worse than ours," Carolina said.

They raised their glasses and threw back their drinks. Stuart let out a loud exclamation of relief. The fire in his throat and stomach was reinvigorating him. Smiling, he refilled their glasses.

"Let's have a toast," Stuart said. "Erm, well, to Manuel's wife and brother-in-law. And to Guillermo."

"Rest in peace," Carolina said.

They drank and Stuart again refilled their glasses.

"And to Manuel's daughter, and, what's her name from the embassy, Molly. Let's hope that they are still alive."

The glasses were emptied and refilled.

"And….to Colombia. Let's hope that this mess will be sorted out."

"I'll drink to that," Carolina said and laughed. "That will be the day."

With a newfound, alcohol based inspiration, they looked at each other for a moment in silence and then smiled warmly.

"We're going to sort this out," Carolina said. She laughed again. "We're really going to take down a cartel, aren't we? It's insane."

"A little bit, yes," Stuart said.

"First, though, we have to find those priests."

She stood up, a bit shakily after the many drinks, and set off after James. She found him sitting at the kitchen table, still on the phone. He was talking in hushed tones and stopped the moment he saw Carolina.

"Father Juan will be here shortly," he said curtly. "Can I get you anything else?"

"No, that's okay."

She looked at him inquisitively for a moment, but then

headed back to the living room and threw herself on the sofa next to Stuart.

"He's still sour," she said and curled up next to Stuart. "We have to wait a bit longer. Let's say some more toasts."

Whilst they were waiting for Juan and Antonio to return from wherever they were spending Palm Sunday, they talked about everything and nothing. Darkness started falling outside and the city began to slow down. Finally, the two priests returned to the friary and entered the living room glowing with positive energy.

"Ah, I see you have found the drinks cabinet," Juan said with a smile.

Juan and Antonio pulled up some chairs and sat down opposite to the sofa. James came in and placed two more glasses on the coffee table and then left, without saying a word. He carefully closed the living room door behind him.

Juan reached into his pocket and pulled out a blue passport, which he handed over to Stuart.

"We went to see Mauricio earlier," Juan said. "What do you think?"

Stuart instantly forgot about James and his mysterious attitude. He took the passport and began to inspect it. He had never seen a Canadian passport before, but as far as he could tell, the document looked and felt real. The picture page shone and reflected the light in the way it was meant to. He could not find any obvious or subtle signs that it was a fake. Stuart was very impressed.

"It looks good," he said.

"Yes," Juan agreed. "You see, the key to making a good fake passport is having a genuine blank one. Just add the photo. Making a fake passport from scratch is very difficult. Mauricio got some blank Canadian ones. It was payment for something...best not to ask any questions, really."

"Who would pay him in blank passports?"

Juan gave him a bemused look.

"This whole not asking questions thing doesn't compute well with lawyers, does it? Mauricio is in the, erm, export business." Juan paused and chuckled. "It would be very ironic, would it not, if this passport was a payment from the very drug cartel we are now investigating?"

Stuart smiled. Lawyer or not, he appreciated that it really was best not to ask any more questions. He gave the passport a final glance and then put it in his back pocket.

"I've done some additional asking around," Juan said. "Speaking to, erm, acquaintances and others, in the most discreet way, of course, and I have an idea of who we should meet." He paused again, looking unhappy. "This is someone whom I have encountered before, but it seems a re-acquaintance is necessary. This individual will definitely know more about the cartel and its leader, the Hermit. So I'm glad the passport has worked out because we need to go flying."

"Thank you," Stuart said. "You don't seem very thrilled about meeting this person?"

"It's been a long time, but we left it on good terms, so I hope it will go well."

"Let's hope so," Carolina said, sitting up on the sofa. "We have, however, a much bigger problem to solve first."

She began to recount the events that had transpired in El Retiro. Stuart interjected with more details about the gunfight, especially the important fact that one of their pursuers was now injured. The priests listened intently. This time Stuart began to wonder why they never seemed shocked or outraged when they heard about his misadventures. They simply absorbed the information and took it in their stride. Maybe Carolina's deep-rooted scepticism of them had some basis in truth after all?

He shook off his concerns and together they agreed that the first order of business was to figure out how the cartel soldiers were able to intercept them at so many different places. The three events, at the bus station, Guillermo's house, and in El Retiro, showed that Stuart was the common denominator. He tried to shrink back into the sofa as the three others bore their eyes into him.

"I really don't know how they keep finding me," he protested.

"There must be something we're missing," Antonio said. "The bus station makes sense, in a way, after the text you sent to the unknown person in the embassy, but the other two times make no sense."

They say in silence for a moment, thinking.

"What about James?" Stuart said, surprising himself at making the accusation. The priests furrowed their eyebrows. "Look, when Carolina and I got back here, he was giving us the evil eye."

"Ah, no, no, it's not him," Juan said, sounding apologetic. "He read the news and voiced some concerns about us helping a suspected murderer. I handled it poorly. I just reminded him that I am in charge in this community and that he should forget about his concerns."

Stuart and Carolina exchanged confused glances.

"So why isn't it him?" she asked. "If he's angry at you, all the more reason for him to do something."

"Oh, I know him," Juan said. "I ask that you trust me on that. Besides, he couldn't have known that you were in El Retiro. And he didn't know that we went to visit Guillermo nor does he know where Guillermo lived. No, it has to be something else that makes them find you."

Stuart and Carolina accepted the logic.

"Yes," Antonio said. "That's it, something that makes them find you." He thought for a moment and then he took his phone out of his pocket. "You have a smartphone, Stuart, you used it to text the embassy. You can track these things, it's quite easy." He pulled up the map function on his phone, which showed them exactly where they were. "If this Ms L, whoever she is, from the embassy has your number, meaning the cartel has your number, they might simply be tracking you."

Carolina sighed and sank back on the sofa.

"How very 21st century of them," she muttered.

Stuart pulled out his own phone and remembered that he had indeed connected it to a local network when he had first arrived. Since it had been for business, his law firm had agreed to cover the charges. However, he had completely forgotten to turn it off. The screen showed him the hundreds of emails and messages that were still unread. Realising that Antonio was correct he suddenly threw the phone onto the table, as if it had just become radioactive.

"But hang on," he said, having quickly reflected on the matter. No cartel was ever going to stop him from reflecting on life. "These cartel soldiers haven't come after us here or at Carolina's place."

"No, they wouldn't," Juan said, but stood up a little bit too quickly and walked over to the window. The darkness outside prevented him from seeing anything other than the reflections of the room. He pulled the curtains shut. "No, there are too many people in this house, and if they went in and killed all of us, it would make for a very big headline. The sort of attention that the cartel wouldn't want."

He returned to his seat.

"Yes, and my apartment building is guarded around the clock," Carolina said. "You really can't get in unnoticed. Unless you killed the guards too, but again, headlines. It's a prosperous neighbourhood. Things like that would get noticed."

"I get the sense that the leader, the Hermit, values his anonymity," Juan said. "All his bribing notwithstanding, he wouldn't authorise anything that attracted the wrong kind of attention. But a mugging gone wrong at the bus terminal, or out in the middle of nowhere, or a side street in some village." Juan shook his head slowly. "Crimes happen, you know, no one would think twice about it. There would be no big headline and the authorities wouldn't take too much of an interest."

Stuart grunted.

"I can't believe that a Colombian drug cartel has my phone number," he said.

"I think we should test this theory," Antonio suggested. "Turn the tables, so to speak. Let's take the phone to somewhere, and wait. If the cartel soldiers turn up, we have our answer. Hopefully, we can deal with them."

"Are you sure about that?" Carolina asked incredulously. "You want to take on the cartel soldiers? They did a lot of shooting earlier."

"Yes," Antonio said with conviction. "We would have the element of surprise. And as Stuart said, one of them is wounded, so perhaps only two of them turn up."

"That still seems a bit much," Juan said uncomfortably. "But if we can prove that they are tracking the phone, we can at least leave it behind and slip their net. Then we can go off and see my contact with peace of mind."

"I guess that would be a safer approach," Antonio conceded. "But we do have Stuart's gun. I say we should deal with these people."

The three men were in agreement with each other and indicated this through solemn and manly nods. They were going to lure out the cartel soldiers and confront them.

"Men are really stupid sometimes," was all Carolina said.

**

A quick dinner was put together by a sullen James. Afterwards, Stuart went into the laundry room to change back into the priest clothes that he had used the day before. Again, the aim was to hide in plain sight. Feeling very apprehensive about what they were going to do, he returned to the living room, where the other three were waiting with gloomy looks.

"I'm afraid there's bad news," Carolina said. "I was checking the news on my phone, which none of us have done all day, and there has been a double murder in Bogotá." She paused and looked at Stuart for a moment. "Your colleague and friend, Roderic, and the embassy worker who was arrested, Robert Hughes. They're dead."

The news stunned Stuart. He stood speechless for a while. The others also kept silent.

"What happened?" he eventually asked.

"We don't know," Carolina said. "The police are looking into it. But I think we can safely have a guess at who's behind it."

"You think the cartel did it? Why would they do that?"

"Roderic and Robert were arrested for something they didn't do, where it seems the cartel wanted to frame you. They might have seen something, heard something, or figured something out. They were another loose end."

Stuart was not convinced.

"But the cartel tried to kidnap me," he said. "Wouldn't the cartel be interested in kidnapping them too?"

"Maybe they tried and it got out of hand?" Carolina sighed. "Then again, they were apparently killed in the city centre. There are some really dodgy areas there and they might have simply walked down the wrong street."

Stuart sat down on the sofa, feeling too exhausted to be angry. Roderic had been a deeply annoying and irritating person, but he had not deserved to be killed on some backstreet in a foreign country.

"The important thing here," Antonio chimed in, "is to have hope. With hope, we will overcome this enemy of ours."

"Not the time for a homily, Father," Carolina said testily.

"No, he is right," Stuart said. "We need to have hope."

"Hope always endures," Antonio continued. "That's the beauty of it."

"I agree," Juan said. "Eternal and everlasting. Surely to feel hopeful is to feel the power of God with you."

Stuart could sense Carolina rolling her eyes, but he agreed with the sentiment. He got up from the sofa and gestured towards the door.

"Yes, and on that, ahem, note, let's go and lure out some killers."

They headed out and managed to convince Carolina

that they should use Juan's car. He explained that it was less flashy and less likely to be seen or stolen by anyone. She begrudgingly agreed. There was very little traffic, perhaps because it was Sunday evening, and they made quick progress. The only geographic references that Stuart had to figure out their destination were the skyscrapers and the flying tracks of the metro, which he occasionally saw further down the side streets.

Finally, Juan parked on a narrow side street. They were out of sight of both the metro tracks and the skyscrapers, so Stuart had no idea of where they were. The only thing he could see around him were large buildings, which told him that they were still in the city. However, the buildings were all lying in darkness.

He stepped out of the car, feeling nervous and queasy about the neighbourhood. Now that he was out here, the priest clothes did not feel very secure. The fact that this time he was the one who was looking for trouble, rather than the other way around, did not assuage his feelings.

Juan led them up a street with a somewhat mischievous smile on his face. That did not assuage Stuart's feelings either.

"You're going to like this place," Juan said to Antonio, giving him a jovial slap on the back.

Carolina took a close look around and seemed to figure out where they were heading. She sighed heavily.

"Really?" she asked incredulously.

"Yes," Juan said enthusiastically, his face beaming.

Close to a small intersection, they reached a series of wide steps. They followed them up and walked out onto a large, open plaza, which was covered in concrete. In the darkness, it was an eerie place.

"This is San Antonio Park," Juan explained, still smiling, and pointed at Antonio. "Your spiritual home."

Antonio smiled weakly. Carolina sighed but did not say anything.

"Is that close to San Antonio metro station?" Stuart asked. "I remember it was the station before I got off at

Berrío Park."

"Yes, we're quite close," Juan said. "It's just down the road."

Stuart stepped out onto the concrete plaza and looked around. However, there was not much that he could see in the darkness. There were a series of two-story buildings, fronted by a line of trees, along three sides of the plaza. On the fourth side was a small road, beyond which there was a genuine, green park, with many trees and bushes. Behind the trees, Stuart could vaguely make out the dome of a small church. Stuart could understand why Juan had chosen this location to ambush the cartel soldiers. The openness meant that there was no good place for them to hide. That is, if they turned up.

"I promise that there's a good reason for choosing this place," Juan said, leading them across the park. "Other than having fun with Antonio."

Through the darkness, Stuart could make out two statues, but there was something strange about them. As they came closer Stuart saw that the statues were of two birds, of unknown species, modelled fat and squat. However, one of them had had its stomach blown open.

Juan explained that a bomb had exploded by the statue in 1995, killing many people. The neighbouring bird was a replica donated by the sculptor after the event. The bomber's identity was still a mystery, but suspicion lay on one of the drug cartels. Juan and Antonio knelt by the statue and recited a prayer for the dead in Latin.

"This is a great place to take a stand," Juan said as he stood up. "Guillermo always enjoyed these birds and I think he would appreciate us being here."

"It works for me," Stuart said. He had always liked symbolism and this made him feel a bit better. However, he soon started looking around, afraid that the killers could turn up at any moment. "So, what's the plan?"

Juan also looked around, furrowing his eyebrows, thinking of a plan.

"You didn't have a plan?" Carolina asked.

"I do have a plan," he replied. "I think... Stuart, just put your phone inside the bird. It's the perfect hiding place for it. We can then wait in the shadows."

Stuart took his phone out from his pocket, checked that it was still connected to a network, and slid it into the bird's right foot. He carefully pushed it out of view, underneath the mangled metal. When he was sure it was out of sight he stepped back and the four of them moved away from the birds.

Stuart looked up at the building behind the statues, on the eastern side of the square. It turned out to be several square buildings, joined together by a single roof, creating numerous passageways through to the main road beyond. Despite the hour, there was the occasional traffic passing by. He could see a few homeless people moving around out by the street, many looking worse for wear by drink or drugs, but they paid no attention to the four of them.

They all spread out. Stuart slowly walked down the tree line, rubbing his hands together to keep them warm, and tried to see through the darkness. The only thing that he could make out was Carolina, hovering a short distance behind him. Juan, who had exchanged his brown friar's habit for a traditional black cassock, and Antonio, who had always been wearing his, had melted into the darkness.

In the darkness, the silence, and the loneliness, his mind could not stop itself from reflecting on the catastrophic events of the past days. Who was Manuel Lopez, the man who seemed to have set all of this into motion? Stuart had to hope that whoever Manuel was, he was worth it. It pained him greatly that five people had now died, even Roderic, with whom he had had an uneasy relationship.

Then there were the two kidnapped women. He knew they had to be rescued but he could not help wonder how many more would die in the process. Would it be him? Would Carolina, or the priests, end up in harm's way? The thought of that pained him even more. They were risking their lives to help him out. He knew he would be doomed without their help, he would have had nowhere to go or hide, but he was not sure how he would live with himself if harm fell on any of them.

He must have spent at least half an hour reflecting before he suddenly spotted movement in the green park, which lay on the other side of the small road which separated it from the concrete plaza. His heart sped up. He stepped up close to a tree and looked carefully into the darkness, trying to make out what the movement had been. He saw it again, shadows moving. Then, three men walked out of the green park and onto the small road. Stuart held his breath. This was it.

They trio hesitated on the road, looking around, but then turned around and walked away. They were soon out of the park and disappeared into the city.

Stuart took a deep breath to calm his racing heart. Once he was more relaxed, he looked around. The concrete plaza appeared empty. Even Carolina had disappeared into the darkness. He started questioning the plan, wondering whether the cartel soldiers would turn up. The fact that they had attacked him at the bus terminal yesterday and earlier today in El Retiro proved that they were not shy from operating in open places, but Stuart could not forget about the blood in the workshop nor the cry of pain as Stuart's bullet had somehow hit its target. One of the trio was wounded, maybe badly wounded.

Just as Stuart had convinced himself that nothing would happen, he again saw a shadow moving between the trees over in the park. He hugged his tree again, straining his eyes to see all the way to the park. The shadow was in the middle of the park and Stuart soon saw two more shadows on either side. They were moving slowly and methodically, as if they were carefully inspecting their surroundings. He knew immediately that this was them. The cartel soldiers had arrived.

The three shadows made it to the end of the park. Like the previous group of people, they stopped at the road and carefully looked around. Stuart saw that one of them, clearly the leader, checked some electronic device, probably a phone. He then looked up, said something, and pointed in the general direction of the bird statues. Stuart smiled. This proved that the soldiers were tracking his smartphone. His eyes followed the three men as they slowly crossed the road and carefully walked up some steps to reach the concrete plaza.

At the top of the steps was another large statue of a bulky male torso. They stopped at its base, looking around. Apart from the line of trees by the eastern side, where Stuart was hiding, and the bird statues in front of them, there were no other obstacles on the plaza. There was no place for the soldiers to hide.

This was exactly what Juan had hoped for. Stuart pushed himself closer to the tree, once again grateful that he was wearing priest's black. Holding his breath, Stuart watched as the three soldiers spread out and moved forwards, heading towards the birds.

At this point, Stuart realised that the no-hiding part of the plan worked both ways. He should have left his tree much sooner, since now there was no way he could leave without the cartel soldiers spotting him. He hoped that Carolina, Juan and Antonio were similarly keeping still in the shadows somewhere, or better yet, had withdrawn and were out of harm's way. As the soldiers moved closer towards the birds, Stuart slowly edged himself around the tree trunk to keep it in-between him and the men, taking great care not to make a sound.

The cartel soldiers walked up to the birds and the leader checked his phone. He started gesturing around, seemingly confused. He knew he was in the right place but he could not see Stuart's smartphone or the people he was chasing. Stuart could not make out what they were saying to each other, but suddenly they pulled out their guns and fanned out, heading away from the birds. Stuart saw that one of the men had bandaged his left arm but clearly did not seem too inconvenienced by the injury.

Carefully, Stuart reached into his pocket and pulled out

his own gun, which he had retrieved from Carolina's car before they left the friary. He was not keen on having to use it again, but he had spent some time mentally preparing himself for the possibility of another gunfight. The injured man was heading in Stuart's direction. He was scanning the tree line and looking down the passageways out onto the main road. Stuart held his breath. The man came closer and closer.

However, he did not spot Stuart in the shadows. As he came nearer to Stuart's tree, which was the last in the line, he suddenly veered out onto the square and headed back towards the statue of the large male torso. Stuart watched him in absolute silence. The man circled around to the other side of the torso statue and then headed off to the western side of the plaza.

Stuart could not believe his luck. He seized the opportunity. With the other two soldiers also on the far side of the plaza, he decided to leave. Huddling down, he moved quickly away from the tree, through one of the passageways and out onto the pavement by the main road. The homeless people had no idea what was going on and he got a few strange looks as he emerged onto the lit pavement, wearing a cassock and carrying a gun. Thankfully, however, he was left alone. The gun probably helped with that.

Stuart walked down the road, jogging between the square buildings so that he would not be seen from inside the plaza. He reached the last building without arousing any attention. He hugged the wall and slowly made his way back in towards the plaza. As he rounded the corner, he came face to face with the leader of the hit squad.

They both froze in surprise.

Stuart recognised the man from last night, in the alleyway near the bus terminal, and from earlier this day, as they had fought in El Retiro. Again, and fast this time, Stuart's instincts kicked in. He raised his gun and pointed it at the man's head. In his panic, however, Stuart's hands fumbled and he dropped the gun. He looked down at it in disbelief. Suddenly, out of instinct rather than any planning, he tried to reach down to pick it up.

A gunshot rang out.

The leader had fired his gun. The bullet hit Stuart's gun, which flew off a few feet away.

"Wow!" Stuart exclaimed. In disbelief, he looked over at his gun, which was now well out of his reach. "That actually works?"

The leader pointed his gun at him.

"What does your boss want from me?" Stuart asked, sounding far more frightened than he wanted to.

The man was silent.

"What do you want from me?" Stuart pleaded.

The man did still not react in any way but kept his gun trained on Stuart. Realising that he would not get any answers, Stuart focused on staying calm and in control. The energy required for that was so immense that it prevented him from thinking about how to end the stalemate.

He saw the man's finger slowly press on the trigger.

Another gunshot rang out.

Chapter 18

William Cooth angrily stepped out of the taxi and strode into the Foreign Office building in London. It was Sunday evening and the building lay in silence. His footsteps echoed as he walked across the central atrium and then he headed up the stairs towards the building's nerve centre. The Foreign Secretary's assistant was sitting at her desk, typing away on her computer. She gave him a friendly nod and gestured for him to go inside.

The Foreign Secretary was slumped in his seat behind the imposing desk, pretending to read a file. Cooth, with his carefully honed instinct, saw that the Foreign Secretary was in fact lost deep in his thoughts. He gingerly sat up as he noticed Cooth entering the office.

"A sad day for us," the Foreign Secretary said.

"Yes, sir," Cooth said. "Why…"

"We are all shocked at the death of Robert Hughes, one of our own." The Foreign Secretary motioned for Cooth to take a seat. "And also your friend, of course, the barrister."

"Thank you, sir. Yes, Roderic Geoffrey Moylan-Roth."

"Mmm." The Foreign Secretary paused. "But beyond that, William, you seem to have made a bit of a dog's breakfast of it all."

Cooth opened his mouth to protest but the Foreign Secretary continued.

"Most importantly, where in the hell is that solicitor you sent to Colombia?"

"I…"

"You know I've had the Colombian Ambassador yelling at me over the phone, asking why British nationals are going on a killing spree across her country."

"Yes…"

"And now I learn there is some crazy Senator, gleefully calling all this a Western conspiracy, and calling for protests during the Prince's visit."

"I know…"

"Thankfully the President is urging calm." The Foreign Secretary, as was his habit when contemplating the difficult questions, stroked his bald head. "Where is that solicitor?"

"Ahem, yes, Stuart Gleeman, sir. He is missing, which is a bit of a problem. We've not had any contact with him at all since he arrived in Medellín on Wednesday evening."

"None at all?"

"No, sir."

The Foreign Secretary stroked his head again.

"Yes, we did have our doubts, didn't we? Your boss and the Home Secretary included. But you said your man would be able to fly under the radar and that the embassy security chief would provide backup."

The Foreign Secretary raised his eyebrows, seeking an explanation.

"Yes, sir, that was the plan, but as you said…"

"And then I learn, not from you, mind, that the embassy security chief was not in Medellín on Friday, but she was in Barranquilla, whatever the hell that is."

"Erm, yes, sir, she accompanied the Ambassador there. As is her job," Cooth dared add.

The Foreign Secretary sighed and stroked his head more vigorously.

"Why the hell was my Ambassador not in the embassy?"

Cooth stirred uncomfortably in his seat.

"Erm, sir, the situation is… he has a mistress in Barranquilla."

"Marvellous! So we're having a major security operation to protect the life of the Prince, and possibly bring down a drug cartel, and the Ambassador is off shagging some poor woman." The Foreign Secretary sighed again. "You so angrily stomped into my building because I recalled the security chief without consulting you. I know she also works for you, but I lost faith in her entirely. Are you saying that I should have recalled the

Ambassador instead?"

"I was very disappointed, sir, that Tara Lawson was recalled. If I may say so, I am also not too happy that you have ordered me to go to Bogotá to take over."

The Foreign Secretary got up and walked over to his favourite window.

"Have you been behind a desk so long that you've forgotten how to run an operation?"

"No, sir," Cooth said.

"Then you are going." He turned around and faced Cooth. "I need someone on the ground who I can trust, and Ms Lawson is certainly not it. She's lost one embassy employee and now another one has been murdered, together with Roderic what's-his-name. The consequences if there is an attack on the Prince, even an unsuccessful one, are grave."

"I understand, sir. I hope that you'll allow Tara to stay and prove herself. I trust her, and I could use her assistance."

The Foreign Secretary furrowed his eyebrows as he slowly walked back to his seat.

"Well, if you vouch for her even after all this, fine. But you're in charge. The tiniest of slip-ups on her part and she's out."

"Yes, sir."

The Foreign Secretary went back to stroking his head.

"I understand that the informant's family is dead."

"Yes, sir, Manuel's wife and brother-in-law are dead. His daughter appears to be missing."

"Maybe she ran off with your solicitor?"

"I really don't think he's behind this, sir."

"No, of course not. I assume that the daughter, Mr Gleeman, and Ms Reed have all been taken by the cartel. We have been preparing ourselves for a ransom demand, but it might come in conjunction with the Prince's visit."

"That would make for maximum impact, sir."

"Which, again, is why I need you on the ground." The Foreign Secretary suddenly looked very worried. "I can tell you, the Palace is very anxious about the Prince's visit to Cartagena. The Prince is wavering. I have impressed upon them that it would be diplomatically insulting to cancel the visit."

"I understand, sir."

"I have to say, I was a bit apprehensive about the Prince visiting so close to a presidential election, but it was the only time that worked for everyone. And we are expressing our commitment to the peace plan. We want peace in Colombia."

"I understand, sir. Though the election will be a good excuse if we feel the need to cancel the Prince's visit." Cooth hesitated. "I was wondering why the visit was so close to the election. Is there something political behind that?"

The Foreign Secretary stroked his head again.

"No, it genuinely was a scheduling issue." He paused. "But, of course, whilst we don't interfere with foreign elections, it's certainly in our long-term interest for the President to be re-elected, and maybe a visit of this nature will help. Securing peace with the FARC and the other insurgents is surely the best way of stemming the cocaine production."

"Yes, sir, I agree. I'm not convinced that the Challenger's plan to go back to military action is an effective long-term solution."

"No. As such, it's probably the most important election yet in Colombia. But if a foreign dignitary was attacked in Cartagena, I don't think the President could convince the people about the merits of a peace negotiation."

"All the more reason to cancel the visit then."

"I don't think so," the Foreign Secretary said emphatically. "If we cancel now, immediately after one of our top diplomats is killed in Bogotá, everyone will believe it was for security reasons. We can cite the election, but people will know. That might also undermine the President."

They sat in silence for a moment.

"I understand, sir," Cooth said eventually. "I'll make the visit a success."

"Good," the Foreign Secretary said. "Also, I need to ask you to do one more thing."

"Sir?"

"The HMS Atholl is bringing Manuel Lopez to the Caymans tomorrow. Can you believe he has been on board for two weeks? But it's probably been the safest place for him. I want you to stop by the Caymans on the way to Bogotá and try to get more information out of him. We might never get this camera evidence now, including the name of whoever in our government is working for the cartel, and we desperately need to learn that information. He also needs to be told about his family."

"Yes, sir," Cooth said. He was not sure how he felt about that task but he understood that it had to be done. "And the Prince and the Duchess, where are they now? I would be happy to brief their team in advance."

The Foreign Secretary did some clicking on his computer.

"They are now in Bermuda. Tomorrow they fly to the Bahamas and will spend the week sailing around the Caribbean. Easter on Jamaica and then they will fly to Cartagena on Monday morning for a two-day visit."

"Sailing the Caribbean, eh? Sounds like a nice trip."

"Yes," the Foreign Secretary said. "Yes, Lord Stuffington, something or other, a public school friend, lent them his yacht." He smiled. "Anyway, I'll let the Palace know that you are going. Our top man from MI6! Hopefully, that will reassure them. I don't think you'll have the opportunity to brief the Prince's team in person, but you'll get to meet them in Cartagena." The Foreign Secretary shuffled around some papers to find a document, which he handed over to Cooth. "Your flight to the Caymans. Guaranteed to be more comfortable than British Airways."

"Thank you, sir," Cooth said somewhat apprehensively and looked at the document. It was more a flight manifest than a ticket. "Erm, sir, this is an RAF transport plane?"

"Yes," the Foreign Secretary said, sounding cheerful for the first time. "Routine maintenance is needed on the HMS Atholl. I'm sure the plane has some spare space in-between spanners and spades and, you know... good luck."

**

The gunshot rang out.

Stuart jumped high in surprise and fell to the ground. Despite the pain, he quickly realised that he had not been hit. He sat up. In front of him, the leader of the cartel hit squad lay on the ground, face down, with blood pouring out from under his chest. In a fit of panic, Stuart started looking around to find the shooter. All he could see though, through the darkness, was the figure of one of the other cartel soldiers, on the far side of the plaza, quickly heading towards him.

Stuart felt a hand grab his shoulder. He let out a shriek.

"We have to run," Antonio said forcefully.

Stuart scrambled to his feet but his legs felt wobbly. Antonio walked over and picked up Stuart's gun. He handed it to Stuart, who reluctantly accepted it. There was a dent on the handle where the bullet had struck earlier, but other than that the gun seemed to be in working order.

His legs thankfully stiffened up as he realised that the other cartel soldier was closing in on them. Stuart followed Antonio in running away, heading along the north side of the plaza, bending down to try and make himself as small as possible. They rounded the top of a small amphitheatre that was carved out in a depression on the plaza's north end and continued on towards the set of stairs that they had walked up when they first arrived.

A gunshot rang out behind him. Stuart somehow managed to run even faster. Clearly, the cartel soldier was shooting at them. They flew down the steps and sprinted towards the spot where Juan had parked the car. They reached the place panting heavily, terrified of the hitman chasing them, but the car was not there.

"Juan and Carolina left before us," Antonio explained in-between panicked and shallow breaths as they kept running down the street. "They were trailing the third member."

"So it's just one member following us?" Stuart asked, his throat quickly drying up from the run.

"Yes."

Stuart had to take that as a blessing of sorts. Despite the pain spreading from his throat and stomach out towards the whole of his body, Stuart kept running, struggling to keep up with Antonio. They reached 51st street, ending up underneath the concrete canopy of the flying San Antonio metro station. Antonio led the way northwards, staying underneath the railway tracks. They were both exhausted and the run had been reduced into a slow jog.

They went past a few homeless people, some of whom said a surprised but polite hello. When they reached Berrío Park, the uninspiring concrete square with its few trees, Stuart was in such pain that he had to stop. He keeled over, panting loudly, and sat up against one of the large concrete pillars that supported the metro tracks above. Antonio stopped as well and carefully scanned the road behind them.

"I can't see him," Antonio said and also leaned over to catch his breath. "But we really should keep going."

"Yes," Stuart croaked and also looked down the road, but other than a few lonely cars, there was no movement to be seen.

They continued on past the concrete monstrosity that was Berrío Park metro station and continued further up 51st street. They walked much slower this time, neither of them having the energy to even jog. After a mercifully short distance, they reached another large plaza.

"Ah, the Botero sculpture park," Antonio said quietly.

Stuart looked around. It was an open plaza, much smaller than San Antonio Park, and it was filled with

Botero's trademark rotund sculptures, many more than the birds and the torso up at San Antonio. They sank down next to one of them, a plump dog of unknown species, and caught their breath.

"He must really have liked fat things," Stuart remarked, having regained some strength but feeling that this was not the time for a more sophisticated art critique.

"Yes," Antonio chuckled.

Their breathing started to slow down. Very sluggishly, they dragged themselves up on their feet and made their way across the plaza. They stayed close to the statues, keeping a close eye on the street behind them. However, there was no sign of the third man. He had probably not pursued them for very long. All Stuart saw were the city's skyscrapers illuminating the skyline around them.

"Remember what I said earlier. Hope, it is a powerful thing. We might yet survive the night." Antonio smiled and reached for his phone. "I'll call Juan. I really hope that they are safe."

He took a few steps away as Stuart continued circling around the statues, still expecting the cartel soldier to turn up at any moment. Stuart only now remembered that his own phone was still inside the bird statue and that he would probably not see it anytime soon, if ever. He suddenly felt very isolated and alone, lost in a foreign place far from home. It made his stomach churn, though that might have been from the exhaustion.

As Antonio was on the phone, Stuart spotted a police car driving down the road. His heart froze and he stood still in a panic. As soon as he regained some sort of composure, he tried to slink away behind one of the statues. However, the policemen must have spotted him, because the car pulled up and two officers stepped out.

Stuart realised that there was no point in hiding or running away. He sighed. This was a strange way for this whole debacle to end. He made sure his gun was well hidden inside his pocket and then he waited for the policemen to reach him. He tried to look relaxed and happy to see them.

"Good evening, father," the first officer said politely but he was carefully studying Stuart. Stuart smiled and nodded as a greeting. He understood that the moment he spoke, the officers would realise that he was not local. The officer had his hand on his gun holster but removed it once he noticed Stuart looking at it. "Apologies, father," he said, smiling gently. "What brings you out here at this time of night?"

It was at this point that Stuart recalled that he was dressed as a priest, and despite being too tall and white not to stand out, there was no reason for the police to doubt the genuineness of his vocation. However, his accent would give him away. He was struggling to decide what to do. He had to do something.

Thankfully, before he had time to reply, Antonio arrived and greeted the officers.

"We are ministering to the homeless in this area," Antonio explained. "It being Holy Week and all."

The officers turned and scrutinised Antonio closely, but seemed to accept his explanation.

"Of course," the first officer said. "We are very sorry for disturbing you, father. Good night."

"Good night," Antonio said. "God bless."

Stuart nodded stiffly, still smiling, but refrained from speaking so as to not reveal his accent. The officers' eyes lingered on him, giving him a final scrutiny, but then they walked back to their car. Stuart and Antonio stood in silence until they had driven away.

"That was interesting," Antonio said once they had disappeared around a corner.

"We should walk on," Stuart said anxiously. "I think they suspect me."

Antonio nodded.

"I'm sure they do, your whiteness and tallness makes you as inconspicuous as an octopus at a garden party."

"What?"

"Something my grandmother said. Don't forget that I

have a foreign accent too. Anyway, Juan will come in the car very soon. I think we can safely wait here for a few minutes."

They walked over to a bench, their bodies still aching from the mad run, and sat down. They kept an eye out for the third hitman, but given the passage of time, it seemed unlikely that he had actually followed them. Stuart left his gun in his pocket, but kept his hand on it, ready to pull it out and shoot, just in case.

The respite gave him a chance to replay what had just happened. He had only one question. Who had shot the leader of the hit squad? Antonio seemed to read his mind and looked at him with a darkness on his face. Without saying anything, he pulled a gun out of his pocket. Stuart tensed up and instinctively pulled his own gun out as well.

"Mauricio gave it to me earlier, when we went to collect your passport. He understood that we were looking into this cartel and he insisted I take it. Juan has one as well."

"Oh, wow," Stuart exclaimed. "He really is a full-service mechanic!" Stuart looked over at Antonio. "But you? You're a priest!"

Antonio put the gun back into his pocket and then rested his head in his hands as if he was in prayer.

"Thank you," Stuart said after a while. "I think you saved my life. I just didn't think that priests were allowed to have guns."

Antonio scoffed, sitting back up.

"You'd think those were the rules, no guns, but the rules are a bit vague." He smiled. "Open to interpretation."

"Really? The Church's rules on guns are…vague?"

"I did what was necessary," Antonio said. "No need to dwell on the past. I'm glad that you are alive. The important thing now is to look ahead."

"No, you should reflect on it," Stuart insisted. "You have to come to terms with it."

Before they could reflect on anything, however, Juan arrived in his car. They got up from their bench and headed over to the road. Stuart was relieved to see that Carolina was sitting safe and sound in the passenger seat. As she saw him, she scrambled out of the car and gave him a hug.

"Let's go," Juan said impatiently. Stuart heard a thud coming from the trunk of the car and he realised that there was someone in there. "Let's go," Juan said again. "The night is not over yet."

Chapter 19

"This is what happens when you send two Colombians to chase down a murderer."

Juan was beaming in the front seat. He seemed bizarrely proud of having captured one of the cartel soldiers and somehow managed to get the man into the trunk of the old car. He was driving fast, heading back towards the church, and with every turn and bump Stuart could hear groaning and banging from the trunk.

"Juan even has a gun," Carolina said with a disturbingly broad grin. Far from the fear that Stuart felt, she was clearly ecstatic. Stuart earnestly hoped that she was experiencing an adrenaline rush and that the night's events had not awoken some latent streak of cruelty.

Juan laughed and smiled at her. They had clearly bonded in the past hour. Stuart and Antonio, feeling more downcast at Antonio having killed the lead cartel soldier, glanced nervously at each other. As Juan continued driving towards the church, Stuart told them about what had happened. Despite being interrupted by continued banging and shouting, he was soon finished. Carolina then described what had happened to her and Juan.

Arriving at San Antonio Park, Juan and Carolina had both moved towards the sunken amphitheatre at the north end. When the cartel soldiers had arrived and started fanning out, one of them headed towards the amphitheatre. From there he continued on and walked down the steps towards the street where Juan had parked the car. Moving in the shadows, Juan and Carolina had followed him. Seeing that they were alone on the street, Juan had pulled out his gun and decided to try to apprehend the man in order to get some more answers. The man, however, had spotted them and quickly disappeared around a corner. Juan and Carolina had gone in pursuit and had managed to take him by surprise near San Antonio station.

"He saw Juan, but I managed to sneak up from behind

and I knocked him out," Carolina said proudly. "I ran to get the car whilst Juan stood guard. I was so pumped up I must have forgotten that you too would be coming for the car. I'm sorry."

"No, this is good news," Antonio said. "We can finally get some answers, right from the source."

"Yes, well done," Stuart said. "I'm glad you're all right."

"I just hope that he talks," Juan said. "But I am worried that the third soldier is still out there. They were clearly following Stuart's phone, but now that they can't do that anymore, I'm concerned about our safety. They already know where the church is, as well as where Carolina lives. I'm not sure that Silvia alone can protect us if the cartel arrives in force."

"I still don't think anyone will come after us at the friary," Antonio said. "There are too many witnesses."

Juan and Carolina exchanged nervous looks in the front seat. Stuart felt a sudden dislike of their newfound bond but quickly realised that it might be unnecessary to be jealous of a priest.

"Don't underestimate them," Juan said.

Shortly after, they arrived at the church. Juan pulled up on the side street and turned off the engine. The man in the trunk was still banging loudly but there were no people in sight. They all remained seated inside.

"We should get some supplies and then go elsewhere," Juan said.

Carolina nodded in agreement.

"My flat has a guard but the guy in the trunk will raise too many questions," she said. "I don't think we should go there."

"What about your uncle's workshop?" Stuart suggested. "Surely they wouldn't expect us to go back there?"

"It's a good idea," Carolina said. "It's a sleepy town, no one will see us at this time of night."

Juan and Antonio headed into the friary to pack some

supplies. Stuart and Carolina stepped out of the car and hovered by the trunk, ready to distract any passers-by. Thankfully though, the man in the trunk had stopped his banging. Stuart wondered if he had passed out, or worse, but this was not the time to worry about that. Instead, they waited in silence until the priests came back, carrying a duffle bag each.

Juan drove the forty odd minutes out to El Retiro. There was very little traffic out on the country roads, and certain that there would be no police around, Juan drove as fast as he could. Stuart, feeling extremely tired now that all adrenaline had worn off, had hoped to sleep, but he was so terrified of Juan's driving that he stayed awake. Antonio and Carolina, apparently feeling more comfortable, slept peacefully. The twists and turns of the winding road had, however, reanimated the man in the trunk, who resumed his banging and shouting.

It was almost two in the morning when Juan drove into El Retiro and woke Carolina to ask for directions. She yawned and rubbed her eyes, trying to wake up, and then directed Juan into the street where her uncle had his home and workshop. Juan parked outside. Stuart's mind flashed back to the shooting earlier in the day. Almost twelve hours had passed. He felt a bit queasy as he sluggishly stepped out of the car and breathed in the cold night air. Stretching made him wake up a bit but he knew he had to get some sleep very soon.

Juan and Antonio walked around to the trunk. Carolina, still bizarrely giddy with excitement, more so now after her nap, joined them. Stuart feared that she was in fact in deep shock. He walked over and stood next to Antonio as the man in the trunk was revealed. He looked up at them in fear but this quickly turned to surprise as he saw three priests looking down on him. He had clearly not expected that.

"Come out," Juan said calmly, and pulled the man out, helped by Antonio and Stuart.

The man stumbled onto the ground and fell over. His

legs had clearly fallen asleep. Juan and Antonio pulled him up to a standing position and then they dragged him towards the workshop entrance, which Carolina had opened. Stuart carefully closed the trunk and then had a last look around to make sure that they were safe. The street was dark and empty. There were no lights on in any of the buildings and there was no sound, except some night birds hooting and the occasional cicada shrieking in the distance. There was nothing to suggest that they had been seen. Happy with that, Stuart walked inside.

Carolina closed the door behind him. He saw that Juan and Antonio had sat the man down on a chair next to some half-finished cabinets.

"You remember this place, of course," Juan said to the man.

Juan, having never been here before, looked around to familiarise himself with the space. The man did not reply but simply stared angrily at Juan. Stuart could see that he was still confused at having been captured by three priests and their female friend.

"You were here earlier today," Juan continued, unfazed. "Your friend was shot. I'm sure you remember."

The man did not react but just kept staring. Stuart apprehensively walked over to the front door and looked down on the pool of dried blood on the floor, next to a splintered chest of drawers. Painful images of the event flashed in his mind and he had to steady himself against another cabinet.

"Right here," he said after he had composed himself again, pointing to the floor. He looked the man in his eyes. The man returned the gaze for a short moment, before turning back to Juan.

Juan pulled up another chair and sat down in front of the man, keeping a reasonable distance. Antonio jumped up on another chest of drawers. Carolina disappeared through the door which led to the stairs and up to the residential quarters. Stuart took up a position behind Juan. He was struggling to stay awake but knew that he could not leave until this was done.

Juan sat quietly, looking into the man's eyes. As the moments passed, the man's eyes started flickering between the three priests, getting increasingly erratic. Fear, confusion and curiosity were getting the better of him.

"What's going on?" the man finally asked. Juan did not move but kept looking into his eyes. They flickered around for a few more moments before he broke down. His voice faltering, he asked again, "Father, why am I here?"

"What's your name, son?"

The man hesitated.

"Raul," he said finally. "Raul Castaño."

Juan nodded but did not say anything. He just kept looking at Raul. The house was silent and Stuart assumed that Carolina had fallen asleep upstairs. He too looked at Raul, scrutinising the cartel soldier up close.

The outstanding feature was the normality of his look, which for some reason annoyed Stuart. He had expected, hoped, for something a bit more sinister. True, Raul had small, dark eyes, and a squat nose, but that was hardly a mark of evil. No, he looked very normal. Stuart tried to remember if Raul had been part of the group that had tried to kidnap him and Carolina at the bus terminal on Friday evening, but he could not be sure. It was possible, but all the faces from that event were blurred. He could not even place Raul in the workshop earlier in the day. He had not got a good look at each of the three men during the shootout. But seeing Raul now, up close, Stuart knew this was a face he would never forget.

The silence was clearly unnerving Raul. Having given away his name, his eyes kept flickering around. The three priests' eyes, however, were constant, piercing him. He must have felt the judgment of God upon him.

"What is going on, Father?" he asked again, sounding increasingly desperate.

"A man was killed last night," Juan said slowly. "His name was Guillermo Adler."

Raul's eyes opened up.

"Yes," he said. He made the sign of the cross, trembling. "Father, I would like to make my confession."

Juan nodded slowly. He turned to Stuart.

"Would you wait upstairs, please?"

"Sure," Stuart said.

He was too tired to be annoyed at having been dismissed. Wearily, he walked out of the workshop and headed up the stairs. Assuming that Carolina was asleep somewhere, he tried to stay quiet and tiptoed across the creaking wooden floor.

To his surprise, he found Carolina in the kitchen. She was sitting in a chair, nursing a glass of whiskey. The bottle stood on the table. She smiled weakly at him as he walked in.

"Were you kicked out?" she asked.

"Yes," Stuart said and sat down opposite her. "He wanted to confess, which apparently means something different to a priest than to a lawyer."

"Not really," she said. "Do you want a drink?" She stood up and fetched another glass from the cupboard. She poured without waiting for a reply. "Hopefully they'll learn something useful."

"He said his name was Raul."

"Well, that's a good start." She handed him the glass and Stuart took a small sip. "Hopefully they can find out why this cartel is so interested in you."

"Do murderous henchmen know such things?"

Carolina scoffed as she sat back down.

"Probably not," she said.

Stuart took another sip of his whiskey, which revitalised his senses. He was too worn out to be thinking clearly and he was amazed that he was still awake. He saw that Carolina was looking at him with equally tired eyes.

"I'm really worried," she said quietly.

The statement took Stuart aback. Carolina seemed to have taken the events in her stride but now he could see that there was something hollow in her look. She must have been in shock earlier, riding purely on adrenaline, which had now worn off.

"It will be fine," Stuart said softly.

Carolina finished her glass of whiskey.

"I'm worried about these...priests," she said with more vigour. "If I hadn't seen them in their church I might have doubted they really were priests."

"Why?"

She sighed and refilled her glass.

"When was the last time you saw a priest with a gun?"

"In The Da Vinci Code," Stuart offered with a soft smile.

Carolina scoffed and emptied her glass again. Stuart looked at her with concern as she refilled it again.

"Be serious," she said, more angrily this time. "You said Antonio shot and killed one of them."

"Yes, but to save me."

"So? I'm grateful, of course, but it's strange. Their willingness to help you, their mysterious contacts, their guns. There's something that just feels strange about it."

"I don't think so," Stuart said. "This is an outlandish situation and they're just being helpful."

"Perhaps," Carolina said but it was clear that she did not believe it.

"They're helping me," Stuart repeated, realising that he was by now sounding a bit too confrontational. "Surely, no matter what, we have nothing to worry about from them."

Carolina leant back in her chair and waved off the argument. They sat in silence for a while, listening, but no sound came from downstairs. The town, beyond the window, was also silent, its people resting peacefully, unaware of the drama unfolding.

Stuart kept sipping his drink, his mind going over what Carolina had just said. He had not figured out why Carolina had this hostility towards the priests, but he had to accept that it was a bit surprising that the priests had accepted the guns from Mauricio. But then, they did know this was a dangerous environment. Better safe than sorry, surely even a priest would accept that logic? They were human, after all.

"I'm sorry you're getting such a warped view of the country," Carolina said after a while. She sounded friendly again.

"Yes, it's living up to every stereotype," Stuart replied. He tried to smile warmly, to exorcise the earlier tension.

"It's genuinely not the reality for most people."

"There are drugs and murder in London too," Stuart said sympathetically. "Criminals vying for power."

"Thank you," Carolina said softly. "You know, you should see one of Congressman Escaso's election adverts. He's local, you know. He talks about making Medellín the best 21st-century city imaginable. Not sure I'm voting for him but that's the city I wanted you to see. I had hoped you would go home with some good memories."

"Yes, well, the first day was quite nice," Stuart said and smiled, fondly remembering the night the two of them had shared.

"Yes, it was," Carolina answered warmly. "If only we could have kept that going."

Before Stuart could reply, they heard footsteps coming up the staircase. Antonio appeared in the kitchen doorway, looking worn out. He leaned against the doorframe, struggling to stay upright.

"How did it go?" Carolina asked.

"He doesn't know much," Antonio said quietly. He walked into the kitchen and leant back onto the kitchen counter. "He, or rather the hit squad, were instructed to find you, Stuart, and ideally capture you, or kill you if necessary. His boss was interested in ransom but he didn't know any more than that. You don't ask why when someone like his boss gives an order." Antonio stopped and as his face clenched he seemed to be suppressing some hidden rage. "Raul did confess to some other murders though, namely the civil servants killed in London and Madrid."

"I hadn't forgotten about them," Stuart said. "So Raul was responsible? Didn't the Spanish guy have a fiancée who also died?"

"Executed, yes," Antonio said bitterly.

"Of course," Stuart said, taken aback by the bitterness. "So he got orders, I assume that means he knows where to find the boss?"

Antonio shook his head.

"No, apparently only the leader of the squad had contact with the higher ups, and…"

"And you shot him," Stuart added.

Antonio made the sign of the cross.

"Yes, I did," he said.

"And I'm grateful," Stuart said, nervously eying Carolina. "So are we back to square one?"

"No," Antonio said. "Tomorrow we'll go and meet Juan's contact. I have faith in this contact, but I'll let Juan explain. Anyway, the plan now is, Juan and I will take Raul to the local police station. We'll tie him up and leave him outside. Anonymously."

"That's a classic."

"Do you need help?" Carolina asked.

"No, thank you. You two should get some sleep. It's been a long day and I fear tomorrow will be just as long."

With that, Antonio left the kitchen and headed back downstairs. They heard the stairs creak and then the door to the workshop closed. Carolina got up from her seat and put the whiskey bottle away. They then heard some muffled sounds from downstairs, ending with the front door closing.

"That's not normal," Carolina said. "Priests don't do these things."

"They're trying to help," Stuart repeated.

Carolina tutted at him.

"How do we know that they aren't just going to put a bullet in his head and dump him in an alley? That's more of a classic move than leaving him at a police station."

"I don't believe it," Stuart said, too tired to sound irate. "Might it be that your dislike of the Church is clouding your judgment? They're helping us."

Carolina stared at him angrily but did not say anything.

"We should get some sleep," Stuart said softly. "I'm sorry."

"There is a sofa in the next room," Carolina said testily. "I'll take the bed. The priests can sleep on the floor, they have a vow of poverty."

Stuart smiled but to no avail. He slowly walked through to the living room and laid down on an old sofa. It was far too short for him but he was too tired to notice.

**

Sunlight was flooding into the living room when Stuart awoke the next morning. His head was pounding from lack of sleep but not even his lassitude could shut out the noises coming from the street below. It was Monday and the town had awoken. With his body protesting angrily, he pushed himself onto his feet. He tried to stretch but his body jolted in pain after sleeping on the tiny sofa. Groaning, he then stumbled out onto the landing, where he heard clanking noises from the kitchen. Inside he found Carolina, looking as dishevelled as he did.

"Hello," he said quietly, feeling apprehensive after the way they had left things last night.

"Good morning," Carolina said. She was brewing coffee and she poured him a cup. "I'm sorry for last night. I was very tired."

"Don't worry about it," Stuart said, pleased that they could leave it at that. He gulped down the hot coffee but it did not seem to have any impact. "It was a difficult day for everyone."

Once they had finished their coffee, they made their way downstairs and found Juan and Antonio sleeping on two old sofas in the workshop. Stuart gently shook them awake.

"What a day that was," Juan said with a hoarse voice.

Stuart could see Carolina holding back the question on her mind.

"How did it go with Raul?" he asked in her stead.

He saw that Juan and Antonio quickly exchanged looks before Juan replied that they had successfully dropped him off at the police station and that no one had seen them out and about.

"That's good," Stuart said slowly, wondering what that look had meant. He clearly remembered the worrying suggestions that Carolina had made last night. "I guess we should be leaving then?"

"Yes," Juan said. "Don't worry though, Raul won't be telling the police anything about us."

Now it was Carolina's turn to give Stuart a look.

"Okay," Stuart said. Was Raul not talking to the police out of fear or because he was dead? Stuart was too tired to wonder.

They began discussing their next steps. Carolina insisted that she had to go back to her office, if nothing else to avoid being fired. She also did not want to have any unexplained absences, in case the police called at her flat again. Juan nodded in agreement.

"I was wondering, though, as we go to see my contact, would you be able to go to Bogotá and see if there is anything you can find out about the murders there? The man from the embassy and the English lawyer, I forget their names. Was it a street mugging or was it the cartel?"

"That sounds very dangerous," Stuart objected.

"I can go later," Carolina said. "The more information we have, the better."

"Thank you," Juan said. "Then the three of us will go and meet my contact. She will definitely know more about this cartel."

"Where is she?" Carolina asked.

"In Cartagena," Juan said. "We have to fly down there. This is why Stuart needs the passport."

"Ooh, you get to be a tourist again," Carolina said smiling. "What's her name?" she asked Juan.

Juan chuckled.

"She calls herself the Red Widow."

"You mean the Black Widow?" Stuart suggested.

"No, the Red Widow," Juan insisted. "When she was younger she killed a lot of communists."

"Of course she did," Stuart concluded apprehensively.

Chapter 20

"I'm an American citizen! You cannot treat me like this."

A red-faced, rotund man was loudly shouting in English at the airport security guards, who were staring back at him with rapidly growing disdain. The man's wife, equally corpulent, was angrily glaring at the guards, vigorously nodding in agreement with her husband.

"You cannot search my bags! I am an American citizen, I have rights."

Antonio nudged Stuart.

"We're in luck," he said, chuckling at the bizarre scene. "The guards are distracted."

"Yes, you can always count on the Americans to help you out," Stuart said.

They were at Medellín Airport, standing in line for the security check, tickets in hand for the flight north to Cartagena. Stuart had been panicking the whole way to the airport, absolutely convinced that the guards would see right through his fake passport, but now he relaxed a bit, amazed at his sudden good fortune.

One of the security guards spotted the three priests and the growing line of passengers behind them, and waved them forward. His colleagues showed the American couple towards a corner. This, unsurprisingly, angered them even further.

"Oi, you, why are you letting these child molesters through before me? I am an American!"

An irritated guard put his hand up in front of the man's face, silencing him, as the first guard helped Juan and Antonio through the metal detector. Stuart followed and nervously handed over his documents. He forced himself to look the guard in the face and tried to smile. The guard, clearly seeing that Stuart was not a local, took a very close look at the passport, but quickly lightened up.

"You are from Canada, Father?"

"Yes," Stuart said, with another smile, relieved that the

guard seemed to have accepted the passport as genuine. "Yes, Canada! We're a bit friendlier than...the United States."

"Yes, go Canada," the guard said loudly in broken English, turning with a broad mischievous grin to the American man, whose face reddened even further. Speaking again in Spanish, he invited Stuart to go through.

Stuart caught up with Antonio and Juan, who warmly patted him on his back. They slowly headed down the length of the domestic terminal, looking through the large windows at the planes parked out on the tarmac, and eventually reached their gate. They sat down on a row of empty seats. The American couple were nowhere to be seen. Perhaps they had not made it through at all.

The seating area quickly filled up with other passengers and, not before long, they boarded the flight. The three of them were fast asleep before the plane had even taxied to the runway. Stuart was awoken by his ears popping. He squirmed in his seat, trying to get his body to wake up once again, and then looked out the window. Gone were the mountains and the high plains of central Colombia. Here, instead, he could see the Caribbean Sea rapidly closing in.

The coastline was crowded with commercial developments, stacks of containers, cranes, and container ships. The sea beyond was busy with all types of vessels, including a large cruise ship. As the plane continued its descent, flying parallel to the coastline, Stuart saw the city itself creep into view. What he saw first was modern, consisting of a large cluster of white high-rise buildings. Further afield, he spotted the Old City, with its imposing church domes. Before he had time to see any details, the city disappeared behind a large hill protruding sharply out of the flat coastline.

Seconds later, the plane touched down.

With only overnight bags carried as hand luggage, it was a quick walk through the terminal to exit out front. It had taken them a few hours in El Retiro to arrange the tickets and travel to the airport, so by now, it was already mid-afternoon. On passing through the main entrance Stuart walked into a solid wall of heat.

"Oh my," he exclaimed and stopped dead in his track.

"It's a bit warmer down here," Juan remarked and laughed. "Welcome to the Caribbean."

They walked out to the taxi ramp and were immediately met with a cacophony of car horn blasts, aggressive driving, and families and friends loudly reuniting. The heat and noise already lent the city a more vibrant atmosphere. This made Stuart distinctly unhappy and he was already dreaming of cooler and calmer climates.

They found a taxi and Juan asked the driver to head for the Old City. Despite the driver's passionate disregard for the traffic rules, they made only slow progress at first. They navigated through congested small roads before eventually coming out onto a freeway that whizzed them down to the sea. On the other side of the road rose the impressive city walls, built in large grey stone blocks. Stuart spotted numerous people walking around on top and surprised himself by being stricken by an explorer's urge to do the same.

They soon reached the other end of the Old City and the driver turned off the freeway. He navigated through an arched gateway in the city wall and parked just within, next to a large townhouse painted in a bright yellow tone.

"This is as far as I can drive. Do you know where to walk?"

"Yes," Juan said and handed over the payment. "Thank you very much."

They stepped out into the boiling heat of the city. Ensconced between the thick wall and the houses, there was no sea breeze, and Stuart felt like he was trapped inside a large cauldron. He was already wiping sweat from his forehead.

They set off for the hotel. Once they turned the corner they entered a large, rectangular plaza, adorned with a variety of trees, including some tall palms. The city wall could be accessed from the western side by a wide ramp. In a bizarre juxtaposition, the modern town, with its imposing white skyscrapers, loomed in the distance. A row of two-story, yellow painted townhouses stretched down the eastern side, and continued southward past the plaza, down the colourful San Juan de Dios street. At its end, Stuart saw the large dome of a church, painted in white and gold, which glistened in the afternoon sun. Two buildings, one in yellow and the other in white, fronted by a hullabaloo of street vendors and buyers, occupied the south side, opposite to where they stood.

"The square is also named for Santa Teresa," Juan explained. He pointed to the opposite side the plaza. "That is the naval museum. If we have time we can learn how we fought off English pirates." He laughed affectionately and patted Stuart on the back. "Not everyone likes the English down here."

Stuart avoided making any comment on the matter. Juan then pointed at the imposing church dome, which in a statement of religious power seemed to overpower the two-story naval museum.

"We must visit that church later to pray for guidance," he said.

It was an oddly definitive statement and it puzzled Stuart.

"Will we get better guidance in that church than one of the others?"

"Yes!"

Stuart sighed to himself. He did not understand Catholicism.

"Yes," Juan repeated and realised that he had to explain. "It has the bones of a saint interred in the altar."

"Ah," Stuart exclaimed. "So it has more of a direct line to God?"

Juan and Antonio both nodded vigorously.

Instead of crossing the plaza, Juan turned left and led them into the warren of old colonial streets. Feeling more relaxed in the shade, Stuart looked up at the buildings and was fascinated by the multitude of bright colours the houses were painted in and the equally colourful panoplies of flowers and plants emanating from the balconies or growing in nooks and crannies between the houses. Stuart was overwhelmed by the beauty.

"This is so very charming," he said, stopping in front of an old wooden door and inspected the large brass knocker, which was in the shape of an iguana.

They continued down the bright streets, passing by colonial palaces and townhouses that in the past few years had been given a new lease of life, as the city had rallied to protect its history following decades of decay due to civil wars and other disasters, which had left the Old City almost crumbling to the ground. The streets were thronged with locals and many excited tourists, clearly from all over the world, including groups of cruise ship passengers being herded around.

After a short walk, which in the heat felt much longer than it really was, they arrived at their hotel. Stuart, who had vigorously objected to the cheaper hotels the priests had initially suggested, was pleased he had offered to pay for something more fashionable. Juan, though, insisted on fronting the money, in case the cartel was also tracking Stuart's bank card. They walked into an old, stone-laid courtyard, surrounded by a ground and first-floor loggia, both overflowing with a colourful explosion of flowers. Checking in went smoothly and Stuart soon collapsed on the bed in his cool, air-conditioned room.

He was not allowed to rest for more than a few minutes before Juan and Antonio knocked on his door. He pulled himself up and gulped down a small water bottle from the minibar. Then they set off again, walking out onto the boiling streets. Juan led them to a café, which was only a few minutes' walk away. Stuart hesitated momentarily when he saw a sign on the front window prohibiting guns from being taken inside, but Juan insisted that it was only for the tourists. Based on the events of the past few days Stuart was not convinced, but he followed the priests inside with the promise of fruit juice and tasty cakes.

"We must prepare for tonight," Juan said softly after they had sat down at a corner table.

"The Red Widow," Stuart said, who felt a bit concerned about meeting someone described as a serial killer. "Yes, who is she?"

Juan took a deep breath.

"It is a long story. I guess it starts where we left off with Guillermo. I met her in my village. She was leading her own death squad at the time, but she had already earnt her nickname. She was working for some emerald miner, chasing down guerrilla fighters on his behalf. It was shortly after my father's memorial service and I was out in a field, looking after my family's cows. I think she took pity on me, because she gave me some money and, of all things, a rosary. Well…I was very angry with the world." Juan sighed. "As you might be if your father had just been killed and his body vanished. I asked her if I could join her group. She said no, thankfully. She had a cousin who, he wasn't a priest, but he did charity work with the Carmelite order. She introduced us, and that's how I got involved with the order, and finally became a priest. I left my mother and my two brothers in the village, which was difficult, but my father's disappearance shook me, and I had to get out."

"I can understand that," Stuart said. "So, we have her to thank for you becoming a priest?"

"Yes," Juan said and smiled. "It's strange, isn't it, how you can get help from the most unlikely of people? Who'd have guessed that I'd be guided to the priesthood by a professional murderer?"

They sat in silence for a moment whilst they were served freshly pressed juice and large glasses with fruit salad and ice cream. Stuart gleefully tucked in.

"That's a serious heat out there," he said in-between spoons. He looked at Juan. "But you said yesterday that meeting the Red Widow might not be a positive experience for you? It sounds like it should be a happy reunion?"

"Well, yes, I guess so. She's still a drug runner and a murderer, and I'm a priest, so I think that we have some insurmountable philosophical differences."

"But she will help us?"

Juan nodded.

"Yes, she said she would. When I called her, she seemed happy. It might be purely out of self-interest though, because undoubtedly this Hermit is a rival of hers. I don't think she would be helping us if the Hermit was her partner."

Once they had finished and felt a bit more relaxed and refreshed, they set off for the church with the saint's bones. Stuart was relatively interested in seeing this direct link to God. Though he seriously doubted its efficacy, he had to admit that if it did work, it could come in handy.

"San Pedro Claver," Juan explained as they were walking. "The patron saint of Colombia. He earnt his sainthood by ministering to the slaves brought over from Africa, who were vilely abused by their, well, owners. I'm not sure it helped much, in the long run, some people would argue there is still a racial hierarchy in the country, but hopefully, he had an impact on the poor souls he did meet. So he's also the patron saint of slaves, and maybe this will help us find the kidnapped embassy worker and Manuel's daughter."

"I have every confidence," Antonio said, indeed sounding confident.

Stuart nodded in support. He remained unconvinced of the utility of asking dead people for help but figured it was unlikely to make matters any worse than they already were.

They kept walking down the hot and colourful streets. They passed by a large, colonial, yellow-painted church, flanked by a tall, beige-brown stone tower, which Juan pointed out as the city's cathedral. The streets were crowded with people; tourists moving around slowly, street traders who had set up shop along the buildings, and hawkers moving around the throngs, some peddling their wares from old wooden carts. It made progress slow, and continuously wiping sweat off his face made Stuart gradually lose interest in the vibrant surroundings.

Eventually, they reached a square, dominated by a large, squat brownstone colonial church façade, above which rose the imposing golden dome Stuart had seen earlier. The square itself was dotted with small, wrought-iron sculptures of people in everyday activities. Stuart had stopped next to one displaying two people playing chess. A little further off was a street vendor with his cart and a barber leaning over his chair.

"The Church of San Pedro Claver," Juan said.

Stuart looked up at the large red door, which was firmly shut.

"It opens only for mass," Juan said. "We must go through the museum."

The museum was in the building attached to the left side of the church. Seeing that they were priests, the smiling museum receptionist, who was dealing with some tourists, waved them through. Stuart felt a bit guilty at the subterfuge but went along with it.

They stepped into an inner courtyard, reminiscent of the hotel, as it was surrounded by loggias on each of the three floors. This courtyard, however, was overgrown with tall trees and shrubberies. A path led through its centre, and in the middle stood an ancient stone archway, whose purpose Stuart could not figure out. He could see various groups of tourists moving around, enjoying their surroundings, which were both cool and serene in the shadows of the trees; a welcomed break from the heat outside. Inside the courtyard were a few overjoyed tourists, who were holding colourful parrots whilst chatting to the birds' handlers.

"This way," Juan said.

Stuart and Antonio followed him through a small door and emerged into the spacious church. The walls were whitewashed, with streaks of deep red around the windows in the nave and around the dome, soaring high above them. Stuart, in an unpriestly fashion, scurried down the aisle and placed himself in front of a large fan.

Juan and Antonio slowly walked up to the sanctuary and kneeled down in front of the high altar, built in elegant pink marble, and sporting a large statue of a man. Stuart guessed that this was Pedro Claver.

Stuart, glad to be cooling down after the walk, observed the two priests with some curiosity whilst they were lost in their prayers. He could not shake the accusations that Carolina had made the night before. What were they up to, exactly? Why were they so keen to help him? What did happen to Raul last night? Why were they so sure that he would not talk? And where were these bones they had come to see? The heat had brought on a headache, which was becoming exacerbated by these questions. With bones on his mind, Stuart decided to walk over to the sanctuary and join the priests. Once he stepped up and got a clear sight of the high altar, he recoiled in horror.

"Oh, my!" he exclaimed loudly and realised he had startled some congregants praying at the back of the church.

"I should have mentioned this," Juan said apologetically and stood up. "Please, come and take a look."

Gathering his wits, Stuart stepped up to the high altar and took a close look. Behind a glass panel, framed by intricate gold carvings, lay a skeleton, dressed in fine priestly garbs in white and gold.

"Pedro Claver, I presume?" Stuart said shakily.

"Yes, indeed," Juan said.

Stuart took a few steps back to avoid looking at the skeleton. Since it was dressed, it was only the skull that was visible, but it had really made Stuart jump. He was not used to skeletons, even finely dressed ones. His heart was beating fast.

"I guess you've never seen a skeleton before?" Antonio said, following Stuart down from the sanctuary.

"No," Stuart said, more firmly now. He was getting his

heart under control. "When would I have done that?"

Antonio nodded.

"Yes, I guess most people haven't."

Having composed himself, Stuart laughed to decompress.

"Strange, this was more of a shock than seeing a dead body."

"Yes, they invite a strange reaction, don't they?"

Stuart nodded.

"Right, okay, I'm back. Let's go ask the skeleton for help."

They walked back to the high altar. Juan and Antonio bowed their heads in prayer. Stuart made himself look more closely at the skeleton. Having adjusted to it, the skull invited a different reaction. Stuart tried to imagine the man alive, living in the city almost four centuries ago, going against social norms to stand up for the slaves brought in from that most evil of trades. He could not make himself communicate with the skeleton, but he did find some inspiration in the man's life story. Taking a deep breath, Stuart realised that he was ready to take on Hermits, Red Widows, death squads, murders, drugs and kidnappings.

Thank you, he whispered to the skeleton.

Chapter 21

It was the middle of the afternoon as a Royal Air Force C-17 transport plane touched down at Owen Roberts International Airport on Grand Cayman. William Cooth stirred uncomfortably in his seat. He was desperate to get off the plane, having spent more than twelve hours in the company of large crates bound for the HMS Atholl and a small contingent of less than chatty engineers.

The solitary flight had, however, given him the opportunity to think about his opponent. The Hermit. Despite extensive investigations, involving both GCHQ and the American NSA, he had no idea who the Hermit was. There was plenty of chatter, from drug smugglers and dealers, mentioning the moniker, but never the person hiding behind it. This troubled Cooth greatly, but at the same time, it surely provided some clues. No one could run an international drug cartel whilst staying completely anonymous, unless that person had great influence, either politically or with law enforcement.

In addition to that, it was clear from what Manuel Lopez had so far revealed, which was also supported by the intelligence collected, that the Hermit did have a wide network of contacts. It did not surprise Cooth that one of those contacts allegedly was somewhere within the British government. It disappointed him but did not surprise him. What concerned him most was that the Hermit was threatening to assassinate the Prince on his visit to Cartagena. That was not an easy threat to actually carry out. Even worse was the threat to attack the warship. Both of those attacks would require serious planning, ideally with inside knowledge, such as knowledge of the Prince's movements and security details. The Hermit seemed to be someone who had access to that information.

None of this revealed who the Hermit was, but it did perhaps narrow down the field. It had to be someone with inside knowledge, most likely with access to sensitive information. It was someone who had the power to remain anonymous and the personal strength to run a cartel. It was also someone who surely had amassed a great deal of wealth but was either disciplined enough not to flaunt it or was independently wealthy, so that the drug money could be displayed in plain sight without arousing suspicion.

Taking all these factors into account, it suggested a politician, a senior bureaucrat, or perhaps a wealthy business leader. Given the international dimensions, with the Hermit seeking contacts in Europe and the US, he or she was unlikely to be just anyone. It had be to someone with enough clout to pull it off. But who was it?

The plane came to a stop on the tarmac. Cooth still did not have an answer. He quickly jumped out of his seat, carrying only his holdall, and raced down the stairs. Immediately, though, he winced at the Caribbean heat and could not help but long for the drizzle they had left behind at RAF Brize Norton.

Down on the tarmac, he was met by a dapper young man in a pink polo shirt, who introduced himself as the Governor's assistant. He was here to drive Cooth to the Governor's House.

"Is the HMS Atholl in harbour?" Cooth asked as they were driving away from the airport.

"Yes, sir. She arrived early this morning. There was a lot of pomp and fanfare, since everyone is so excited about the Prince's visit on Friday."

"Yes, I can imagine," Cooth said quietly.

The drive to the Seven Mile Beach did not take long. Cooth was relishing the air conditioning inside the car but was soon captivated by the brightness outside. It was a world apart from the grey and depressing light of London. White and blue, he thought, everything was white and blue. Except for the palm trees. Past the flashy hotel resorts, he could see the Caribbean Sea glistening in the sun, as well as some cruise ships anchored out at sea. This slice of paradise cheered him up.

Soon the assistant drove past a pair of large, white gates

and parked in front of the Governor's House. It was a long, whitewashed, single-story house. It looked exactly as Cooth had imagined a Caribbean house; elegant but thoroughly unimpressive. Cooth stepped out of the car and did an awkward dance to wake his legs up. He would need to go for a long walk later or his legs would be burning in pain all night.

The assistant led him through the main entrance and into a spacious reception room. He explained that the Governor would see him shortly and then he left. Once alone, Cooth walked up to the windows and looked out across a large lawn. Through the tree line, he could see the beach and the sea beyond. Then, whilst waiting, he began taking large strides around the room as exercise.

"Pleasant flight?"

Cooth spun around, somewhat embarrassed, and came face to face with the Governor. She was a pleasant-looking woman in her fifties, with dark-blonde hair and a warm smile. Despite the heat she was wearing a heavy and formal-looking blue dress.

"Good afternoon, ma'am," he said. "Just stretching."

The Governor sat down on one of the sofas and gestured for Cooth to do the same. He sat down on a chair facing her.

"I received the most interesting house guest this morning," the Governor said. "He looks like hell, but maybe you would too if you've spent two weeks on board a warship. Not many luxuries there, I guess. I understand you want to meet with him."

"That's right, ma'am," Cooth said. He assumed that the Governor did not have a clue as to what was going on, and he intended to keep it that way. "How are your preparations for the Prince's visit?" he asked instead, to move the conversation in a different direction.

"Everything is going well. They arrive on Friday afternoon and fly to Jamaica on Saturday. Everyone is looking forward to the celebrations on Friday evening. It's a bit more festive than usual on Good Friday, but no one's complaining." She tilted her head. "Is this man connected?"

"No, ma'am," Cooth answered, truthfully. As far as he knew, there was no threat to the Prince in the Caymans.

"Well, that's good." She stood up. "I'll get Samuel to take you across to the guesthouse. There are two bedrooms, you can have the other one. I understand you're staying the night."

"Thank you, ma'am," Cooth said.

The Governor left and her footsteps quickly receded down the tiled floor in the corridor beyond. Cooth returned to stalking the room for a few moments until Samuel, the assistant, returned and led the way across the lawn to the guesthouse. It was a small cottage, nestled by some trees, situated just a few short steps from the main house. Samuel opened the front door and showed Cooth into the cramped living room.

Sitting on a sofa, watching a small TV, was a tired-looking old man. He was wearing a rating's trousers and a dark t-shirt, undoubtedly provided by the HMS Atholl's crew. He turned the TV off as Cooth walked in and stood up to greet him.

"Good afternoon, Mr Lopez," Cooth said. His Spanish was acceptable, a necessity if spying on South American countries. He decided to invoke one of his covers. "I'm John Spence, call me John."

"Nice to meet you," Manuel said.

Cooth sat down in one of the chairs and Manuel returned to the sofa. Samuel placed Cooth's bag in the spare bedroom and then left. Cooth followed him with his eyes as the young assistant returned across the lawn back to the main house.

"How was it to spend two weeks on board the warship?" Cooth asked, to get the conversation going. He was eager to get to the point but he needed Manuel to open up first.

"It was good," Manuel said. "Very different to my little house in Medellín." He paused, looking at Cooth for a while, before deciding that he might as well be completely honest. He had come this far already. "I used to drive the drug boats for the cartel, to Jamaica, Miami, and Mexico. I'm used to living at sea."

Cooth was excited about the prospect of learning more about the drug routes straight from the horse's mouth, so to speak, but first things first. He felt it was only fair to start with the bad news. He sighed, not sure at what the best way was to break it. This was not what he was used to doing. He opted for the band aid technique, quick and to the point. He explained that their attempts to help his family in Medellín had horribly backfired. His wife and brother-in-law were dead and his daughter was missing. He added that one embassy employee was also missing and that another was dead.

Manuel sat silently as Cooth spoke, and when Cooth finished, he simply nodded a few times.

"I should have expected this," he said, speaking very calmly. "This is all my fault."

"No," Cooth said. "The situation is very clear, we're fighting a dangerous enemy. You did the right thing, coming to us, and I promise that we'll keep looking for your daughter." Cooth was not sure how he could offer any further reassurances. "I'm personally going to Bogotá," he explained. "I will assist my colleague, Tara, the lady you met on the ship two weeks ago."

"She was very friendly," Manuel said. "The gentleman too, but I forget his name."

"Robert. He was the man killed in Bogotá on Saturday night."

Manuel nodded again a few times.

"And Tara, is she the one who is missing?"

"No," Cooth said. "No, she's safe, and as I said, she's doing everything she can to find your daughter."

"That is a great comfort to me," Manuel said. "Yes, I trusted her."

"As do I."

They sat in silence for a moment, contemplating the view across the lawn. A gardener was working his way through some rose bushes in the distance. Cooth was pleased how well it had gone, giving Manuel the bad news. Outwardly, at least, he did not seem too shocked by what he had heard.

"Perhaps we underestimated our opponent," Cooth said after a while. "You said that they have a person inside the British government working for them."

"Yes," Manuel said. "I saw it in the book. The evidence is on the camera." He sighed. "I should have brought it with me, but leaving it was the only way to make sure that you would help my family. I'm sorry I didn't trust you."

"No, no, I understand," Cooth said, truthfully. He would have done the same thing had the situation been the opposite. "But I must ask you, please, what can you remember?"

Manuel nodded his head again but did not speak. Cooth became concerned that Manuel had retreated inside himself over the past few weeks. Who knew what hell Manuel was experiencing in his head?

"You said it was someone who worked inside the government," Cooth pressed gently.

"Yes."

"What made you think that?"

Manuel closed his eyes and tried to remember. Cooth waited patiently.

"There was a list inside the book. Initials and payment details. This was the evidence I photographed. But, the list also mentioned the city where the person lived. I was going through it and I saw London next to one of the names."

Cooth took a deep breath. That confirmed that it was someone in the government. But who?

"Do you remember the initials?"

"No. Maybe it was Mr D."

Mr D. Maybe. It was not much to go on.

"How do you know this person works for the government?"

"I...I don't know," Manuel said slowly. "Most people

they bribe are public officials, police, and people like that."

"Hmm," Cooth muttered to himself.

Mr D in London. Technically it could be anyone, but realistically it was someone who could be useful to the cartel. Like James Westbury would have been, and Carlos Muñoz in Madrid; both worked with the ports and could have ensured that containers with drugs in them slipped through customs. That narrowed it down a little bit. Civil servants, port officials, police, customs. Anyone who could do something to expedite the drugs into the country. Sadly, the initial D was not much to go on.

"Is that the only person they have in Britain?" Cooth asked.

"I don't know," Manuel said. "Look, I was in a hurry, I photographed as many pages in the book as I could. I'm sorry I don't know more."

"No, no, I understand." Cooth smiled, remembering his colourful career as a spy. "I've been in similar situations. Sometimes you're in a hurry."

He decided to move on.

"What do you know about the attack on the Prince?"

Manuel sighed and seemed to retreat further inside himself.

"They wanted my son to do it," he said quietly. "My son said no, it is crazy, it would ruin everything. The police, the army, everyone would come down on us. My son wanted out." Manuel paused. "So they killed him."

"I'm very sorry."

"And now my wife, and her brother."

Cooth waited patiently for Manuel to get his head around the facts.

"But my friends told me a little of what the plans were," Manuel continued. "For my son's sake."

"Yes?"

"There is to be a ceremony at the Fortress of San Felipe. There are some exposed areas. The plan is to shoot the Prince there."

Bingo! Cooth tried not to smile. Granted, the ceremony at the Fortress had now been publically announced, but it had not been when Manuel surrendered, more than two weeks ago. Still, there were a lot of officials, both in Bogotá and London who had known, but this could help narrow down who Mr D was. Maybe even help identify the Hermit. If the Hermit was someone senior, he or she might have had first-hand knowledge of the draft plans for the Prince's visit.

"Yes, I know about the event," Cooth said. "The President of Colombia and the Mayor of Cartagena are going to be there as well. There is a dinner afterwards and there'll be quite a few dignitaries there."

"Oh my God," Manuel said. "They plan on killing the President too?"

"Erm, you tell me?"

Manuel shook his head.

"I cannot believe this."

"Two birds with one stone," Cooth suggested, his mind racing. "Make a statement to the world and scupper the President's peace process in one attack."

Why would they want to do that, Cooth wondered? Then it hit him. It was fairly obvious. A Colombia in chaos, with the civil war raging on, was surely good for drug smuggling. The war keeps the military and police focused on the guerrillas, not the drug cartels.

"We'll deal with it," Cooth said. "Don't worry."

"Worry? What else can I do?"

Cooth tried to smile reassuringly before standing up.

"I have to go to another meeting now," he said. "Thank you, Manuel. I'm staying in the other guest room, so I'll see you later."

Manuel turned the TV back on as Cooth left. Cooth walked back to the main house, worrying about Manuel's mental health, but that was something that would have to be dealt with once he made it to England. In the meantime, Cooth had many questions to find answers to. Who was Mr D? Was he acting alone? And most worrying of all, was the Prince the only intended target or was the Hermit gunning for the President as well?

**

Once the trio had left the Church of San Pedro Claver, darkness was falling over the city. The streets, still bustling with tourists and hawkers, were livening up even more as a variety of street performers had started playing. Juan led them to what appeared to be the city's main square, Santo Domingo, a spacious plaza in front of a yellow-washed colonial church, which was now pleasantly lit up. The square had been filled with outdoor seating for a variety of restaurants, which were filling up with diners. There were a couple of bands playing at opposite corners.

"Right, let's eat," Juan said and checked his phone messages. "The Red Widow will join us soon."

"Wow, she'll come here?" Stuart asked incredulously. By all accounts, she was a notorious criminal. "In public?"

"Oh, yes," Juan said nonchalantly. "She's dating some senior police detective, I think, so she's pretty free."

"That's convenient," Stuart muttered.

They sat down at one of the tables. It was not clear which restaurant the table belonged to, but it would undoubtedly be fine.

"I don't think she'd date him otherwise," Juan said.

"True love."

Juan and Antonio laughed cheerfully.

"Oh, Stuart," Juan said. "You make it hard to believe that you're a man of the world."

"I fear I've been living under a rock," Stuart confessed. "I must learn the ways of the world, don't I?"

"Ah, I don't know," Juan said. "No, the lack of cynicism is refreshing."

They ordered a few pizzas from the restaurant the table happened to belong to and sat in silence for a moment, enjoying the uplifting accordion and guitar music coming from the nearby band. It was a nice way to relax whilst waiting for the serial killer to arrive. Whilst they were eating, the entertainment lived up as a man dressed up as Shakira performed a few hits, with both Juan and Antonio happily singing along. Stuart vaguely recalled some of the tunes from the CD his boss had given him.

As they finished dinner Juan sighed and looked at his phone again.

"She says she's going to be late," he said.

"That sounds Spanish enough," Antonio said with a smile.

Stuart was not impressed. Surely serial killers could be punctual?

They decided to leave the bustling square. Juan led them towards Café del Mar, a bar situated on a massive expanse on top of the city walls. As they walked up one of the ramps, to reach the top of the wall, Stuart delighted in a fresh sea breeze. He let it envelop him and cool him off. Once at the top, Stuart leaned across the cold stones and looked out across the sea, which was shrouded in darkness. A few moving lights on the horizon revealed that there were some boats sailing about.

At the café, they found a table at the edge of the wall, with a commanding view of the sea beyond. Flying above them was a large Colombian flag, fluttering gently in the breeze.

"This is a nice place to hang out," Juan explained, once they had ordered fanciful cocktails from a young waitress in a tiny dress who was clearly somewhat surprised to be serving three priests. "They have invigorating drinks."

They cooled down a bit as the sea breeze intensified. The flag was surprisingly loud as it fluttered above them. Not before long, another waitress walked up with their drinks on a tray, and she also seemed confused at serving a group of priests. They enjoyed their drinks in a short-lived bliss.

"Juanito, my darling," came a shrill voice through the night.

Stuart looked up to a surprising scene. In his mind, he

had pictured a female serial killer in many different ways, but this was not one of them. Charging down the wall with outstretched arms came a rotund woman in her sixties, with a cheerful disposition and a beaming smile, dressed to match her name in a red, flowery summer dress. Her hair, too, was coloured in an absurdly light red colour, which was interwoven with the natural greying hair underneath.

Juan stood up and embraced her, assuring her how nice it was to see her again. He introduced her to Antonio, who she also embraced warmly. Juan then introduced her to Stuart, who fluttered awkwardly with his arms, but she stood still, boring her eyes into him, and did not embrace him. In an instant, Stuart could see murderous menace lurking deep in her soul. He smiled faintly.

"Let's sit," Juan suggested quickly, breaking the awkward moment.

The Red Widow sat down opposite Stuart and continued to study him carefully. Stuart's eyes spun around, not sure where to look as he avoided her gaze. Finally, she scoffed.

"I once saw some meerkats in the zoo in Buenos Aires," she said, looking around at Juan and Antonio. "They were viciously bullying a member of their group, standing in a circle around him, pointing and shouting. That little meerkat in the centre had the purest expression of fear on his face that I have ever seen." She looked back at Stuart. "I don't know why you reminded me of that. But I don't think you carried out the murders you are accused off on the news."

"I'm sorry?"

"Those two people in Medellín and that young girl from your embassy," the Red Widow said in an annoyed tone. "Have you forgotten that you're accused of triple murder? Anyway, it's impossible that you're responsible for that."

Stuart opened and closed his mouth. He was not sure how to respond.

"Thank you," he said slowly. "No, I've never killed

anyone."

He recalled the previous night, coming face to face with the cartel soldier in San Antonio Park. He did not know what would have happened if Antonio had not shot the man. The earlier shooting in the workshop had been different. Even though he had shot one of the men, he had been shooting blindly. He had not been looking the man in the eyes. Importantly, the man had only been wounded, not killed. Stuart had reflected on the incident numerous times, but each time he failed to relate to the Stuart who had done the shooting. It was as if the act had been done by someone else entirely.

"Well, not everyone can kill," the Red Widow said with a dismissive tone, consigning Stuart to some inferior and less capable class of people. "I'll never forget my first, of course. Some lowlife..." She stopped, looked again at Juan and Antonio and chuckled lightly. "Maybe the priests don't want to hear about it."

"We're no strangers to your sins, Red Widow," Juan said politely.

"Some unemployed lowlife harassing my mother. I took a gun my father owned, tracked him down, and shot him in the back." She reflected for a moment in silence. "My first time. I was too afraid to look the man in the eyes. I confess to my weakness. I confess! But the next time I killed, I looked the man in his eyes."

Stuart listened with a terrified look on his face, feeling a chill tingling down his spine. He nervously drank his Piña Colada through a straw. Who the hell was this woman?

"So, you've asked for my help. First, tell me, what's really happened?"

Apparently unperturbed by her admission, perhaps because he had heard it before, Juan started explaining everything that had transpired over the previous three days, starting with how Stuart had been asked by someone in London to deliver a package. The Red Widow listened carefully, and could not help smiling when Juan recounted the gunfight in the workshop, with amazing detail despite not having been present, and she grinned even broader when Juan explained how Antonio had killed one of the cartel soldiers. However, she seemed rather unimpressed by their decision to dump Raul outside the town's police station.

"This shares some similarities with my weekend," she remarked once Juan had finished. "More on that later, perhaps. So, two priests and a gangly lawyer bizarrely dressed up as a priest have decided to take on the Hermit?" She laughed. "This is too good to be true!"

"Someone has to stand up to evil," Juan said. "Might as well be two priests and a lawyer."

"Yes," she said slowly. "Yes, and you know about evil, of course." She turned to Antonio. "I'm not sure where you found the strength to kill, being a man of God, but good on you. I can respect that." She turned to Stuart. "But you…I don't know about you. What do you bring to the table?"

Stuart hesitated. He had never thought about that and now he could not think of anything to say. With Carolina's words echoing in his mind, he could still not be sure why the priests had agreed to help him in the first place.

"A real dedication to the cause," Juan said on his behalf. "True grit."

The Red Widow seemed unconvinced.

"My father did a lot of business with Englishmen," she said.

"Here in Colombia?" Stuart quickly asked, deciding he had to say something.

"No, no, I've never heard of Englishmen doing business in Colombia. My family is from Argentina. He did a lot of business with Englishmen back in the 1920s, 1930s, before…before it changed." She paused for a second, suggesting to Stuart that whatever had happened had been painful in some way. "He always described those entrepreneurs as strong, upstanding, they could take care of themselves, whether in the boardroom or in a bar fight out in the Pampas. You give the impression you couldn't do either."

"I can certainly fight in the boardroom and the courtroom," Stuart said, trying to sound as impressive as he could. "So, what happened after the 30s?" he added as a snide remark to prove the point. If it was something painful, he might as well ask her to relive it.

The Red Widow did not flinch.

"The insanity of Peronism," she said. Suddenly she smiled again. "You know my parents always told me I was the result of an amorous celebration the day Evita died."

"Sounds a bit harsh," Stuart said.

This time the Red Widow flinched, almost imperceptibly.

"You know of Evita?"

"Yes," Stuart said, involuntarily curling his lips in a smile. "I've seen the musical."

The Red Widow looked at Juan in exasperation.

"Good God, Juanito, where did you find this idiot?"

"Come now," Juan said cheerfully, clearly having enjoyed the sparring. "If he's brave enough to give you the run-around, he must be good enough to take on the Hermit." Juan gave Stuart a wink. The Red Widow was pondering the remark and did not notice. "We really do need your help," Juan added.

The Red Widow nodded.

"Yes, of course, what have I to lose? The Hermit believes it's possible to build up a great criminal empire, like Escobar. How foolish!" She paused for a moment and sighed in annoyance. "The worst part is that the Hermit's ambitions are forcing the police and army to wake up again, which is really bad for me. I've lost shipments of my own to checkpoints and overzealous customs inspectors."

"We're sorry for the inconvenience," Juan suggested hesitantly, looking searchingly at Antonio and Stuart. He wanted to keep her happy.

"Yes," Antonio said, utterly unconvinced.

The Red Widow looked at them both and smiled gratefully. She then drilled her eyes into Stuart again.

"First, I want your help with a small matter. Don't think of it as doing me a favour in return for me helping you, think of it as you proving to me that you are a real man."

Stuart hesitated, which made the Red Widow scoff.

"Real man, indeed."

"I'll help you out," Stuart said, looking directly at her. "What do you want me to do?"

The Red Widow chuckled.

"I love that I always get what I want by questioning men's manhood."

Stuart did not say anything but stared at her angrily. Antonio was looking out into space but Juan smiled.

"See, that doesn't work on priests," he said.

"No, Juanito, I know," she said with a surprising air of motherliness. "But this Englishman here, I feel it, he needs to prove himself."

"What do you want help with?" Stuart asked again.

The Red Widow explained that she had had a busy weekend. She freely accepted that she was a murderer and a drug trafficker, but she did not accept anyone else acting immorally in her city. Stuart raised his eyebrows in disbelief but she ignored him. The previous day, Sunday of all days, would you believe it, she had learnt about a new gang that was selling cheap drugs in one of the poorer neighbourhoods. They all agreed that this was horrendous, and Stuart had to accept that maybe the old lady had something of a moral compass spinning inside her. With limited information, the Red Widow had not yet been able to track down the gang, to deal with them, the meaning of which was abundantly clear, but she had caught one man who had bought drugs from them.

"Would you believe it, he is an old, fat man from the US. I have been questioning him all afternoon, but I think I'm getting too old to be scary."

"Never!" Juan exclaimed.

"He isn't talking anyway, which I why I was late. All he's told me is that he has a wife waiting in some hotel."

"He has a wife with him?" Stuart asked incredulously.

"I know, it's insane," the Red Widow said. "Now, I'm itching to kill this man, maybe the wife too for good measure, but not before he tells me where I can find this gang." She paused. "I had an idea just now. I told him I was going to kill him, but I'm not sure he believed me. You go in there, pretending to be a priest, offer him his last rites, get him to confess and tell us where the gang is."

Stuart nodded.

"I think I can do that. I'm a lawyer after all."

"And if this man talks, what will you do to him?" Juan asked. "I know you are friendly with some senior police officer, will you hand this man in?"

The Red Widow laughed dismissively.

"No, I'm going to kill him anyway, Juanito," she said casually. "Surely you did not expect anything else?"

The three men shook their heads.

"Would you excuse us for a moment?" Juan asked, and indicated for Antonio and Stuart to follow him.

They left the Red Widow at the table and walked a short distance down the city wall. At this time of night, it was empty. The Old City behind them was lit up, providing enough illumination to see where they were going. They stopped once they were definitely out of earshot from the bar.

"Well, she is some lady," Stuart exclaimed.

Antonio nodded slowly.

"I'm glad you didn't join her crew," he said.

"This is getting far more complicated than I had anticipated," Juan said. "I don't think she's going to help us unless we help her first."

"I'm really sorry," Stuart said. "I feel this is my fault entirely. She doesn't like me for some reason."

"Not your fault that you're English," Juan said. "But even so, if it wasn't this, it would have been something else, whether you were here or not. I'm just glad she's not asking us to drive a speedboat to Miami. Even as priests we wouldn't have a good excuse to give the US Coast Guard."

They stood in silence for a while, staring out at sea. A few lights were still moving around far out from the coast.

"I should just point out," Stuart said lawyerly, "that anything we do now to help her, knowing that she is going to kill this man, makes us accessories to murder."

Juan looked at him quizzically.

"Really? After everything that's happened, that's your main concern?"

"It's a concern." Stuart chuckled. "Sorry. I can't turn off the lawyer inside my head."

"He's right," Antonio said. "Law school is like an alien abduction. They mess with your head and you never see the world the same again. We haven't actually done anything wrong up to this point. Stuart did not kill Manuel's family, and everything else we've done has been in self-defence."

"Except for my fake passport," Stuart added. "For which I'm very grateful."

"Oh, yes," Antonio muttered.

"So, we're already criminals," Juan said. "If we don't help her, she won't help us, and we're no further along. And she definitely kills that man. If we help her, she'll help us, and maybe we can intervene and save that man somehow. Drug user or not, he doesn't deserve to be killed and dumped in some swampland somewhere to be eaten by vultures."

Antonio seemed to be shaking his head slowly, but Stuart accepted that Juan was correct.

"I agree," he said. "Let's go help a serial killer."

Chapter 22

The Red Widow invited them to sleep over at her estate, which was located a short distance outside the city, but they insisted on staying at their hotel. All things considered, that felt like the safer option.

It was late by the time they returned. In the courtyard they saw an old woman sitting by herself, apparently waiting for someone to arrive. Stuart was filled with dread at the possibility that this was the wife of the American that the Red Widow had kidnapped. From his look, it was clear that Juan had had the same realisation, but he motioned them upstairs, and they left the old lady to her own thoughts.

In the solitude of his own room, Stuart collapsed on the bed. He thought about using the room's landline phone to call Carolina but decided against it. If nothing else she would probably be asleep. Moments later, Stuart too was fast asleep.

He was tormented by his dreams, a bizarre phantasmagoria as his mind tried to rest, recover, and make sense of the past few days. He saw his ex-girlfriend, Kate, in Argentina, cuddling with penguins, which suddenly transformed into demons. The demon penguins of Patagonia was an image that would haunt Stuart for the rest of his life. Later, he found himself being chased by shadows down the narrow streets of a large, nondescript city, but almost every turn led to a dead end. At some point, his mind must have come to terms with the nightmare because one road led out into a large, open field, where he spent the rest of the night playing with a collection of friendly animals. When he awoke, for the first time since Friday morning, before he encountered the bodies of Manuel's family, he felt relaxed and energetic. He laughed at the idea of demonic penguins and got dressed, looking every bit the part of a Catholic priest about to take confession from a tormented soul.

By the time the three of them left the hotel the city was wide awake. Stuart was relieved that the old lady was no longer in the courtyard; hopefully she had met whoever she had been waiting for. Outside, groups of tourists, hounded by hawkers, were walking down the streets, and cars and small vans used what streets they were allowed to make deliveries to the stores, cafés, and restaurants. Though the buildings provided shade, the heat was pressing down on them, and Stuart was soon awash with sweat.

Juan had agreed on a place where the Red Widow would pick them up for the drive to her estate. They walked through the colourful and flowery streets of a city in which a nightmare should have been impossible. They passed the imposing Church of San Pedro Claver, continued down the narrow square, filled with its metal statues, and into an altogether larger, triangular square. To their right was a pleasing whitewashed two-story colonial building with deep red balconies, flying the Colombian flag, and the other two sides had picturesque assortments of colourful buildings. They crossed it quickly and entered another, rectangular, square. Along one side were various buildings, fronted by a long, covered walkway, which was full of traders selling street food. Along the other side ran the city wall. In the middle of the square, the wall was interrupted by a large gate, consisting of three arched passageways, on top of which stood a tall clock tower painted in bright yellow.

Juan led them through one of the passageways and out of the Old City. Beyond the wall lay a large, open area through which ran a wide road, clearly the main artery serving the city as a whole. To their left was the furthest inlet of the harbour, filled with an assortment of small ships. Juan pointed to the other side.

"Behind there is the less glamorous, but still vibrant, side of the old city of Cartagena. It is called Gethsemane." Juan looked at Stuart to see if he knew what that meant, but Stuart's face was blank. "It's the garden where Jesus spent his last night, contemplating death, before his capture, torture, and crucifixion." Stuart nodded, appreciating the importance of the name. "And beyond Gethsemane stands the old fortress," Juan continued. He then looked around searchingly. "The car should be meeting us here."

They found some shade under a nearby tree and waited for a while. The traffic was noisy since the drivers here seemed to think that hitting the horn was an integral part of driving. Whilst the heat was growing in intensity, they were blessed by the occasional gust of cool air coming in from the harbour. Just like yesterday, Stuart felt his head starting to spin.

Thankfully, a car finally pulled up outside the main gate in the city wall. It was a large, black SUV, and it looked exactly what Stuart thought a crime cartel car would look like. Juan led them over and greeted the driver before they climbed into the back seat. The driver was a burly, old man with a thick moustache. The heat was undoubtedly playing tricks on Stuart's sense of propriety, because he found himself smiling at how perfectly stereotypical this scene was. It was only once the air-conditioning had cooled him down that he remembered that a heavyset and moustachioed henchman was now driving him to the estate of a maniacal serial killer, who based on last night's conversation really did not like him. There was some cause for concern.

They drove out of the city. The new part, with its tall, white residential buildings, disappeared on their right-hand side and was replaced with flat, open fields, visible through the interstices of an almost constant wall of trees. It was a vista of boiling serenity. After a while, the car turned onto a narrow and winding country road. The landscape, beyond the trees still lining the road, was dotted with a few buildings, including plantations growing bananas and oranges.

Soon, the driver passed through a set of gates, which opened automatically before the car even slowed down, and continued down a perfectly paved driveway. They passed over a ridge and the sea appeared in front of them. Pleasantly situated by the beach was a grand colonial-style villa, whitewashed with a wraparound terrace on the first floor. The villa was surrounded by gardens with orange trees, and an assortment of appropriately red flowers, including roses, hibiscuses and bougainvillaea. For a moment Stuart forgot that he was not in paradise.

The car pulled up in front of the main entrance. Stuart was quick to jump out but was almost knocked back by the thick wall of heat.

"This is very nice," he said once he had made it out of the car and had put on his Panama hat. He looked up at the sun. "If only it could be a bit cooler."

"No chance of that happening," Juan said, climbing out of the car with less enthusiasm.

As the three of them assembled outside the villa the car drove off. They looked around, wondering what to do next, but before they could decide the front door swung open and the Red Widow made a triumphant appearance. Wearing another flowery dress she hooted and then jogged over. She had clearly spent the morning dyeing her hair since it was now a sort of cotton-candy pink, which startled Stuart.

Once she had jogged all the way over she enthusiastically embraced Juan and Antonio. Stuart did not fall for this again, and just stretched out his hand. This, however, was also too optimistic, as she only gave him a curt nod.

"You have a really nice house," Stuart said, trying to sound kind. However, the sentiment was somewhat undermined by him wiping the sweat from his forehead, which had started running down into his eyes and nose.

"Of course I do," was all she said.

She led them around the house. On the other side, the gardens were shaded by an assortment of larger trees, including a number of palms which were just barely swaying in a light sea breeze. In the distance, hiding between the trees, Stuart saw a number of small outhouses. He shuddered at the thought that the American might be held inside one of them. The back of the villa opened up to a long garden, which led down to the beach. Stuart saw a large yacht moored to a wooden jetty, but this was a luxury yacht and not a drug-smugglers' speedboat. The villa itself opened up to a large patio, laid with large stone slabs, which included a sizeable pool and an assortment of lawn chairs and sunbeds. It was everything one would expect from a dream home by the beach.

The Red Widow invited them to sit down around a table next to the pool. A young woman, who avidly avoided making eye-contact with anyone, emerged from the villa and brought over glasses from a small cabinet.

"Do you want some homemade orange juice?" the Red Widow asked, and even when just offering a drink she made it sound like declining could be lethal.

"Thank you," Juan said, speaking for the group.

The young woman scurried inside and promptly returned with a large carafe of orange juice, which she carefully poured into the four glasses. She then retreated into the house but Stuart could just make out that she was waiting attentively, just inside the door.

"So, have you made any progress with this man you, erhm, kidnapped?" Juan asked.

"No," the Red Widow said. "I don't know, it might be old age, but I got bored with him. But I did hold off from killing him, as promised, because I want to see what this Englishman is capable of. My men kept him awake most of the night, so he should be primed and ready."

"I am ready to go," Stuart said, trying to sound assertive. He had to show the Red Widow a little bit of backbone. Just enough, but not too much.

"That's good," the Red Widow said but she did not move from her seat. They waited patiently for her next move. "Did I ever tell you, Juanito, my uncle was in Bogotá in 1948? He was some liberal thinker from Buenos Aires, excited about the ceremony to create the OAS. Then

Gaitán was assassinated." She turned to Stuart with a soured look. "The Organisation of American States. Gaitán was the leader of the Colombian Liberal Party." I didn't ask, Stuart thought, but said nothing. She turned back to Juan and her face lightened up. "He was caught up in the riots that followed the assassination. Then years of yet more civil war, which apparently the Colombians had already been doing for more than a century. Hundreds of thousands killed." She chuckled, which made Stuart wince. "We don't do mass killings like that anymore."

She looked sad. Juan cleared his throat.

"Which is a good thing, thank God," he said.

The Red Widow laughed loudly.

"Oh, Juanito, you're too squeamish." She paused and looked serious for a moment. "Yes, we don't do mass killings anymore." Stuart could not help but feel that she had just revealed some sibylline prophecy of a new hell to come. "I know what the Hermit is up to," she continued. "I understand why you are here, even if I'm a bit torn."

"His cartel, are they planning on assassinating someone?"

The Red Widow laughed again, which sounded more and more like a crazed witch's cackle.

"Yes," she said rather gleefully.

"There is an English link to this," Juan said. "I read that an English Prince is visiting next week."

The Red Widow winked at him, still grinning broadly.

"And the President is going to be there as well."

She laughed again, almost maniacally this time.

Stuart was aghast. This confirmed what they had guessed. The cartel had gone insane and was planning on assassinating the Prince. He now understood why the British were interested. Manuel had information about this assassination, and in return for sharing it, his wife and daughter would get British passports so they could leave Colombia. But the extraction had been scuppered because there is a traitor inside the British embassy, this mysterious Ms L. This would also, surely, undermine any security arrangements that were in place for the Prince's visit.

Finally, the big picture made sense to Stuart and knowing the cartel's plan filled him with greater resolve. He had to stop them.

Juan made the sign of the cross.

"An energumen," he said quietly, looking afraid.

"The Hermit is hardly the devil," the Red Widow said dismissively. "Look, I have enough ears in Cartagena so I found out about this a long time ago. If it works, I'm sure the Army will hunt down the Hermit and execute him, and I always like it when the Army deals with my competition for me." She laughed again, which now, despite the heat, sent chills down Stuart's spine. "And hopefully new opportunities will open up for me."

Juan shook his head.

"Even if this assassination was successful, what makes you think the country would descend into another bloodbath?"

"I don't know," the Red Widow said and waved it off. "I was just nostalgic for an era I did not get to experience."

Nostalgic for mass murder! Stuart could not stop himself from rolling his eyes. The Red Widow glared at him angrily.

"Oh, the things I would have done if I had met you in an alley," she said menacingly.

Stuart believed it for a moment, before remembering that she was a somewhat overweight lady in her sixties. He could definitely outrun her. He looked at her again, trying to see the reality instead of the legend. If not for the armed guards and the kidnapped man, she would have been a truly ridiculous character, but in this Bond villain's lair, he could see that she was dangerous.

"I will prove myself," he said. He understood now that he really needed her help in finding the Hermit and his cartel. He would do what was necessary.

"Of course you will," the Red Widow said, smiling. "Remember, I want to know where the American bought those drugs, where those dealers are operating from. The

American had a large quantity, so he didn't get it from some street corner."

"I will find out," Stuart said.

The Red Widow stood up and scuffled over to an outdoor fridge, standing by the wall in the shade of an awning, and grabbed a bottle of water. Then she led them down a path through her gardens. As they walked, Stuart was struck by an overpowering aroma from her flowers. It was a beautiful garden. He had believed that the American was being held in one of the outbuildings, but the Red Widow instead led them towards her yacht.

One of her henchmen, with a machine pistol slung around his shoulders, stood guard at the base of the jetty. He respectfully stepped aside as the Red Widow walked past. The yacht was sizeable and greatly impressed Stuart. It had the name Red embossed on its rear hull.

They boarded and the Red Widow told them to take a seat on the sofas on the rear deck.

"Where is this man?" Juan asked as he sat down.

"In a safe place."

The engine started with a low grumble. Two crew members removed the mooring lines and pushed the ship away from the jetty. Stuart looked on, feeling confused. What was going on? The yacht sped up and headed out to sea. The villa was soon a small dot in the distance.

"I have a place on one of the little islands off the coast," the Red Widow explained. "I never keep such guests at home, in case of unexpected visitors."

"Makes sense," Juan said.

A crew member served more drinks. Stuart tried to relax as best he could, telling himself that being on a yacht in the Caribbean was a one-off event in life and that he should savour the moment. At least out here, the tropical heat was tempered by the sea breeze as the yacht continued to cruise further out from shore. However, his mind was spinning from what the Red Widow had confirmed. An assassination threat to the Prince. It was beyond belief. He could hardly make sense of what the consequences would be if such an attack was successful and even worse if the President was assassinated as well. Could it unleash, in essence, another civil war? His crazy host certainly seemed to hope for that. But would that really happen? Based on everything he had learnt about the country, there was certainly a chance, even if remote.

"Do you like my yacht?" the Red Widow asked suddenly, lounging on the sofa with a colourful cocktail.

"It's very nice," Juan said, and Stuart and Antonio nodded along.

"It's a relaxing way to smuggle drugs. I send it north the first week of every month, and it has never been stopped because it looks like a wealthy man's toy and the Americans never bother rich people."

"It doesn't feel like a smuggler's boat," Antonio remarked. "I thought that they all used speedboats so they could outrun the coast guard."

"Exactly," the Red Widow said and sat up. "So if you're in a speedboat out on open water, you will be stopped. But not if you're casually cruising on this thing. Buying this thing was one of my better ideas."

The yacht eventually slowed down and Stuart could see a number of small islands up ahead. There was lively sea traffic near most of them, with fishing vessels and pleasure crafts sailing around. Stuart could spot various estates on the islands, including a few which looked like hotels and restaurants. The crew navigated the Red to one of the smaller islands and moored it at another wooden jetty.

The Red Widow led the way down a narrow path over to a small, single-story house. The gardens around it were sparse but were surrounded by tall hedges for maximum privacy. The house was guarded by another henchman with a machinegun, who opened the door as the Red Widow walked up. She stopped on the small veranda and turned to Stuart.

"He's inside," she said smugly. "And whatever you do, don't pretend you're Colombian. You look like a pale, white gringo, who's turned lobster red in the sun, and you speak Spanish like one too."

"I have not forgotten," Stuart assured her, as Juan and Antonio chuckled silently in agreement behind her. "I'm here as a Canadian."

"Canada, huh? Good, that you're used to living in a snow hut will explain why you're all red and sweaty."

She handed Stuart the water bottle and he stepped inside. The door closed shut behind him. He was momentarily blind in the darkness and he stood still as his eyes adjusted from the bright sun outside. His surroundings slowly came into focus. He was standing inside a large room, which was apparently empty. Once he could see more clearly he spotted a single chair and a dark mass in one corner, which turned out to be a mattress lying on the floor. A shape, like a round ball, lay on the mattress.

Stuart took a single, hesitant step forward, trying to see the body better. As described, it was an old, very heavy set man, seemingly in his sixties. His chest heaved as he breathed, and Stuart was pleased that the man was alive. Eventually, Stuart could see clearly enough to appreciate the dishevelled state the man was in, his clothes dirty and torn. His face was stubbly and filled with dark marks that were clearly bruises and dried blood. Stuart felt sorry for him. It was hardly an appropriate fate, even for someone who had bought a large quantity of drugs.

"Hello," he said loudly in English to wake him up. The man stirred and groaned but was clearly still asleep. "Hello, wake up," Stuart said again, taking another hesitant step forward. The man stirred and opened his eyes. He recoiled with surprising agility as he saw Stuart. "Good morning," Stuart said softly. "My name is…I'm Father, erhm, John," he said, unhappy with his obviously fake name.

"Why are you here?" the man asked hoarsely, speaking in an unmistakable southern US accent.

A corpulent old man from the US south; Stuart marvelled at meeting another living stereotype. The man was staring at Stuart, clearly terrified, covering his face with his chubby fingers. Stuart wondered how he himself might react if faced with a priest after a period of captivity with a crazy, maniacal criminal.

Stuart stepped forward and handed over the water bottle.

"Drink this," he said. "Slowly. Don't hurt your throat."

"Thank you," the old man said and grabbed the bottle.

Stuart waited for him to take a few gulps of water.

"What's your name?"

"I'm Donald, Don."

Stuart pulled up the lone chair and sat down, leaving a bit of a distance between himself and the mattress. He knew the value of silence and he needed a moment to think of something to say. He fingered the rosary which Juan had given him. He had no idea if this was something priests did, but it seemed religious enough. Don looked at him in fear. Stuart finally had to relent and say something.

"So, Don, how did you end up here?" he asked, trying to sound casual so as to not reveal that he knew the answer.

"I…I…I don't know," Don stumbled. Despite his condition, Stuart could sense his mind spinning to come up with a good story. That was disappointing. Stuart had hoped that he would tell the truth right away. "I had visited that big, old castle in Cartagena, and I was walking back towards town, but before I got there I was grabbed. Is this a kidnapping for ransom? Because my wife's in town and she must be out of her mind with worry."

Stuart did not say anything in response. It sounded like a plausible story.

"That neighbourhood is called Gethsemane," Stuart said after a moment. "Do you know the meaning of that?" he then asked knowingly, despite only just having learnt it from Juan.

"Yes," Don said quickly. "Where Jesus spent his last night."

"Mm, contemplating his death."

Don looked up at Stuart with real fear in his eyes, perhaps now fully understanding why he was meeting with a priest.

"Is that lady going to kill me?" he asked.

"She invited me to hear your confession," Stuart said slowly.

"I understand." Don leaned back on the mattress. "Will you tell my wife that...what has happened?"

Stuart nodded.

"Yes, I will convey the news."

Don lay in silence for a moment, contemplating his fate. Stuart remained silent, waiting for him to come clean on his own accord. Why had he bought the drugs? This man did not seem like a mastermind drug trafficker, but why else buy such quantities?

"I'm not some rosary rattler, like the one you have there," Don said after a while. "My pastor says Catholics are the Devil incarnated." He looked at Stuart, waiting for a reaction, but Stuart remained still. "But at the end of the day, I guess we're all the same." He paused again. "The Devil has tricked me into doing some bad things." Stuart sighed, apparently too loudly, but was amazed that the stereotype was getting better. A heavyset, southern US man who was clearly a Christian fanatic. Don looked at him, puzzled. "You don't believe the Devil can force you to do evil?"

Stuart was racking his brain for something priestly to say but he could not think of anything. He really had to avoid getting into some theological argument with Don, since he knew nothing about the subject.

"So you recognise that you have done some bad things?" he asked instead.

"Yes, yes, I have," Don said quietly. "Did she...did she tell you?"

Stuart nodded and despite the darkness in the room, he could see a deep shame in Don's eyes.

"The Devil," he started but stopped himself.

"You understand the havoc caused by the drug trade, in

this country and elsewhere?" Stuart said, steering the conversation away from the Devil.

"I do," Don said and buried his large face in his hands.

Stuart could hear soft sobs.

"It's no good blaming the Devil," Stuart said, again trying to sound priestly. "You need to, erhm, reconcile your soul to God." Don nodded and Stuart was pleased with his choice of words. "You already know the best way to do that. Where did you meet these people? How can we bring them to account?"

Don hesitated for a second.

"Are you working with this crazy woman?"

"No," Stuart said, perhaps reacting too quickly. "No, I just heard that someone wanted an English-speaking priest."

"Can you get me out of here?"

Stuart remained silent for a while. Don had seemed resigned to his fate earlier and Stuart knew he could not give Don any false hope.

"We're not in the United States," Stuart said. "It's a different world here. You should focus on saving your soul."

Don nodded.

"If you promise to try to get me out of here, I will tell you."

Stuart weighed up his options.

"All I can do is try," he said. "But I don't think it was a coincidence that you were taken in Gethsemane."

"I understand," Don said. "My soul is more important than freedom anyway. On that, at least, you and my pastor would agree. I'll tell you what you need to know."

Chapter 23

It was boiling inside the room and Stuart was continually wiping sweat off his face. Despite his discomfort, he listened patiently as Don explained why he had bought the drugs. Don said that he was in a desperate financial situation, owing hundreds of thousands of dollars. He had been approached by someone who knew about his circumstances and offered a deal. If he took his wife on a cruise around the Caribbean and acted as a drug courier, the mystery man would pay off Don's debt. Don was crying generously as he told his story, insisting that he knew it had all been a bad idea, but that he had been out of options. He had agreed to the deal. Stuart, having taken his own deal from a mystery man, listened with a great deal of sympathy.

He did not know how long it had been by the time Don had finished. Stuart was struggling to stay focused in the oppressive heat and he wondered how Don had endured it over the past few days. He thanked Don for sharing what had happened, promised he would talk to the Red Widow about sparing his life, but for good measure, he ended by pardoning Don for his sins. He did not know if what he said was religiously correct, but Don seemed relieved and thanked him profusely. With that, Stuart stepped outside.

He took a few deep breaths of the mercifully cooler air which was blowing in from the sea. The guard told him that the others had gone back to the yacht. Before he set off, Stuart begged the guard to leave the door open so that Don could get some fresh air. The guard did not reply, but as Stuart looked back once he was halfway down the lawn, he thankfully saw that the door was still ajar. Maybe there was a sliver of humanity even in the henchmen?

Stuart headed out onto the jetty and boarded the yacht. He was greeted by cold water and more orange juice. Drinking quickly to quench his thirst, he sat down on the sofa on the rear deck. He closed his eyes and tried to cool down, but despite the shade from the yacht's superstructure and the drinks, he still felt like he was boiling.

The Red Widow, with the two priests in tow, came out from the indoor stateroom. Juan and Antonio seemed relieved to see him. The Red Widow, however, looked at him impatiently.

"Well?"

"How can you live in this heat?" Stuart asked, almost angrily, his eyes still closed.

The Red Widow flung her arms out and grunted.

"Grow up," she yelled. "What did he say?"

"I have an address," Stuart said softly. "I know where he got the drugs."

"Excellent!" She now had a kinder look on her face, which somehow frightened Stuart even more. "Perhaps you're not completely useless, after all."

The Red Widow stepped back inside the stateroom to speak to her crew. Stuart closed his eyes and tried not to move, but his sweaty clothes were clinging to him and his whole body was starting to itch. He felt his mind reeling until he completely lost it. To Juan and Antonio's amazement, he jumped out of the sofa and, fully clothed, threw himself overboard into the sea. He kept his head below water for as long as he could, before finally coming up for air.

"Are you all right?" Antonio asked, leaning over the railing.

"Yes, I think so," Stuart said.

He dropped below the water again, feeling its coolness envelop him. His mind was coming back into action, but his happiness was short-lived. When he re-emerged from the water he saw the Red Widow glaring down at him.

"What the hell is wrong with you?" she screamed.

Stuart swam to the rear of the ship and slowly climbed up the metal ladder, weighed down by his water-drenched clothes.

"I had to cool down," he explained.

"Unbelievable, fucking Englishman!"

The Red Widow stormed off, heading back into the stateroom. Juan and Antonio laughed heartily at the bizarre scene. Stuart stood still in the sun for a moment and dried off, but quickly realised that his clothes were now clingy because of the seawater. It was not ideal.

"You're really not cut out for this climate," Juan said. He continued in a quieter tone. "If this goes well I'm sure we can fly back to Medellín tonight."

"That sounds like a dream," Stuart said. Once he felt like he had dried off enough, he slumped back down onto the sofa, hoping that he would not leave a seawater stain on the serial killer's yacht. "Will she give us the information that we need now?"

"No," Juan said and sighed. "She said she wants us to join her in taking down these drug dealers."

"Oh, come on," Stuart said. "Are we sure she's not just playing with us?"

"She said it will be a practice run for when we go after the Hermit, which I guess makes some kind of sense," Juan explained.

"I guess," Stuart accepted.

A crewman came out and dumped a pile of clothes next to Stuart. He ruffled through it and found a pair of old, tattered jeans, a t-shirt and a pair of underwear he would never in his life have put on. Nonetheless, he was grateful, if only because the Red Widow had not killed him.

As the yacht departed from the island, Stuart headed inside to find a secluded spot to change out of his salty clothes. The Red Widow sat by a large table, having a hushed conversation with a grumpy looking man, who was obviously one of her henchmen. Stuart nodded to her, in thanks for the clothes, and thought he saw the tiniest of smiles in return. The serial killer obviously had something of a maternal instinct hidden deep inside her. Below deck he found a spacious bathroom, complete with marble countertops, where he changed, washing as best he could in the sink. By the time he was finished and had returned to the deck, the yacht was mooring back at the Red Widow's estate.

They all disembarked. The Red Widow sternly told them to wait back on the patio. As the three of them slowly headed across the gardens, the Red Widow swaggered down a path towards the outbuildings, undoubtedly to gather more of her men for the attack. Taking the opportunity when the Red Widow was out of their way, Stuart recounted what had happened in the house with Don.

"Do you think we can get him out alive and hand him over to the police?" he asked when he finished.

Juan shook his head.

"We'll try, of course. But I don't know, she made it quite clear that her boyfriend, the assistant, deputy police commissioner or whatever he is, would just hand Don back to her. I don't like it, but I don't think there's anything we can do."

Juan and Antonio dutifully made the sign of the cross, looking distinctly unhappy about the situation.

"We have to see this as a step on the journey," Antonio said. "This helps us take down some local criminals, make a minor blow to the drug market around here, and it leads us to the Hermit and his cartel."

"So Don's execution serves some useful purpose?"

Juan and Antonio shook their heads.

"I'd never say that the ends justify the means," Antonio said, "but, maybe, sometimes you have to accept the inevitable."

"Maybe," Stuart said.

They returned to the patio and waited in silence until the Red Widow came bobbing back up the path, followed by almost a dozen burly-looking men carrying an assortment of weapons. She directed the men towards the front, no doubt to round up some cars, before walking up to the patio. She looked angrily at Stuart.

"Are you ready now or do you need another swim?"

"I'm ready," Stuart said, trying his very best to sound

determined.

She shook her head angrily and motioned for them to follow her. The large, black SUV they had arrived in was parked by the front door. The Red Widow sat down in the front passenger seat and Stuart joined Juan and Antonio in the back. As they slowly drove down the drive Stuart noticed that they were followed by another three cars. They were all ordinary, old sedans that would pass unnoticed in the city. Stuart could see that the first car was crammed with men. The Red Widow was clearly on the warpath.

On the approach to the city centre, Stuart caught sight of the fortress that Juan had mentioned earlier, which was an impressive brownstone pile rising high above the old buildings of the Gethsemane neighbourhood. He then lost sight of it as they headed into the narrow side streets. This was clearly a poorer neighbourhood, with depressed and dark buildings, the very opposite to the colourful and flowery look of the Old City. After making a few turns the SUV pulled up in front of a grey three-story building. Paint was chipping off the façade and various tied up refuse bags were scattered on the sidewalk.

"You have to be a real lowlife drug dealer to be willing to live in a place like this," the Red Widow muttered to herself. She turned around and faced Stuart. "Right, this is the place. Don told you it was the ground floor apartment, which makes our lives easier. Now, you go in, make sure everyone is there. My men will follow after and take care of these idiots."

Stuart opened his mouth in amazement.

"Wait, you want me to go inside?"

"Yes, of course," the Red Widow said.

"And ask some criminals if I could buy some drugs?"

"Yes," the Red Widow said impatiently. "What did you think was going to happen here? You're the one being tested."

Stuart took a deep breath.

"I'm not sure about this."

"What's not to be sure about?" she asked angrily. "Go in, ask to buy some drugs." She offered him what was supposed to be a supportive smile, but it made her look even more evil. "Look, if my men went in, there would be immediate trouble. You, on the other hand, look like a typical idiot, gringo customer. It will put the sellers at ease." She handed over a small mobile phone. "Just hit call once you've established contact," she explained. "Keep them occupied until my men come in."

"Fine," Stuart said.

The Red Widow handed over a roll of money.

"This is what Don told you it cost for a bag. Try not to hand it over before you see the product, and if it gets lost you're in real trouble."

Stuart apprehensively took the money.

"Don't worry about looking nervous, it will keep the sellers' guard down, and make it easier for us. The more nervous you look the better."

"Good," Stuart said. "I'll be looking very nervous, you can be sure of that."

The Red Widow sighed and shook her head.

"Just make sure your guys don't shoot me by mistake," Stuart said, trying to find some inner strength. After receiving another angry stare from the Red Widow, he stepped out of the car.

Stuart took a quick look up and down the street. Some old and scruffy men were congregating on the steps of a building a bit further down, but they paid no attention to him. Other than that the street was quiet. Stuart realised it was an ideal place for murky criminal activities, but it was also clear that any white tourist with money to spend would stand out like a sore thumb. That might put a dampener on business.

He opened the main door to the building and stepped into a hallway. There was a staircase heading upstairs, and a single apartment door to the left. His heart pounding, Stuart walked up to the door and knocked a couple of times. There was no turning back now.

The door opened. Stuart came face to face with a dishevelled, middle-aged man wearing jeans and a disgustingly stained undershirt. This was worse than anything Stuart had ever met in his career as a lawyer. The apartment behind the man looked equally messy, with a dirty sofa and a TV which was showing some nondescript show. Stuart almost recoiled in horror but fortified himself by the thought that he had to prove himself to the Red Widow.

"Hello," Stuart said. He did not know how best to proceed, but he had to say something as the man remained quiet. "Erm, a friend of mine, well, this American man I met, erm, yesterday, said I could, erm, get a good service here."

Stuart trailed off, waiting for some sort of response.

"Come inside," the man said and stepped away from the door.

With a great deal of apprehension, Stuart walked inside and took a few steps towards the sofa. He turned around and saw the man quietly close the door.

"You want product?" the man asked.

"Yes," Stuart said and fiddled with his hands. "Yes, I would like that please."

He was stumbling on his words, still not sure what to say. The man had an ugly leer on his face which sent a chill up Stuart's spine.

"This is the best place in the city," the man said with a misplaced sense of pride. "You from the US?"

"Erm, no, Canada," Stuart said.

The man laughed.

"You need this to stay warm, yes?"

"Something like that."

"Take a seat," the man said.

He gestured towards the sofa. Stuart very reluctantly sat down since the sofa was stained with who-knows-what, but then, he was wearing a cartel henchman's jeans, so what was the harm? The man headed over towards Stuart, clearly expecting the payment. Stuart patted his pocket to indicate that the money was there.

"Can I just see it first, make sure everything is good?"

Stuart remembered that this was a request often made in films, so maybe it would work in real life. The man hesitated. At this point, another man walked into the room. This one wore jeans and a clean t-shirt, and was altogether less scruffy that his colleague.

"Is there a problem here?" the new man asked, scrutinising Stuart.

"He wants to see the stuff up front," the first man said.

"No, no," the second man said. "Show the cash, gringo. It's business, you understand."

Stuart nodded. It was not his cash anyway, but he was very sure the Red Widow would shoot him on the spot if any of it went missing. But she had clearly given him the wad for this very reason. Slowly he pulled the cash out of his pocket. It turned out that he had been given significantly more than what the price was, since the two drug dealers seemed suitably impressed by Stuart's purchasing power. The fact that they were clearly inexperienced and out of their depth calmed Stuart down significantly.

"I like your style, gringo," the second man said.

Stuart counted up the cash and handed it over, accepting that he did not have another option. To placate the men he handed over a little extra cash, which was met with two broad grins. Stuart noticed that they both put the extra cash into their pockets, whereas the main bundle went into a box. Hiding cash from the boss, it was always a gutsy move.

The second man disappeared through a door whilst the first one waited with Stuart. Whilst he was preoccupied with the TV, Stuart put his hand inside his pocket and reached for the phone. All he had to do was press one button, once he saw the product. The second man soon returned with a heavy duffle bag. He opened it and showed Stuart. It contained numerous small, clear plastic bags, each filled with a white powder.

"Excellent," Stuart said.

He still had his hand in his pocket and now he pressed the button. The second man handed Stuart the plastic bags. Stuart took them and remained seated on the sofa, pretending to closely inspect the product. The two men anxiously looked at each other, clearly wondering why he was not leaving.

"This is really good," Stuart said loudly as he heard the building's front door opening.

Seconds later the apartment door flew open and the Red Widow's henchmen rushed in. Stuart rolled down on the floor, which was somehow more disgusting than the stained sofa, and curled up into a ball, hoping that he would not get shot, either by accident or on purpose. He heard two shots being fired and then the apartment door closed.

He slowly opened his eyes and let out a shriek as the Red Widow's chubby face, with her cotton-candy pink hair, was right above him.

"You survived," she said, but Stuart could not tell if she was pleased or disappointed.

"Yes," he said and stood up. "Yes, I did."

He looked around and saw her henchmen going through the apartment, tearing it apart as if they were forensic investigators in a hurry. Juan and Antonio were there too, kneeling in prayer over the dead bodies of the two drug dealers. By now, dead bodies did not shock Stuart, but he nonetheless averted his eyes.

"Your money is in there," he said and pointed to the box. "And some of it is in their pockets."

"Excellent," the Red Widow said. "Right, we now have to go and find their boss."

Stuart sighed. He had hoped that this would be the end to his ordeal and that they would be able to go back to Medellín.

"Who is the boss?" Stuart asked.

The Red Widow held up an old mobile phone.

"The idiots had his number in here. I know who he is.

He wanted to work for me once, but he was too reckless."

The drug dealing community must be really small, Stuart thought. Everyone knew everyone.

"Don't worry," the Red Widow said. "This will not take long. He works close by."

"Where?"

The Red Widow fortified herself, as if about to say something she really did not believe.

"He's a tour guide up at the fortress. Fleeces tourists with his crazy stories." She laughed loudly, which again reminded Stuart of a witch's cackle. "We're going to have to storm the fort. Like real, outlaw pirates. Woohoo!"

Stuart laughed weakly.

"Sounds like a dream come true," he said, somewhat sarcastically.

The Red Widow ignored his remark. Without saying anything, Stuart, Juan and Antonio followed her out onto the street. The Red Widow's henchmen came after, leaving the dead bodies to their own fate. Back in the cars, it was a short drive around a few corners before they arrived. They parked on the street below the mighty fortress, which was built on a small hill. The open plaza in front of it was filled with tourists and traders, and the henchmen all hid their guns under their shirts.

"My treat," the Red Widow said kindly, again demonstrating something of a maternal kindness.

Stuart looked on in amazement and disbelief as the eccentric old murderer joined a queue to buy tickets for herself and her henchmen. Do serial killers actually buy entrance tickets, he asked himself. To him, the whole situation had become completely surreal.

He looked up at the long, rectangular fortress, which towered above him. Its heavy stone walls slanted inwards the whole way to the top, which was crowned with large tower. A footpath zigzagged its way up the base of the hill and into the fortress. The tower, still sloping inwards, was defaced by a bizarre red, wooden staircase, which led to the top. On the north side of the fortress, separated from the tower by a large expanse, was another structure, in front of which flew an enormous Colombian flag, which was fluttering gently in the wind.

The Red Widow came strutting back with the tickets. They followed her and the henchmen up the zigzagging path, a taxing exercise in the afternoon heat. It was crowded with many happy tourists, who were heading up and down, enjoying a nice day out. Stuart realised that their party must have looked rather odd; an old woman in a flowery dress and pink hair, a group of burly men, two priests, and a really white guy. However, no one seemed to pay them any attention.

At the entrance to the fort, which was already a good way up the hill, they faced a ticket check, and then they were finally inside. At the top of the path was a large opening, in-between the tower and the smaller structure with the flag. Stuart looked around and saw several levels of gun emplacements, though very few actual guns. That took something away from the might of the location.

The Red Widow explained that the man they were looking for was called Carlos. She provided a general description and said that as a tour guide seeking easy money, he would be around somewhere. She ordered her men to spread out before she swaggered away towards the tower. Juan, Antonio and Stuart remained standing where they were.

"I guess we should look somewhere," Stuart said.

Antonio nodded and was already looking around for anyone resembling a tour guide, but everyone around was clearly a tourist. Juan explained that the most interesting part of visiting the fortress was to run around inside the old tunnels, which ran for great lengths inside its bowels.

"Most of them are not lit up, so they are a likely place to bring a tour guide, who has a flashlight and some geographical knowledge," he concluded.

"Sounds good," Antonio said.

They made their way up to the small terrace where the enormous flag was hoisted. It provided a fantastic view over Gethsemane and the Old City beyond it. Antonio had started looking around with an increasingly anxious look, which Stuart did not understand. Juan led the way through a small doorway and down a narrow staircase, which took them further and further inside the hill. There was no lighting in the staircase, so each step down brought on an increasingly impenetrable darkness. Juan and Antonio took out their mobile phones and used them as flashlights. Stuart, whose phone was probably still inside the bird statue in Medellín, fumbled behind them.

Finally, they reached the bottom of the staircase, from which the entrance above was just a bright square in the distance. From where they were standing, several tunnels headed off in various directions. None of them were lit and Stuart felt a growing sense of unease. There was no way to tell what kind of enemy lurked behind the next corner.

"Gut feeling, this direction," Juan said.

He turned left and led the way into that tunnel. They walked slowly, relying only on the weak light from their phones. Stuart had to feel his way with his hands, and touching the old, cold and damp stones sent shivers down his back. He could feel a panic coming on.

Suddenly, they heard the voices of some other visitors coming from somewhere, but they quickly disappeared.

They carried on, Stuart still feeling increasingly uneasy. After many long minutes of walking in the dark, they reached another staircase, which too led up to a doorway through which they could see a bright square of sunlight.

Before they could decide on what to do, Stuart heard footsteps behind him. He spun around and stared into the darkness. Antonio followed suit but by the time he managed to point his phone in the right direction, there was nothing to be seen. At least not in the few metres the light beam was effective.

"You heard that, right?" Stuart asked.

"Yes," Antonio said, sounding scared. "I was looking around before. I feel as if I keep seeing the same face."

Juan huddled up, also pointing his phone down the

tunnel.
"Is there someone following us?"

Chapter 24

"It sounded like footsteps."

Stuart peered into the darkness but he could not see anything. Juan took a few steps back down the tunnel, moving his phone around to get a better view, but there was only emptiness. Antonio and Stuart followed after him, all of them moving slowly and methodically. There were alcoves carved out of the tunnel at regular intervals, each filled with impenetrable darkness. Stuart's dread and panic increased with each alcove he passed because, despite Antonio shining his phone into them, there was still the possibility of someone hiding in a corner.

Finally, they returned to the base of the staircase that they had originally come down.

"That was weird," Stuart said, breathing deeply to steady his racing heart.

"Could have been an animal," Juan said, looking quizzically at Antonio. "What did you say about someone following us?"

"I don't know," Antonio said, sounding much calmer now as they were back in the natural sunlight coming down the staircase. "I thought there was a face which kept reappearing."

"Let's keep our eyes open," Juan said.

He led the way down the tunnel to the right. It was no different to the other one. Juan and Antonio continued to shine their phones into every alcove, nook and cranny, but there was no one to be seen. Stuart managed to keep his panic in check. Eventually, they reached a lit up section of the tunnel network, where they met a group of enthused Chinese tourists. Antonio asked them in English if they had seen a tour guide around, but they had not, and soon they had disappeared around a corner.

Juan led the way around the network for another ten or fifteen minutes, but the only people they encountered were more tourists. After a while, they gave up and left the tunnels through one of the staircases. They found themselves, somewhat surprisingly, on top of the tower, far above the terrace with the flag from where they had first descended into the underworld.

Beneath a lookout turret, placed in one of the corners, they spotted the Red Widow and some of her people talking to a young, clean-shaven man. They quickly headed over. The young man looked really confused as two priests and a pasty foreigner joined his captors.

"You finally turn up," the Red Widow said dismissively.

"I'm sorry we missed out on the chase," Juan said politely.

"Well, a search party with an Englishman in it is bound to get lost," the Red Widow said snarkily. "Anyway, this is Carlos. He's cleaned up a bit since he tried to come work for me."

Carlos laughed nervously. The Red Widow nodded to her men, who grabbed hold of Carlos and led him away. Stuart was surprised that he did not put up a fight, but then it was him against ten heavily armed, burly men, who each could probably kill him with two fingers. The Red Widow leaned against the turret, looking like a somewhat eccentric queen of all she surveyed.

She retrieved an envelope from her purse. Stuart looked at it nervously, feeling a bit unhappy about envelopes in general. She handed it to Juan.

"Go and meet this man," she said. "He'll be expecting you. He'll tell you where to find the Hermit. Well, where you might find him." She smiled warmly to Juan. "Good luck taking him down. All this assassination nonsense, I don't need that in my town. It's bad for business, you know."

"Thank you," Juan said slowly.

The Red Widow looked at Stuart.

"You have been acceptable."

"Thank you," Stuart said and smiled. It was the best he could have hoped for.

Juan tucked the envelope away safely and then took a deep breath.

"Can you please now let Don, your prisoner, go free. We took down Carlos. Let the man go back to his wife."

"Oh, Juanito," the Red Widow said and cackled again. "You know I can't do that."

"I beg of you," Juan said.

"There's nothing you can do, Father," she said. She took out another piece of paper from her purse and handed it over. "But you can go tell the widow, well, wife for a few more hours. I'm sure the news will come better from a priest. Tell her to go home, don't expect a body."

After another gleeful cackle, the Red Widow bobbed away, her red dress and pink hair swaying in the late afternoon breeze. In front of her, out over the western horizon, the sun was starting to descend, slowly turning the sky into a deadly yellow-reddish tone. Stuart, overwhelmed, sank down on a cannon barrel and hid his face in his hands.

**

The note revealed that Don's wife, whose name apparently was Annabeth, was staying at a different hotel from them. It was not her that they had seen the previous night, waiting for someone in their hotel courtyard. The three of them made their way over and knocked on her door. It was opened by an old lady in her sixties, quite heavyset like her husband, whose eyes expressed horror as she saw two priests in the corridor. Stuart, in his ill-fitting jeans and t-shirt, tried to keep out of view. Having spent the morning with her husband, he had no wish to meet the wife.

Juan introduced himself and asked if he could come inside. As he stepped in he motioned for Antonio and Stuart to stay in the corridor. Juan was in the room for a few minutes and then he stepped back into the corridor. Stuart heard the woman sobbing inside as the door was closing.

"Let's leave," Juan said quietly.

A while later they back at the Church of San Pedro Claver. They sat down on one of the pews and admired the bones of the saint from a respectable distance. After a while, Stuart broke their contemplative silence.

"This is getting a bit...much."

"I'm really sorry, Stuart," Juan said. "I did not foresee this. But we had to do it to get the information. The note inside the envelope, it has a name and a promise of help. Think of Molly, the embassy worker, and Manuel's daughter, both kidnapped by the cartel. The Hermit is trying to kill your Prince and maybe our President." He stopped and sighed. "Perhaps it had to happen this way."

"Perhaps," Stuart said.

He remembered the feeling he had had yesterday when he had first encountered the bones of the saint. The sense of hope and strength he had got had not lasted for long, but now that he was back, he realised that he had somehow made it through, and he had to be ready for the next, and hopefully last, step of their journey.

They sat in contemplative silence for another moment, before Antonio spoke up.

"I'm reminded of the words of the royal philosopher," he said. He recited from memory the words of Ecclesiastes. For everything there is a season, and a time for every matter under heaven: a time to be born, and a time to die; a time to kill, and a time to heal; a time to weep, and a time to laugh; a time to mourn, and a time to dance; a time to keep silence, and a time to speak; a time to love, and a time to hate; a time for war, and a time for peace. "I guess this is our time to kill, hate, weep and go to war. Tomorrow, I hope, we will have peace."

"I hope so as well," Stuart said.

**

They got an evening flight back to Medellín. They travelled in silence, contemplating what had occurred and the fate that Don was most likely facing at that very moment. Once they landed, however, Stuart was overcome with joy at having left the tropical heat behind. He hurried through the terminal, headed outside and deeply inhaled the cool mountain air, even though it was thick with fumes from the cars, coaches and taxis waiting to pick up their passengers.

"This is a climate more fit for humans," he remarked a few moments later as they were collecting Juan's car from the parking lot. Stuart felt like his mind had quite literally melted during his two days in Cartagena, and he had started to worry about his mental acuity. It turns out a hot brain is a slow brain. "Still rather warm, though," he added sullenly, despite the sun having already set behind the mountains.

"We'll let you cool down at the friary," Juan said, smiling.

They joined the evening traffic, heading along the winding roads back towards Medellín. Stuart asked Antonio to call Carolina and invite her to the friary. She said she would be happy to meet them there in a few hours' time since she was just about to leave Bogotá. Stuart had completely forgotten that she had gone there to see if she could find out anything about the deaths of Roderic and the embassy official, Robert. He blamed the heat. They offered to wait for her back at the airport but she said she needed to pick up her own car anyway.

They stopped at a roadside restaurant, realising that they had not eaten anything all day, except the drinks offered by the Red Widow for breakfast and the much-appreciated juice box on the flight. The rice and bean stew restored some of their lost energy. The evening had turned to night when they finally returned to the friary. Stuart had a quick shower to wash off the sweat and the seawater which had clung to him all day, and he felt like a prince as he got dressed in fresh clothes. He returned downstairs and joined Juan and Antonio, who were lounging in the small courtyard between the friary and the church.

"Did that really happen?" he asked incredulously, as he poured himself a glass of pineapple juice. He drank as quickly as he could and then slouched back in a rickety plastic chair, which almost toppled over.

"I think it did," Juan said slowly.

Antonio flicked through some photographs he had taken on his phone.

"I wouldn't believe it if I didn't have pictures," he said. He suddenly looked rather worried. "Is it dangerous to have a sneaky photo of a serial killer?"

"I would think so," Juan said and laughed. "Did you really take a picture of her?"

Whilst Antonio continued looking at the photos on his phone, Juan pulled out the envelope that the Red Widow had handed him. He placed it on the table, and pushed it away from him, reluctant to look inside. Stuart, still having a strongly bittersweet feeling about envelopes, grabbed it and swirled it around, but did not open it either. They sat there for a while in silence. Stuart slumbered off in the cool night air, and maybe even slept for a minute, before they were roused by Carolina walking in.

"Good evening, everyone," she said cheerfully and winked at Stuart. He felt a sudden, overpowering urge for a comforting intimacy, so he stood up and tightly embraced her. "I've missed you too," she said in a surprised tone, unsure of what was going on.

"I've been to hell," Sturt offered as an explanation.

"Really? I've always liked Cartagena." She disentangled from his embrace, arched back and looked him over. "You do look rather red. Did you use your sunscreen?"

"Yes," Stuart said. "I accept, it was paradise too." Stuart sighed and returned to his seat. "We had an interesting but rather difficult trip."

Juan let Stuart reflect in peace, which Stuart greatly appreciated, and gave Carolina a quick rundown of what had happened. She turned pale as Juan described the events in Gethsemane and the deadly outcome for all the men involved.

"That's absolutely horrendous," she said as Juan came to an end. "So, your friend, the Red Widow, she sounds…interesting."

"Yes, she's quite something," Juan said.

"What's her name?"

Stuart suddenly looked up and realised that he had never asked nor wondered about that. The heat must have turned his legal mind into Swiss cheese. Juan chuckled.

"Would you believe it, it's Ana-Maria Alejandra Alvarez de Ámbar."

Stuart whistled.

"That's quite a mouthful."

"Argentineans, eh," Juan remarked.

Carolina looked over at the table and saw the envelope where Stuart had left it.

"So, is this the next step on the journey?" Without hesitating, she picked it up, opened it, and pulled out a single sheet of paper. Her face was unimpressed. "The name 'Felipe Hernandez' and an address, his I guess, in Guatapé. Is that all?"

Juan took the note and looked it over himself.

"Yes, this is her friend, or contact. We'll go and meet him tomorrow."

"Good thing it is Easter Week," Carolina said. "I've managed to take the whole week off work. I told my boss I was traumatised after Stuart's disappearance and Roderic's death."

"Good thinking," Stuart said. "But first, how was your trip to Bogotá?"

Carolina looked at them gravely and then smiled.

"You remember the mysterious Ms L, the cartel's contact in the embassy? I met her. I know who she is."

**

At about half past ten that Tuesday evening, Avianca flight 8553 thundered down the runway at Cartagena airport, and quickly climbed into the night air. Leaving the colonial city behind, it banked south and started its ascent into the Andes, bound for Bogotá. After it, the airspace over northern Colombia usually fell silent. This night, however, the keen observer would note that something was different.

There was another plane trailing the commercial jet, similarly racing southwards on the jet route to Bogotá. It was a grey C-17, with the markings of the Royal Air Force.

William Cooth was sitting in a passenger seat, crammed between a mixture of large and small crates, the contents of which he knew nothing about. This was not the C-17 that had flown him to the Caymans. It had unloaded its cargo and returned to Britain as quickly as possible. This was a different C-17. It was technically bound for RAF Mount Pleasant on the Falkland Islands, but its captain had grumpily but dutifully agreed to make something of a detour. Transport Cooth from the Caymans to Bogotá. The Foreign Office request to the Air Force had helpfully pointed out that Bogotá was, sort of, on the way.

Cooth felt like his visit to the Caymans had been a success. He had learnt something about the identity of the cartel informant, a Mr D, who worked somewhere in the British government. Manuel Lopez seemed to have taken the bad news as well as one could have hoped, and whilst concerned for his missing daughter, he had agreed to fly to Britain, where he would be settled in somewhere. Cooth had escorted him onto the British Airways flight earlier in the day, where he had been momentarily jealous of the absence of wooden crates on the passenger deck.

Despite being afflicted by seasickness even on smooth waters, Cooth had also made a quick visit to the HMS Atholl, which was docked in port whilst undergoing some minor engine repairs. Captain Cranston had assured him the ship would be up and running by Thursday at the latest, ready to welcome the Prince on Friday, before spending the weekend sailing to Cartagena to be present for the Prince's arrival there on Monday.

Cooth had spoken to captain Cranston and the lieutenants about the assassination threat to the Prince and the President. They had seemed shocked, which was understandable, but had accepted the news professionally, which encouraged Cooth. He explained that he would now be spending the week investigating the threat on the ground, but he put them on notice that they were not in Cartagena just to look nice. The captain had promptly called a drill, and as Cooth hurriedly disembarked, the ship's sirens rang out for battle, which really only served to alarm the locals spending the day by the seafront.

It was almost midnight by the time the C-17 touched down at El Dorado International Airport and discreetly taxied over to the Colombian Air Force hangar. It parked by an assortment of military aircraft, including the President's transport plane.

Cooth was met by a welcome party. His embattled colleague on the ground, the embassy security chief Tara Lawson, was the first to greet him, followed by the Ambassador. He was then introduced to an unimpressively squat figure who he recognised, from some old intelligence report, as a Colonel in the Colombian National Police named Wilbur Zapata. Cooth had not fully understood why so many Latin Americans had been given English names, and strange ones at that, but at least it made it easier for him to remember them.

"It's nice to have you in Bogotá," Tara said apprehensively, in English.

"It's good to be here," Cooth said.

He fully understood her concerns. It had been on her recommendation that asylum be given to Manuel Lopez's family, and it was her failure to supervise the handovers that had resulted in Molly Reed and Stuart Gleeman going missing. By association, she also had some responsibility for Robert Hughes and Roderic Geoffrey Moylan-Roth being murdered. Cooth was certain that everything was connected and he understood why the Foreign Secretary wanted Tara removed from office. However, he had known her for many years and he trusted her. His only interest now was ensuring that the Prince and President would be safe when they met in Cartagena. He would have to deal with Tara later, and the coming few days would be her chance to prove herself.

"I am very excited for Monday," the Ambassador said. "It will be such an honour to welcome the Prince and Her Royal Highness to Colombia."

"Of course it will," Cooth said, trying not to sound sarcastic. He had never understood the need to rub shoulders with the great and the good, but it was clearly something which excited the Ambassador.

"Colonel Zapata here is in charge of security for the event," the Ambassador said. "I invited him along to meet you. I think you have a lot to discuss."

"I have arranged for your plane to be refuelled," Colonel Zapata said in English and gestured towards a refuelling truck which was heading in their direction. "Where is this flight headed now?"

"It's going to the Ascension Island," Cooth said without missing a beat.

They started heading towards the embassy car, which was waiting a few steps away on the tarmac.

"Ah, you mean the Malvinas."

"I don't know anything about the Falklands," Cooth said, worried that this was now going to become a thing.

"Uh-huh." The Colonel smiled. "Just don't tell the Argentineans we let you land here. They get grumpy."

Once they were in the car and heading for the city, Cooth leaned in to whisper to Tara.

"I have a lead on who the cartel's contact is," he said. He thought he saw a flash of panic on Tara's face, but waved it off. "A Mr D."

"Right, yes, good." She seemed to chuckle nervously, and Cooth wondered if she actually was a bit off her game. "That doesn't tell us much."

"True, but a step in the right direction." Cooth sighed. "There's so much to sort out in the next few days."

**

"The embassy chief of security?"

Stuart was shocked.

"It makes sense," Juan said, and Carolina and Antonio both nodded in agreement. "The chief of security knows a lot, has unlimited access, and can snoop around without raising suspicion. It's who I would bribe, if that's something I did."

Stuart furrowed his eyebrows and looked at Juan, still remembering the constant warnings Carolina had made about the priests.

"You seem to have thought about this a lot," he said.

"I have," Juan replied. "Ever since we found out that the cartel had a contact inside the British embassy, I have wondered who it might be. The Ambassador, no, why would he, and also it's a very risky approach to make. A low-level person, like a cleaner, yes, they're on low pay so maybe more amenable to a cash reward, they do have access, but it quickly raises questions if they poke around too much. The security team is often very loyal, but worth their weight in gold if you can get hold of them. The head of security, that's a real gold mine."

Stuart listened in amazement.

"When did you have the time to think about all this?"

Juan chuckled and turned to Carolina.

"So, how do you know it's the chief of security?"

Carolina explained what she had been up to. Yesterday, she had gone to her office in Medellín. The paperwork from Friday's signing ceremony was filed away. She had spoken with the boss of the English company that Stuart and Roderic worked for. He had expressed his shock that Roderic, after failing to turn up to the signing ceremony, had in fact been arrested for murder, released, and then been murdered himself, and further expressed his anxiety that Stuart was missing and was the subject of a police hunt. Carolina had played along, saying that she too was shocked, which was true, because the real story was as shocking as the one told in the media. Thankfully, the English company still wanted to proceed with their deal to overhaul the hydroelectric power plant, and Carolina had assured them that they would not regret moving forward. She hoped that she was right.

She told her bosses the good news and then stated that she was too upset about everything and asked for the rest of the week off. Her bosses had agreed. She had spent yesterday evening reviewing every news article, especially the ones about Robert and Roderic's murder. She knew where to go when she got to Bogotá.

Today, she had taken an early morning flight to Bogotá. From the airport she had taken a taxi to the Presidential Palace. From there she had walked to the site of the murder. It was a long, uphill walk through the colonial district. During the day, it was charming and pleasing, though the buildings became increasingly dilapidated the further up she got. She kept having to consult the map on her phone to find the street where the bodies had been found. It made no sense at all as to why Robert and Roderic had gone there. It seemed completely removed from anything two Englishmen, or indeed anyone, would visit on a Saturday night.

To her, the only logical explanation had been that they had been killed elsewhere and dumped there. Then she looked around some more and started to question her logic. The area was poor, true, but there was a clear and discernible community. There were houses and shops, people walking around, and a steady flow of cars and motorbikes. If you wanted to hide two bodies, there were far better options available. Here, the bodies would be noticed immediately, as indeed they had been. If the cartel was responsible, what was their interest in the bodies being discovered? Who were they sending a message to?

Whilst all these thoughts were swirling around in her head, Carolina had stopped at a local shop, which was simply a hole-in-the-wall. It was manned by a spry, old lady, who had carefully scrutinised Carolina.

"I'm interested in the two dead bodies," Carolina had said softly.

The old lady had made the sign of the cross. With a frightened look on her face, she had hissed that the devil's spawn was responsible.

"Yes, murder is bad," Carolina had offered, assuming the old lady had simply lost her mind over the years.

"No, the Devil's child," the old lady had insisted. "I saw it from my window. A woman, with flaming red hair, like hell itself! She led those two men to the slaughter."

The old lady had explained that she had been looking out at the street because she was waiting for her son to come home. Then, she sees a group of people arriving and lurking in the alley across from her house. Carolina had looked behind her. There was a narrow alleyway, which led to a set of stairs. The next street must be on a higher level, further up the hillside. The old lady had been terrified of being spotted but had kept looking anyway. She was concerned for her son's safety now. Not long after, three people had come walking up the road. Two men and one woman. In the streetlight, she had seen the devil's daughter. The woman with red hair. They had passed the alley. Two of the men who had been lurking around jumped out and quickly stabbed the two new men from behind. Their bodies had been dragged into the alleyway. Another man, whom she had not seen before, walked up to the redheaded woman, kissed her, and then everyone had disappeared.

Carolina had thanked the old lady. Bizarre superstitions aside, the old lady had provided more evidence than she could have hoped for. Robert and Roderic had been led to their deaths, like lambs to the slaughter. The redheaded woman surely was Ms L.

"I agree," Juan said.

"I know she is," Carolina said. "Because I had a genius, if somewhat dangerous, idea."

Carolina had decided to go to the British embassy to see if she could do some scouting. At this point, the only information she had was that she was looking for a female employee with red hair, and maybe she could use that information to her advantage. She took a taxi to the upmarket street in north Bogotá where the embassy was located. She entered a reception area, which seemed to serve the consular section. She truthfully explained to the receptionist that she had worked with Stuart Gleeman and that he was missing, and she simply asked if there was anyone she could speak to about him. She had been told to wait in a hallway, where she had spent twenty minutes looking at photos of the Queen before she had been invited into an office. To her horror, she had come face to face with a redheaded woman.

"Luckily I managed to compose myself," Carolina said. "I explained who I was, that neither Stuart nor Roderic turned up on Friday, that I had read in the news about his arrest and murder, and that Stuart was wanted by the police, and I mentioned that the police came to see me on Saturday morning. I said that I was naturally concerned and wondered if there was anything she could tell me."

"The truth is always the best cover story," Juan said sagely.

"Yes," Carolina said and looked at him quizzically. Stuart sensed that she was still harbouring some animosity, or at least serious concern, towards the priests.

"What did she say?"

"She said she didn't know anything, other than that the police were investigating. I did not believe her, but I didn't want to press too much. I didn't want to come across as anything other than a concerned colleague."

"No, that was the right approach," Stuart said. "But are you sure it was her?"

"Yes," Carolina said. "There was something in her demeanour when we talked. Obviously, she knew far more than what she told me, but I had a feeling. And the description from the old lady matched. The security chief was in her thirties, quite tall, attractive, natural red hair."

"And did the name match? Ms L?"

"Yes," Carolina said. "Her name is Tara Lawson."

"Seems very conclusive," Antonio said.

"So what do we do now?" Stuart asked. "Do we tell anyone?"

"Tell who?" Juan asked. "We don't trust anyone and I doubt what we have amounts to legal evidence. We should continue according to our plan. Tomorrow, let's go to Guatapé and meet the Red Widow's contact."

Stuart glanced over at Carolina. Despite apologising, they had left it rather frostily last time they spoke. It had only been yesterday morning, back in El Retiro, but it felt like a lifetime ago. Nonetheless, Carolina invited Stuart to spend the night at her place. She insisted that it was more comfortable than the friary. Juan and Antonio did not argue but pointed out that one cartel soldier had got away and still posed a danger.

"I'm so relieved that you survived," she said to Stuart once they had curled up on her sofa.

"Let's just focus on the future," Stuart said, desperately trying to suppress the images of the day's events. It was a hard thing to do, especially for someone with a passion for reflecting on life's events. He realised that Don was probably dead by now. He wondered how his widow was surviving the night.

"I'm sorry about how we left it the other night," Carolina said. "I know you trust those priests, I won't say anything more about it."

"Yes, I trust them," Stuart said. "But I have thought about what you said. I can't explain why they have been so willing to help me, even before Juan's friend was killed. But even so, I do trust them."

"That's good enough for me," Carolina said. She smiled, leaned in and kissed Stuart. "Tonight it's just the two of us."

Chapter 25

They had allowed themselves a late start and Stuart felt refreshed again when he awoke on Wednesday morning. By the time he and Carolina set off for the friary it was again unbearably hot. Stuart tried not to grumble too much. On arriving, Father Pedro showed them into the sitting room and explained that he would get Juan and Antonio at once.

Shortly thereafter, Juan and Antonio appeared and greeted them. They too seemed rested and more relaxed.

"It is a new day," Juan said.

"Definitely," Stuart agreed. "So, where is Guatapé?"

"Oh, you're going to love it," Carolina said. "It's a small town out east from here, but every bit as colourful as Cartagena. But not as warm!"

"I like that last part," Stuart said.

They agreed that Stuart should once again change into a priest's attire, and having done so, they left the friary and drove off in Juan's unassuming car. As always, the car protested loudly as it slowly inched its way up the steep eastern valley.

"I'm starting to get very familiar with this road," Stuart remarked once the car had finally made it to the top, as he once again looked at the road signs pointing towards the airport.

"Yes," Juan said. "I'll try to make sure our next stop is somewhere out west instead," he added with a laugh. "Maybe we'll go sailing on the Cauca River?"

"It's a big river," Carolina whispered in response to Stuart's confused look.

They quickly drove past the airport, greeted by the roar of an airplane flying closely overhead, and continued further eastwards on a winding and empty road. Stuart, cooped up in the small backseat, observed the passing landscape intently, but other than hills, farmsteads and the occasional village, there was not much of interest to see.

He remembered that it was a full week since he had first arrived in Medellín and, to his surprise, he found that it was all starting to feel familiar, almost like home.

Suddenly, however, at a sharp turn in the road, overlooking a deep valley, they passed a roadside restaurant with a large parking area, which was hosting an army checkpoint. They zoomed past quickly, but Stuart managed to count at least ten soldiers with machineguns positioned around a large armoured vehicle. Any happiness he might have had immediately drained away.

He knew that the police were still looking for him. Carolina had shown him a news article about the murders just this morning over breakfast, which said as much. It had been accompanied by the rantings of Senator Reyes, who said it was proof that the Imperial Westerners were not trustworthy, and that this was grounds for cancelling the Prince's visit. Stuart had laughed it off at the time, but now his worries returned. If the police were still looking for him, then surely the army was also doing the same? He had also not forgotten that one of the cartel soldiers was still at large, no doubt trying to chase him down, nor had he forgotten the mysterious footsteps in the fortress in Cartagena yesterday. There were too many parties trying to capture him. The fact that their best option was getting help from a friend of a serial killer did not fill him with much optimism. Who is friends with a serial killer, especially someone as lethal as the Red Widow?

After about an hour's drive, which was thankfully uneventful, they arrived in the picturesque town of Guatapé. It was pleasantly situated on the slopes of a hill, which led down to the banks of a large lake. Juan expertly navigated through the narrow streets and up to the main square, where he parked underneath a ceiba tree. Stuart stepped out of the car and stretched, getting his circulation back. Though the sun was still shining, clouds had started gathering, and the temperature had dropped to moderate. Stuart smiled and breathed in the fresh country air. This was more to his liking.

As the others got out of the car he took a closer look around. The town had a colourful, colonial look. The square was encircled by one and two-story whitewashed buildings. The doors, window frames, balconies, and decorative panels on the façades, were all painted in a wide array of bright colours. The buildings were fronted by small, youthful palm trees. As all colonial squares, it was dominated by a large church, whose whitewashed walls were enhanced by red highlights around the doors, windows, and the two towers.

Juan took out the envelope and looked at the note the Red Widow had given him.

"This way," he said confidently and pointed down a road that continued past the church. "The address is down here."

"We should probably ask for directions," Carolina said, unconvinced.

"No, no," Juan said. "I think I know it."

Juan quickly set off down the narrow and almost psychedelically colourful road and the others followed closely behind him. After a few wrong turns Juan did ask for directions and soon thereafter they arrived at the town house where Felipe Hernandez was said to live. His house was painted mint green, with the door and window frames sporting yellow, orange, red, and blue details.

"This is not the place you'd expect to meet a friend of a serial killer," Stuart remarked, looking at the neighbouring houses, which were painted pink and blue and also sported multicoloured doors and window frames.

Juan knocked on the door. They waited a while but there was no response. He knocked again but there was still no answer.

"If only the Red Widow had given us a phone number," Juan said dejectedly.

"Surely she let the guy know we were coming?" Stuart asked.

Carolina sighed loudly and started pacing up and down the street, looking at the buildings. Having noticed something she returned close to the group.

"The neighbours are watching," she whispered.

Stuart looked around and there were indeed a few faces hiding in the neighbouring windows.

"I'm sure they're wondering what Felipe has done to warrant a visit from three priests," Stuart said, not feeling any concern. "And a nice lady," he added, to which Carolina smiled.

At this point, Juan's phone buzzed. He looked at it and scoffed.

"I just got a text from Felipe Hernandez," he said and looked around. "I guess the neighbours told him that we have showed up."

"What does it say?" Antonio asked and took the phone.

"*Meet me at the Rock of the Gods*," Juan said.

Everyone paused.

"What does that mean?" Antonio asked and read the message again.

"I'm not sure," Juan said.

Carolina returned to angrily pacing around.

"Meet me at the Rock of the Gods," Stuart repeated, irritated. He had no idea what that could mean.

Carolina suddenly stopped pacing and came back with a big smile on her face.

"There's only one rock around here," she said and grimaced at Juan, whose face lit up in recognition.

"Ah, yes, of course," he exclaimed. "You two are in for a treat," he added, looking at Stuart and Antonio.

"What kind of a treat?" Stuart asked suspiciously.

"It's a good one."

They returned to the car at a brisk pace and Juan drove it back out onto the main road. When they were out of the town, Juan began explaining some of the local features. In the past, the area had simply been a rolling landscape on the vast Andean plateau east of the Medellín cauldron. In the 1960s, Medellín had explored different ideas on how to expand its electricity supply, and it was agreed to build a large dam coupled with a hydroelectric power plant, which was built near Guatapé. The lake that they had seen was, in fact, an expansive reservoir, which had filled up after the dam was built. In this middle of all this, close to Guatapé, was a tall, mysterious monolithic rock, rising some 200 metres out of the ground. Its bizarre appearance, a massive grey rock protruding out of the green landscape, had led to numerous local legends and superstitions.

They had only been driving for a few minutes before Stuart spotted the Rock, as it was simply called, and he was immediately spellbound by its mystique. He had never before reacted in this way to any geological feature, but its presence in this gentle, rolling green landscape defied reason, and its height dominated the surrounding area. It was not long before Juan turned off the main road and headed up a small access road, which led to the base of the Rock.

Stuart should not have been surprised that the Rock was a popular tourist destination. Arriving at its base they found a large parking area, together with a cluster of souvenir shops and restaurants. As the morning was quickly turning to midday, the parking lot had already started to fill up. Though it was at the base of the Rock itself, Stuart noticed that the edge of the parking lot lay on a precipice, leading to a steep drop. Stuart saw that they were already high above the reservoir. Antonio joined him in staring out over the magnificent vista, whilst Juan and Carolina started looking around for any signs of Felipe.

"Oh, got another text," Juan said. "Strange, we only just arrived."

"What does it say?" Stuart asked.

"*Meet me at the face of God.*" Juan scoffed. "I should've guessed."

"What?"

Juan and Carolina both sighed heavily and looked at the Rock with deep exasperation. Stuart turned around and also looked at the Rock. It was the first time he had seen it from this side and the nature of the problem became abundantly clear. Built into a deep fissure, running all the way up the side of the Rock, was a zigzagging staircase. The first section was complete with an exquisitely decorated balustrade railing, but the builders must have run out of money since the rest of the railing was made in redbrick, which jarred against the grey rock behind. At the top, Stuart spotted a redbrick tower, undoubtedly hosting an observation platform of some sort.

"I guess the face of God is up there," he said in agony, realising that this was going to be a long climb.

"That would stand to reason," Juan said. "Just be glad it's not boiling hot today."

They walked over to the base of the Rock, passing groups of tourists hanging around the shops and restaurants, and set foot on the first step. It had a brightly painted number 1 on it.

"It's 740 to the top of the observation tower," Carolina said. "This will be a healthy exercise."

Stuart grimaced but set off. There was nothing else to it.

Once the reality of the long climb had set in, his earlier excitement and curiosity returned, and soon he was speeding up the steps well ahead of the others. With each step, he continued to gaze in fascination at the wonderful panoramic vista spreading out all around him. The dam had not just created a reservoir, it had created an inland archipelago of breathtaking beauty, its turquoise-blue waters playing off the rolling hills beyond. Most of the islands, peninsulas and isthmuses dotting the landscape were covered in thick forests, though numerous houses and farmsteads were dotted amongst the green. As he was looking around he also spotted several eagles, who were elegantly and effortlessly floating around in the air around the Rock. He marvelled at how majestic they were now that he could see them up close.

Eventually, his heart, not used to strenuous exercise, caught up with his enthusiasm. Pulling his gaze away from the vista, Stuart slowed down and focused solely on getting to the top. The steps were regularly numbered and he knew that 740 was his target. It still felt like a long way off. Halfway up, built on a natural ledge in the rock face, was a viewing platform, and Stuart took the chance to stop and rest. The others soon caught up with him.

"I'll say a prayer here," Juan said and walked out onto the platform, followed by Antonio.

Stuart saw that there was a statue of the Virgin Mary at the far end. By now these things did not surprise him. Whilst he rested, he saw a family walk up the stairs, but their children refused to stop at the platform and continued running upwards. Stuart smiled sympathetically at the parents, who had looks of pained exhaustion. Then, another group of visitors pressed on up the stairs without stopping. Stuart looked at one of the men, thinking he looked familiar, but brushed it off.

When Juan and Antonio were finished, the four of them congregated together.

"It is hard work tracking down a cartel boss," Juan said, smiling. "Come on."

They continued climbing and, with his long legs, Stuart again ended up ahead of the others. He sighed heavily when he finally reached the summit. Immediately to his right stood the observation tower. He looked to his left and saw that the top of the Rock was a flat surface, which was enclosed by a handrail. In the middle stood a kiosk, surrounded by a few tables with parasols. It had a few customers enjoying cold drinks and ice creams. Stuart stopped and took some deep breaths, calming his heart, and he felt invigorated by the fresh air up in the sky.

"I guess he means right at the top," Juan said unhappily once the others had caught up.

They looked up to the top of the observation tower. Stuart shook his head in annoyance but they stepped into the tower and climbed up its circular staircase. They emerged onto the circular roof, the centre of which hosted a few final steps. Without giving Felipe Hernandez another thought, Stuart sprinted up and planted himself on top of the number 740. He had made it to what felt like the top of the world. Antonio followed after him, equally caught up in the moment. Having accomplished the climb, they patted each other on the backs, smiling.

"Whoa!" Antonio exclaimed and looked at the world around them. "This is really something special."

Juan and Carolina also climbed up the final steps.

"How do we find this person?" Carolina asked.

They looked around the observation deck. There were quite a few visitors around, some sitting on the final steps, others standing by the railings, but none stood out as a friend of a serial killer, whatever that looked like. Everyone looked like they were tourists enjoying an exciting day out, talking animatedly, taking photos, eating ice creams.

"I don't know what he looks like," Juan said. "He's been leading us here. I hope we're in the right place."

"Is there another divine rock around here?" Stuart asked.

Juan laughed.

"That would be a nightmare."

They stepped down to the railing and looked out over the Rock's surface. Stuart saw various visitors sitting around the kiosk. Beyond it, he saw a couple huddling up next to the railing. At the far end stood a solitary figure, looking out over the reservoir and the world beyond, appearing deep in thought.

"Could that be him?" Stuart asked, pointing.

"Yes," Juan said. "It definitely could be. Let's go."

They quickly headed back down the spiral staircase, left the observation tower and started walking across the Rock towards the solitary figure.

Then, Stuart noticed the man who had looked familiar on the steps coming up. The man wore baggy trousers and a big t-shirt. Stuart slowed down and took a closer look at him. He was also standing by himself at the railings, about halfway between the observation tower and the kiosk. Stuart's mind was racing, trying to figure out why the man looked familiar. Suddenly it hit him.

It was the third, surviving cartel soldier. His wound must have healed quickly. In surprise, Stuart stopped. The man had spotted him and was now slowly walking towards Stuart. He had one hand on his waist, and Stuart spotted a bulge, which had to be a gun of some sort.

Stuart panicked. What was he going to do? In a heartbeat, he realised that there were only two options. The first was to run forwards, to catch up with his friends and the figure they assumed was Felipe Hernandez. This, however, would trap them on top of the Rock with a cartel soldier blocking their access to the staircase. The other option was to run to his left, back to the staircase, and down off the Rock.

His mind reached a snap decision. He turned left and ran towards the stairs. Through his panic, he managed to be thankful that the cartel soldier started running after him. At least that did not trap the others. Unless, of course, the cartel soldier had brought new friends with him.

At the stairs, Stuart realised that there was a different staircase for people heading down, set further into the fissure in the Rock. He ran down as quickly as he could. At each turn he looked up and saw the cartel killer just a few turns above him, panting heavily as he tried to catch up.

It was a long way down and Stuart soon found that his pace was dropping. His heart was beating way too fast and he was struggling to breathe. The midday heat was starting to bear down on him, though thankfully the outer staircase, for people heading up, provided shade for the inner staircase. By the time he got to the bottom Stuart was drenched in sweat and his jelly legs were refusing to go on. He staggered out onto the large parking lot. Numerous tourists looked at him but seemed to assume that the climb had simply been too much for him. He looked behind him and saw that the cartel soldier had also reached the bottom of the stairs.

Stuart was not sure where to go next. There was no point going further out to the parking area since it was a plateau and the precipice led to a straight drop. He turned right and started struggling down the access road, heading away from the Rock towards the main road beyond. He had no idea what he would do when he got there.

However, he did not get very far.

A large SUV pulled up and stopped in front of him. Another burly man with a thick moustache, a stereotype upon a stereotype, stepped out and discretely pointed a gun at Stuart. The soldier behind him caught up and pushed Stuart into the back seat. They pulled a hood over his head and then the car rapidly pulled away.

Stuart did not even have time to scream for help.

Chapter 26

His phone buzzed. He carefully placed the gun, which he had been cleaning, on the table. He checked who was calling and then answered.

"Yes?"

"Hi," Tara said over the phone. "Are you free to talk?"

The man looked around. He knew he was alone, his life depended on knowing whether he was alone, but he checked anyway. He was alone.

"Yes."

"My boss arrived last night," Tara said.

"William Cooth?" The man was surprised. "You said he never left London anymore."

"I know." Tara paused. "He means well, but the pressure's getting to him. The threat to the Prince has spooked him, and he seemed addled, acting in panic. I don't know why he's come here in person."

The man shook his head, but not because the old SIS boss had travelled to Colombia.

"The threat to the Prince? Fuck sake, speak plainly, Tara. Our paymaster's plan is to have him assassinated. You said the plan would never leak to London. You have to control your boss now."

"How was I to know that Manuel was going to be captured by the HMS Atholl, or that Robert would come with me to interrogate him?"

"I don't give a damn about your excuses, Tara," the man said angrily. "I'm just here for the paycheque. Control your boss!"

"I will," Tara said. She paused. "That's why I'm calling. Cooth visited Manuel in the Caymans. Manuel apparently decided to remember what he knows about you, or what he thinks he knows about you."

"Fuck you, Tara," the man said.

"It's not my fault. Anyway, all they know is your initial, D."

"Bloody hell."

"But they think you work in the government." She paused again. "They think you work in the Home Office. That you've been bribed to ensure that Colombian containers are allowed into the country without being checked for drugs."

"Marvellous. Isn't that what they wanted with James Westbury, who was killed when he said no?"

"Exactly, and they assume you said yes where he said no. I've strongly encouraged that belief."

"That better fucking work."

"It will." Tara paused again. "Where are you?"

"In my cabin, cleaning my gun. Some other idiot's guarding the Prince and the Duchess now."

"The schedule says you're in the British Virgin Islands."

"Yes."

"How is the Prince?"

"Fucking spoilt. But happy. He's been briefed about the threat to him, but I think he's suppressed it by now. No one's bothered to tell the Duchess, so she's having a bloody lark."

"That's good," Tara said. "Thankfully, Cooth still trusts me, even though his superiors want to remove me from my post."

"I should think they'd want to remove you. One employee kidnapped, one killed."

The line was silent for a moment.

"Anyway, he has told me about his plans for the Prince's security on Monday. It's not finalised yet, and he keeps wondering whether to call in the SAS. I'll keep you informed."

"Fucking hell. Look, I've got a bloody big paycheque to look the other way on Monday as someone takes a shot at the Prince. Now, I don't give a fucking toss about royalty, so I accept the paycheque, no problem. But fucking hell, no one was meant to know about this in advance. Now the plan has leaked, we've been briefed the whole consignment of the HMS Atholl will be there to provide additional security, and now you're banging on about the bloody SAS. It's getting a bit much."

"I know. I've accepted a paycheque too. There's no backing out now."

"Yeah, you've gone and taken a bit more than just a paycheque, haven't you? Shacked up with the bloody second-in-command of the whole bloody cartel." He heard her scoff. "What the fuck do you think's going to happen to you if SIS fires you? Think your boyfriend's just going to let you go back to England, knowing all you know?"

"Let's worry about one thing at a time, thank you," Tara said sternly.

"And what the fuck's happening with those two girls you kidnapped?"

The line was silent again.

"They're fine," Tara said. "I haven't seen them, obviously, I can't have Molly recognising me, but she's fine. Manuel's daughter Sara is fine. I have insisted, as forcefully as I can, that they are treated well."

"That's good. What's the plan with them?"

"The Hermit wants to issue a ransom demand on Sunday. He thinks it will be symbolic, being Easter."

The man scoffed.

"I don't give a fucking toss about that fairy-tale either, but I guess it'll hit home in a Catholic country."

"Yes, that's what the Hermit hopes for. Anyway, the Prince and the President meet in public on Monday, suitably humiliated by this. And we assassinate them. It's a good encore."

The man could not believe what he had just heard.

"What the fuck, Tara, you're going to fucking assassinate the President as well? No one said anything about that. I think I want a fucking bigger paycheque."

Tara chuckled.

"You're not getting that. You just look the other way."

"Two major hits in one strike? The paymaster's fucking insane. What happens to the girls after that?"

"I don't know," Tara said. "We might demand ransom again. If the attack is successful we might actually get paid."

The man sighed.

"Look, I don't care about being paid to look the other way, it's a fucking Prince so who cares? But I'm fucking unhappy about kidnapped women. It's fucking dishonourable."

"Really, that's where you draw the line?" Tara paused. She continued in a softer tone. "I agree with you. This has got too messy, too complicated. Listen, if the assassination is successful I'll try to get them released, unharmed."

"And if the assassination fails?"

The line was silent again.

"I'll do what I can. I promise. You just worry about looking the other way on Monday."

**

The car drove at great speed.

Stuart, blinded underneath the suffocating hood, was thrown around in the backseat with every sharp turn. He assumed that they were driving at this breakneck speed to ensure that no one, neither Juan nor Felipe Hernandez, if indeed it had been him on the Rock, was chasing them. After a while, the driver must have been satisfied that they were safe, because he slowed down a bit, and Stuart could finally sit up. His hands had been tied behind him and were painfully pushing into his lower back, but even so, he could now try to relax and recover his composure.

They had been driving for at least a full hour when the cartel soldier, who had jumped into the backseat next to Stuart, removed the hood. Stuart squinted, dazed by the bright afternoon sunlight. As his sight recovered he looked around. The soldier sat next to him, the other burly man with the gun and the moustache sat in the front seat, and there was a third man, equally beefy and moustachioed, who was driving the car. No one said anything. Stuart guessed that there was no point in asking questions. At any rate, he knew who they were and he was fairly certain of where they were heading. The cartel base. Hopefully, he would get to meet the boss.

The boss. The mysterious Hermit.

The man who had framed Stuart for the murder of Manuel's wife and brother-in-law, and spread the rumour that he had also killed Molly Reed. The man who had ordered the murder of Guillermo, and who had ordered the hits on a civil servant in London, and another civil servant and his fiancée in Madrid, and who was responsible for pumping drugs into North America and Europe.

Perhaps, after all, it would be best if he did not meet the boss.

To distract himself from the fear of encountering the Hermit, he looked outside the car window. The view was very different from the gently rolling hills around the Rock. The landscape here was steeply mountainous. They were driving, much slower now, on a narrow road, snaking its way around the almost vertical valley sides. The valleys they passed through were each as lush as the next, covered in a forest intensely displaying all shades of green. Occasionally they drove past small, impoverished settlements, with ramshackle dwellings built of planks and corrugated steel. From time to time, a side road would wind down to a larger village at the bottom of a valley, which would have more robust structures, built with stone or brick, as well as the obligatory church. Stuart's eyes traced other paths, which led to large, enclosed estates, owned by the wealthy and used as relaxing retreats, away from the stress of the cities and hidden from the poverty of the country.

After a while, the driver grunted and the hood was put back on. Stuart guessed that they were getting close to their destination. The precaution was unnecessary, however, since Stuart did not have a clue where they were. The valleys, settlements and villages had all been nondescript, and he had not seen any special landmark that he might have been able to use for navigation back to Medellín.

He felt the car turning off the main road. It entered onto a dirt track, which they bumped along on for a good ten minutes before the car came to a stop. The henchmen all stepped outside and pulled Stuart out after them. They then pushed Stuart down a path. Through a narrow opening between the hood and his chest, he could see that he was walking across grass. It was too nondescript to reveal anything. After a while, he was told to stop. He heard a door open and he was pushed inside a building of some sort. He then heard the door close behind him.

Stuart stood still, listening.

There was absolute silence. It did not seem like any of the henchmen had followed him inside. He tried to wiggle his hands free from the rope tied around them, but it was hopeless. He did not know what kind of room he was in and he had to use his feet to feel his way around. Hesitantly he took a few steps forward, but stopped, realising that there was little point inching around the room blindfolded. He was bound to hurt himself. Instead, he carefully lowered himself and sat down on the floor.

Sitting in the darkness beneath the hood, he had an opportunity to reflect on what had just happened. Somehow the cartel soldier had caught up with him again, without the need to track his phone. How they had done so confounded him. He then wondered what had happened to the others. There was no indication that they had been captured. Stuart had seen the soldier climbing up the Rock, and he had been by himself when he started chasing Stuart. His colleagues had been waiting in the SUV. No, by all account, the others had not been caught.

Hopefully, they had seen Stuart being chased off the Rock, but realistically there was nothing they could have done to help him. If they had chased after him in Juan's car, the cartel driver had ensured that they had lost the trail. Stuart's best bet was that they had successfully met with Felipe Hernandez and had got the information that they had been promised by the Red Widow. If so, they could come after him, perhaps with the help of the army unit they had driven past on their way to Guatapé.

Stuart took a deep breath. The certainty, well, hope, of some sort of rescue kept him calm, together with the fact that he was sure of where he was. The Hermit's base. All he could do was wait.

In the darkness, he listened, carefully. He could not hear anything inside the building, but there was plenty of noise from outside. However, it was all natural noises. Birds and insects hooting and screeching. He thought he could hear the swooshing of running water, but through the hood, he could not be sure. The absence of any industrial noises told him that he was out in the countryside, probably on a large estate, like the one the Red Widow had outside Cartagena. That is definitely how he expected the Hermit to live.

Sweat was running down his face, and he tried to shake it off, but the only effect was that the bag started clinging to him. Sitting on the wooden floor, with his arms still tied behind him, he was in deep discomfort. He could feel a panic growing. He wanted out.

Suddenly a door opened, not behind him, but in front of him. A different door. He furrowed his eyebrows and listened. A single pair of footsteps walked into the room and stopped abruptly. Stuart expected a deep, burly voice from some henchman, but was taken aback when a young woman screamed out in surprise.

"Who are you?" she asked in Spanish, her voice trembling.

"My name is Stuart."

His voice was muffled by the bag and he was not sure if it was understood. He heard the woman walk up to him. He braced himself, not sure what would happen. The hood was removed from his head. He looked up and saw a young woman in her early twenties, with blonde hair tied up in a ponytail, wearing a light summer dress. She was clearly European.

"Molly Reed, I presume," Stuart said in English, taking a chance. He thought he recognised her from the photo Carolina had shown him on the news site, and beyond that, how many young, blonde Europeans had the cartel kidnapped recently?

She looked at Stuart in surprise.

"How did you know?"

"I'm here to rescue you," Stuart said.

She stepped behind him and untied his hands. Stuart thanked her, stood up and started waving his arms around to regain circulation.

"Not a very successful rescue," Molly said, holding up the hood and rope. She threw them into the corner.

Stuart chuckled.

"How do you know this wasn't my plan all along?"

They both laughed at the misfortune.

"Are you, erhm, with the British government?"

"Well, in a manner of speaking," Stuart said. He would no doubt tell her the full story in due course.

For now, he looked around and saw that they were inside a large, single room. There was a door behind him and another one across the room, which Molly had come in through. There was a wooden pillar in the centre. Molly showed him to some chairs and a wooden table, which stood in a corner. They sat down facing each other, both full of questions to ask the other. The first thing that came to Stuart's mind was Molly's apparent freedom.

"How are they treating you?" he asked. "You seemed to have walked in here on your own, when I had a hood over my head."

He realised that he had made it sound like an accusation, and he apologised. Molly shook her head.

"They're treating me surprisingly well," she said. "I say surprisingly, I've never been kidnapped before, but in context, I can't complain. There are guards all around the perimeter, but I have relative freedom within the estate. I stay in this building, but I can walk around outside. There is another girl, Sara, who's staying in another hut like this one, just a short walk away. When the boss is not around we've even been allowed to use the pool up by the main house."

"I'm relieved to hear that," Stuart said, partly because he had been concerned for Molly and Manuel's daughter, but also in the hope that he too would be treated with the same leeway.

"You know, I'd read Ingrid Betancourt's book, about her captivity with the FARC in the jungle. I was so afraid that I'd end up like that." Molly paused for a moment. "I don't think I could have survived in the jungle."

"You'd be surprised," Stuart said with a sympathetic smile. He thought about the unexpected strengths he had found in himself over the past few days. "How did you come to be here?"

Molly leaned back in her seat.

"It was a Friday, but I've lost track of the days…"

"Week and a half ago," Stuart said.

"Good to know." She paused. "A short story, really, but it started with the strangest thing I've ever been asked to do! The security officer at the embassy asked me to go to Medellín and deliver a message. I've been fretting over why she asked me to go, though she said she was too busy herself. I think the Ambassador was travelling to Cali that day. Anyway, I was close to the meeting point in Medellín when a car pulled up. Some men got out and pushed me into the car. There was nothing I could do to stop it and no one else on the street who could help me. We drove off. I had a hood over my face as well and I ended up here."

Stuart nodded. It added up with the information they had learnt, not least their belief that it was Tara Lawson who worked for the cartel. He could not understand, though, why Molly had been sent. Why did Tara not just instruct the cartel to kill Manuel's family, as they had done anyway, and just leave it at that? There had to be a reason why she had sent Molly. The henchmen, when they had tried to kidnap him and Carolina the first time, when they had been chased from the bus terminal, had spoken about a ransom. Perhaps Molly had been delivered up like a lamb to the slaughter? Is that what Robert and Roderic figured out and why they were killed? Stuart took a deep breath to calm his nerves again.

"I think I can fill in some gaps," he said. "You were on your way to meet the family of a man called Manuel. He's an informant and the government was trying to get his family out of the country. I was sent to meet with them a week after you."

"Okay. But that's not when you got kidnapped?"

"No," Stuart said, and sighed. He found that it was difficult to speak of death. "No, I found his wife and brother-in-law, but they had been killed." He stopped, remembering that Sara was also at the estate. "You do know that Sara is his daughter?"

"Oh my God," Molly said. "No, she was here before me. She said her father worked for this cartel, but he had gone missing. Then she was forcibly taken here. She said she didn't know anything about her parents' fate." A tear rolled down her cheek. "She's such a nice girl. So, her father was actually captured by us and became an informant, but her mother and uncle is dead?"

"Yes."

"You said you found them, what does that mean?"

"I found their bodies when I was attempting to deliver their passports. The cartel, as well as the police, have been chasing me ever since. I guess my luck ran out today."

He then told her about Roderic and Robert being murdered in Bogotá but left out the suggestion that Tara Lawson was responsible. This was not the time to start inflammatory and potentially false rumours. He wanted to get more proof first, if that was possible. Molly sat in silence for a moment, taking it all in.

"Is that why you're dressed as a priest?" she asked. "Disguise? Or are you really a priest?"

Stuart laughed softly. He had not been thinking about his clothes for a while. He removed the priest collar and unbuttoned his shirt. He breathed easier inside the hot and stuffy cabin.

"No, it's a disguise."

Briefly, he told Molly his story, from meeting William Cooth last Tuesday in London, to being framed for the murder of Manuel's family, being assisted by Juan, Antonio and Carolina, ending with being captured at the Rock. He finished by explaining that the cartel had an inside person, possibly working in the Embassy. Molly's eyes widened in horror.

"In the embassy?" she asked. "Who?"

"I'm not sure," Stuart said. He still did not want to make potentially false accusations. Carolina had been certain, and he did trust her, but somewhere his legal mind was shouting for more proof.

Molly pondered the information for a moment, but then tilted her head slightly.

"So, you don't really work for the government, then? You're a lawyer?"

"Yes," Stuart admitted. "But lawyers have some useful skills too."

"Really?"

Stuart chuckled.

"Yeah."

"So," Molly asked slowly, suspecting the worst. "Are we going to be rescued?"

"Oh, yes," Stuart said, trying to sound enthusiastic. "Yes, I have a rescue team. Two priests and a lawyer! I guess maybe also the lawyer's uncle, who was mayor of some local town and who I suspect was a paramilitary leader, oh, and Felipe, the friend of a serial killer."

Molly sighed.

"I sort of meant, do the police or the army know where we are?"

"Oh…no. Not unless the others tell them." Stuart considered that. "I hope they do." He did not know what else to say. He really hoped that Felipe was able to give them all the information that they needed. He looked around. "Is there any water here?"

"Of course," Molly said, standing up. "I'm so sorry, I should've asked right away."

She walked over to the other side of the room, where Stuart spotted a mini-fridge. She fetched a bottle of cold water and handed it to Stuart.

"Like I said, they're treating me surprisingly well."

"I guess an international drug cartel can afford it," Stuart observed, but it did seem a bit strange. However, if it was Tara Lawson who was working for the cartel, maybe she had asked for her colleague to be treated with some respect.

They kept on talking for what must have been a few hours and Stuart settled in as best he could. Then, the rear door was suddenly flung open and a henchman walked in. A couple of others followed, carrying a mattress which they threw on the floor. They returned shortly after with a bowl of food and a single spoon, which they put on the table.

"The boss will come tomorrow," the henchman said. He pointed to Molly. "You, go and sleep in the other house."

They then left. Molly slowly got up.

"Well, enjoy dinner and get a good night's sleep," she said. "I'm sure I'll see you tomorrow."

"I hope we will," Stuart said. "I hope it goes well, telling Sara the news about her family."

Molly nodded and then left. After she had closed the door, Stuart heard it being locked.

"The boss," he said to himself, tucking into the bowl of beans and rice. "Tomorrow is going to be interesting."

Chapter 27

The church bells in Bogotá and Medellín triumphantly rang in Maundy Thursday. At the British Embassy, Cooth, Tara and the Ambassador started the day with their daily security briefing, preparing for the Prince's visit to Cartagena. At the Church of Santa Teresa, a distraught Father Juan led morning mass, which even had Carolina in attendance.

Meanwhile, in a remote valley south of Medellín, Stuart was having a far more leisurely start to his day. He woke up on his own accord, having managed to sleep through the night, despite having a few loud cicadas as neighbours. He was hot and his throat was dry, but he did not feel any immediate panic. Knowing where he was and what was happening had kept him calm.

He got up and drank from another water bottle he found in the mini-fridge. Water was all that the mini-fridge contained but he was grateful for it. He walked around the room, as he had last night after dinner, but there was nothing of interest to see or do. There was a small window set in the rear door, but all he could see were some trees. It did not tell him anything useful.

At some point in the morning, the guards returned with breakfast and also removed the pot from last night. It had been an enjoyable stew, even though it was beans again. Stuart told the guards that he had liked it but there was no reaction from them. They left and locked the door. Stuart was somewhat disappointed, however, when he realised that breakfast consisted of more beans. Maybe an hour later, another guard came in and threw a duffle bag at Stuart.

"From the boss," he grunted and left.

The bag contained a pair of chinos, some t-shirts, swimming trunks and a towel, as well as a set of men's toiletries. The friendly gesture did wonders in calming Stuart down. He understood that he was here to be bartered for ransom, and he guessed that it would be asked for when the Prince was visiting, in order to generate maximum embarrassment. The friendliness shown by his captors was surprising, but he was not about to start complaining. However, he also wondered what would happen if the ransom was refused. This led to some deeply troubling thoughts, but somehow he managed to push those concerns away.

He remembered that Molly had said that she was free to use the pool. The swimming trunks in the duffle bag surely suggested that he had the same liberty. He grabbed them and the towel and headed for the door. This time it had not been locked. He stepped outside and joyfully breathed in the fresh air, feeling energy coursing through his body. The cabin had become hot, stale and full of the smell of beans.

Some survivalist instinct, which he did not know he had, then kicked in, and he began to carefully survey his surroundings. It was obvious that he was on a very large, rural estate. Based on the position of the sun he guessed that the cabin was situated on the northern slopes of the valley. Through an interstice in the trees, he could see across to the southern slopes, which seemed a long way away. Above the southern ridge rose a very tall peak, which loomed ominously above the valley, its contours disappearing in the heat haze. There was no other building in sight, although the cabin where Molly and Sara were being held must be somewhere around. He tried to look for it, but the woods were too thick, so he could not see very far. Around the front of the cabin were large tracks leading back up the valley, but the car he had been brought in was no longer there.

He spotted a footpath, which wound its way through the trees along the side of the valley. He set off, somewhat tentatively, but his confidence grew as he realised that there were no guards around. The path revealed the most amazing things. Despite his captivity, he could not help but stop and marvel at it all. Inside a bush with long, spiky leaves he saw a cluster of tiny pineapples. So that's where they come from, he thought. He continued past assortments of palms, banana and orange trees, and he took deep breaths, marvelling at their powerful aromas. He stopped and looked at a bright red flower, and on hearing a buzzing sound, he leaned in closer. To his amazement, he spotted a tiny nightingale hovering next to it.

He carried on. After a few turns, he came to a large clearing. At the top of the clearing lay a spacious, whitewashed two-story house. He spotted two armed men walking around the front, which demonstrated that despite his apparent freedom, trying to escape would be futile. Further down the clearing, connected to the house by a path made of large stone slabs, was a pool, complete with a covered bar and seating area, as well as a small hut.

The clearing opened up a view of the whole valley. Large fields covered its base, which stretched for a great distance until the southern slope rose up again. Stuart saw an enclosure with horses and several pastures filled with cows. The whole area looked like a large, working farm, and perhaps that was the cartel's cover, in case anyone looked too closely.

He headed down towards the pool. There were two women there. One was Molly. The other must be Sara. Seeing her made Stuart's mind flash back to the jewellery store and the image of her mother's and uncle's bodies. He had to steady himself before continuing on.

Molly waved as Stuart came closer.

"Good morning," she said. "I'm glad you've been allowed out as well. I wanted to see you earlier, but the guards said no."

"Good morning," Stuart said.

Sara was young, around twenty, and was short and slim. She had long, brown hair, which was frazzled and unkempt. She was staring blankly into space, a haunted look on her face. Stuart guessed that she was still processing the tragic news.

"Hi, I'm Stuart," he said, introducing himself.

She looked up at him with pleading eyes.

"What happened to her?"

Stuart sat down on the adjacent sunbed, and images from the jewellery store once again flashed in his mind. He did not know what to say, so he very briefly explained how he had found the bodies. He did not mention the bullet holes or the copious amount of blood on the walls. Sara started crying but did not say anything.

He walked away, leaving her alone to grieve. He saw that there was a changing room behind the small bar, and he quickly got out of his priest's attire, which was unpleasantly malodorous from the previous day's running up and down the Rock. He quickly stepped underneath a shower before jumping into the pool. He kept his head under water for as long as he could, trying, perhaps in some spiritual way, to wash off the evil of the past week. His head came up above the water and he looked out across the illusory paradise he was in. He found himself thinking of the simple pleasure of home. How he longed to be there.

Molly walked over to the other side of the pool, away from Sara who was still staring blankly into space. She sat down at the edge and let her feet dangle into the water.

"I've spent many hours in here," she said quietly. "Day and night." She laughed softly at some memory. "I panicked the first night. Bats came out, in large numbers, diving into the pool. I guess they were drinking the water. I ran out as quickly as I could. But the next night I stayed in. You know they say that bats never hit you, and they didn't." She paused. "I dreamt for while that I was Batwoman or something. It's silly, I know."

"Not at all," Stuart said. "I think you're allowed to dream in captivity."

They stayed by the pool for as long as they could but escaped when the midday sun became too much. They returned to the cabin where Stuart was staying. The guard had brought lunch; another pot with another stew. It had gone cold, but with the heat outside Stuart was more than happy with a cold meal. They had to persuade Sara to eat, and she eventually relented. She and Molly walked off after lunch, back to their own hut. Molly said she would look after her.

Stuart carried his mattress outside and lay down in the shade underneath the trees, patiently waiting. It was many hours later when a couple of cartel soldiers came down the path and roused Stuart from his drowsy afternoon rest.

"Let's go," one of them said.

Stuart rubbed his eyes to reenergise himself and then got up. He walked between them as they headed up to the main house. The stone path in the clearing led up to a large wooden terrace, which continued around the building. It was kitted out with various tables, chairs, and plush sun loungers, and had a commanding view of the valley below. There was a large opening into the house itself, and Stuart saw that the entire wall had been rolled away to one side.

The guards pushed Stuart through the opening and into a large wooden chair, which stood just inside. Stuart sat down, facing out into the valley. His hands and legs were tied tightly to the chair. He started sweating profusely from the heat and the fear.

He looked to his right and saw a large dining table. A burly henchman was standing next to it, holding a large kitchen knife. Stuart gulped. On a tray on the table stood a few pineapples. The henchman picked one up and started slicing it. Stuart managed to wonder whether the pineapples were locally grown but mostly he hoped that the knife would not come any closer to him.

Stuart's head began to spin in the heat and he lost track of time. Eventually, another man entered from the terrace, giving a quick nod goodbye to someone who was out of Stuart's sight. The man was tall and well built. He was smartly dressed in long trousers and a shirt, and he had rolled up the sleeves above his elbows. It was a strange choice of attire given the climate, and it suggested the man had high status. The henchman with the knife nodded in respect.

Stuart wondered if he was finally meeting the boss, the Hermit. He then tilted his head in contemplation. He had a feeling that he had seen this man before.

Before Stuart could place him, the man stepped forward and struck Stuart with impressive force. Stuart's head flew to one side and quickly bounced back. His whole body would have toppled over had it not been for the sturdy chair he was tied to, and his knuckles turned white as he clenched the wooden armrests.

The man waited a moment for Stuart to regain his senses.

"Would you like some pineapple?"

Stuart's head was still spinning, but he looked up at the man.

"What?" he mumbled.

"Pineapple?"

The man looked in the direction of his burly employee and gave a slight nod, calling for the plate to be brought over.

"Well," Stuart said, taking a deep breath. His mind was starting to defog. He found the question odd, but he had to buy some extra time before the henchman put the knife to another, bloodier, use. "Yes, thank you."

The employee brought the plate with pineapple slices over and handed it to his boss. He then quickly retreated to the table, placing his hand on the knife.

"The house belongs to my boss, Mr Gleeman," the man said, still standing over Stuart. He did not offer Stuart any of the pineapple slices, which did not matter much since Stuart's hands were still securely tied to the back of the chair. "But you know that, of course. What I want to know, do your companions know where we are?"

Stuart's mind was clearing up. They know my name, he thought, but after the escapades of the previous week, he was not too surprised. The man slowly ate a slice of pineapple, looking intently at Stuart. Stuart was not sure how to proceed. All he could do was hope that Felipe Hernandez had told Juan and the others about this location, and that rescue was on its way. He also knew that he had to keep silent.

"Well," the man insisted, with a sterner tone. "Your companions?"

Stuart looked away and out over the valley. Even though the tall peaks beyond were disappearing into the heat haze, it truly looked like paradise. Then he noticed that the henchman came back over. He had the knife in his hand.

"I am disappointed," the man said. He subtly nodded his head at the door. With some effort, the henchman slid the rolling door shut.

"I really am disappointed, Mr Gleeman."

Stuart looked up at the man.

"Do your companions know where we are?" the man asked again.

The man struck Stuart one more time, and once again the sturdy chair kept Stuart upright, which meant his body absorbed all of the force. He struggled through a few shallow breaths before his mind reset.

"I don't know," he said quietly. "How could they?"

"Very well."

The man again made a quick, almost imperceptible nod, this time towards Stuart's back. The henchman hurried to untie Stuart's hands. Stuart was finally offered the pineapple. He took a slice and ate it slowly, his jaw screaming in pain. The pineapple though was very succulent and its sugars brought his mind back into play.

"My name is Julian," the man said and pulled up a chair of his own. He sat down facing Stuart and studied him carefully for a moment, as if inspecting his prey. "You are a surprisingly difficult man to catch. You somehow kill two of my men." Julian shook his head slowly. "But now you are here," he concluded triumphantly. "Welcome."

"Thank you," Stuart said. "But you're mistaken. I haven't killed anyone." He rubbed his jaw, which was still hurting. "And only one of your men has been killed, after he threatened me, and it was in self-defence."

Julian nodded slowly, still studying Stuart closely.

"You genuinely believe that. Well, the priests then, that you have recruited to be your soldiers, they killed one of my men in Medellín and one of my men in El Retiro. I am…disappointed."

Stuart's heart skipped a beat. At once he remembered all of the concerns that Carolina had spoken of at her uncle's house in El Retiro. Juan and Antonio had said that they had brought the captured cartel soldier, Raul, to the local police station, but Carolina had wondered whether they had just killed him.

"They didn't kill anyone in El Retiro," Stuart protested without conviction.

Trying to rationalise it, he thought that maybe Julian was lying, but for what reason? If Raul was dead, maybe he had been killed by the local police, but what was their motive? What was the priests' motive? Nothing made sense to him anymore.

Julian pulled out his phone, tapped a few times, and showed Stuart a photo. He recognised Raul immediately. His body was lying dead in a dumpster. Stuart took a deep breath, trying to stay in control of his spinning mind. He did not understand what was going on. All he could do was shake his head.

"Well, there you are," Julian said. He stood up and motioned for the henchman to untie Stuart's legs. Julian chuckled heartily. "I saw you last Friday in Medellín, outside the jewellery store building. My colleagues and I had just killed Manuel's family. You were waiting for midday, no? You looked so nervous, so anxious. I did not expect any of this to transpire in this way."

Stuart remembered the wait outside the building. He had seen a group of four men, one well dressed, leave just moments before he had gone in at noon.

"Why didn't you capture me there and then?"

"We were hoping our friends in the police would get you," Julian said. "Then you escaped and we reassessed our interests. Well, the good news is that you'll meet the boss tomorrow. You can ask him anything you want."

Stuart slowly got up from the chair, his body still weak from the blows. The henchman, with some effort, rolled the big door back open and Stuart stepped out onto the terrace. Evening had arrived and darkness was quickly falling. The peaks to the south now rose like looming shadows. What a difference a few minutes could make.

He spotted a woman at the far corner of the terrace, lying on one of the sunbeds. She looked European, tall, athletic, with long, flowing natural red hair. Stuart jolted again, remembering what Carolina had uncovered in Bogotá. The woman in the Embassy had long, red hair. Was this her? Was this Tara Lawson?

She looked at Stuart for a second but then turned away. The henchman gave Stuart a push and they walked back to the hut.

Stuart found Molly waiting for him inside.

"Oh my God!" she exclaimed as Stuart walked in. "Your face."

Stuart realised that his face must had swelled up from the two blows.

"It's all right," he said. "I'm all right."

"Did you meet the boss?"

"No," he said. "Someone else. Julian."

"Yes, I have met him too."

Stuart gave her an inquiring look.

"Don't worry," she said. "No one has mistreated me."

Stuart sat down by the table.

"He promised me that I would meet the real boss tomorrow. The Hermit. Have you met him?"

"No, never."

"I saw who I guess is Julian's girlfriend. A European woman, I think. Tall, bright natural red hair. It was surprising, I haven't seen anyone else like that here."

Stuart looked at Molly to see if there was any reaction. There was. Her face strained.

"No, no me neither." She paused. "I…there is one person who matches that description, but no, it can't be

her."
"Who?"
"No, she can't be here with the cartel."
"Who?"
"Tara Lawson. The embassy head of security."
Stuart nodded slowly. It seemed to be confirmed.

Chapter 28

Stuart was now certain that it was Tara Lawson who was working for the cartel. The embassy's head of security. Stuart found it difficult to get his head around that fact. Maybe she was not responsible for all the crimes committed by the cartel, but she was certainly behind getting Molly kidnapped and undoubtedly responsible for what had happened to Manuel's family. He was sure that she was also responsible for his own predicament.

Whilst Stuart had had time to ponder this possibility ever since Carolina had told him on Tuesday evening, Molly had just heard it for the first time. She was pacing around the cabin, with a look of shock and disbelief.

"It doesn't make any sense," she said eventually. "Or does it?" she asked after a few more paces around the room.

"I don't know, does it?"

"I don't know! It can't be," she protested. "Why?"

"I don't know why she's done it," Stuart said. "All I know is that there's a tall redhead up at the house, who looks exactly as the old lady in Bogotá described the murderer, and who looks exactly as my friend described the lady she met at the Embassy. Unless this country is suddenly swarming with redheads, it's her."

"Fuck!" Molly exclaimed.

Stuart chuckled.

"Yes, we are that. She'll just steer the Colombian police somewhere else, at least the ones that the cartel hasn't cosied up to, and we'll never be rescued."

"So it all depends on your priest and lawyer friends?" Molly asked.

"I think so."

Stuart's mind then sank to a new low. He started thinking about everything that Julian had revealed. There was no harm in telling Molly, so he explained about Raul being found dead in El Retiro. He talked about the doubts that Carolina had expressed about the two priests and how he had started to think that maybe, after all, she had been right. Why had Juan and Antonio been so willing, so eager, to help him, a complete stranger? Had they actually killed Raul?

He could tell that Molly was struggling to maintain hope.

"That doesn't mean that the priests killed Raul," Molly said, trying to sound positive. "I mean, anyone could've killed him. Even Julian himself, just to mess with your mind."

"I guess so."

"And a photo of a dumpster doesn't prove that the dumpster is in El Retiro."

Stuart sighed.

"I don't really know anything at this moment."

"That's the point," Molly said. "Psychological warfare."

"They teach you about that in the Diplomatic Corps?"

"Yes."

Before Stuart could enquire how effective Molly was at resisting psychological warfare, the cabin door opened and two guards walked in, carrying dinner. It was another bean stew.

"Don't you cook anything else?" Stuart asked, but the men simply left without saying a word.

"Fill up your bowl," Molly said. "I'll carry the rest down to Sara."

"How's she doing?" Stuart asked, helping himself to a fair amount of stew.

"Not good. First her brother, now her mother. And who knows where her father is."

On that sad note, Molly picked up the stew and left.

Stuart ate and then went to lie down on the mattress, which the guards had thrown back inside after Stuart's restful afternoon under the trees. He tried to sleep but peace eluded him. Too many thoughts were spinning around in his mind. After many hours he got up and tried the door. To his surprise he found it unlocked. He stepped outside into the mild night.

The valley lay in darkness, but a thunderstorm raged beyond, and the contours of the mountains were illuminated by the almost constant lightning strikes in the distance. It was mesmerising and awe-inspiring, but he remembered that it was the same phenomenon he had seen the night that Guillermo had been killed. Had that been, perchance, a bad omen?

He took a few steps away from the cabin and looked around. Out front, two guards were relaxing around an open fire. They were merrily chatting and exchanging cards with pictures on them. Football cards. Stuart could not help himself sighing. Why was everyone so preoccupied with the upcoming World Cup? He could also see some bottles of aguardiente strewn around, suggesting the guards were making the most of their assignment. They did not seem to pay him any attention.

About ten or so metres away from the cabin was a large boulder, standing as a monument, as it was encircled by a few palms. Stuart slowly walked over to it, anxiously awaiting protests from the guards, but none came, and he sat down on the grass, leaning back onto the rock. He closed his eyes and listened, hearing the soft rumble of the thunder rolling in from the distance, the gentle rustling of the winds in the leaves above. Just occasionally the cheerful voices of the guards carried across. In context, he could not complain about that. Finally, he had found an almost perfect spot where he could reflect on life.

He had so many questions. Why was the cartel killing people in Europe? Why had they kidnapped him? What problem did they have with the Prince and the President that had led them to plan an assassination? And the biggest question, who was the Hermit?

Though Carolina had brought it up repeatedly, he had never really thought about the people who were at his side, helping him. Who exactly was Father Juan? By day, a seemingly respected Carmelite prior. What were his motives for helping? And who exactly was Father Antonio? A lawyer and a priest, in the service of the Archbishop of Madrid. What were his motives for helping? Antonio had killed one of the cartel soldiers, but that was to save Stuart. But had the two priests killed Raul? Stuart could not make himself believe that.

For that matter, who was Carolina? A well-to-do lawyer, from a family she had never mentioned, except uncle Paulo in El Retiro, who had a decidedly questionable past. Why was she helping him?

Stuart sighed. The long days of the past week had not revealed the answer to any of these questions. He thought that he had seen glimpses into the lives of Juan, Antonio, and Carolina, but now, when he was finally able to reflect on it all in the peaceful solitude of the night, he realised that he really did not know any of them at all.

What did he know about Juan? He came from a small town not too far away, with a name that had been left unmentioned. There, his father had been killed by a paramilitary outfit, hired by the mayor and some business leaders. Stuart strongly hoped that the mayor had not been Carolina's uncle. Juan, at the time just a confused teenager, had somehow come across the Red Widow, who had been operating in the area. He had asked to join her team, but she had sent him to the priesthood instead.

Juan had known Manuel, as he had explained when Stuart had first met him at Arví Park. Manuel had come to the church, seeking guidance. The murder of his congregant may have been what had spurred him to help Stuart in the first instance, as well as his familiarity with the senseless violence which seemed to have plagued the country since its birth nearly two centuries earlier. Juan's desire to help must have strongly increased when his friend, Guillermo, was murdered.

Maybe that explained Juan's involvement. Maybe. But Stuart's mind returned to the death of Raul. Had that truly been the priests' doing?

What about Antonio? He had had no idea why Stuart

wanted to meet him when he had invited Stuart up to Arví Park. The priest in training, James, who Stuart remembered was also a big question mark, had called Antonio, and all Stuart had said on the phone was that he needed help. Was Antonio's involvement since then just following Juan? After all that Antonio had done over the past week, that was a serious commitment to his friend.

No, Stuart could not make sense of Antonio, the man who had become a priest because he had been rejected by a woman he had met only once. Stuart had never grasped the notion of love at first sight, which to him seemed like a Hollywood construct, but perhaps it did exist? Maybe he had not found it? Yet? It had certainly not been the case with Kate, though he had probably grown to love her before she had left for Patagonia. It had not been the case with Carolina, though he had certainly come to admire her greatly over the past week. Well, he would have to leave true love for another time.

What confused him was that Antonio had shot a man. True, it had been to defend Stuart, and Stuart could not see any other way in which he would have survived that standoff. The cartel soldier had been pointing his gun at Stuart, and surely Stuart would be dead now if Antonio had not intervened? But it was a bizarre act by a priest. He could not square it with his understanding of the world, however limited that understanding was. His mind again returned to the death of Raul. Had Antonio been involved in that?

Then there was Carolina. But what could he say? He had to try to see beyond her warm embrace and question why she was helping him out. Bizarrely, despite staying at her flat, and meeting her uncle, he probably knew the least about her. She had effortlessly lied to that police officer on Saturday morning. For biological reasons he had to assume that she had parents somewhere, whether dead or alive, but that was all he could do. There was uncle Paulo, but he had not revealed much about his niece. What else? She was a lawyer, working for an energy company that owned a hydroelectric power plant which was in dire need of upgrading. That was about it, and it did not reveal much about her character.

He simply could not figure out why she was helping him. She too understood senseless violence, perhaps from her background, which might be why she did not mention her family, and maybe that had been enough to want to help him. He thought about her warnings about the priests, and how prescient those warnings seemed to have been. She must have known something.

His mind turned to the coming day. He would hopefully get to meet the boss, the Hermit. Having already met the Red Widow, another crime boss did not daunt him too much. For all his queries about his companions, the most important question was to understand who was behind all of this. Who was the Hermit?

No one seemed to know the Hermit's real name. He had searched the news sites with Carolina, but they said very little about the Hermit and the cartel. No names were ever mentioned. He scoffed. Maybe Julian was the real boss, and had invented the legend of the Hermit to deflect attention? It the Hermit was a made-up person, it would explain why he had evaded capture.

But maybe the Hermit was a real person. To have been so successful yet secretive, it had to be a powerful person behind the mask. Someone with money, connections, and insight. Maybe it was Tara? In her security capacity, she surely knew plenty of state secrets. As a spy, she surely knew both British and Colombian state secrets. Maybe she could pull off running a drug cartel? She would certainly have all the inside knowledge to successfully assassinate the Prince.

Stuart accepted that he would not be able to guess the correct answer. He also understood that asking such questions came with certain risks. If he knew too much, would he be allowed to leave, even if a ransom was paid? The old saying, if I told you I'd have to kill you, might be a cliché, but Stuart sensed that in this place, amongst these people, it had a certain truth to it. Having met Julian earlier, maybe he already knew too much?

His curiosity, which had grown rapidly during the past few days, still held the upper hand over his fear of continued incarceration and death. Tomorrow would tell. Hopefully, finally, he would get to meet the Hermit.

A loud thunder rolled in through the valley, startling him from his reflective peace. It was followed by silence. An idea walked into his mind. Why wait for tomorrow? Was there a chance he could escape now?

**

Stuart stood up and carefully looked around. In the darkness, there was nothing to be seen, other than the two guards in front of the cabin. They were still happily chatting away about their football cards and seemed to have found some additional bottles of aguardiente. He was certain that he could get away from them without being noticed. After all, he had been sitting by the boulder for an hour or so without being detected.

Very slowly he started walking away, staying close to the trees, trying to find the path that Molly had taken earlier towards the second cabin. There was no way that he would try to escape without her and Sara. After some careful tiptoeing around, during which he cracked a few tree branches lying about, he found the path. He held his breath for a few seconds. He could hear the guards laughing out front. They were completely oblivious to his movements. Satisfied that he was in the clear, he set off down the path.

He had no idea where the second cabin was. All he could hope for was that the path would be sufficiently clear to follow in the dark and that it would lead straight to his target. He walked slowly, quickly alternating between scanning the path for obstacles and looking for any movement around him. He had to assume that there were other guards at the second cabin. However, the only sound he could hear was the distant rolling thunder and the occasional screech of a bird or an insect.

After what felt like hours, but was at most five minutes, he spotted another cabin located inside a small clearing. Like his, it was small, square, and built out of wood. He snuck up to the treeline and carefully scanned the clearing. There was no movement to be seen. There were clearly no drunk guards discussing football out front. It was possible that one of the two guards at Stuart's cabin had in fact been assigned to this cabin, but had left his post. Molly and Sara seemed to have enjoyed a great deal of freedom and perhaps they were not considered a flight risk.

Stuart crouched down and legged across the opening to the door. He knocked softly. The door was soon opened by Molly, who was very surprised to see him.

"What are you doing?" she asked.

"There is no one around," Stuart whispered. "We should try to escape."

He anxiously looked around but the woods were quiet and still. Molly dragged him inside the cabin.

"Are you insane?"

"We have to try," Stuart said. "We can't just accept our fate here."

He heard a stirring from the corner and he saw Sara blankly looking up at him from her mattress.

"They'll kill us if they catch us," Molly said, sounding scared. "You know who these people are. You've seen the guns."

"They won't kill us," Stuart said. "They want us for ransom. There is no ransom for the dead. Surely we have to take the chance?"

"I don't know," Molly said. She looked down at Sara. "She's still out of it from grief."

"No, we must leave now," Sara said, startling them both with the intensity of her voice, and jumped onto her feet.

"Wow, from lethargic to lithe in one second flat," Stuart exclaimed. "Look, we have to go for it. By the way, do you have water here? We should bring some."

"Yes," Molly said and quickly fetched a couple of bottles from their mini-fridge, as Sara was already out the door.

Stuart rushed after her outside and held her back. He scanned the clearing again but thankfully it was still empty.

"Just slow down," he said quietly. "How do we get out of here?" he asked as Molly joined them outside.

"Not sure," Molly said. "Going uphill is probably no good, it leads past the main house and some other buildings I saw earlier."

"My dad said there is a village in the next valley over," Sara explained and pointed south, towards the tall peak. "We have to climb that ridge."

"That's a long way to go at night," Molly said.

"Let's go then," Sara said and set off without waiting for a reply.

She briskly crossed the clearing and into the trees on the other side. Stuart and Molly hurried after. He was already starting to regret bringing Sara along, if she was going to be this nonchalant about scouting for the guards who surely were stationed around them.

There was no discernible path going downhill, which slowed their progress. They had to navigate around large boulders, cross streams, and pass through thickening undergrowth. Stuart had seen that parts of the valley were cultivated, but this particular area seemed almost like virgin forest. He could feel a variety of insects, perhaps awoken by their progress, crawling around his feet and legs, but in the darkness he could not see what they were. He could only hope that they were friendly.

Eventually, when they were all feeling exhausted, they came across a larger stream. It flowed downhill inside an exposed rock bed, which was littered with boulders and rocks of all sizes. They stopped and drank from the cold but refreshing water. Stuart did not know what time it was, but it was probably a few hours past midnight. The thunderstorm in the distance seemed to have run its course and a myriad of stars were starting to make their appearance in the sky. It was heavenly.

"Let's go," Sara said.

Without waiting, she set off, following the stream downhill. It was even more difficult than cutting through the undergrowth in the forest, but at least they were following a clear path into the valley. The rock bed was slippery and their feet and ankles were freezing in the cold water. The rocks and pebbles posed a constant hazard and they occasionally had to heave themselves over the large boulders. Thick trees and bushes lined the stream, forming a natural barrier which forced them to stay in the water.

After a long and precarious descent, with their feet now completely numb, the ground finally flattened out. The trees and shrubs along the stream began retreating away, and they finally managed to leave the water and enter dry land. They followed the treeline instead, making more rapid progress now, and soon they reached a wide river which the stream flowed into. Stuart looked around and saw that the river ran in its own gorge and that the banks rose steeply on both sides. They would have to cross the river somehow and then climb up the opposite bank. It was the only way forward. He sighed, realising that climbing the opposite bank would be nothing compared to then having to scale the entire southern ridge.

The flat river bed was entirely made of rocks. Stuart saw that the water itself actually was not that wide, most of the width of the gorge was the rocky ground on either side. As he looked downriver he saw an old wrought-iron bridge spanning the gorge and he instinctively crouched down. He was grateful that Molly and Sara followed his example. They all looked at the bridge for a moment, but there was no movement on it. Satisfied, they carried on. Thankfully, the river was not very deep and they managed to quickly wade across, their feet again screaming in pain from the cold.

The bank on the other side rose more than ten metres

and they had to crawl up it on their stomachs. Stuart used the grass and tree roots as best he could to pull himself upwards. Though the night was mild, almost cold, he was drenched in sweat by the time he reached the top and the ground flattened out. Sara again took charge and led them onwards. The ground climbed slowly but steadily upwards. Soon, they came across a wide gravel path. It led uphill, so they continued to follow it, staying as close as possible to the treeline.

The only interruption for a long time were a few sleeping goats, with impressively long goatees and bizarrely oblong ears, who were tied to wooden posts along the path. Eventually, rounding a bend in the road, they came upon a large clearing in which stood a large stone house. Stuart halted and tried to crouch down, but then had to chase after Sara who had simply kept walking onwards.

"Just wait a bit," he said, starting to sound rather impatient.

The building lay in darkness, but several cars, glistening in the moonlight, were parked outside. There was still no movement to be seen or sound to be heard but the cars suggested that there were people around. Stuart had to assume that the owners of the cars belonged to the cartel.

Satisfied that there was no one standing lookout, Stuart motioned for them to carry on. Pointing rather than saying anything, he gestured for them to continue on the road past the building and further up the slope. Sara again hurried in the lead, with Stuart and Molly chasing after.

They were halfway across the open area when Stuart heard a group of male voices coming from the stone house. He looked over and saw some people hurrying out the door, one of them having a phone in his hand. He froze, wondering whether to run forwards or head back. Sara, however, was still walking on, apparently not having noticed the men. Molly gave him a push and they rushed after her.

They had almost reached the treeline on the other side when they heard shouting. Stuart started running, heading for the trees. He called for Sara to follow him and he hoped that Molly was still right behind him. Despite the moon, high in the sky, the woods beyond lay in darkness. He rushed in between two trees, but could only see a few steps ahead of him.

He managed to find Sara and Molly, and staying close together, they rushed further into the woods. There was a lot of shouting coming from behind them. He dared to cast a quick glance behind him and he could see rays from flashlights flying between the trees.

"They must have noticed our escape," he panted as they kept on running.

After rounding many trees and boulders, Stuart and Molly crouched down in an opening underneath a large boulder, which was perched over a small depression with a little stream in it. They sat in silence, listening to the yelling of the men chasing them. Sara, however, was nowhere to be seen. They had lost her in the darkness.

"Oh, God," Molly whispered. "I'm so worried for her."

"What was her rush?"

"I don't think she's thinking straight," Molly said.

They huddled up as the voices came closer. Stuart could see flashlights illuminating nearby tree trunks. He held his breath, but to their luck, the voices soon carried on further up the slope.

They sat in silence for a good ten minutes, before Stuart dared breathe out. Carefully he crawled out from the hole and tried to look around. Once again, only silence and darkness surrounded them.

"Do you think we can find her?" Molly asked.

"I have no idea."

They carefully kept walking onwards, up the slope, well aware that the men chasing them were now up ahead somewhere. However, with their shouting and the flashlights, they should not be too difficult to spot. Stuart paused every few steps to look around but it was difficult to see anything. From time to time he thought he heard sounds up ahead, but unless his ears were playing tricks on him, the sounds were far away and posed no danger.

Eventually, they saw a road up ahead and beyond it the southern ridge of the valley. The trees were thinning out and Stuart realised that they would be fully exposed if they tried to cross over the ridge. They slowly moved up to the treeline and looked around. To their dismay, they saw a guard posted some fifty metres down the road, and despite the darkness, it was clear that he had a rifle slung over his shoulders.

"Let's move along the treeline," Molly said, motioning in the opposite direction.

They moved slowly, staying within the treeline. However, after walking for only a minute they spotted another guard further up the road. They crouched down behind a large tree.

"Well, either we try crossing the road, or we have to go back down again."

Molly shook her head.

"No, we can't go back down," she said. "We've come this far."

"Crossing the road it is then. But it's quite exposed on the other side."

They both looked across and tried to plot a safe route on the other side of the road. There were clusters of trees leading all the way to the ridge, but there were exposed areas in-between them. Molly rubbed her eyes and smiled.

"Let's assume these guards are as tired as we are. Maybe they simply won't notice."

"Let's hope," Stuart said.

Very carefully they crawled out from behind the tree and up towards the gravelled road. Stuart stopped once he reached it.

"Crawling over gravel is very loud," he said. "We should walk."

Slowly they got on their feet and as quickly as possible tried to soundlessly traverse the road. They were almost across when they heard the guard up the road yell out.

"Run," Stuart said.

He dashed after Molly towards the nearest cluster of trees. Behind him, he could hear the two guards on the road shouting towards each other, and then the sound of them giving chase. He did not know how far behind they were, but it could not be far. He reached the trees, Molly just ahead of him, and they ran through the trees in a zigzag pattern, trying to evade their pursuers. This time, however, it seemed hopeless. The pursuers were right behind them.

They rounded a big boulder and came face to face with a gun.

Chapter 29

Stuart was awoken by a loud banging on the door. He opened his eyes and felt his whole body screaming out in pain. He tried to roll over but could not even manage that. He remained lying on his back, staring at the cabin ceiling, whilst the pounding on the door continued.

"What the hell?" Molly muttered.

She slowly got up from the mattress and shuffled over towards the door. Stuart again tried to get up from the cold, wooden floor, and with all his might he managed to roll over and sit up on his knees. He then slowly stood up and tried to stretch out his body. It was very painful.

After they had been captured on the southern ridge, the guards had bound both of them and driven back to the cabin where Stuart had been kept. They were both thrown inside with the door locked behind them. Stuart had let Molly stay on the single mattress, whilst he had spent the night lying directly on the floor. It had been uncomfortable.

Molly tried to open the door, but it was locked.

"What?" she yelled loudly.

The door was unlocked from the outside and two guards stepped in, guns in hand. Ignoring Molly, they walked up to Stuart.

"The boss wants to see you," one of them said. He handed over a Panama hat. "The boss wants you to be careful in the sun."

"Thank you," Stuart said hesitantly.

The two guards then bundled Stuart out of the cabin. A third guard was standing outside and immediately closed the door and locked it. He remained standing by the door as the other two pushed Stuart forwards on the path towards the main house. Despite having been given a hat, the guards' attitude was far more violent than yesterday. They had clearly not appreciated the escape attempt.

Stuart tried to keep his mind focused despite his

throbbing body. Mostly he felt a deep disappointment that their escape had failed. They had come so close to the ridge and potentially freedom beyond it. In addition to his disappointment, he felt a deep worry, because he did not know where Sara was. She had not been returned to the cabin. The best he could hope for was that she had been returned to the other cabin. Or maybe, against all odds, she had managed to get away? He cautioned himself from getting his hopes up.

They walked quickly. He realised that he had slept for a long while as the sun was already at its zenith. The heat and humidity was pressing down and he was grateful for his hat. Up above, in the sky, Stuart spotted a family of eagles soaring past, then diving rapidly for some quarry further down in the valley. He felt a twinge of envy for their freedom.

When they reached the large clearing below the main house, the guards turned down towards the centre of the valley. The walked past the pool and reached the start of a wide path, which wound its way through the fields beyond. Stuart walked on his own accord now, with the two guards remaining a few steps behind. There was nothing he could do but carry on.

They passed a cow enclosure, where a handful of cows eyed Stuart with their customary curiosity. Beyond it was a paddock, where a few ranchers were handling a group of uncooperative horses. They walked on and on, across fields, past more cows and through an orange grove.

To his left, Stuart could see a large wooded section of the northern slope, and he guessed that it was the forest through which he, Molly and Sara had descended last night. Walking across the fields was certainly easier. All the while, the imposing peak which rose over the southern ridge came closer. In the daylight, he could see what an obstacle the ridge itself was, and what a folly it had been to have tried an unplanned escape attempt in the dark of night.

As he and his guards reached the centre of the valley,

Stuart dared looked around properly, and he could see numerous small houses perched on the hillsides all around, many of them hiding behind outcrops and in clearings in the forest. The path eventually led them to the old wrought iron bridge, which Stuart had seen last night, and they walked across it.

They continued on up another path. In the distance, across an open field, Stuart saw the large stone building where the guards had spotted them last night, and based on that he could visualise whereabouts he and Molly had been captured. It had not been much further up the slope at all. He doubted whether they had actually stood a chance of making it across the ridge before daybreak, when they certainly would have been spotted. How foolish he had been to even have suggested an escape.

They carried on. By now Stuart was feeling so weak that he started to stumble. The heat and exhaustion was getting to him and he was sweating profusely. The guards, however, who seemed to be similarly exhausted, egged him on. After a while, Stuart spotted a small building which was sitting at the base of the tall peak. It was built out of round logs and reminded him of an Alpine chalet, which he, of course, had only seen on TV. There were several cars parked around it.

Stuart was ushered onto a patio and through the open north wall into the living area. There were a sofa and some large armchairs placed around a low table. Stuart saw a well-dressed man sitting in one of the armchairs, closely observing as Stuart was pushed inside. It took Stuart a moment to figure out who the man was.

"Nice to see you, Julian," Stuart croaked.

"Welcome to my humble retreat," Julian said.

Stuart sank down in another armchair without waiting for permission. His legs had given up completely. Julian gestured to a servant who had been standing in the back of the room. Stuart was offered a bottle of water, which he quickly drank.

"You're not here to be tortured," Julian remarked

casually, but after the long march from the cabin, the statement was rather ambiguous. "Anyway, it is a pleasure to see you again. I hope I didn't punch you too hard yesterday."

"Don't worry about it," Stuart said. He nervously glanced around, realising that he was sitting with his back to the open patio, which made him feel anxious. Who knew what could sneak in from behind? He then looked at Julian. His mind had caught up to the situation. "So, you're the Hermit?"

Julian shook his head before starting to laugh.

"I'm flattered," he said. "But no, I am only a lowly servant. Unfortunately, the Hermit cannot be here to meet you today."

The servant brought in a hot meal, presumably lunch. Stuart was offered juice, toast and fried eggs. He had little appetite for hot food, but Julian insisted, and it was a welcomed relief from bean stew. He forced himself to eat it all, as he knew he would need the energy. Julian stepped outside for a few minutes, leaving Stuart to eat in peace. He was not sure where Julian or the guards had gone, but they returned once he had finished. He felt more energetic, which apparently was what Julian had hoped for.

"We will go for a walk now," he said.

He gestured for Stuart to join him outside. With loud groaning and wincing, Stuart made it out of the armchair and walked out through the patio. Julian led the way as they started to climb up the tall peak, crossing straight over the thick grassland. They seemed to be heading for a large wooded area up ahead.

"I have heard much about you, Mr Gleeman," Julian remarked on the way. "As has the boss. He does hope to meet with you over the weekend."

"Really?" Stuart asked. Though his head was still throbbing, he realised that he had to take the opportunity to find out as much as he could about the Hermit and the cartel. If he was lucky he could get confirmation about Tara Lawson. "How have you heard about me?"

Julian's nose twitched.

"The newspapers, of course," he said quickly. It was a lot to hope for that he would reveal his prize source right away. "You've been in them quite a bit, accused of many murders. A man and woman in Medellín last Friday. And Molly Reed, though, of course, she is not dead. But then, it was us who put your name out there."

"Yes, why did you do that?" Stuart asked. "If you wanted ransom money, surely you'd tell the authorities that Molly and Sara were alive?"

"Amateur move," Julian explained. He had started breathing more heavily as the slope got steeper. They had now reached the wooded area, but the trees stood far apart and only offered sporadic protection from the sun above. "To be honest with you, I wanted to ask for ransom right away, but the Hermit knew better. Ask for ransom and the authorities keep looking. Tell them the victim is dead and in a ditch somewhere, they lose interest after a while. Then you can re-emerge and ask for ransom on your own terms. You understand, yes? Despite that, after the police failed to capture you, the Hermit realised that he wanted to meet with you himself."

"Why?"

"We have many questions for you. Maybe I can ask some of them today?"

Stuart took a deep breath, trying to keep his legs moving. He needed strength.

"What's happened to Sara?" he asked.

Julian stopped and looked at him gravely.

"She's dead."

The news hit him hard. Stuart lost his strength and he sank down onto the ground. This had been his greatest fear since losing sight of her last night.

"Trigger-happy guards," Julian said. "But these are the consequences of trying to escape. Come on, Mr Gleeman."

Stuart was consumed with guilt. It was his fault. He should never have tried to escape without a clear plan, without properly talking it through with Molly and Sara beforehand. Two guards scooped him up and pushed him onwards. He tried to get his mind back on track. He was out in the middle of nowhere with a violent cartel lieutenant, who might actually be the boss himself. Stuart had not forgotten his idea that Julian had invented the myth of the Hermit. Current events would suggest that Stuart had had the right idea. So this was not the time to get lost in dark emotions.

Before long they reached a larger clearing, which was occupied by old earthworks. It looked like a house might have stood there a long time ago, its rectangular foundation now overgrown by bushes and long grass. Julian sat down on a boulder and seemed genuinely at ease with being outdoors. This was far removed from the palatial splendour of the Red Widow's estate. Stuart could not imagine her trekking up this peak. He perched himself down on a smaller, neighbouring boulder.

"What would happen if someone assassinated the English Prince?"

"What?" Stuart asked sheepishly.

It took a while for his mind to recall what they had uncovered about the Hermit's plan. Assassinate the Prince, and possibly the President, when they visited Cartagena. He recalled that the Prince was visiting on Monday. Today was Good Friday. The clock was ticking.

"The Prince. The English guy who makes his own cheese." Julian looked contemplative for a moment. "I respect that, you know. I also make my own cheese. It's for my restaurants in Bogotá. What would happen if he was assassinated?"

Stuart did not really know what to say. At least the question confirmed what they had uncovered about the cartel. It explained, without doubt, the British government's interest in the Hermit. It emphasised the danger that Tara Lawson posed, if she indeed was working for the cartel.

Stuart's legal mind, greatly shrivelled up after more than a week in the tropical heat, tried to assess the evidence against her. A redheaded woman had been seen when Robert and Roderic were killed. Carolina had met a redheaded woman in the embassy. Stuart had seen a redheaded woman last night at the main house. Was this all the same person? Then there was the damning initial in the photograph Manuel had taken. There was the person on the other side of the text message Stuart had sent last Friday, which had led the cartel to the bus station in Medellín. No, ultimately it did not look good for Tara Lawson.

But how could he be sure she was on the cartel's side? Maybe she was one of the good ones, and had managed to infiltrate the cartel in order to help take them down? How could he be sure of anything?

"What would happen?" Julian asked again.

"Not much, I think, if I'm to be honest."

"Really?"

Now it was Julian's turn to be taken aback.

"People would be sad for a bit, like when any public figure dies. They'd leave flowers at Buckingham Palace."

"Yes?"

"What do you think would happen?" Stuart asked.

"Would it overthrow the government?"

Stuart managed to smile to himself. It was an interesting question. As a lawyer, Stuart knew very well that you learn more about your opponent by the questions they ask than by the answers they give.

"There would definitely be questions asked. There would be an investigation into what had happened and why it wasn't prevented."

He thought about the tragedy of Princess Diana. The cynic in him recalled that the government had managed to come out stronger after it.

Julian sighed.

"That is not what I wanted to hear," he said. "Perhaps we overestimated the impact when we agreed on this plan?"

"What did you expect would happen?"

Julian stood up and animatedly walked around the clearing.

"National outcry. Riots. The government falling."

"An opportunity for you to establish yourself in Britain?"

Julian stopped and looked at Stuart with a broad grin.

"I knew you would understand."

"That's unlikely, at least in Britain. Anyway, the next election is scheduled in thirteen months. The government would just hold on until then." He chuckled. "And the coalition government is very unpopular, no one expects them to be re-elected. Then you'd just have to start all over again."

Julian sat back down on the boulder.

"That is very disappointing. The Hermit will be displeased." He paused for a moment. "What if someone blew up a British warship? Maybe at the same time as the assassination?"

Now Stuart started to get worried. Not at the plan, but what the plan revealed. This was not just an ambitious drug cartel, this was starting to sound like a madman who had lost grip of reality.

"I think you'd be insane to attack a British warship," he said.

"No, not at all. One of them is coming to Cartagena, together with the Prince. I would use our submarine to plant explosives on its hull. They wouldn't be expecting that whilst docked."

"You have a submarine?" Stuart asked incredulously.

"Of course. No self-respecting drug cartel is without one."

Stuart felt bewildered.

"Is that what you wanted to ask me? Confirmation that your plan would topple the British government and you could reign supreme as a crime lord?"

"The Hermit wishes for many things," Julian said. Now he instead sounded like a rational man who dismissed the plans as ludicrous. "As I said, we might have been too optimistic."

"I would think so," Stuart said.

"Of course we could ransom you and Molly, as well," Julian added, almost as an afterthought. That sounded like the most rational part of the plan.

However, Stuart knew that the British government had taken the whole thing seriously. Seriously enough to send him to meet Manuel's family. He knew the clock was ticking down. He would have to think of something, other than another foolhardy attempt at escaping. Despite the insanity of the plans, having this knowledge made him relax. Now he knew what he was up against. He took a deep breath and looked around the clearing. He became aware again of the birds twittering around him, and he saw another eagle soaring through the valley. It made him smile, for a moment.

He then remembered where he was and who he was with, and his face hardened again. Julian understood.

"You mustn't think that I enjoy the violence," Julian said. "But this is a kill or be killed world. You understand? I execute violence only when necessary. It establishes authority. The Hermit will be very powerful once we carry out the assassination. Very powerful indeed."

Stuart thought back to Juan and the Red Widow. They both seemed to have had a point in their lives when everything changed, perhaps when some anger inside them welled up and they had to let it out. The Red Widow had started killing. Juan had thankfully managed to contain it and joined the church.

"So where did your path of violence start?" he asked Julian.

"My family is from a run-down town near Cartagena. Some of us have managed to get out, make a success out of our lives, live up to our family name. I realised that I had to fight for success, and ultimately kill for it. And here I am, living in splendour."

"And you have a girlfriend to match," Stuart dared suggest.

Julian glared angrily at him and Stuart had to backtrack as quickly as he could.

"I'm sorry I couldn't give you the answers you wanted," he said, trying to sound polite and genuine. "Assassination or not, I don't think you'll be successful, whatever your plans are."

Julian scoffed.

"Well, at least we should get some ransom for you and Molly," he said. He stepped off the boulder he had been sitting on. "I have appreciated our conversation. I will report your observations back to the Hermit."

Stuart tilted his head and dared ask the question.

"Does the Hermit really exist?"

Julian chuckled.

"Oh, yes. I promise, I am not the Hermit. Your thoughts will be appreciated but I'm sure that we will proceed as planned." Julian now gestured vaguely towards the sky. "We must head back now. The storm will come soon."

Stuart was taken aback. He looked up at the clear blue sky, from where the sun was beating down with the same ferocity it had every day.

"What storm?"

"It is Good Friday," Julian said. "The day of Jesus's crucifixion. There is always a storm at three in the afternoon. The hour of His death."

Stuart looked up at the blue sky again but did not say anything. Baseless superstition, he thought and realised the priests had not really rubbed off on him. He sighed. The priests. What was he going to do about them?

They had almost returned to the Alpine chalet when Stuart, to his amazement, saw that the sky was darkening as black clouds emerged from the east. He heard thunder rumbling, just as it had last night. Good Friday, Julian remarked again. There is a storm every year. Stuart was perplexed but his eyes and ears were not lying. The storm was quickly closing in.

Once at the chalet, they jumped into an open-top Jeep

and set off across the base of the valley, following a dirt track back towards the main house. As they crossed the bridge, thunder rumbled again, closer and louder this time, but through it, Stuart heard something else. A rapid, mechanical beating, coming from above.

He looked up and in addition to storm clouds he saw two large helicopters swooping into the valley.

Chapter 30

Back on Wednesday afternoon, Antonio was walking across the top of the Rock at Guatapé, towards the solitary figure at the far end, hoping that it was Felipe Hernandez. His mind was focused on the task at hand, to take down the Hermit and his vicious drug cartel. He had spent every spare moment over the past few days mentally preparing for the end and what he would do once he finally got to meet the Hermit. He knew what he wanted to do, that was always the easy part, but he did not have a clear plan for how to actually carry it out. That would be the challenge. He would have think of a way.

He had passed the kiosk, which stood at the centre of the Rock's top, when he heard a commotion behind him. He turned around. A few tourists were gawping confusedly towards the top of the stairs, but the kiosk blocked the view and he could not see what they were looking at. He would have turned back towards Felipe Hernandez but some of the tourists started shouting towards him, waving him over.

"I think the other priest was chased off by some man," a young, foreign tourist said in broken Spanish when Antonio had walked over.

"Explain," Juan demanded, catching up.

The tourist described, alongside interjections from his friends who had gathered around, that he had seen the third priest hang back a bit, and after being approached by some tough looking man, had turned and rapidly run down the stairs, chased after by the tough man.

Alarmed, Juan and Antonio quickly moved to the edge of the Rock and looked down. The Rock extended out a bit and they could not see the bottom of the stairs, but a bit further out, on the road, they saw a tiny figure in priest's black being pushed into a car, which quickly sped off.

"Oh, Mother of God," Juan muttered quietly and dutifully made the sign of the cross.

Antonio was astonished. It took him a few moments to make sense of what he had just seen.

"The third cartel soldier," he said.

"Yes," Juan said and nodded. "We have been found."

Carolina looked equally astonished. She stood still, leaning over the railing, and followed the car with her eyes for as long as she could, as it sped down the winding roads off into the distance. It disappeared from view behind the large precipice on which the car park was situated, but then returned on the other side, passing by a large hotel resort, over a long bridge, and then finally disappeared in the thick forests on the islets beyond.

Antonio also followed the car with his eyes and sighed heavily once it finally disappeared. There was nothing they could do. Even if they had immediately raced down the stairs towards their own car they had had no chance of catching up with Stuart's captors. They also did not know where the car was heading.

He was nudged by Juan, who gestured towards the solitary figure they had believed to be Felipe Hernandez. The figure had walked over to the railings on this side of the Rock and had been observing Stuart's capture as well. Antonio and Carolina followed Juan as he walked along the top of the Rock, past the kiosk again, and up to the man.

"Mr Hernandez?" Juan asked.

"Yes," the man said and extended his hand.

They greeted him in a dampened mood. Antonio kept glancing towards the islands where he had last seen Stuart's car. He felt a surge of anger. Felipe Hernandez better have all the answers.

"The Red Widow told me what you want to know," Felipe said, also glancing out over the archipelago. "I have a sense that the information is suddenly more urgent."

"Yes, it is," Carolina said forcefully. "And what the hell was the point of dragging us up here?"

"I have all my preliminary business meetings up here," Felipe said in a carefree manner, which further angered

Carolina. "Climbing those stairs is proof of commitment. I certainly didn't expect that one of you would get kidnapped." He looked down towards the parking area far below and shook his head. "I was going to ask if you really knew what you're up against, but you clearly do." He paused again. "So, who is the Hermit? No one knows, right?"

Carolina's heart sank as she heard this.

"But, I know where you might find him, or at least, one of his top lieutenants. There is a large estate in the Herrera Valley, south of Medellín." He retrieved a printed map from his pocket and handed it to Juan. "I have marked it for you."

Antonio leaned in and studied the map together with Juan and Carolina. He saw the Herrera Valley, which was marked by a red X, in the sparsely populated area south of Medellín. He guessed that it would take perhaps an hour or so to drive there. This seemed like a remote estate and was a perfect base for a drug lord to hide out in. He had a strong feeling that he would find the Hermit there. Then he would finally get closure and his pain would be lifted.

"Please tell the Red Widow that I have delivered as promised," Felipe said and indicated that he was leaving. "I don't want any trouble from her."

"You haven't really delivered," Juan said. "But with someone as elusive as the Hermit, maybe this is as good as it gets."

"It is."

With that, Felipe hurriedly left and headed down the stairs. Still in disbelief, Antonio, Juan and Carolina looked out over the archipelago below and the rising mountains beyond. An eagle soared by, which lifted Antonio's spirits. Yes, he was certain that it would all work out in the end. As long as he did not lose hope.

"We must plan what we do next," Juan said carefully. "At least we have the final piece of the puzzle."

"Well, we have to go there and get him out," Carolina said anxiously and tried to walk off towards the stairs.

Antonio and Juan shook their heads and held her back.

"That seems reckless," Antonio said. He did not want to take any unnecessary risks that could compromise his endgame. He had to remain calm. He turned to Juan. "Do you think we should go there and explore the area?"

"Yes, but we have to be very careful," Juan said. "Who knows how many locals are loyal to the Hermit?"

They walked back to the stairs and quickly headed down the staircase. Many of the tourists were staring at them with curious looks but no one said anything. Once they were back in Juan's car they studied the map once more and then Juan set off. As they were about to leave the access road they saw a police car speeding up the main road. It turned off and sped up towards the Rock. Juan grimaced.

"I completely overlooked that someone might have called the police," he admitted.

Juan drove down the winding roads, going as fast as he dared, heading back towards Medellín before turning south, passing the airport in Rionegro, then through the town of La Ceja and its bustling main square complete with colonial-era church, and finally onto increasingly poor and winding roads into the mountains. Despite the decrepit state of the roads, there was a steady flow of traffic, including buses and trucks, most driving with scant regard for anyone's safety.

"Does this road actually lead anywhere?" Antonio had to ask after a while.

They had passed a few hamlets and settlements but he could not work out where all the traffic was coming from.

"Oh, yes," Juan said. "Eventually you reach Manizales, the capital of coffee country. Or you can turn left after a while and go up to Bogotá."

A while later, Juan pulled up by a small roadside shop, which was nothing more than an old wooden cabin. The road was running high up along the side of the valley and the parking space offered a commanding view. They headed in and bought the bright orange Colombiana soft drink and a bag full of cheese balls which were freshly fried to order. They ate by the edge, keenly filling up on energy after the long morning, and looked out over the valley. On the opposite side, roughly to the north, a tall peak rose up, dominating the skyline. Down in the valley was a small, sleepy village, complete with a disproportionately large church.

"Is this the valley?" Antonio asked, biting into his first cheese ball.

"No," Juan said. He pointed towards the tall peak. "It's the next valley over, beyond the ridge."

"How do we get there?"

"We'll drive down to the village and then climb up the ridge," Juan said. "From there we can observe the Herrera Valley from above. Hopefully, that will give us a better understanding of how to approach the cartel."

Once they had finished eating Juan bought some water bottles from the shop, and then they returned to the car and drove down into the village. It consisted of only a few streets with old, whitewashed buildings, some of which were in great disrepair, and even the good ones had façades that were slowly chipping away. Juan parked in front of the church, which was firmly and securely locked up. Antonio looked up at the peak towering above them. Thankfully the ridge of the valley was only about halfway up, and he hoped that that would be all they would have to climb.

They set off walking down the empty street. The afternoon sun was pressing down on them and Antonio soon felt himself dripping with sweat. He focused on the task and managed to keep going at a good pace. At the edge of the village, they found a path and headed out across the uncultivated fields. In the distance they saw some farmers tending the land, but no one seemed to have noticed them. Soon the ground started tilting upwards and the climb got more and more challenging. His legs were aching, and he started to get annoyed by the high, unkempt grass which kept brushing up against them.

It took more than an hour to reach the top of the ridge. They were all breathing heavily and Juan handed out the water bottles. They sat down on the ground in silence for a moment, looking back down on the village they had come from.

"Let's turn around," Juan said once they had regained their strength.

They carefully crossed over the top of the ridge and got their first glimpse down into the Herrera Valley. It was long and deep, and mostly empty. A small river ran through its centre, which could be crossed by an old iron bridge. Some of the land was split into pastures and Antonio thought he could see a group of cows in one enclosure. A few buildings were scattered around, including, on the opposite side of the valley, a very large house. At this distance, it was difficult to make out any details as the house was shimmering in the heat haze.

"That must be the base," Juan suggested.

"I wonder where they're keeping Stuart?" Carolina asked, but there was nothing that pointed to an obvious location to hide prisoners.

They spent a few minutes studying the valley and they all took numerous photos with their phones. Suddenly, Antonio spotted movement on a path further down the valley. Two men were walking along, guns in their hands.

"Let's move," Antonio said. "Someone's coming."

They turned around and quickly scurried away, heading down the other side. It was a few minutes' sprint until they reached the first cluster of trees. They stopped inside the treeline and looked back towards the ridge. There was no movement to be seen. Antonio wiped the sweat off his face and finished one of the water bottles.

"I guess those were guards, patrolling the perimeter," Carolina said. "We certainly found the right place."

"Well, we got the photos," Antonio said, making sure his phone was safe in his pocket. "We can study them in peace back in Medellín."

Satisfied that no one was observing them from the

ridge, they quickly headed back down to the village. It was still bizarrely empty and quiet. They got in the car and drove away as fast as they could.

"Who do we call to help us?" Antonio asked as they were back out on the main road, heading northwards towards Medellín.

"The army," Juan said. "They have special units to deal with this. They're our best bet. We haven't seen any army personnel in the photos from Manuel's camera."

"Sounds good. So, do they have a phone number?"

Carolina sighed in the back seat.

"I'll call my uncle," she said. "I know he has some contacts." She sighed again. "We should probably look at those photos again, make sure we haven't missed anything."

"Agreed," Antonio said. "But let's start with your uncle."

After a few conversations on the phone, Carolina had good news. The commander of the local Gaula Group, the army's specialist hostage rescue unit, would meet them the following morning at an army base outside Medellín.

"Isn't time of the essence?" Antonio asked incredulously. "To rescue Stuart and Molly?"

"They said tomorrow morning," Carolina said. "I'm not going to argue with the army."

They returned to Medellín and dropped off Carolina at her apartment building. They agreed to meet early the following morning to head out to the army base. Their aim was to convince the army to stage an assault on the Hermit's base and rescue Stuart and Molly. Carolina agreed that it was a good plan and she was certain that the Gaula unit would assist them.

Juan and Antonio returned to the church and sat down in peace in the inner courtyard. James was scurrying around preparing the church for its Maundy Thursday services. Juan explained to him briefly that he and Father Pedro would have to take the lead. James seemed very curious but Juan did not provide an explanation.

"You should probably tell him what's going on," Antonio said when James had left. "He seemed very unhappy earlier that we were helping Stuart."

"Maybe," Juan said slowly. He turned and looked solemnly at Antonio. "Are you sure you want to proceed with this?"

Antonio took a deep breath.

"I need this weight lifted off me," he said. "Please don't back out now."

"*Vengeance is mine, says the Lord*," Juan said, quoting from the Bible.

"Yes, I know."

"The Lord also commands: *You shall not murder*."

Antonio nodded.

"I fear you're risking your eternal soul, my friend," Juan said. He paused and looked closely at Antonio. "But then I'm not sure you believe in the eternal soul."

"I try," Antonio said slowly. "I really do try."

Juan sat in silence for a moment.

"I'm no stranger to revenge," he said. "I guess all the more so since Guillermo was murdered. But I do worry about you."

Antonio smiled.

"I appreciate that, but I know what I have to do."

**

Maundy Thursday dawned. At the Church of Santa Teresa, Juan led an early morning service. Carolina had driven down and sat silently at the far back. After the service had finished, the three of them got into Juan's car and headed off towards the army base. Antonio was sure that they had almost reached the end of the journey. His mind was focused like it had never been before.

In Bogotá, William Cooth left his hotel and walked to the Embassy. His mind was gradually descending into a state of paralysing panic. The past few days had not turned up any further information, which was becoming a very real problem. How could there be no evidence about the identity of the Hermit? To be able to operate with such deadly consequences, and still maintain total anonymity, spoke of someone with serious power and influence.

There was also no new information about the threat to the Prince. All the spy agencies assured him that there was no mention of this attack in any of the communications that they monitored. This told Cooth that they were monitoring the wrong people, another remarkable achievement by the Hermit. However, Monday was steadily coming closer. Cooth had spent the night thinking through the implications of cancelling the Prince's visit and he had finally agreed that it was a decision he was prepared to take.

Tara and the Ambassador were waiting in the Ambassador's office.

"Her Majesty is celebrating Maundy Thursday in Blackburn today," the Ambassador remarked with a certain amount of disdain. "What an awful place that is."

"Isn't Mrs Ambassador from Blackburn?" Cooth asked pointedly with a faint smile. He enjoyed reminding the diplomats that he really did know everything about them.

The Ambassador squirmed and nodded.

"Indeed," he said.

"So, do you have any new leads, Tara?" Cooth asked, keen to move on.

"No," Tara said. "I've been reaching out to my contacts, but I am not getting anything. Either they genuinely don't know or they're too afraid to tell me. I'm almost at a dead end."

"Almost?"

"There are a few people in Medellín that might be helpful, and perhaps even more so if I go and meet them in person."

The Ambassador shook his head.

"No, I can't let anyone else go to Medellín."

"Not really your call," Cooth pointed out. "But I do have some misgivings myself."

The Ambassador angrily leaned forward over his desk.

"What the hell do you mean, not my call? It's my bloody staff..."

"If you say so," Cooth said calmly.

"Look," Tara interjected. "I'm getting nowhere on the phone. Meeting them in person could make all the difference, and we need answers."

Cooth agreed with her.

"What's your plan?"

"I can fly down right away and have some meetings," she said. "I'll stay the night if necessary, keep at it tomorrow. Honestly, I'm out of options at this end."

"What has the Colombian national police said about this cartel?" the Ambassador asked. "You met with that Colonel yesterday."

"Colonel Zapata, yes." Cooth shook his head. "Well, the situation is this. The police only have limited information on the cartel."

"How limited?"

"Well, they know it exists."

"Huh," the Ambassador said and leaned back. "Anything else?"

"Maybe. The police have their eye on a few professionals in Medellín, who might be helping the cartel, not least with banking, but there doesn't seem to be much to it. They keep arresting low-level members, both in Medellín and up north by the coast, but that has no long-term impact."

"Have they spoken to those professionals?"

"Yes."

"And?" the Ambassador pressed.

Cooth shook his head.

"They haven't been able to climb up the food chain. Colonel Zapata said they know of someone who might be senior enough to make some decisions, but this is far from being able to identify the top lieutenants, let alone identifying the Hermit."

"All the more reason for me to go down there myself,"

Tara said.

"I accept that," Cooth said. "Have we got anything else on this Mr D?"

"No," the Ambassador said. "The information is a bit vague."

"Too vague," Tara said. "We can't do anything with that, if all we know is that he works for the government."

"Yes, and the government can mean anything," the Ambassador pointed out.

They contemplated this in silence for a moment. It really was a dead end.

"Are you happy for me to leave now?" Tara asked.

Cooth nodded.

"Good luck. Call me immediately if you learn of anything."

"I will."

Tara stood up and walked out of the office. The Ambassador stared blankly into space for a moment.

"Do you know anything about who this Hermit is?" he asked.

"No," Cooth said. He glanced down on one of the newspapers that the Ambassador had on his desk. "For all we know it might be her," he said and gestured towards the headline.

The Ambassador picked up the newspaper and chuckled.

"Really? Wouldn't surprise me, you know."

"She meets all the criteria," Cooth said. "She has a position of power. She is the ranking member of the Intelligence Committee in Congress, so she will have detailed knowledge of military and law enforcement operations, including the security arrangements for the Prince's visit. With that knowledge and power, it's understandable that the Hermit has remained anonymous whilst being so successful. And, she has a passionate hatred of the West, so I doubt there are any moral qualms in exporting drugs or assassinating the Prince. And if the President was assassinated too, I guess her chances of success would go up."

The Ambassador listened carefully.

"Bloody hell," he said eventually. "Senator Reyes, the Hermit? Blimey, she might be the next president!"

"That would be alarming."

"Have you asked Tara about this?"

"No," Cooth said. "I just thought of it now when I saw the headline. Why?"

The Ambassador could not stop himself from grinning.

"So much for knowing everything. Her boyfriend, Julian Reyes. He is a distant cousin of some sort to the Senator. He owns some restaurants in town. I even had dinner in one of them once."

Cooth quickly absorbed the news.

"This boyfriend, is he close to the Senator?"

"No," the Ambassador said. "From what I understand, the Senator is estranged from her family. You know, Congressman Escaso, from the Foreign Affairs Committee, he was adamant that none of the Reyes family would even be voting for her."

"Well, this is a delicate matter to put to Tara. I'll look into it. I don't know that Senator Reyes is the Hermit, it was just a thought, but she meets the criteria."

"Indeed, but so do many others, I guess," the Ambassador remarked.

"I'm not sure if the list is actually that long," Cooth said. "To have the authority and insight to pull this off, sure, there are others than Senator Reyes, but it's not a long list."

The Ambassador sighed.

"Anyway, I have reached a decision," Cooth said. "I need you to go and see the President. We have to seriously explore the option of cancelling the Prince's visit."

"They'll never agree to that," the Ambassador said immediately. "They'll just insist on bringing in more security."

Cooth nodded but looked insistent.

"Fine, I'll go to the Presidential Palace," the Ambassador

said.

Cooth spent the rest of the morning in Tara's office, where he had installed himself, reading through the national police file on the Hermit's cartel, detailing the low-level arrests that had taken place. The file, however, was discouragingly brief. Colonel Zapata had insisted that the police had been focusing on more important criminals and that until all these Englishmen had started going missing and being murdered, the Hermit cartel had not been seen as a major problem, even though it was clearly bringing in a lot of money from cocaine smuggling. There are always going to be low-level criminals, the Colonel had explained. They are always going to be greater in number than the police's resources. Unfortunate, but true. Cooth had hesitantly accepted the Colonel's reasoning.

At lunchtime, Cooth tracked down the details of Julian Reyes' restaurants and took a taxi to the only one that served lunch. The young and busty waitress recommended bean stew and explained that Mr Reyes sadly was not in today. Cooth stayed for lunch anyway and was on his way back to the embassy when Colonel Zapata called and asked to see him immediately. Cooth diverted his taxi to the National Police building.

After a brief meeting with the Colonel, Cooth left feeling uplifted and energetic. Perhaps things were going to work out after all. He waited patiently for the Ambassador to return from the Presidential Palace and then went to the Ambassador's office.

"The President is adamant," the Ambassador said as Cooth stepped in. "He's going to Cartagena on Monday morning."

"As expected, then."

"Yes, he's afraid he'll lose the election if he backs down to this threat, and that would likely mean the end to the peace negotiations with the FARC. It is too important, and he accepts the risks involved."

"He manages to sound like a politician and a president at the same time," Cooth observed. "I'm impressed."

"Well, there's a rich history of assassinated politicians in this country. He takes the threat seriously but he can't be seen as being weaker than those other guys. And he reminded me that I'll be standing next to him and that hopefully I can stop the bullets for him."

"A valiant end to your diplomatic career."

"Indeed."

"At any rate, I have good news, which should save you from being cannon fodder. Colonel Zapata finally has a lead!"

"That's good news," the Ambassador exclaimed.

"An unexpected lead, I must say, but it seems credible. A priest in Medellín came forward to a local Gaula team, with information about where the Hermit cartel might be based and, indeed, where they might be holding the hostages."

"A priest?"

"Yes, I don't know what that is about. First of all, there is a suggestion that Molly Reed might be one of the hostages held there."

The Ambassador took a deep breath and clapped his hands.

"That's the best news I have heard."

"The other hostage is Stuart Gleeman."

"The lawyer?"

"Yes." Cooth nodded. "Yes, I don't understand what happened to him, but being kidnapped by the cartel would explain his disappearance and radio silence."

"So what's the army doing?"

"Things are moving surprisingly fast for this large bureaucracy. Given the severity of the situation, with the threat to the President, the Gaula team wants to storm this location tomorrow. They'll spend tonight making preparations."

"That would be a forceful end to the cartel," the Ambassador said resolutely. "It would alleviate all concerns for Monday. How very wonderful!"

"Yes, indeed." Cooth hesitated. "It's a lucky break,

which always worries me. I'm spending the afternoon digging up what I can about this priest. Anyway, the Colonel will let me know the final details when he has them, but he did invite me to ride along."

"Are you happy with that?"

"It has been a while since I stormed a place by helicopter, but yes. I'll be sitting in the back, anyway. I think they just want someone to blame if it all goes pear shaped."

"Ah, yes, the foreign consultant who duped the army into raiding Medellín. The Foreign Secretary is not helping you out of that one."

"Of course not." Cooth chuckled at the reality of his life. "Officially, the Foreign Secretary doesn't know I'm here, doesn't know who I am or that I even exist. But I should be there, see if I can secure our people."

"Good. Where is this place?"

"Some valley, south of Medellín. Rather remote, hence the choppers."

"Have you told Tara?"

Cooth shook his head.

"No, I tried calling but I didn't get an answer."

"What?" the Ambassador exclaimed and stood up. "You've lost contact with her too?"

"Relax," Cooth said. "I haven't lost her. As I said before, I trust her, and she can look after herself. She led the British Army through the Iraqi desert. If her phone is off, it just means that she's meeting with her contacts."

"Okay," the Ambassador said. He walked over to his window and looked out on the street below. It was clear that he was very worried. "Yes, let her do her thing."

"Hopefully I can catch her before the show starts, let her know what's going on. Otherwise, I'll fill her in afterwards."

"Good. Well, flying a helicopter and raiding a Colombian drug cartel, freeing hostages, and saving the Prince and the President from their assassins. That'll be one hell of a show."

Chapter 31

The valley erupted into chaos.

Two large helicopters zoomed in out of the storm and began hovering angrily over the pastures near the main house, searching for a landing zone. Stuart looked up towards the house, which was hardly more than a dot in the distance, and he could see a lot of movement around it. To his alarm, a few gunshots echoed across the valley, overpowering the noise of the helicopters, which were now setting down on the ground and unloading groups of soldiers.

Julian yelled at the driver to get the truck off the path, and soon they stopped inside a clearing. Julian ordered the driver to head up to the main house on foot and help out the other men. The driver picked up a rifle from the back of the truck and set off. Julian produced a gun from his pocket, which he must have been carrying all day. He pointed it at Stuart and motioned for Stuart to follow him.

They ran through the forest, heading uphill. Never getting a step wrong, Julian led Stuart through the trees, past boulders, and over the streams. After a long day of trekking, Stuart was exhausted, and with his whole body soaked in sweat, he was struggling to keep up. He soon realised that they were heading towards the hut where Molly was held. If his mind had been working, this should not have surprised him, since Julian was obviously interested in protecting his other hostage. All Stuart could do was to keep up and hope that Molly had already been rescued.

As they came closer, Julian slowed down. Struggling after him, Stuart tried to spot the cabin through the trees. Finally, he saw it, and to his great relief, he saw a few soldiers standing guard around it. They were all carrying assault rifles and were carefully scanning the treeline.

Julian swore softly, tugged on Stuart's shirt, and led him away. They ran back down into the valley, racing through the trees and the thickening undergrowth, which slowed their progress. Time and again they heard gunshots echoing through the valley. At least one of the helicopters was airborne again and Stuart could see it hovering through the treetops. By now, he was drenched in sweat, his throat was burning and he struggled to breathe.

"Slow down," he croaked, but Julian simply waved the gun in his direction.

They continued on towards the eastern end of the valley. Julian seemed to have a specific destination in mind since he rushed as fast as the vegetation allowed without any hesitation. By now, the storm was upon them and it had started to rain. The water poured down with increasing ferocity but the humidity was not letting up.

This section of the valley, which Stuart had not been in before, was covered in thick woods and they made it down to the riverbed without crossing any fields. Stuart could see that both of the helicopters were airborne again. One was close to the main house and the second one was further away on the other side of the valley. Neither had any chance of seeing Stuart. Julian praised their luck and then sprinted across the riverbed and into the water. The river was shallow and though Stuart's soles did not provide much protection from the rocky bottom, they were quickly across and made it into another patch of trees, which offered some shelter from the heavy rain.

"There is a cabin at the end of the valley," Julian explained, now also struggling for breath. He wiped sweat and rain from his head. "I have supplies there." He tried to take some deep breaths but was clearly struggling with a burning throat. "There are more men waiting there. We must get out of the valley."

Stuart nodded. There was nothing else he could do. Julian set off, occasionally waving his gun towards Stuart as a reminder not to resist, and Stuart followed after. His throat had dried up completely but he had recovered his breath during the short break. He kept looking around, hoping to see some soldiers, but there were none in sight.

To his dismay, he remembered how big the valley actually was. If the soldiers were concentrating on the main house, there was every possibility that there would be none at this supply cabin.

They trekked for a good half hour. Julian was emboldened by the fact that the helicopters were still hovering around the main house, which was now a good distance away. The pilots were clearly not searching for anyone trying to escape and through the heavy rain, it was not clear how much visibility they actually had. Stuart had not heard any gunshots in a long time, but he tried to imagine the chaos that was undoubtedly surrounding the main house, as the army was rounding up the cartel soldiers. At some point, surely, they would realise that he was not amongst them. Then they would come looking.

Finally, they reached the cabin. It was situated at the base of the eastern slope, which did not rise very high up. Crossing the ridge would be fairly straightforward, which dismayed Stuart. The longer they were inside this valley, the better the chance that the army would spot them. If they got out of the valley, all bets were off. Julian slowed down and carefully scanned the area, but there were no soldiers around. Julian smiled but Stuart's heart sank. The odds of being rescued were rapidly diminishing.

Two men jumped out of the front door as they approached, aiming their guns at them. Stuart stopped, hoping they would be soldiers, but quickly realised that the scruffy, middle-aged men worked for the cartel. They entered a sparsely decorated sitting room, where a handful of armed men were hanging around, waiting for instructions.

As he was pushed further into the room, Stuart saw that Molly was sitting on one of the sofas, a gun pointed at her head. She looked terrified, and as they saw each other, both looked equally disappointed that the other had not been rescued.

"We have been betrayed," Julian said angrily. "We must leave immediately."

"What about the men at the house?" Stuart asked, desperate to slow down their escape in the hope of being rescued.

Julian did not reply but simply gave Stuart a push forwards. There was nothing more he could do to stall. They hurried out the back door, where two large but battered SUVs were parked under the protection of a few palm trees. The rain had let up and it seemed like the sun was about to break through the clouds again.

"Wait, where is Sara?" Molly asked, desperately looking around.

"Your little friend is dead," Julian said, cutting in before Stuart had the chance to reply more diplomatically.

Molly went pale and stared at Julian with surging anger. Suddenly, with an anguished squeal, she lunged forward and attacked him. Julian, taken by surprise, staggered a few steps backwards but did not topple over. He quickly grabbed her by her arms and pushed her off him. His men, who had quickly formed a circle around the spectacle, were sniggering and gleefully shouting encouragements. One of the men grabbed a tight hold of Stuart and stopped him from intervening.

"Relax," Julian said as Molly eventually gave up the fight. "But remember, it will be you who dies if you try to escape again."

Subdued, Stuart and Molly were bundled into the backseat of the first SUV, together with a henchman who kept his gun pointed at them. Julian sat down in the front together with a driver. The two SUVs set off down a grass path, heading eastwards. The path was almost entirely flanked by trees, making it ideal for a quick and safe exit. The army would need to know exactly where to look if they were to spot the vehicles through the vegetation.

The path followed the river through a narrow gorge and they had soon left the valley behind and entered another one, just as spectacularly verdant. A family of eagles soared above, undisturbed by the helicopters on the other side of the ridge.

The dirt path wound its way up the slope of the valley and eventually, after many twists and turns, they reached the main road. They joined it and headed north, now wedged between cars, trucks and buses. To Stuart, still a captive, it was a bizarre interaction with civilization. He looked out the window but it was tinted black. No one on the outside could see his desperate plea for help.

The driver expressed a concern about a roadblock, but at the moment everything seemed fine. Julian, with his hostages, seemed to have escaped unscathed.

**

"What the hell happened?"

The Ambassador was staring at Cooth, who looked rather beaten. Friday evening had set, and Cooth had returned to Bogotá and gone straight to the embassy. He felt exhausted after the raid but had to fill in the Ambassador on the failure.

"No one of importance was there," Cooth explained. "Not the Hermit, not his lieutenants, not any hostages. But the army is still searching the valley. It has a lot of properties and hideouts."

"It's a fucking nightmare," the Ambassador yelled and violently pounded his desk with his fists.

"At least it was the right place," Cooth said. "This priest came through. The army captured about a dozen men, who confessed to working for the cartel. They confiscated weapons. I don't think the National Police knew about this house before, so who knows what will be uncovered."

"So what? It's less than seventy-two bloody hours until the Prince will be traipsing around Cartagena with a target on his back."

"It's time to cancel."

The Ambassador opened his mouth but did not say anything.

"It's time," Cooth repeated more forcefully. "We can't

let the Prince come. I spoke to Colonel Zapata before I flew back here. He agrees."

The Ambassador buried his head in his hands, elbows on his desk.

"The Foreign Secretary's going to hit the roof," he said suddenly. "And they're going to send me to fucking Mongolia!"

"Well, it's very nice out there."

"Fuck you!"

"I need you to remain calm, sir," Cooth said sternly.

The Ambassador sank back in his chair and nodded slowly.

"Yes, I'm sorry."

"I need you to call London and then speak to the President."

"Yes."

"I also have work to do. The priest was at the Hermit's house this afternoon."

"Really?"

"Oh, yes. Him, another priest, and a lawyer. Colonel Zapata spoke to them, but I didn't have the chance, unfortunately. An interesting group, he said. They admitted to having helped Stuart Gleeman over the past week, but that the cartel finally captured him."

"So he's alive?"

"I would think so. They also said that Molly Reed was a hostage and that they were sure that she was alive as well."

"That's, well, that's better than her being dead."

"Quite. The trick now is finding them."

The Ambassador nodded again.

"Yes, how are you going to do that?"

"Well, I spoke to Tara, after the raid. It was only then that I managed to get hold of her. She sounded shocked when I told her about the raid. I think she was disappointed that she had not found out about this house on her own. Anyway, the cartel thinks the Prince's visit is still on. The only logical assumption is that they are now heading for Cartagena. The airports are on lockdown, and there is only one road to Cartagena, Route 25, and the National Police have already set up roadblocks. Tara said she had managed to get some intelligence, which is that the cartel might have a safe house of sorts further up that road."

The Ambassador grunted.

"Sounds promising, I guess. I'm glad she has some intelligence."

"I agree. It isn't always easy to obtain. For good measure, Colonel Zapata said they also have a roadblock on the other road heading north from Medellín, Route 62, but it only leads to smaller towns near the Panamanian border."

"Good. Did you ask her about the identity of the Hermit?"

Cooth sighed.

"I asked her about the Reyes family. She insisted that her boyfriend has no contact with the Senator, but she found it hard to believe that the Senator was the Hermit."

"So her contacts had no information as to his identity?"

"No."

"Too bad. So what's Tara doing now?"

"She offered to go to Cartagena, to see what she can learn there. If the cartel is not apprehended tonight at the roadblocks, or elsewhere, I propose to go to Cartagena myself tomorrow."

"Sounds good." The Ambassador sighed. "Right, I have a very bad phone call to make."

**

Stuart watched in agony as the two SUVs drove through central Medellín. There was absolutely nothing he could do. He tried banging on the window, but the henchman who sat in the backseat together with him and Molly reached over and rapped him on the head. Stuart stopped. Molly just shook her head. It was a hopeless situation.

It was evening now and darkness had fallen. The Medellín valley was, as always, lit up by the shimmering lights of the city. It was a world apart from the rural tranquillity of the country estate they had just escaped from. It was Good Friday and the traffic was light, which ensured they made quick progress.

Once past the city centre, they crossed over the river and headed northwest, climbing the western slope of the valley through a part of the city that Stuart had not been to before. He tried to keep track of their direction but was interrupted when Julian suddenly turned on the radio and started singing along to some folk song about lost love. It was so bizarre that Stuart became transfixed long enough to lose sight of where they were. When he looked out of the window again he could see that they were on a main road, heading through a wide gorge up and out of the Medellín valley. Soon they were in the open countryside.

Their progress was then blocked by a toll booth and the henchman in the backseat carefully pointed his gun at Molly and Stuart. The implication was very clear. Neither of them made any sound as the driver paid the toll to the old booth attendant. They then proceeded into a long and narrow tunnel, which was cut through a prodigious peak.

A very long while later, they emerged on the other side. The moon, rising in the early night sky, struggled to illuminate the verdant peaks ahead. The road followed the sides of the valleys as it pressed on northwestwardly, occasionally passing through narrow gorges cut into the mountains. From the road signs, Stuart soon guessed that they were heading towards the town of Santa Fé.

It had been maybe half an hour since they had emerged from the tunnel when Julian received a text message on his phone. He read it, grunted angrily and then told the driver to pull over. Julian and the driver got out and Stuart saw them walking back to speak to the men in the second SUV behind them. Through the trees which lined the road Stuart could see something glinting in the moonlight, which he finally recognised as a being wide river.

"The Cauca River," Molly muttered.

It was the first thing she had said since they had left the valley.

"Thank you," Stuart said.

He was not sure what else he could say. He did not know how she was processing Sara's death, but she did not seem to be taking it well. Additionally, the disappointment of the failed rescue was clear to see, especially since the army had come so close. Stuart did not know how he could possibly hope to cure all that distress now. All he could do was hope that some sort of endgame would eventually present itself.

A few cars and trucks drove past, but the road was fairly quiet. After a while, Julian and the driver returned to the car.

"There is a roadblock up ahead," he said. "On the bridge over the river. We will not be crossing tonight."

"So where are we going?" Stuart asked.

"Always inquisitive! Well, there is a small village further down the river, on this side. We have a house there, where we will stay the night."

Stuart did not say anything else but immediately started plotting ways to escape. If they were staying in a village, then surely he could get someone to come to his assistance?

The driver pulled out and continued down the road. It went inside another ravine and on the other side was a sharp bend, leading to a bridge. A police car was parked at the base of the bridge and police officers were occupied with searching a small truck. The SUVs left the main road at the bend and entered a dirt track, which followed the river back southwards. Trees and bushes grew on both sides, but the river, or rather its reflection in the moonlight, could occasionally be seen through the interstices.

They bumped along for a good twenty minutes before they reached their destination. The village was pleasantly seated on the eastern bank of the river. It was very small, with only a few streets but it did have the obligatory church in the central square. Large fern and palm trees were growing amongst the houses, which were almost all surrounded by large rose bushes. All the houses were single story, again painted in the most vivid colours; whilst some had tiled roofs other had traditional thatched roofs, which gave the village a historical charm.

They drove past the main square, where the Easter revelry was still ongoing, and then up another path which led out of the village. After a while, they reached a secluded farmhouse, which was situated further up on the ridge and provided a panoramic view of the river basin. As he stepped out of the car, Stuart could see both orange and banana trees being grown in orchards, which were laid out around the house. The air was hot and humid, despite the lateness of the hour. The noise from the party down in the village square was clearly audible, but above it, Stuart could hear the clucking of numerous poultry, who were undoubtedly being kept awake.

Julian was greeted by an old man and woman, clearly the couple who owned the farm. Everyone was welcomed inside. The living room was sparsely decorated, with an old and tattered sofa standing next to a wooden table. A colourful quilt adorned one of the whitewashed walls, which were otherwise bare. Some chairs were brought in from the kitchen and Julian and his party were invited to sit.

Stuart and Molly, however, were shoved onto the floor in one of the corners. The old lady offered them each a glass of orange juice, which she explained was freshly pressed from the orchard outside. Julian casually gave her a nod, indicating his approval. Stuart drank greedily, relieved to finally get some energy in his body.

"This is a terrible situation," the old farmer said, speaking to Julian. "I'm sorry to hear about the raid."

"Your hospitality will not go unnoticed," Julian replied.

"When you called earlier, to say you were coming to stay the night, I took the liberty of calling the boss."

Stuart's ears pricked.

"The Hermit will join us in the morning," the farmer said.

Julian sat still for a moment.

"I look forward to it," he said finally. He then turned and spoke more generally to the cartel soldiers. "After we meet the Hermit, we must press on. I need a plan for crossing the river."

Stuart smiled. Despite everything, he was pleased that he would finally meet the Hermit.

**

Antonio rubbed his eyes.

It was late at night and he was sitting by himself in the friary's living room. He tried to understand what had gone wrong. He had spoken to a Colonel in the National Police, a Wilbur Zapata. The Colonel had said that the house definitely belonged to the cartel. There was no doubt that they had raided the right place and the captured cartel soldiers had been very clear: the hostages had been there. Stuart was alive, but somehow the cartel had managed to whisk him away.

However, it was not just the failure to capture the Hermit that made Antonio feel particularly gloomy. Rather, it was the painful and indeed soul wrenching disappointment that he had not been able to carry out his own plan. The very reason he had come to Medellín.

"Vengeance is the Lord's," Juan had reminded him as they had stood on the spacious veranda outside the Hermit's house. Maybe he was right, but Antonio was not ready to accept it just yet. Somehow, somewhere, he was sure that he would be able to put his plan into action.

Suddenly, there was a loud knock on the front door. Antonio suppressed his brooding thoughts and walked into the hall to open the door. Outside stood a young girl, hardly more than twenty, with a dishevelled and exhausted look on her face, giving the impression that she had just stepped out of a horror film.

"Is this the Church of Santa Teresa?" she asked weakly.

"Yes," Antonio said, sounding concerned. "How can we help you?"

"My name is Sara," she said. "I've just escaped from the Hermit."

Chapter 32

Stuart slept uneasily on the floor in the sitting room and it was early in the morning when he was violently awoken. His head was pounding from the heat and exhaustion. Grunting, he managed to sit up and rested his head against the wall. The two henchmen then forcefully shook Molly awake as well. She too groaned in pained enervation but slowly managed to sit up.

"Where are we?" she asked softly.

"The farmhouse," Stuart whispered. "Remember, we fled from the valley."

"Yeah," she sighed. "Yeah, I remember."

As the cartel soldiers were getting together, the farmer and his wife entered. She carried a plate with a large stack of maize pancakes, called arepas, which she offered to everyone, including, finally, to Molly and Stuart. The arepas were still warm and each had a generous helping of molten cheese on top. Stuart ate heartily, realising how hungry he was after the previous day's ordeals. The farmer was chatting to the men but Stuart was too tired to listen. The wife returned with a large carafe of orange juice, which she poured to everyone, Molly and Stuart last. She handed them their glasses with an apologetic look but she did not utter a word. Stuart thanked her, guessing that she was not fully on board with having a group of cartel soldiers and their kidnap victims in her home.

After everyone had eaten, Julian walked into the room and smiled gently.

"I'm afraid the Hermit couldn't make it," he said. Stuart sighed, still not convinced that the Hermit was a real person. "But I have a message from the Hermit, to share with you all."

Julian stopped as he saw Stuart and Molly in the corner. He motioned for them to be removed into the kitchen. The farmer's wife, still not uttering a word, led them to the kitchen and closed the door. However, the door was old and did not close fully, meaning Stuart and Molly could just about hear what was being said in the sitting room.

"Today is a great day," Julian said. The announcement seemed to please the cartel soldiers and the farmer, who had stayed in the room, because they all started cheering. "We weren't raided in the dead of night. The army doesn't know where we are." There was more cheering. "Today, we will press on northwards, to Cartagena, where we will carry on with our plan, undaunted by the army and police."

This was met with further vocal approval. Preaching to the choir, Stuart thought, but he was very unhappy, because he knew what terror awaited at their destination, and it was not just the pressing Caribbean heat.

"Thank you," the farmer said. "I want to thank the Hermit and yourself for taking a stand against this immoral President! You know, all my life I have worked hard on this farm, as did my father before me, and his father as well. And all my life we have been terrorised by the FARC and other of these communist heathens. And they have stolen my workers and poisoned them against me and other honest men in the villages around here. And they have killed many of us. And then they killed the workers who said no to them."

The cartel soldiers were vocally expressing their outrage at everything that had happened.

"They are criminals, all of them," the farmer said. "And this President wants to make peace with them!" There was strong indignation in the room. "And he wants to give them pardons for murdering honest people. And he wants to guarantee them seats in Congress, making a mockery of our democracy. This President must be stopped!"

Again, there were loud cheers of approval.

"Would you believe, the communists have poisoned so many minds, we can't even trust that the President will be ousted in the election," Julian added, and the farmer vigorously shouted his agreement. "So why wait a few weeks for an untrustworthy election, when we can take action on Monday? With the President gone, and all blame placed on the communists, of course, there will be chaos over here, and with the Prince of England gone, there will be chaos over there! Which is good for all of us, especially our drug trade overseas."

"That's what this is really about, isn't it?" Stuart whispered to Molly.

"Of course," she whispered back. "The cartel surely doesn't give a damn about some farmer and his troubles. But yes, if there is peace with FARC and the other guerrillas, the army and the police might suddenly have much more time for the drug dealers, which they're not happy about."

"So they're mad enough to assassinate two prominent statesmen!"

Molly shook her head and leaned in closer.

"No, don't you see. If they can blame the FARC, or whoever, for even the vaguest attempt at an assassination, they have got their chaos. Success is irrelevant. An attempt, even just a scare; that's all they need. The peace negotiations will fail and the civil war will re-escalate."

They stopped talking as there was now silence in the sitting room.

"Before we get to the violent part," Julian said, "we will humiliate the President and the Prince by showing off our trophies!"

The men cheered again. They were clearly referring to Molly and Stuart.

"I spoke to the Hermit earlier, who will meet with us in Cartagena on Monday, ready for battle!"

There was a lot of cheering in the room, which eventually died down. Suddenly, Julian appeared at the kitchen door. He led Stuart and Molly back into the sitting room, where all the men sneered at them.

Before Stuart had time to be frightened, the farmer received a text message on his phone.

"Good news," he announced. "A friend of mine passed the bridge, on his way to Santa Fé. It seems the police got bored, so the roadblock is gone. You can safely head off now."

"That is wonderful," Julian said.

He motioned for his men to head outside. Two of the cartel soldiers took hold of Stuart and Molly and led them outside as well. Stuart breathed in the fresh countryside air, pleased to be outdoors. Despite it still being early in the day, the heat was already punishing, and the smell from the farm animals was becoming increasingly noticeable. He wrinkled his nose as they walked past some characteristically curious cows. A few steps down a dirt path was a large chicken enclosure, which was heard before it was seen. The SUVs were parked right in front of it.

"It's a long drive to the Caribbean," Julian said. "Let's go!"

※ ※

"God is dead," Antonio said sullenly.

He was sitting on the front pew in the church, looking gloomy and despondent. Carolina walked up to him, having hovered around some candles, keeping a watchful eye on him.

"I know," she said in a motherly fashion and sat down next to him. "But don't worry, He'll be resurrected tomorrow, like every Easter Sunday."

Antonio raised his head with a confused look on his face.

"Yes, that's not..." He sighed. "You're right. I should have hope."

"Good. In the few days I've known you, you have often talked about hope, so my hope is that you actually have some."

"I do."

Antonio chuckled.

"How is Sara?" Carolina asked. "I couldn't believe it when you called last night to tell me."

"She is still sleeping, I think. She was too exhausted to

say anything last night. I hope she has something good to tell us."

Carolina frowned.

"That she escaped is good news in itself, Father," she said admonishingly.

"Yes, of course."

"Why are you so gloomy, anyway?"

"Because I didn't get him," Antonio said, but then stopped himself.

Carolina studied him for a moment.

"That's an odd turn of phrase," she remarked. "Did you mean, because we failed to rescue our friend, Stuart?"

"Yes, of course."

"But that's not what you said."

"Oh, please don't be a lawyer with me."

"No, you're supposedly one yourself, but still you said…"

"Let it go," Antonio yelled out, violently.

His voice echoed around the large church before finally coming to a rest. Carolina kept looking at him, unfazed.

"I told Stuart that there was something strange about two priests, that he had just met, helping him out so eagerly. Maybe I was right? Who didn't you get?"

Antonio took a deep breath to control his anger and gave her a piercing look. Carolina leaned forward slightly, with a mischievous smile on her face.

"Are you after someone? The Hermit?"

Antonio did not move but kept breathing heavily.

"You can tell me," Carolina said. "I'm not here to stop you. All girls want a bit of excitement, I think. Not that you'd care. But tell me this, why is a Spanish priest interested in some Colombian criminal? What has he done to you?"

"He…" Antonio stopped and took another deep breath. He tilted his head back and looked up at the large, gilded image of the Virgin Mary which was painted on the ceiling above the altar. He recalled the admonition, which Juan had repeatedly reminded him of. Vengeance belongs to the

Lord.

"So he has done something to you," Carolina said. "You can tell me. I'm no stranger to violence. Certainly not after the past week."

"I am praying on the fifth commandment."

"Interesting," Carolina said. "Don't murder other people." She then looked at Antonio in a whole new light. "Wait, are you trying to kill the Hermit?"

"I haven't met the Hermit, so I'm still praying."

"Isn't the commandment very clear-cut?"

"There are many exceptions."

Carolina scoffed.

"Fine, I'll bite. As a lawyer. Don't murder. So, I guess you can kill in self-defence and you can kill in war if you're defending yourself." She thought in silence for a moment before articulating her final suggestion. "So, if you have an evil crime boss, who brings misery to thousands by selling drugs, who kills to maintain his power, are you allowed to kill him, in defence of the community, in protecting the common good?"

"There is much to pray on," Antonio said.

Carolina also looked up at the image of the Virgin Mary.

"You know, I had a wicked old nun as a Sunday school teacher. She's dead now, and probably substitutes for the Devil when he's on holiday."

Antonio chuckled quietly, nodding.

"Some of them are rather strict."

"She still managed to teach me a few things. Doesn't God say that vengeance is His? If the Hermit has done something to you, are you allowed to go after him?"

Antonio's body seemed to sag.

"I keep getting reminded of that saying."

"Maybe people don't want you to do something stupid, such as killing someone? Even if that someone is a really bad person."

"Maybe."

"If, when, we find the Hermit, I won't stop you,"

Carolina said. "But I hope you are certain about what you want. And I hope sometime you can tell me why."

**

It was early on Saturday morning when Cooth returned to the embassy. He walked up to Tara's office and relaxed in her chair. Last night, the Ambassador had sent the request through to London to cancel the Prince's visit, citing the mounting security concerns. Cooth was sure the cancellation had been approved by now. There was not much more for him to do. Tara was out tracking the two kidnap victims, Stuart and Molly, but even so, that was really a job for the Colombian authorities. They had the experience. They were used to it.

Cooth was just about to try to call Tara, to see if she had any updates, as the phone on the desk buzzed. A tired and grumpy assistant, who had probably been up all night facilitating the cancellation of the Prince's visit, summoned Cooth to the Ambassador's office. He hurried up, making a mental note to call Tara immediately afterwards.

The Ambassador was slumped in his seat, looking like he too had been working all night.

"We have bad news," he said as Cooth walked into the room and took a seat.

"What?" Cooth asked.

The Ambassador groaned quietly.

"The government insists that the Prince's visit to Cartagena must go ahead as planned."

Cooth's heart sank.

"That's outrageous!" he said. He really had thought that the government would approve the cancellation. "I will speak to the Foreign Secretary myself, right away."

"He made the decision," the Ambassador replied. "Well, him, the Prime Minister, the Lord Chamberlain, I'm sure many other Lords. The Palace."

"Unbelievable! I'll call him anyway."

"No. He said the decision is final."

"Unbelievable," Cooth fumed. He thought through the implications. "And what the hell happens, what the hell do we do, if the Prince is assassinated in Cartagena?"

The Ambassador sighed.

"The government wants to show their unwavering support for the Colombian President and his goal to bring this civil war to an end."

"Unwavering sounds like a dangerous word in politics."

The Ambassador smiled but did not reply.

"But, the Prince?" Cooth shook his head. "I support peace and goodwill to all as much as the next guy, but isn't risking his life too high a price to pay for showing our support? What is the government thinking?"

The Ambassador looked queryingly at Cooth. He was exhausted and replied testily.

"I don't know what kind of twisted mindset you have developed in the Secret Intelligence Service, but there is never a price too high for peace. Never! I'm sure His Royal Highness will be the first to agree with me on that."

Cooth shook his head.

"Twisted mindset? Do you hear yourself? Sometimes, even for peace, the price is too high. And peace notwithstanding, how are you possibly going to explain to the British people that the Prince has been killed, with us having had advance notice? That he was a victim of some foreign, civil war that the British people have never heard of?"

"A martyr on the path to peace. Everyone can understand that."

"Really?" Cooth was almost shouting by now. "We have advance notice! We know this is going to happen, and we still let the Prince come here. You know what will happen. The government will fall, we will all get fired, and who knows if they'll send us to prison for being complicit in it all."

The Ambassador lent back in his chair.

"We are showing our unwavering support for peace, Mr Cooth. I think the government is concerned that we haven't done enough of that recently, especially if you ask our Arab friends. There will be peace in Colombia, come what may." He paused his Churchillian moment and continued in a calmer tone. "Besides, you're a spy and don't officially exist, so you can neither be fired nor go to prison. You're a shadow and you'll get a terraced house with a small garden in Exeter, and no one will ever hear from you again." He suddenly looked very resolute and concluded firmly. "But there will be peace."

Cooth shook his head again.

"Furthermore," the Ambassador continued. "As you well know, having spied on Latin America for God knows how long, the Colombian army has been trained by British Special Forces, and by US Special Forces, so let's give them the benefit of the doubt and trust that they know how to do their jobs."

"I know."

"And the Prince has his own security team."

"He does. They are quite good as well."

"There you are. We'll stop these maniacs, rescue the hostages, the President will be re-elected, and there will be peace."

"I hope so," Cooth said. "I really, really hope so."

Chapter 33

There was some lingering tension in the friary kitchen. James, who had been sullen all week, had now complained about the number of female guests. Father Juan, who generally felt he had a pious duty to be patient, had decided that enough was enough. He had, therefore, thrust the old Rulebook of Saint Benedict, which was of a hefty size and contained, somewhere, the call to welcome all guests as if they were Jesus himself, into James' arms, and told him to go and read the whole thing. That was probably not the Easter that James had been hoping for.

Carolina had arrived early and had prepared breakfast for herself as if it had been her own kitchen. This was what had apparently been the last straw for James. Juan had asked her if she could wait in the church, mainly to watch over Antonio, who was in a rather dismal mood, until Sara woke up. Juan had then dispatched Father Pedro to the nearby hospital to visit the sick, and, finally alone, he had sat down in the kitchen to write his Easter Sunday homily. Its preparation had been somewhat delayed.

Juan was not sure where to begin. He could go with the obvious, of asking people to be happy that Jesus had been resurrected, but he felt that that did not truly capture the momentousness of the occasion. Instead, he started writing more generally about war and peace, of which there were plenty of examples in the Bible, and then more specifically about the peace negotiations with the FARC as well as the upcoming election. It was a crossroad, a choice between the President's desire for a peaceful negotiation and the Challenger's wish for a final military annihilation of the enemy. It was time for everyone to choose.

"Blessed are the peacemakers, for they shall be called the children of God."

Juan nodded and underlined the exhortation, which he had written down at the end of his homily. He then sighed and thought about the Hermit, and their quest to bring down his cartel. He thought about Stuart, kidnapped somewhere, hopefully still alive.

"What does it mean to be a peacemaker?" he asked himself out loud.

Feeling rather pleased with his own deep thought, he turned over the page and scribbled it down. It would be a rather long homily, but he remembered that the Archbishop had droned on for quite a while the other week. Hopefully, his parishioners would indulge him.

What does it mean? To reconcile people and bring harmony to discordant groups. He jotted that down. That could be difficult though, when other side had killed and kidnapped, and the other had felt the pain of loss. Even more difficult, perhaps, when the opposite was also true. Still, he thought, there had been repeated civil wars in Colombia since its independence, so peace had to come somehow. Even if it meant reconciling. If the FARC was disbanded and stopped producing cocaine to fund its work, it would hopefully be an opportunity to finally disband the last remaining drug cartels as well. Reconciliation with those who had killed was the price of peace, the price for an end to violence, and surely a price worth paying. So, "love your enemies and pray for those who persecute you", he wrote as an ending. Peace can be difficult but has a divine reward.

He felt rather pleased with himself. He then heard movement outside the kitchen, and he folded up the paper and put it in his pocket. He first guessed that it was James who was returning with Saint Benedict's rulebook, but the book was much too long for it to be him. Instead, it was Sara who hesitantly looked in through the door.

"Good morning," Juan said. "Come in."

Sara walked into the kitchen and sat down at the table. She looked rested and more composed, a big difference from the pale and exhausted girl who had turned up last night.

"Would you like some breakfast?"

"Yes, please."

"I'm not much of a cook, but I can fry up some eggs, and prepare some toast."

"Sounds nice."

She sat in silence as Juan started preparing the meal.

"Did you sleep well?" he asked.

"Yes, it was very comfortable. I didn't sleep anything the night before."

Juan put some juice and bread on the table.

"When you're ready I would like to hear about your escape."

"Yes."

Juan served up the fried eggs. There was one important question he had to ask. He could not think of a very tactful way to ask, so he simply put it out there.

"Tell me, how did you know to come here?"

"Stuart told me," Sara replied, tucking into the eggs. "He said you had helped him."

"Yes, we tried," Juan said slowly.

"And my father told me about you."

Manuel Lopez. With everything, Juan had almost forgotten about him. He suddenly panicked, wondering if Sara knew about the death of her mother and uncle. He had never enjoyed being the bearer of bad news, but perhaps Stuart had already told her?

"Yes, I met your father. It was…well, a few months ago now, I think."

"Did you tell him to betray his boss and put his family in danger?"

Juan's heart skipped a beat. Sara, though, looked more sad than angry.

"I'm so sorry about everything that has happened," Juan said. "Manuel told me that the cartel had killed your brother. Your father was in deep agony. I told him what I tell everyone who seeks guidance, what God asks of everyone. Do that which is right and good. I don't know exactly what your father planned, but I know he tried, did everything he could, to protect you. That man you met, Stuart, he was sent here to help your family."

"But it didn't work."

Juan thought about Sara's mother and uncle, killed in the city. He thought about the evidence on the camera, which they had died for, and what it revealed about Tara Lawson at the British embassy.

"You father, your family, and Stuart, all of us, we were betrayed. I fear your father might have put his trust in the wrong person."

"Is my father alive?"

"I don't know, Sara. I pray that he is." Juan paused. "Do you mind if I ask another question?"

"No."

"We want to rescue Stuart and Molly and punish the Hermit. Did your father ever mention, say, any houses that the cartel has up north, perhaps close to Cartagena?"

"No, he didn't."

"I see."

"But my brother did."

Juan smiled.

"Yes?"

"Yes, he often drove things for them there. They have a farmhouse outside Turbo."

"Do they have their drug boats there?"

Sara nodded.

"It's not that close to Cartagena, but it is remote," Juan mused. "It would be a good place to hide away kidnap victims." He looked at Sara. "Do you know any details?"

"I think my brother said that he drove there on the main road from Medellín, through the town, and it was a bit further beyond." For the first time, there was a glimmer of excitement in Sara's face. "Can I come with?"

"This is going to be very dangerous," Juan said.

"My family is dead, Father," she said with a serious tone. "I only knew Molly for two weeks, but now she's the closest I have to a sister. I want to help."

Juan nodded slowly.

"I understand," he said.

**

"That sounds very promising," Carolina said.

Having left Sara to finish her breakfast in peace, Juan had walked over to the church and recounted the information about the Hermit's house in Turbo to Carolina and Antonio.

"So, how do we get to Turbo?" Antonio asked.

Carolina looked at him, searching for bloodlust. Juan furrowed his eyebrows.

"She knows about my, erhm, desire," Antonio told him.

"You told her?" he asked in a whisper.

"God can hear you whispering," Carolina said. "As can I, I'm sitting right here. And no, I figured it out based on all his gloomy moanings."

"Right."

"And now I have to figure out why two priests want to kill a cartel boss."

"Want is a strong word," Juan said.

"Oh, this is far more exciting than Sunday school. What did the Hermit do, kill a priest or something?"

Both Juan and Antonio looked angrily at her.

"Oh God, he did?"

"No," Juan said. "And whilst I usually encourage curiosity, I kindly ask you to refrain from speculating."

She could see the darkness in Antonio's eyes and she nodded.

"You must think we are very bad people," Juan said, for the first time looking nervous.

"Oh, nonsense. Having got to know you, you are very nice people, even if you're priests. I think that if the opportunity presents itself, neither of you will be able to go through with it. But who hasn't wished someone dead?"

"Don't underestimate me," Antonio said darkly.

"Well, one thing at a time," Juan said. "We have to get to Turbo first. Let's wait and see if the opportunity comes."

"What about tomorrow?" Carolina asked, gesturing around the church. "Easter Sunday mass."

Juan pulled out the written homily from his pocket. He felt it was the best one he had ever prepared.

"Rescuing our friends and stopping this assassination is more important," he said. "I can ask Father Pedro to lead the mass. James will assist, if he has finished with Saint Benedict by then."

"Excellent," Carolina said and stood up from the pew. "But this time we're taking my car. I'm not spending all day going to Turbo in your old heap. Follow me."

**

"Why did I agree to this?" the Ambassador moaned.

Cooth was driving their hire car, leaving the airport in Medellín and heading for Route 25, the road that would take them on their journey north, towards Cartagena.

"Because me telling Mrs Ambassador about your heroic antics in chasing down a drug cartel was favourable to me telling Mrs Ambassador about the young lady in Barranquilla," he replied softly.

"Oh, yes."

Cooth smiled sinisterly.

"And you get to show your unwavering commitment to peace, and all that."

The Ambassador looked at him angrily.

"What did Tara say when you called her earlier?" he asked.

"She said she's further up Route 25, in a town called Santa Rosa, where she says the cartel has a safe house. Her contacts came through. She's been watching the house during the night and says there is movement."

"Okay. But you said there were roadblocks in place?"

Cooth shook his head.

"To be honest, they're quite ineffective when the police don't know who they're looking for. We don't have any names, no photos. The cartel must have slipped through somehow."

"Fair enough," the Ambassador said. "But why are we here?"

"We're joining her," Cooth said enthusiastically.

"To do what?" the Ambassador asked flatly.

"Look, the National Police and the army are locking down Cartagena and following up on other leads from the Herrera Valley. The least we can do is help out a bit."

"Yes, but you two are spies. I'm just a civil servant."

"True, but don't let that hold you back."

Cooth smirked and the Ambassador's face twitched.

"Did you find anything on Senator Reyes?" the Ambassador asked sullenly.

"No," Cooth said. "I can't prove or disprove that she's the Hermit. No more can I prove or disprove that your unctuously friendly Congressman Escaso is the Hermit. I can't even prove or disprove that the bloody President is the Hermit."

"So we're stuck?"

"For now."

They drove on in silence. Thankfully, the Easter Saturday traffic was light and they made good progress. The police roadblock, still in place, did not hold them up for long either. They made it through the northern suburbs of Medellín and then the scenery improved. The road followed the Medellín River as it twisted its way northwards in-between the green hilltops towering above it. After a while the road started to climb up the side of the valley and soon they were driving across the Andean high plains, passing by colonial haciendas, redbrick huts, fields with cows, and verdant hilltops which looked like there should be Hobbits living in them.

They arrived in Santa Rosa about three hours after leaving the airport. Cooth navigated into the town centre and parked by the main square, which was dominated by the redbrick cathedral.

"So, where is she?" the Ambassador asked as they stepped out of the car. He winced at the pressing heat.

They were definitely getting closer to sea level.

Cooth took out his phone and called Tara but soon he twisted his face in disappointment.

"She's not answering."

"Well, how convenient!"

The Ambassador took a few steps around on the pavement, looking disgruntled.

"Where is this house she told you about?"

"I don't know," Cooth said.

"This is a bloody long trip for nothing," the Ambassador said angrily but was sufficiently alert to speak quietly, to avoid being overheard by the locals walking up and down the pavement.

Cooth tried calling again but to no avail.

"This is why the Foreign Secretary wanted to get rid of her," the Ambassador fumed. "I don't know what happened but these past few weeks she's become completely unreliable."

"Nonsense," Cooth replied defensively. "If she's observing the cartel house she might just be unable to answer."

"So what do we do? Randomly walk around and see if we can find her?"

"This place is a bit too big for that, and it would be very conspicuous too! No, I'll call Colonel Zapata, and see if he knows anything. Maybe he can get the local police to help us out."

Many minutes later, Cooth was looking more despondent than before.

"Apparently the local police don't know anything about the Hermit's cartel."

The Ambassador sighed.

"Well, that's helpful."

Cooth tried calling Tara again.

"Do you think something's happened to her?"

"I don't think so," Cooth said. "She's really good at this."

"I'm glad you still have faith in her. I don't know what

to think anymore."

Cooth did some checking on his phone.

"It's too far to drive to Cartagena today," he said. "Let's find a hotel here. Maybe we'll hear from Tara later. Otherwise, we drive on tomorrow morning."

"Ambassadors usually have a more glamorous lifestyle," the Ambassador muttered but agreed to the plan. "So, what do you do for fun around here?"

**

"Are we there yet?"

Carolina smirked at Juan, who was consulting an old paper map that he had brought along.

"Almost," Juan said, folding the map back up. "We've made really good progress."

Carolina took it as a compliment on her ability to drive very fast down the twisting mountain road, despite its poor condition. As the afternoon pressed on, the road had made it down from the last hilltops of the Andes, as the rugged peaks which had run uninterrupted from the very end of the continent gave way to the tropical Caribbean flatlands. The port town of Turbo was steadily coming closer.

The traffic picked up as they approached the town. The afternoon was coming to a close and the sun was beginning to set. They drove through the dilapidated outer areas of the town and finally reached the centre, which did not look much better. Carolina parked by an open square, framed by a few trees, which was next to a small inlet where the sea came into the centre of town. A few fishing boats were tied up along a wooden pier. The four of them stepped out into the pressing heat and stretched after the long drive.

"Well, this is an awful place," Carolina remarked. "We should leave immediately."

"We need to figure out a plan first," Juan said. "Let's go in here and have a coffee."

As they walked down the street to a nearby café,

Carolina noticed that quite a few locals were eyeing them suspiciously. It was not difficult to figure out why.

"Do you think you two should have changed into more appropriate clothes?" she asked Juan, who was still wearing his friar's robes. She nodded her head in the direction of the watchful locals. "Two priests and two women travelling together might look strange."

"I wouldn't worry," Juan said as they sat down by a table. He ordered coffees for everyone from the proprietress. "Maybe we are on a pilgrimage together."

"In a way, I guess we are," Carolina said and looked at Antonio.

"Let's remain focused," Juan said. "We're here. Now we have to find this house."

They waited in silence as they were served their coffee, and then they looked at Sara.

"I think my brother said it was on the other side of the town. Obviously by the sea."

"And I guess somewhat secluded?" Antonio suggested. "To avoid unnecessary attention."

"That makes sense," Juan said. "Well, I don't know anyone here to ask. I suggest that we drive to the north part of the town and just start looking."

"What are we looking for?" Carolina asked. "We can't just stop at every seafront house and ask if it belongs to the cartel."

Juan looked at Sara.

"Can you think of any other details? Anything at all?"

"I'm really sorry," she said and shook her head.

"Then all we can do is look."

Having finished their coffee, they started to head back towards the car. On the way, Juan spotted something in the square.

"Antonio, come with me," he said.

The two of them walked across the square. On the other side, Antonio saw an old man sitting on a bench by the seafront. He looked rather worse for wear and it was clear from his mannerisms that he was under the influence of some drugs.

"Good afternoon," Juan said.

The old man seemed friendly enough but his eyes turned to horror as he saw Antonio.

"Why have you brought Death with you?" the old man exclaimed.

"This is why priests shouldn't wear black," Antonio muttered.

"I…I just wanted to ask a question," Juan said, trying to sound as friendly as he could.

"Will Death take me if I don't answer?"

Antonio started nodding slowly, and the old man's eyes widened in horror, but Antonio then quickly shook his head as Juan gave him a rebuking look.

"You're not in Samarra yet," Juan said. "You have nothing to fear. I was wondering, do you know of a man called the Hermit?"

The man cowered on the bench, still looking in terror at Antonio.

"Is that why you brought Death?"

"So you do know the Hermit?"

Antonio slowly leaned forwards, which seemed to motivate the old man.

"There is a house by the sea, outside the town. Past the banana fields."

"Thank you," Juan said.

"Go with God," Antonio said and stepped backwards, which seemed to relax the old man, who sat up straight again. "I wonder what reality he was living in," Antonio remarked to Juan as they were walking back towards the car.

"I know," Juan said. "Try not to convince any other poor soul that you are Death."

They climbed back into the car and revelled for a moment in the air-conditioning.

"There are apparently some banana fields outside the town," Juan told Carolina once he had cooled down. "The house is beyond them."

"Excellent. How did you find that out?"

"It's all about asking the right person," Juan said. "And, apparently, offering the right incentives."

Carolina pulled out and drove back through the centre of the town, heading north. The rundown two-story buildings were soon replaced by rundown one-story buildings and eventually, the dusty road was lined only by wooden shacks. The sun was quickly disappearing behind the horizon and darkness was setting in. The buildings stopped after a while, as did the street lights, and they were guided only by the car's headlamps.

"This does look like a banana plantation," Carolina remarked, peering out into the twilight.

"I think so, yes," Juan said.

After carrying on for another mile or two through the banana fields, they came across a side road which led into a wooded area. The only marker was a wooden sign, on which a pineapple was carved. Carolina turned around and looked at Sara.

"Pineapple symbol, does that ring a bell?"

"Yes," she said, having just thought of something. "Yes, my dad said that apparently the Hermit liked pineapples."

"We did see some pineapple plants in the valley yesterday," Antonio pointed out.

"That's good enough for me," Carolina said.

She turned the car onto the side road, which was simply a bumpy, old path.

"We should probably hide the car," Juan said. "We have to be careful now in case the cartel is up there."

Carolina parked the car in a narrow opening in the treeline. Juan found some old palm leaves lying on the ground, which he rested against the car as a rudimentary form of camouflage. Juan and Antonio then retrieved two guns from a bag they had put in the trunk.

"You didn't get me one?" Carolina asked impatiently.

"Oh, no, Mauricio only gave us the two," Juan said.

They started to slowly walk down the path, staying

close to the trees, not knowing what lay ahead. The heat of the day was slowly dissipating, and they were further energised by a cool sea breeze. Juan and Antonio walked in front, keeping their eyes open for any guards or lookouts from the cartel. The area, however, was very quiet.

Quiet, in the sense that there was no human noise. There was, however, a cacophony from cicadas, grasshoppers, and a veritable ensemble of annoyingly energetic birds. On top of that, in the distance, they heard the occasional engine of a truck or bus travelling on the main road as it carried on north of Turbo.

After ten or so minutes they saw a clearing. In the centre of it stood a sizeable wooden house. By all accounts, it was empty. There were no lights, no movement, and no human sounds. Juan sighed quietly.

"I don't know about this," he whispered.

"Let's be very careful," Antonio said. "Looks can deceive."

They continued to creep forward and stopped at the end of the treeline. The house was right in front of them and to the left was the sea, glistening in the last light of the day. Juan was about to step into the clearing when Carolina grabbed hold of him and pulled him back.

"I saw a shadow inside," she said.

**

The Ambassador sighed and Cooth rolled his eyes. Again.

"It's Easter Saturday," the Ambassador said.

"You've mentioned that already."

"The Prince is in Jamaica. Do you know what the High Commissioner in Jamaica is doing right now? Having a lavish dinner with the Prince! What am I doing?"

"Moaning?"

"Eating beans in some half-rundown town."

"Don't be rude! And did you join the diplomatic service only for the champagne and caviar?"

"That was part of it."

"Well, on the bright side, if everyone survives, you'll be having a lavish dinner with the Prince on Monday. Try to keep it together until then."

The Ambassador sighed once more but did not say anything. A while later, after they had ordered ice cream for dessert, Cooth's phone buzzed. His face lit up as he read the text message.

"It's from Tara," he said.

"Thank God," the Ambassador said. "That's a relief. You know, I never doubted that she'd come through for us."

"Of course you didn't."

"Where is she?"

Cooth read on for a moment.

"She's tracking members of the cartel, they're almost in Cartagena by now."

The Ambassador threw his hands into the air.

"Wonderful! That would've been useful to have known a few hours ago. We could have flown straight there!"

"Yes, being an intelligence officer doesn't mean a gunfight a day and a martini for dinner. Sometimes it's just a lot of waiting around."

"Well, civil servants never wait."

"No, you usually go in circles."

The Ambassador scoffed.

"What do we do now?"

"No point in changing the plan," Cooth said. "We drive to Cartagena in the morning. We'll start early, but it'll take all day no matter what."

"Wonderful." The Ambassador sighed. "But I'm glad she's alive and in control of the situation."

"I told you, don't doubt her. She'll rescue the hostages and save the Prince."

"Good." The Ambassador managed to smile gently. "You know, I'm looking forward to that lavish dinner on Monday. Too bad you aren't invited."

**

"What shadow?"

They crouched down and stepped further back into the treeline. Carolina carefully observed the house.

"I swear I saw a shadow in the window, the one to the right of the front door."

They waited in silence, but as the minutes ticked by, there was no movement to be seen. There were no signs that any other person was around. There was only the sea breeze, rustling the leaves in the trees above, and the birds and insects hooting and chirping. Though the night air was still hot, Carolina had to shrug off some chills running down her back.

"All right, I might have imagined it," she accepted but kept her eyes firmly on the window.

"Perhaps," Juan said, but did not seem entirely convinced.

The four of them started taking hesitant steps out into the clearing, heading towards the house. The priests held their guns in their hands, ready, just in case. They had come almost halfway when a shadow passed by the same window. They all froze and crouched down in fear.

"Come on," Juan said.

Still crouching, they sprinted up to the main door and stopped right outside it.

"What do we do?" Sara asked, a look of terror on her face.

Juan held his gun out to Carolina, who took it with furrowed eyebrows.

"Be prepared," he said.

Before anyone could ask for clarification, Juan calmly knocked on the door.

"What are you doing?" Carolina hissed, just in time before the door swung open.

Behind it was a young, scrawny man, whose eyes widened in shock as he saw Juan, though as he took in the three others standing behind Juan, his face turned to confusion. Carolina was not sure what to make of him, but he clearly did not belong to a vicious drug cartel. For starters, he did not have a gun.

"Good evening, son," Juan said.

"I...I...I wasn't stealing anything," the young man stuttered.

"Of course not," Juan said.

Emboldened by the young man's fear and lack of a weapon, Juan walked straight past him and into the house. The three others quickly followed suit, with Antonio and Carolina still tightly gripping their guns. Inside a large, open-plan kitchen and sitting room they encountered another young man, who also seemed confused and somewhat uncomfortable by the interruption.

"So, what's going on here?" Juan asked calmly.

"We were just looking around," the second young man said. "Who, who are you, Father?"

"We seek the man who owns this place."

"You mean the Hermit?"

Juan smiled.

"Yes, exactly."

"Is that why the cartel is on the run, why there was that big raid in Medellín? God has come after him?"

"Well..."

"The cartel came to town earlier today, with many of their men. They fled north, they didn't stop here."

"That's good to know," Juan said. "Was the Hermit with them?"

"No," the second young man said. "The Hermit is never here."

"Right," Juan said dejectedly. "Still, what are you two doing here?"

The two young men looked down on the floor, clearly feeling guilty about something.

"Our boss told us to come and look around," the first one said eventually.

"And who is your boss?"

"He...he sells drugs in town."

"A friend or rival of the Hermit?"

"Both, I think," the second young man said. "He thought, maybe with the Hermit's cartel on the run, they had left some valuable, erhm, goods here."

Juan took a deep breath.

"I understand. Go, tell your boss there's nothing here. Your boss never finds out about us. Don't come back until tomorrow. We'll be gone by morning."

"Okay," the young men said hesitantly, wondering how to lie to their boss. Without saying anything else, they left and started walking down the dusty road towards the town.

Once alone, the quartet sat down on the sofas in the living area and breathed a sigh of relief.

"Don't just knock on a door like that again," Carolina said angrily once she had collected her thoughts.

"They were clearly not from the cartel," Juan said. "There was no security, no guards, and no vehicles. And, you'll only get an answer if you knock."

"Unbelievable."

"What do we do now?" Antonio asked. "Press on?"

"No," Juan said. "We should get some sleep. They're heading to Cartagena, we know that now. We'll do the same, first thing in the morning."

"The final showdown," Antonio said, with a darkness in his eyes.

Chapter 34

"So the Englishman got himself kidnapped?"

"I don't think it was entirely his own fault," Juan said.

"I told you he didn't deserve your help, Juanito."

Juan sighed.

"This isn't just about him."

The Red Widow cackled, rousing Antonio and Sara from their deep thoughts. Carolina, however, was gazing at the old serial killer with a fascination which was probably not all that healthy. The four of them had left Turbo early in the morning and had reached Cartagena in the afternoon on Easter Sunday, and without any better destination in mind, they had driven to the Red Widow's estate, where, in Stuart's absence, they had been enthusiastically welcomed.

"No, I heard what happened at the Herrera Valley," the Red Widow said. "And I heard that the police raided various properties yesterday and this morning. Those captured cartel soldiers really revealed a lot of secrets, didn't they?"

"News travels fast," Juan said.

"I like to stay informed."

"I'm not surprised."

"So you want my help to give the Hermit the final, fatal blow? As well as rescue your little friend?"

"It's a lot to ask," Juan said.

There was another round of cackling, sounding more sinister than ever.

"My pleasure, I promise."

"Thank you," Carolina chipped in with a smile on her face, prompting a discouraging look from Juan.

"Yes, thank you," he said more gravely. He glanced at Antonio, who had returned to his deep thoughts, before looking back at the Red Widow. "Do you know where the Hermit might be?"

"Oh, Juanito darling, I'll tell you the truth." The Red

Widow leaned in and continued in a softer tone. "I have honestly no idea who the Hermit is."

Juan and Carolina looked at her with raised eyebrows.

"What?" Carolina asked in amazement.

"I guess the top lieutenants know the Hermit's identity, but I certainly don't."

"So, wait, is the Hermit even a real person?" Carolina asked. "Or just a smokescreen?"

The Red Widow cackled again.

"She's thinking like a drug lord, isn't she?"

"I'm thinking like a lawyer," Carolina insisted.

"Oh, sure," the Red Widow said. "No, the Hermit is real. Very real."

"Do you know any of the lieutenants?" Juan asked, starting to sound desperate.

"Oh, yes," the Red Widow said. "I met one of them, Julian Reyes, a while back. I have to say, he's a very bad person."

"What do you know about him?" Juan asked.

"Not much. I prefer his cousin, the Senator. She's getting my vote!"

"Wait a minute," Juan interjected. "Senator Reyes? The presidential candidate and head of the Intelligence Committee in Congress? That Senator Reyes?"

"Yes."

"So, is she the Hermit?" Carolina asked, sounding horrified.

The Red Widow pondered that for a moment.

"I hadn't thought about that," she said. "I must be going senile!" She sighed. "Anyway, as to finding them, if we go based on Julian Reyes, I do have an idea of where they might be." The Red Widow looked certain but her voice betrayed her uncertainty. She glanced at the clock on her phone. "First, though, I want to show you something."

Juan's heart skipped a beat.

"You haven't kidnapped someone else, have you?" he asked nervously.

The Red Widow gave him a rebuking look.

"No, of course not. It's Easter."

"Erhm…Well, I'm glad you're restraining yourself."

She leaned in and gave him a quick embrace.

"It's a bit late for you or God to reform me now, Juanito," she said softly. "But I have to say, when I met you and you asked to join my team, I couldn't say yes. You were so angry at your father's murder. I sent you to the church instead, mainly to calm that anger. I didn't expect to see you here, now, asking me for these kinds of favours."

"I know," Juan said. "Funny how that works out."

"I don't want to think it was God's plan to make you into some kind of warrior monk."

"Well, I'm neither a warrior nor a monk," Juan said. "I am but a friar, trying to right a wrong."

"Hmm, by asking me to go to war with my competitor, on Easter Sunday, of all Sundays. That must be some wrong!" She leaned in again. "Or are you still just angry about your father's murder?"

"That is not the reason why I'm here," Juan said.

"So, it's really just about the Englishman?"

"No, Red Widow, it's not about him. I got involved when a parishioner came to see me, many, many weeks ago. I learnt some things from him, about the Hermit's cartel, and my advice had deadly consequences, it seems." Juan glanced at Sara. "A mother and an uncle were killed. A father is missing, maybe killed as well. Then, out of the blue, the Englishman, ahem, Stuart, dropped in, caught up in the same story."

"Hmm." The Red Widow tilted her head. "You make him sound unimportant, a peripheral player. Are you sure we should waste our time rescuing him? We could focus on taking down the Hermit?"

"No, we have to rescue him," Carolina said determinedly.

Juan had forgotten that she was listening to the conversation.

"Yes," he said, slowly, though he could not help but

agree with the Red Widow, to an extent. Stuart had become an added player in a quest he and Antonio had already embarked upon. The thought, however, made him feel guilty and he tried to push it away.

"Fine," the Red Widow said and stood up. "As I said, there's something I want to show you."

Her movement again rose Antonio and Sara from their thoughts, and together they all made their way down to the pier, where the Red Widow's yacht was moored.

"She's delightful, if somewhat scary," Carolina whispered to Juan as they walked.

"She's ruthless, though thankfully rather helpful," Juan replied sternly. "Don't get drawn in by her."

"I know. But she has a certain magnetism."

"True."

"Imagine having her as a mother!"

"A rather uninviting prospect, I think," Juan said. He whispered even lower. "Though there is a rumour that she has a child left behind in Argentina."

Carolina's mouth fell open at the scandalous gossip, but she kept silent.

Down at the pier, they climbed on board the yacht, Red, and its crew quickly took it out to sea. The pressing afternoon heat was tempered by the rushing wind as the yacht sped up, passing the island where the Red Widow had kept the American, and continued out into the openness. The openness, however, was rather crowded, with ships large and small hanging about, seemingly waiting for something.

"How kind," Juan said as a crewman served them champagne. He gestured at the flotilla around them. "What's happening out here?"

The Red Widow led the way as they climbed up the staircase onto the upper deck.

"You can't fault them on punctuality," she said, sounding rather annoyed.

It was easy to see what she was referring to. Less than a nautical mile in front of them, a long, sleek, grey ship glided effortlessly through the sea, heading for Cartagena, whose colonial cupolas were glistening on the horizon. From the ship's radar mast flew the Union Jack, and the gun on its bow deck was unmistakable.

"Your worst enemy, I take it?" Juan said, trying to keep the mood light.

Sullenly, the Red Widow unfolded a piece of paper she had kept in her purse. It looked like a printout from an online encyclopaedia.

"The HMS Atholl, Type 23 frigate. Does anti-drug smuggling patrols in the Caribbean, and is visiting Cartagena together with the Prince, who arrives tomorrow."

"Well, now that you know what it looks like, you can avoid it in the future."

"Don't try to be funny, Juanito."

"No, if nothing else has, it brings home the seriousness of the situation," Juan said. "The English Prince is coming tomorrow, as is the President. We have to save Stuart and stop the Hermit, right now."

"Fine," the Red Widow said. "Fine, I'll kill my competitor and save the President. It's something for me and something for the country. I guess it balances out."

Feeling pleased with the equation, the Red Widow ordered her crew to follow the warship, and take the yacht to Cartagena.

**

"That's a magnificent sight, isn't it?"

"Certainly."

Cooth and the Ambassador were standing on Cartagena's city walls, looking out to sea where the HMS Atholl was slowly heading towards the naval port, situated on the inside of the Bocagrande peninsula. They waited in the murderous sunlight, protected only by cheap Panama hats bought from a street hawker, until the ship disappeared from view behind the white, high-rise apartment buildings that crowded the peninsula, and then they started walking along the city wall.

They sat down in the welcomed shade under a parasol at the Café del Mar, situated on top of the city wall, and, feeling they needed a kick after the long drive from Santa Rosa, ordered some suitable cocktails. A light sea breeze cooled them down a little before the waitress returned with their drinks.

"I've heard this one before," the Ambassador said. "Are you sure she's coming?"

"Yes," Cooth said sternly. "Tara said she would be here imminently. We just have to wait."

They waited for another ten or so minutes before they spotted Tara walking up the nearby ramp from the street below. She joined them with a grave look on her face.

"I'm sorry I missed you two yesterday," she said and ordered a soft drink. "I was shadowing a convoy of SUVs to Santa Rosa, where I was told the Hermit has a hideout. They left very abruptly yesterday afternoon and I had to follow them. It was difficult to stay in contact with you."

"I understand," Cooth said. "Where did you end up?"

Tara paused as she was served her drink.

"They went to an estate just outside Cartagena."

"Excellent," the Ambassador said. "So, Molly and Stuart Gleeman, were they in the convoy?"

Tara shook her head.

"I couldn't say with certainty. I haven't been able to get close to the estate today. I hope to do so tonight, after dark."

Cooth and the Ambassador looked disappointed.

"So we're nowhere further on that? Where are we for tomorrow?" The Ambassador looked a bit nervous. "Remember I'm going to be with the Prince almost all day."

"And you don't want to get shot," Cooth added. "We understand."

"I've spoken to all my contacts," Tara said. "In the police, military, as well as with the Prince's security team.

Everyone is on alert."

"That's it?" the Ambassador queried.

Tara nodded.

"I'm not sure what you're looking for, sir. We know the cartel is here. We know that Manuel Lopez said there would be an attack on the Prince, and possibly by extension, on the President. We don't really know anything else, certainly no details. We don't know what to look out for."

"But with all these murders and kidnappings, we know this is happening for real, right?"

"Yes, sir," Tara said. "This is happening."

"Unfortunately none of the men captured on Friday knew anything," Cooth said. "Low-level foot soldiers, all of them. They led the police to some other properties, there have been a few raids, but we got nothing of value anywhere. Well, they seized some drugs, but only small quantities. What we need is to capture a high-ranking member of the cartel or find this mysterious Mr D, their contact in London."

"Any progress on that?" Tara asked.

"No," Cooth said. "GCHQ is working overtime, but nothing. I'm starting to think that Mr D might not be working in central government or at the English ports. It might be time to widen the net."

"To look at what?"

"Foreign Office staff working where the cartel might have an interest. Latin America, the Caribbean, the US, Spain. Could be anyone, anywhere."

"And the D initial might be a cover, anyway, right?" the Ambassador asked.

"Yes, sir," Tara said.

"This is a nightmare," the Ambassador sighed. He turned to Tara. "Is your boyfriend's cousin behind this?"

Cooth looked alarmed but Tara smiled.

"I'm certain that Senator Reyes is not the Hermit, sir. Though as chair of the Intelligence Committee she does have all the details for tomorrow's security operation."

"Is what wise?" the Ambassador asked.

"I'm sure it's fine, sir," Tara said. "She's not the Hermit."

"What about Congressman Escaso?"

"Why do you ask, sir?"

"Well, he's on the Foreign Affairs committee. He worked so hard to get the Prince to visit. Maybe there's a reason he worked so hard?"

Tara smiled.

"You're getting paranoid, sir," she said. "All that Congressman Escaso talks about the 21st-century economy, making Colombia a world player. I'm very sure he's not the Hermit."

"Well, who is the Hermit?"

"It's going to be some wealthy individual we've never heard of, sir."

"I don't know," Cooth said. "But we mustn't get paranoid, soon we'll be suspecting everyone."

"Yes, what about Colonel Zapata?" the Ambassador asked. "He also knows a lot, doesn't he?"

Tara shook her head.

"I really doubt it's him, sir. We need to stay calm and professional."

"Fine," the Ambassador said, rather angrily. "So what do we do?"

"Tonight, I suggest that we investigate the estate," Tara said. "See if we can find the hostages."

"We?"

"Yes, sir. You can drive."

"Well, that's sorted then," Cooth said. "Tonight, we rescue our countrymen. Ahem, well, man and woman."

**

They trailed the frigate as she sailed past the old fortress on the island of Tierra Bomba, guarding the entrance to Cartagena's harbour. Slowly, escorted by numerous small, local vessels, the warship docked at the naval port. The yacht carried on to a nearby marina, where the Red Widow's crew moored. The boss confidently led everyone ashore and up to a couple of SUVs, which were waiting by the nearby road. Juan, Antonio, Carolina and Sara all looked queryingly at the Red Widow, hesitant to get into the cars without any more information.

"I'm sure we can resolve this quickly," she said impatiently. "I know that Julian Reyes is associated with an apartment here in Bocagrande. We'll go there right away."

"Is that safe?" Juan asked. "If the cartel is there?"

The Red Widow nodded and thought for a second.

"Maybe that's where you two come in. Same as we did with the Englishman, send in the priests first to see what's what."

"Great idea!" Antonio exclaimed.

"It could work," Juan said more hesitantly. "Though I fear the Hermit knows who we are."

"Sure," the Red Widow said. "Well, it's an element of surprise nonetheless."

With that, she jumped into the front car, followed by a number of her armed henchmen. Juan led his team to the second car. Not before long they pulled up beneath a towering high-rise building, painted all in white, sporting no doubt some forty floors. They all stepped out of the cars and looked around. A few locals and tourists were walking around on the pavements, many heading towards the nearby beach. No one paid them any attention.

"What are you going to do to the security guard?" Juan asked the Red Widow.

"We'll lure him away," she said. She saw Juan's concerned face. "Don't worry so much, Juanito, we won't kill him."

"Thank you."

Carolina and Sara were told to wait inside the car, which they happily did as the air-conditioning was still running. The Red Widow explained that they were looking for the north-facing penthouse. With that, Juan and

Antonio headed to the entrance and stepped inside, which was like entering an icebox. A security guard was sitting behind a desk and greeted them with a friendly nod.

"Good afternoon, Fathers," he said and stood up. "Are you here to see Mrs Palacios?"

Juan and Antonio both hesitated.

"Yes," Juan answered slowly.

"She was so upset she couldn't go to Easter Mass this morning."

"Uh-huh."

"She's in 31A. I'll call the apartment and let them know you're coming up."

"Thank you very much."

They walked to the lift and, duty bound, pressed the button for the 31st floor.

"What are we doing?" Antonio asked.

"I don't know. Let's just say hello and hope that no other priest suddenly turns up."

They stepped off on the 31st floor and knocked on the door. It was opened by an old maid, who politely welcomed them in. She showed them into the bedroom, where an old lady was lying asleep in bed, looking deathly ill. She was bathed in sweat, despite a fan blowing cold air across the bed. Juan and Antonio exchanged worried looks. This was far worse than just missing Easter Mass.

"Exactly how ill is Mrs Palacios?" Juan asked the maid.

"The doctor was here this morning," she replied, her voice breaking. "She is very poorly. Erhm, do you know where Father Teófilo is?"

"No," Juan said, wondering who that was. "I hope he will come soon. For now, we'll say a prayer for Mrs Palacios."

The maid stayed in the room as Juan started performing the last rites, preparing Mrs Palacios for the end. Whilst Juan was focused on the task at hand, Antonio thought about the possibility that the Hermit, and maybe Stuart and Molly too, were in the penthouse apartment just a few floors up. His heart beat quickly, knowing that the end of his journey might be just minutes away. He was also afraid of what the Red Widow would do if she discovered that they were not at the penthouse. It seemed unlikely that she would be moved by the plight of a dying old lady.

"Thank you so much," the maid said as Juan finished.

"I'm afraid that we are needed elsewhere," Juan said in the kindest way possible. "I'm sure that Father Teófilo will come soon."

"I understand." She showed them back through the apartment and to the front door. "Thank you again," she said as they stepped outside.

They quickly took the lift up to the top floor. The corridor was empty and quiet.

"There's only one thing to do," Juan said and knocked on the door to the north-facing penthouse apartment.

There was silence.

Juan knocked again, but nothing happened. Out of curiosity, he tried to open the door, and to their surprise, it swung open without a sound. They stepped into a large entrance hall, which had magnificent white marble flooring. Slowly they carried on into a spacious living room, which opened up to a terrace. From the terrace, there was a clear line of sight out across the Caribbean, lit up in red as the sun was slowly setting in the east.

"What the hell took you so long?"

They jumped in terror and then managed to look around. The Red Widow was emerging from the kitchen with a large cocktail in her hand.

"What?" Antonio stuttered. "What is going on?"

"We came up a few minutes after you and found an empty apartment. My men are searching the other rooms, but there's nothing here."

"But…we knocked!"

"Yes, I heard, but I was making myself a piña colada. Would you like one?"

"We're all right," Juan said, having regained his composure. "So, the Hermit is not here?"

The Red Widow shook her head.

"No, but maybe it was too obvious, if it belongs to a top lieutenant."

Juan sank down on the sofa. Antonio did not move. He had mentally built himself up for meeting the Hermit and ending this, once and for all. Now, he just felt drained of all energy.

"So, do you have any idea where the Hermit and the hostages might be?" Juan asked.

The Red Widow calmly drank her piña colada before answering.

"I have to think," she said.

**

"Is this legal?"

The Ambassador looked very nervous as he was driving the car out of Cartagena, heading towards the estate where Tara had tracked the cartel members.

"No," she said. "This is very illegal."

"Yes, trespassing on private property," Cooth added from the backseat, where he had spread out in relative comfort.

"That, and all the guns we have in the trunk are hardly legal," Tara said.

The Ambassador's face paled but he did not say anything. It was already gone midnight when Tara instructed him to pull up. Somewhat wearily, they all stepped outside. The Ambassador groaned and sighed in the heat, which despite the hour was still pushing down on them. Tara had arranged some guns, which she now fetched from the car's trunk, and handed one to Cooth and one to the Ambassador. He looked at it in terror but finally accepted it.

"Just in case," Tara said.

The Ambassador's face went pale but again he did not say anything. Tara led the way as they walked along the quiet road. It was narrow and probably did not see many cars on a busy day, let alone on Easter Sunday. Rows of orange trees were planted in the fields on either side, offering up a pleasant aroma. The Ambassador followed gingerly, quietly complaining about the loud insects that were out in a multitude. When they had walked for a while they reached a stone wall, some two metres high, which clearly enclosed a large farm of some sort.

They left the road and followed the wall as it ran along the edge of the orange field. They passed each tree as slowly as they could, but it was inevitable that they had to push branches and leaves out of the way, creating a rustle that sounded deafening to their strained ears. To anyone else, however, it could hardly be heard over the birds and insects, who seemed to be in a celebratory mood.

They had almost reached the far end of the wall when they came across some wooden crates, which were clearly used to carry the oranges once they were picked. They stood absolutely still for a minute, listening for any human sounds from the other side of the wall. Thankfully, there were none.

"There might be guards nonetheless," Tara said in a single breath, barely audible.

With practised skill, she noiselessly placed one of the crates up against the wall, and then stood up on top of it. She peered over the wall. The Ambassador held his breath, expecting Tara to be shot at any second by a guard on the other side. However, no shot rang out.

Effortlessly, Tara slid over the wall and disappeared on the other side. Cooth motioned for the Ambassador to follow her. He realised that he had not climbed over any obstacle since his early schooldays, but with a bit of effort he made it up onto the crate and over the wall, where Tara caught him before he almost crashed onto the ground.

"Silently," she said. In the dark, where the Ambassador could barely see her, it sounded like an eerie, disembodied voice.

Cooth quietly came over the wall next. They crouched down and headed for a nearby hedge, which clearly formed part of a well-kept garden. In its cover, they kneeled down and again listened for any human noises. There were none.

The Ambassador peered over the hedge. A large, single-story building was situated about thirty metres away. A pool and patio spread out in front of it, followed by the garden, which had rosebushes and hedges. By all accounts, it was a pleasant estate and no doubt fit for a drug lord. The lights were on inside but there were no visible movements. The Ambassador tightened his grip on the gun.

Tara started crawling along the hedge. After a while, they carefully peered over it again. The front drive of the house was now visible and parked there were two dark-coloured SUVs. They were clearly the ones that Tara had followed from Santa Rosa. There were still no guards to be seen, however.

"Do you think that they're here?" Cooth whispered.

"It seems so," Tara said. "We have to get closer."

They both looked around, scouting the terrain. The Ambassador had no idea what to look for but he did see that it would be difficult to approach the house without being spotted by anyone inside.

"Let's divide," Tara said. "I'll carry on around the front. You two approach the house from the back."

"Sounds good," Cooth said.

"What are we looking for?" the Ambassador asked.

"The hostages," Cooth said impatiently.

"Yes, but what does that look like?"

"Come!"

Cooth started crawling back along the hedge and Tara kept moving forwards. The Ambassador had no choice but to follow Cooth. Slowly they made it to the back of the house, carefully moving between the end of the hedge and some large rosebushes, hoping that no one would happen to spot them at that exact moment. They paused behind the rosebushes and listened. The Ambassador strained his ears and suddenly motioned to Cooth.

"I think I heard talking," he said as quietly as he could.

Cooth nodded and motioned for the Ambassador to keep following him. They crawled on, trying to get closer to the back wall. There were a few open windows overlooking the garden and the lights were on inside, spilling out in long lines on the ground. They were careful to stay in the darkness in-between. Eventually, they reached the wall and sat up against it, trying to listen for noises from inside. It was very quiet.

Cooth turned around and tried to look inside. The Ambassador followed suit, crawling over to the next window. He carefully peered inside. It was a large, open room, and he could make out a sofa group. By the wall there was a TV, and his heart jumped as he saw that it was turned on, though the sound was muted. There was definitely someone in the house. He tried to arch his head to get a better view inside.

He suddenly felt a presence behind him.

The Ambassador turned around and came face to face with a gun. It was held by a young man with an angry, determined look on his face. The Ambassador slowly put his hands up over his shoulders and glanced to his right, where he saw another young man pointing a gun at Cooth. Cooth seemed disappointed but resigned to their failure.

"Come with us," the young man pointing his gun at Cooth said.

The Ambassador slowly started to get up, and his young man grabbed his back and helped him along. Together, Cooth and the Ambassador were disarmed, before being shoved forwards and into the house. They were led into the sitting room and told to sit down on the sofa. The young man who had captured Cooth turned the TV off.

"Who are you?" he asked sternly, still pointing his gun at his captive.

"Oh, we're looking for our friend," Cooth said, sounding rather calm. "Perhaps we have the wrong address?"

The young man smiled but shook his head.

"No, I don't think so," he said and smiled sinisterly. "No, you see, our boss said you would be coming."

"Oh? Are you sure? Who is your boss?"

The young man stepped closer, still grinning evilly.

"The man you are looking for."

The Ambassador's heart sank as it finally sunk in. He had been kidnapped by the Hermit's men. A foreboding swelled up inside him. He knew this was going to end badly. His heart sped up and he struggled to breathe. Finally, as the room around him started spinning, he began to scream, louder than he ever had before.

**

When he woke up he realised that he was paralysed. He could not move. Everything was quiet and dark. He wondered for a moment if he had ended up in Hell. Then he heard breathing to his right. He turned his head, realising he was not entirely paralysed, and saw Cooth. He took a moment to look around and saw that they were still sitting on the sofa in the living room. He looked down and saw that several thick ropes had been pulled around his body, tying him and Cooth to the sofa.

"Are you awake?" he asked.

"Of course," Cooth said.

"What happened?"

"You had a panic attack." Cooth looked at him angrily. "It was most inopportune."

"I'm sorry."

"You should be. There was no way to engineer an escape with you passed out."

The Ambassador looked around the room but could not see anyone else.

"Where are those boys?"

"Around. There have been noises in the next room and outside. I think they're patrolling."

"Okay. So, can we escape now?"

Cooth sighed.

"Don't you think I've tried to get out of these restraints whilst you were napping?"

"Unconscious."

"We're unfortunately stuck, for the time being."

"Don't say that to a man who just had a panic attack!"

"Well, just so you know, this will reflect poorly on your next performance review."

The Ambassador ignored the barb and tried to wriggle out. He now realised that his wrists and legs were firmly tied together and no amount of straining would change that. Maybe if he had been twenty years younger and a bit more athletic, but his current body quickly told him to stop trying.

"Maybe Tara will come and..."

"Shhh. Don't mention her name. They might be listening."

"I'm sorry," the Ambassador said. They sat in silence for a moment, listening, but there was no indication that the young men were anywhere nearby. "Maybe we'll be rescued somehow."

Cooth sighed and for the first time looked deeply concerned.

"I don't know what happened to her. There's no indication that she's been captured. But you've been out for hours, and there has not been any indication that she's tried to help us, either."

"That's not good," the Ambassador said. "If there's just the two boys around, surely she could deal with them?"

"I would've thought so," Cooth said. "She's more than adequately trained for that."

"So this is like Santa Rosa again? She's just left us?"

"I'm starting to think that this will go on her next performance review as well."

"Is there any indication that Molly, or your guy, Stuart Gleeman, are actually being held here?"

"No," Cooth said. "That's what Tara said, and maybe they're being held elsewhere in the building. For all we know, there might be additional buildings on the estate as well."

"But this is definitely the Hermit's house?"

"Yes, it is! I learnt as much from the young men after you had, ahem, checked out."

"Passed out. But that's good. We're in the right place."

"Yes. Maybe now we'll finally get to meet the Hermit."

"I want to know who he is," the Ambassador said. "Do you think he's going to ransom us to the Prince tomorrow?"

Cooth chuckled.

"Yes, he will. There was nothing in the news today, no ransom for Molly or Stuart. But tomorrow, with the Prince here, oh yes. And with us as prizes, it will be the mother of all PR disasters."

"How so?"

Cooth frowned.

"How so? You're the bloody Ambassador! Have you forgotten? And I'm a senior SIS agent."

"Yes, of course," the Ambassador said and bowed his head. "I'm the Ambassador." He glanced over at Cooth. "Why can't you say MI6, like everyone else?"

"Secret Intelligence Service sounds rather more impressive."

"Well, not as impressive as ambassador. Which I am!"

"Yes, I know, I just told you!"

"Should we stop bickering and figure out a plan?"

"I've been thinking of plans all along, but I can't break these restraints."

The Ambassador tried wriggling around some more.

"Do you think we can slide out underneath these ropes?"

"I tried," Cooth said. "Nearly suffocated myself, they are wrapped so tight."

"Can we stand up and try to smash the sofa against the wall or something?"

Cooth shook his head.

"I tried pushing it with my feet. It's too big and heavy, even for the both of us. Not to mention, it would be very loud."

"There's a lot of negativity here," the Ambassador said.

"Well, it's easy to be upbeat when you've been napping for a couple of hours."

A gunshot pierced the dark night.

The Ambassador sat up straight and listened. It had come from outside, perhaps from the front drive. There was some scuffling in the room next door, perhaps as one or both of the young men headed outside to see what was going on.

Then there was silence for a while.

"What do we do?" the Ambassador asked in a whisper.

"Nothing we can do," Cooth replied.

Another gunshot rang out, closer this time.

Then a third.

There was some grunting from the room next door.

Suddenly two men burst into the living room, guns in their hands. The Ambassador instinctively tried to cower, but his body could not move. He looked at the men closely and his fear turned into confusion. They did not look like cartel soldiers.

"Yes, we are priests," one of them said by way of explanation.

He was dressed in a brown habit, which extended for almost his entire body, held together by a thick, black leather belt with a brass clasp. The other one was simply dressed in black, with a white priest's collar. This one was limping slightly. They quickly untied the two captives. The Ambassador stood up and stretched his body, which was aching from the hours in the sofa.

"Thank you," he said apprehensively. "Are you all right?" he asked the one in black, who was still limping.

He was not sure what to make of being rescued by two priests. Cooth, on the other hand, seemed less perturbed. The Ambassador felt jealous for a second. Nothing seemed to affect that man.

"Yes, thank you," the priest said. "I think I twisted my ankle coming in here."

"Are you the priests who spoke to Colonel Zapata?" Cooth asked. "He said you came out to the valley during the raid, but I didn't get a chance to meet you."

"We are," the priest in the brown habit said.

"Ah, right," the Ambassador said, and relaxed a bit. "Cooth here mentioned you."

The four men quickly introduced themselves.

"We must get you to safety," Juan said to the Ambassador. "You can't be kidnapped or absent when the Price arrives."

"Before we leave," Cooth interjected, "are there any other captives here? Stuart, Molly, or our colleague, Tara Lawson?"

Juan and Antonio exchanged nervous glances as Tara's name was mentioned.

"There's no one else here, as far as we know," Antonio said. "Our friends are searching the whole compound, but there were only the two guards. It seemed like another dead end, until we found you."

"Another?"

"We searched an apartment in the city earlier," Juan explained. "It belongs to one of the Hermit's lieutenants, and we hoped that Stuart and Molly would be there, but no luck. Our friend did some digging and found out about this place. We really thought, hoped, that this would be the Hermit's main base. It clearly isn't."

"Damn it!" the Ambassador exclaimed. "Erhm, apologies," he added to the priests.

The two priests exchanged another nervous glance.

"You asked whether Tara Lawson was here," Juan said slowly.

"Yes, she came with us," Cooth said, "but we separated before the two of us were captured. Hopefully, she managed to get away somehow."

Juan nodded slowly. The Ambassador frowned. What was going on? As he waited for the priest to explain, he could see the first light of dawn through the window. It was only hours before the Prince arrived.

"There's something you two should know," Juan said gravely. "Something about Tara Lawson. And after I've told you, we have to get back to the city. This has to end, now."

Chapter 35

Somehow he managed to get a full night's sleep. When he awoke on Monday, the sun was already high in the sky. It was warm, he could feel it in the air, but the air-conditioning in the luxurious room kept a constant stream of cool air flowing across his body. For an instance, he forgot where he was. Then he remembered.

Stuart sat up in the bed. His eyes adjusted to the brightness beyond the window, and he looked out over the high-rises in Bocagrande. In the distance, the Caribbean glistened. An enormous cruise ship was making its approach to port. He got out of bed and saw that someone had placed a fresh set of clothes on the chair by the door. His captors clearly wanted him to look his best as they mounted their attack on the Prince.

As he dressed he felt his chest tightening. So much had happened during his days in captivity, some of which had involved a rather luxurious lifestyle, but he had not managed to get one step closer to stopping the Hermit. He knew that today something had to give. He had to do something. The question was what.

Once he was dressed in some linen trousers and a white shirt, he made his way through the apartment and into the living room. He appreciated that he had the freedom to do so, but he took care to notice the two armed guards sitting in the entrance hall. There was no way out. Unless he wanted to jump, but there were some forty floors to the ground.

In the living room, he found Julian Reyes. He was talking to some other men who Stuart had not seen before. He looked around and saw Molly sitting at a table in a corner, looking upset. He walked over to her.

"It'll all be fine," he said, trying to sound reassuring.

"They're going to kill the Prince today," she said. "And there's nothing we can do to stop it."

"Yes, there is," Stuart said. "There has to be."

"No, you don't understand," she said slowly. "There's nothing we can do. The Hermit is here." She paused for a moment. "He's too powerful."

Stuart looked around, and out on the large terrace, leaning up against the railing and surveying the world beyond, stood a man in the finest linen suit. Intrigued, Stuart slowly walked to the doorway and out onto the terrace. Upon sensing his presence, the Hermit turned around and smiled at him.

Stuart recoiled. He had seen that smile before. His mind raced through the events of the past two weeks before he remembered. A smile on a poster, on a wall, in Medellín.

"I know who you are," Stuart said.

**

The Ambassador nervously waited on the tarmac as the large Royal Air Force transport plane taxied from the runway. He was in a daze. Everything that had happened in the past few hours, and the past few weeks for that matter, were spinning around in his mind. The black suit that he had to wear despite the tropical heat did not help either.

Out at the farm, the priests had told him that Tara Lawson was the traitor. At first, he had refused to believe it. Granted, he had been disappointed in her performance ever since they received the tip from Manuel Lopez, but he could not accept that that meant she was working for the cartel. Anyway, it was Mr D, he and Cooth had insisted. The priest said yes, they had found Mr D in Manuel's photos when giving them a second look, but Tara Lawson was in there as well. As they had all shared their respective stories, it had gradually dawned on the Ambassador that the priests were telling the truth. Not only did Mr D work for the cartel, so did Tara. The final blow was when the priests revealed that the only senior member of the cartel they knew by name was Julian Reyes.

The Ambassador took a deep breath to steady himself.

Julian Reyes! He had eaten at Julian's restaurant! What nerves of steel Tara must have had, to have invited him there. Despite Cooth's objection due to the lack of evidence, the Ambassador was now convinced that the Hermit was Senator Reyes. Their family feuding was probably just a show. Together, the Senator, Julian and Tara knew enough to successfully run a drug cartel under the radar, as well as stage the attack on the Prince and the President. But now, standing on the tarmac, what really worried the Ambassador was getting killed himself, if he somehow got caught up in the crossfire.

Last night, Cooth had made some calls and then they had both, somehow, managed to get a few hours of sleep. The priests had disappeared, still on the search for the Hermit and the captives. Cooth had started searching for Tara when he woke up. The Ambassador had been forced to suppress all this from his mind. He had attended a final security briefing, where at least they had some faces to look at, before heading out to the airport to meet the Prince.

As the aircraft parked and turned off its engines, the Colombian Army music corps struck up a lively rendition of the British national anthem. Military officers and local dignitaries eagerly looked on as the Prince and his wife, the Duchess, disembarked, followed by their staff and security officers. The Ambassador was lucid enough to properly greet the Prince and the Duchess, but as they moved on, his mind went back to thinking about Tara. Where was she? What was going to happen today?

The Ambassador could not reach Cooth on the phone for the next few hours, which made him panic even further. He trailed the Royal party as they made their way through the colonial streets of the Old City, occasionally stopping to admire a particular building or monument. Uniformed and plainclothes security officers were everywhere, including a team of Royal Marines who had come ashore from the HMS Atholl. The Ambassador, however, was not paying much attention to anything. His mind had lost its ability to focus. Before he knew it, they were in the official cars for the short drive to the Fortress, where the Royals would meet the President, and a short speech would be delivered.

This is where Manuel Lopez had told Cooth that the assassination would take place. The Ambassador tried calling Cooth again, but no answer. Where was Cooth? In his panic, he started wondering if Cooth had run off with Tara. Why was he not answering his phone?

**

"It is very nice to meet you in person, Mr Gleeman," the Hermit said. "I am sorry I didn't get to meet you earlier."

"I guess you were busy running for re-election, Congressman Escaso," Stuart said.

Stuart did not know what to feel. He was not surprised, that was all he knew. He had guessed that the Hermit was someone powerful, so why not a congressman? Stuart remembered that he had seen Congressman Escaso in many news reports, always speaking so highly of the future, of establishing a 21st-century economy that worked for everyone, and always praising the Prince's upcoming visit, even when others, such as that Senator Reyes, had so roundly criticised it. Even Carolina had been enthusiastic about the Congressman's vision for the future. He remembered reading that the Congressman was the senior member of the Foreign Affairs committee in Congress, which clearly gave him influence and no doubt made him privy to a lot of secret information. Maybe the security details for the Prince's visit? Then, perhaps, Molly was right. There was nothing that Stuart could do to stop it.

He looked at the Congressman, standing by a railing, looking exuberant. A simple push would do it, Stuart thought, but then he shuddered. He was not built for such cold-blooded murder, no matter what the circumstances.

"What do you have planned for today?" Stuart asked instead.

Congressman Escaso pointed up towards the sky.

"The Prince's plane, it is landing just now. He and his wife will tour the city. In a few hours, they will arrive at the Fortress of San Felipe. I will be there, of course, in my official capacity. They will meet the President. There will be a short speech."

"And then you kill them?"

Congressman Escaso smiled.

"They are obstacles, Stuart. Obstacles to free trade."

"The free trade of your drugs?"

"Free trade that brings in millions of dollars, which I share with my people."

"You know you will be stopped, right?" Stuart asked boldly.

Congressman Escaso laughed.

"I understand why you think that. But last night your friends, the Red Widow and the priests, raided another apartment nearby, thinking I was there. It is owned by Julian's cousin's cousin someone or other, I can see why they thought I would be there. Then they raided a farmhouse, which was a clever decoy on my part." His nose twitched. "It didn't go exactly as I planned, but never mind. So, you see, your friends are running around like headless chicken, but they will not find me. I will succeed."

Stuart's heart sank. The Congressman would be on the podium, no doubt directing the attack somehow. Tara had surely done something to pave the way for an assassin. No one in the security detail would think it strange if Tara, or indeed the Congressman, gave them instructions. Stuart thought it was unlikely that Tara would do the deed herself. And after it was done, no one would suspect Tara or the Congressman of being involved.

"Why?" Stuart asked. "Is it just about the money?"

"Not at all," Congressman Escaso said. "In the valley, Julian took you to a clearing, remember?"

Stuart remembered. He and Julian had climbed up the southern slope in order for Julian to ask what would happen if the Prince was assassinated. Julian had not liked it when Stuart said that the consequences would not be as major as the cartel had hoped for. He also recalled earthworks in the clearing, as if a house had once stood there.

"It was my ancestor's house," Congressman Escaso explained. "I was born in it. Escobar, you know, had it burnt down when he was on the run from the law, twenty or so years ago. I was a younger man, enraged by the unnecessary cruelty, and it led me to revenge."

"You killed Escobar?" Stuart asked incredulously.

"Of course not," Congressman Escaso said and laughed. "No, no. But I knew some people who were involved. It was a period of great moral ambiguity. Who sided with who, who was good, who was bad? I learnt that through the chaos could come order, but only through strong leadership."

"So you became a Congressman?"

"Yes, in time. But I also learnt to take pity on those caught up in the chaos through no fault of their own, and my political message is very genuine. I do want to help my people."

"How does an assassination help people?"

"Indirectly, of course. No, today's events will lead to two things. One, it is a message of my power. It is important for certain partners, and enemies, of mine to know that this is what I can and will do. The people who take my drugs to the United States and Europe need to know that they work for me, and me alone, and that they must never cross me. Secondly, today's event will create chaos."

"And how does that help people?" Stuart asked.

"Through the chaos comes order, like I said. And who do you think will provide that order?"

"You?"

"Exactly! With the President gone, anything can happen in next month's election. I will establish myself as the only true leader, the one who got our country through and out of the chaos of assassination. I will be respected and admired, even abroad. I'll fly to London, as Congress' representative, and cry at the Prince's funeral, and speak of a brighter future. This is when I will sweep to power!"

"I'm still not sure how this will help people," Stuart dared say, marvelling at the man's political delusions.

"When I am president, we will become the greatest country in Latin America," Congressman Escaso said proudly. "We will have global power, wealth, trade, and respect. And when I'm finally in power, I won't need the drugs. I can wipe out all guerrillas, insurgents, and criminals. I'll scrap the President's nauseating peace deal with the guerrillas, who have no sense of civility, honour, or tact. He is a dishonourable man for even proposing it. No, the future, Mr Gleeman, the future that I will create, is going to be great!"

Stuart was amazed.

"Will you really give up all the money you get from this?" he asked, not sure how to respond to Congressman Escaso's bizarre vision.

Congressman Escaso chuckled.

"Yes. There are crazy people, like Julian in there, or the Red Widow out there in the city somewhere, who simply seek money. For me, it is just the springboard to power. There are great days ahead, Stuart, and I'm just sorry that you will not be alive to see it."

Stuart's heart jumped, but he understood.

"You'll ask for ransom, but I know too much."

"Yes," Congressman Escaso said. "Tara Lawson, did you ever meet her? Anyway, she insisted you be treated well. I have indulged you and Molly for a few weeks, but I am afraid that today is the day you die."

Stuart froze in fear.

As his mind slowly got around to accepting what the Congressman had just said, he started to wonder whether this was his last chance to act. The Congressman was still standing by the railing. He was only a few steps away. Stuart could rush up on him and push. Maybe the

Congressman would grab hold of Stuart and pull him over the side as well, but perhaps that was a worthy sacrifice? Queen and Country, and all that? But would that stop the others in the cartel? No, it would not. They would probably kill Molly right away, which was no good, and then carry on with the assassination. As Stuart hesitated, the Congressman walked away and headed into the living room. Stuart remained still, breathing heavily. It took a while to calm down. Carefully, he peeked over the railing. It was a long way down. He quickly stepped backwards and steadied himself.

Julian came out on the terrace and motioned for him. The Congressman was waiting in the living room, a phone in his hand.

"The Prince will soon be at the Fortress," he said. "Let's go."

**

Congressman Escaso left in his own car, no doubt to go straight to the podium. He had ordered Stuart and Molly to come along in a separate car, which would wait somewhere not too far from the Fortress. The Congressman wanted his hostages nearby, just in case. Stuart felt dejected and powerless. He was struggling to wrap his mind around it being his last day alive. As they got closer, desperation was starting to grow inside him.

The driver parked the car on a narrow side street, alongside a row of colourful townhouses. They saw some soldiers in the distance, so Stuart guessed they were just outside the security zone. Julian was sitting in the front seat. He turned around and looked at Stuart and Molly in the back.

"This is the place," he said. "I have to go out there. But you two stay. You'll be under guard, so don't think you can escape."

"What do you think is going to happen if you succeed?" Molly asked angrily. "Do you really think you can just walk away?"

Julian nodded gravely.

"Yes, Ms Reed. That is exactly what will happen. I will walk away, as will the Hermit, and we will come back and get you, and we'll ransom you off. Once they know our strength and capabilities, they will pay handsomely for you two."

Stuart shook his head in disbelief.

"Stuart, you have seen the lovely lady with the red hair. You can only begin to guess what powerful people work for me. I will succeed."

Molly gasped for air.

"You mean Tara really works for you?"

Stuart had not told Molly anything of what Congressman Escaso had said on the terrace. Julian only laughed.

"You finally understand."

Before he could continue there was a rap on the window. Julian turned around and lowered it. A woman leaned in, looking rather nervous. She wore a brightly coloured scarf over her head, but the red locks falling out underneath it were unmistakable. Molly yelled out in anger.

"Hello, Molly," Tara said. "It's nice to see you again."

Molly stuttered but could not form the words to reply.

"And Stuart, I'm sorry we didn't have the chance to say hello up at the estate. I hope you are both well."

"Well, this was a nice reunion," Julian said and slowly opened the door, as Tara stepped away. He turned around one last time. "Stuart, Molly, see you when this is over."

Julian stepped out of the car. Stuart reached forwards to try to stop him, but the driver beat him back with his gun. Another cartel soldier then sat down in the front passenger seat and pointed his gun at the captives. Stuart admitted defeat and leaned back. He saw Julian and his men head down an alleyway, leading towards the Fortress. Tara, however, rapidly walked down the road, along the townhouses, perhaps trying to reach the Fortress from a different approach. It was probably a good idea to attack from multiple fronts.

"What the hell do we do now?" Molly asked quietly.

"Don't know," Stuart said. "There's no way out that I can see."

"If Tara is working for the cartel, who else might be? Do you think they'll actually succeed?"

She sounded petrified.

"They might have a chance," Stuart conceded.

He looked out the window, staring aimlessly down the street. He was reflecting on the possible outcomes and their consequences. What all the outcomes had in common was complete chaos.

He then saw the worst possible omen.

Up ahead, Death was crossing the street, a scythe in his hand. His heart jumped and his whole body with it. Molly looked at him curiously, but before she could ask what was going on, Stuart realised who Death was.

Instinctively, he lunged forwards, taking the guards by surprise, and started beating on the car's horn. He managed to sound it for a few seconds before the guards pulled him off it and started pushing him back towards the rear. Molly, by some instinctive reaction, pushed him in the other direction, trying to keep him up front so he could press the horn again. Hopefully, someone would come and see what was going on.

There was suddenly a light knock on the driver's side window. Everyone in the car froze for a second, as the guards reached for their guns. The front doors were flung open on both sides, and the guards were dragged out, leaving Stuart slumped between their seats. As he struggled to sit back up, he could hear some grunts from outside, and then the sound of two bodies being thrown up against the car.

"What a small world, eh?" Father Antonio said, opening the rear passenger door and letting Stuart out. "You're lucky we found you."

"I think I found you," Stuart said and embraced his old

friend. He noticed that he was carrying a long walking stick.

"I never gave up hope."

Stuart did not confess that he had completely given up hope. He also embraced Father Juan, who was stepping around the car, having just let Molly out from her seat.

"How are you?" Juan asked pastorally. "Have you been treated well?"

"We have, yes," Stuart said. There was no time to ask questions, not even why Antonio suddenly had a walking stick. "The assassination of the Prince and the President is happening right now at the Fortress. Julian Reyes and Tara Lawson, they left here just minutes ago."

"I've just texted Mr Cooth," Juan said. "He'll be here in a second."

Stuart's mouth fell open. Cooth, the man in the suit from London, was here? Maybe, after everything else that had happened, that should not surprise him.

"You have met him?"

"Yes," Antonio said. "He's been a very useful friend these last few hours."

"Is…is Carolina here?" Stuart asked.

Antonio grinned.

"Yes, she's with the Red Widow, somewhere. They were heading to the Fortress from a different direction. We were out looking for you and the Hermit. She'll be so relieved to hear that you are safe."

Before Stuart could say anything else, Cooth appeared around a corner and greeted Stuart and Molly in a very formal tone.

"The Ambassador will be pleased," he concluded. "Now, we must pursue the enemy. What can you tell us?"

"You know about Tara?"

"Yes," Cooth said, clearly suppressing his anger.

"And the Hermit. It is Congressman Escaso."

Cooth and the priests stared at him for a moment, before regaining their composure.

"That's not good," Cooth managed to say. "Juan,

Antonio, take Molly, get eyes on the Congressman, and don't lose track of him. I want to go after Tara."

"Sounds good," Juan said.

"Colonel Zapata and his men are up there, along with the Prince's security detail. Tell the Colonel about the Hermit."

"Will do."

"Be safe," Stuart said.

Juan and Antonio cumbersomely lifted the two cartel soldiers back into the car. Stuart left them to it and started following Cooth, who was already sprinting down the road. He felt light. Now that he was free, it was as if a literal weight had been lifted from his body. His mind was focused solely on finding those responsible, first of all Tara, who might have masterminded his capture. Not even the pressing Caribbean heat was bothering him now.

They had almost reached the end of the road, where it merged into the main road leading to the Fortress, when Cooth stopped abruptly to answer this phone. Stuart stopped as well and realised that he was completely drenched in sweat, but he pushed that to one side and looked around. He could see a crowd gathering up by the Fortress, and a fair number of police officers and soldiers posted by the street corners and along the main road. However, they would not do much good unless they knew exactly who they were looking for. He was convinced that neither Tara, Julian, nor Congressman Escaso would actually carry out the assassination themselves.

"Bloody hell!"

Stuart looked at Cooth.

"What's going on?"

"There was a Mr D mentioned in those photos that Manuel Lopez took."

"I didn't know that."

"Yes, Mr Lopez told me that when I met him. We thought that Mr D was working in the British government. GCHQ has been, ahem, you know."

"What did they find?"

"Talk about coming through in the nick of time. Unexplained payments to an Alan David."

Cooth paused for a second, shaken by what he had found out.

"Alan David is on the Prince's security team. He's on the security team!"

Cooth started sprinting down the main road towards the Fortress, with Stuart following close behind. He could hear music playing up ahead, suggesting that the ceremony had begun. As they got closer Stuart saw that the main road in front of the Fortress had been closed off, and it was now a teeming mass of people, looking at a podium built halfway up the ramp which led to the top of the fort. Stuart thought that he recognised the Prince, but from this distance, he could not be certain.

However, their progress was quickly impeded by the crowd. Stuart tried pushing on but was met with angry responses from the other people around him. Then, the music stopped. A man stepped up to make an introduction. It was Congressman Escaso.

**

Alan David was standing just below the platform, looking out over the crowd. The Army music corps was still playing. He knew that once they were finished, the Prince would be introduced by some congressman, and then take to the podium to deliver his royal speech. That was the moment when the assassination was to take place. David was positioned on the embankment, to the front and left of the podium. A cartel hitman was going to come up the embankment. David's role was to let him through and not intervene. The hitman was meant to shoot the Prince and then the President in quick succession. During this, David was meant to hold back other people and let the hitman slip away in the inevitable chaos. If all went to plan, he would get the rest of the money the cartel had promised him.

Of course, he was worried about getting exposed. That would mean spending the rest of his life in prison. Tara Lawson had made assurances though, on behalf of the cartel, that he would be safe if anyone suspected him of being involved. That was a bit flimsy, perhaps, but he trusted her because of her senior position. She was not some low-level secretary pretending at greatness. She was the real deal.

He saw her in the crowd. For some reason, she was wearing a scarf over her head. It seemed odd to him, and he did not like surprises, but there was nothing he could do now. She nodded at him, almost imperceptibly, and he quickly nodded back. The music corps was reaching the climax of their performance. It was time.

He lost sight of Tara. The crowd was growing. He thought he could see some shuffling amongst the audience, but nothing that was of any concern to him. This was not the first time he was guarding a podium with VIP speakers. His eyes kept scanning from left to right and back, taking in the whole scene as well as details about the nearby people at the same time.

The music corps finished. The congressman, who David knew nothing about, stepped up to the podium and introduced the Prince. David knew that the Prince was only going to speak for a few minutes, essentially to say hello and thank you to the city for inviting him. The crowd was watching the congressman speak and then the Prince stepped up. David kept his back to the podium, now searching for the cartel hitman.

A young man moved forwards through the crowd. David kept a close eye on him. The young man came closer. They made eye contact, and the young man gave a small nod. This was it.

**

Somehow he managed to break free of the crowd. He was standing on the embankment. The sloping stone walls of the fort towered above him. He could clearly see the makeshift podium on which the Prince was currently speaking.

Stuart looked around, trying to find anything suspicious. He was not sure what he was looking for. He heard the Prince say something about friendship. Then he saw what he was looking for. A fairly tall man, wearing a jacket, scanning the crowd below. That had to be one of the Prince's security team since both the Colombian police and army were in uniform. Was this Alan David?

Stuart started walking up towards the man. What would he do? How would he apprehend the man? Stuart felt a presence to his side. He looked over and saw a young man walking up the embankment. He passed close to David, but David did not react. Was this the plan, Stuart wondered. David would let the young man shoot the Prince? Stuart tried to take a few quick steps forward to stop the young man, but he suddenly felt a strong hand press backwards on his chest.

"Stay back."

He looked up and saw David's face staring back at him. He tried to look past David and could see the young man reach for something underneath his shirt. It was a gun.

Stuart tried to lunge forwards, but David held him back, a surprised look on his face. As Stuart battled on, the young man ahead carefully raised his gun with his right hand, trying to keep it hidden from view beneath his left hand. The man was a second away from pulling the trigger.

Stuart was about to shout out as another figure stepped into view and overpowered the young man. Cooth grabbed hold of his arms and, with the help of a soldier, pushed the young man back down the embankment. David began flicking his head back and forth, but he quickly realised that the game was up. He tried to sprint away, but now it was Stuart's turn to grab hold of him. Soon, two more soldiers arrived and firmly grabbed David by both arms, dragging him away.

Stuart was left panting. Many of the nearby onlookers were staring curiously at him and the two men being led away by the soldiers, but no one intervened. As he caught his breath, he could hear the Prince finish his remarks, and handed over the podium to the President, who was met with loud cheers. Stuart followed the two captives, confident that Congressman Escaso was still up on the podium, and snaked through the crowd to the main road beyond. There he saw that David and the intended shooter were being put inside police vehicles. Cooth was also there, speaking to an older police officer who seemed to be in charge. Stuart kept his distance, figuring he would speak to Cooth when things had calmed down slightly.

Suddenly, he was tackled from behind. He yelled out and spun around, ready to defend himself, but he quickly let his guard down.

"You're safe!"

Carolina embraced him properly.

"Yes, I am," he said. "It's so good to see you."

"I was worried there for a moment."

They held the embrace in silence.

"Juan and Antonio said you were with the Red Widow," Stuart remarked finally. "Where are they?"

Carolina smiled.

"Well, the Red Widow was pointing out her competitors to her police boyfriend, all over the place. They have arrested several people. She was overjoyed."

"I can imagine."

Carolina's face then went very grave.

"There was a bit of chaos when they arrested the shooter. Juan told me and the Red Widow that Congressman Escaso is the Hermit. I couldn't believe it! I almost voted for him!"

"Chaos?" Stuart asked. He had a bad feeling.

"Escaso got away. He left the podium. Juan and Antonio began chasing after him, but I lost them." She paused, looking even more nervous. "About Antonio…I'm worried about him."

"Why?"

"Look…do you have any idea where the Hermit might be going?"

Stuart nodded. Congressman Escaso was probably going back to the penthouse apartment. He had seemed safe and confident there, sure that the place could not in any way be linked to him.

"Let's go," Carolina said.

"We should tell the police," Stuart said, pointing to where Cooth and the officer were still engaged in conversation.

"I'll text them on the way."

With great urgency, Carolina led the way down the road to a parked SUV. It looked like the ones that belonged to the Red Widow. Carolina got a key from her pocket and jumped into the driver's seat, and impatiently hurried Stuart on. He got into the passenger seat and without a second wasted they were hurtling into the traffic.

Stuart directed her the best he could away from the Fortress, through Gethsemane, past the Old City and back out to the glistening white high-rises in Bocagrande. Congressman Escaso had not tried to conceal which building he was in from Stuart, which now seemed like an act of great overconfidence. It did not take long before Stuart recognised it. Far up, he could see the penthouse balcony. If Congressman Escaso was anywhere, it was up there.

As they pulled up to the main entrance, Stuart saw someone he had not expected.

"You survived," the Red Widow said with a clear tang of disappointment as Stuart got out of the car.

"I did."

"So, this is where it ends."

"Is Escaso here?"

"Yes, who knew?" The Red Widow shook her head. "A congressman! He and your holy friends are upstairs. I am waiting for the police. They should be here soon."

Stuart felt very confused.

"Why are Juan and Antonio up there?"

"Come on," Carolina said impatiently, already walking up to the entrance. "I should have stopped this earlier."

Stuart ran after her, leaving the Red Widow lounging out on the sidewalk.

"Stopped what?"

"Come on."

They got into the lift and rode all the way up to the top floor. Carolina was shaking her head and Stuart fortified himself for whatever was going to happen. Only now did he realise that he was still unarmed. If Congressman Escaso was holding the priests as hostages, there was nothing he could do. Other than trust that the Red Widow really was waiting for the police.

Carolina barged into the penthouse, Stuart just a step behind her.

"Oh, no," Carolina said and stopped as she saw what was happening in the living room.

Stuart pressed on past her but similarly stopped in surprise. He saw Congressman Escaso sitting on the sofa, looking surprisingly calm. His hands and legs were carefully tied up with some rope. Juan and Antonio were standing next to him. Antonio had a gun in his hand, pointing straight at Escaso's head. Stuart stared in disbelief.

"What the hell is going on here?"

Chapter 36

After the speech, during which Congressman Escaso had rudely left, everyone departed for a reception by the waterfront, close to the Old City. The Ambassador was feeling relieved. Cooth had sent a text, saying that the would-be assassin had been arrested. He was too tired to worry about Tara. He was too tired to even consider who the Hermit might be. Right now, he had a glass of champagne in his hand, and he was happy.

He got a text on his phone. He tried to read it discreetly, to avoid seeming rude to the Prince and the President, who were sitting around a nearby table. It was another message from Cooth. The Ambassador's mouth fell open. Congressman Escaso was the Hermit. He was reported to be in an apartment in Bocagrande, and the police were responding.

It took a few minutes for the Ambassador to process the news, but it made sense. They had expected the Hermit to be someone powerful. Congressman Escaso fit the bill. He glanced over at Senator Reyes, who was chatting animatedly to some other guests nearby. He felt a bit guilty at having accused her. No, if he was being honest with himself, he had been convinced that it was her. He thought about apologising to her, but after all her anti-British rhetoric he thought that perhaps they were even.

He looked at her again. Why was she even here? After so vehemently opposing the Prince's visit, her presence seemed strange. No, he shook off his suspicion. She was probably here to be seen and photographed. She was running for president, after all.

He sipped his champagne, but it only made him feel more tired. Where was Tara, he wondered? Where was her boyfriend, Julian? Hopefully, they were in the same place as Congressman Escaso, and they would be arrested together. That would be a nice way to wrap up this whole debacle. He sighed. How was he ever going to look the

Foreign Secretary in the eyes again? His own head of security, working for a cartel and trying to assassinate the Prince. This would be the end of his career.

He suddenly saw a face which he thought that he recognised. It was a man in his thirties, heading confidently through the crowd towards the table where the Prince and the President were seated. The Ambassador followed his progress, trying to remember who the man was. Then it struck him.

It was Julian Reyes.

How had he got in here? The Ambassador did not know what to do. There was no security in here, they were all outside. How had Julian managed to get in? What was he here to do? He was still heading towards the Prince and the President. The Ambassador panicked. Was he here to carry out the assassination?

The Ambassador tried to make his way towards the Prince's table.

"You must die," Julian's loud voice boomed out.

The Ambassador saw that he had pulled out a gun and was pointing it at the President. All around him, the other guests started screaming and ran towards the exits. The Ambassador tried to move forwards but his path was blocked.

"What are you doing, you idiot?" a shrill voice said, overpowering the screaming of the other guests.

"He must die," Julian repeated.

The Ambassador broke free and hurried forwards. He could see security guards racing in from different directions. Someone was grappling with Julian.

"You can't do this, cousin."

Julian pulled the trigger. The Ambassador screamed in terror. Senator Reyes groaned and clutched her chest.

"You can't kill the Republic," she said to her cousin, and fell to the floor, blood pouring from a bullet hole.

**

Stuart took a few more steps into the living room, looking around. It was clear that there was no one else in the apartment. Carolina also took a few steps forward, stopping next to Stuart.

"He ran the moment he realised that we were on to him," Antonio said. "The fact that you're here suggests that you stopped the assassination."

"Yes, we did," Stuart said. "The Prince and the President are alive and well."

The Hermit did not react. He kept calmly looking up at the gun.

"What the hell is going on here?" Stuart asked again. He turned to Carolina. "Did you know about this?"

"He's a priest," she said defensively. "I never thought he'd go through with it."

"First and foremost I'm just a man," Antonio said. He took his eyes off the gun and looked at Stuart. "I didn't expect that you would come here."

"I bet you didn't."

Antonio had his finger on the trigger. He must have been holding the gun for some time because his hand had started shaking gently from tiredness. That was not a good sign. When no answer came, Stuart again demanded to know what was going on. Juan opened his mouth but did not say anything. Instead, he looked at Antonio, who seemed increasingly uncomfortable.

"This is the reason I came here," Antonio said slowly.

"To kill the Hermit?" Stuart asked incredulously.

Antonio nodded.

Finally, the last pieces of the puzzle began to come together for Stuart. He had reflected on this for so long without ever getting an answer, ever since Carolina had warned him about the priests. The dark look in Antonio's eyes, which he had first seen on the flight from Madrid. His willingness, eagerness even, to help Stuart. Why he had accepted a gun, why he had shot the cartel soldier in San Antonio Park. Perhaps the priests really had killed Raul in El Retiro, as Julian Reyes had claimed. As Stuart's mind raced through everything that had happened, there was one last thing that did not add up.

"The reason you came here? To Colombia?"

"Yes," Antonio said, more resolutely.

Stuart took a deep breath and swore loudly, which he immediately regretted since it made Antonio jump.

"I can't believe this," Stuart said. "You...I came to you because I had been implicated in a murder. Manuel's family. I came to you!" He stopped, trying to make sense of what had happened. "I thought you were helping me, clearing my name, rescuing Molly. But...what, you weren't helping me? I was just coming along with you? On some murderous quest?"

Stuart had been shouting towards the end, but neither Antonio nor Juan had reacted. Juan kept looking at Antonio, who was really starting to struggle with the gun. Carolina placed her hand on Stuart's shoulder, and he took a deep breath to control his emotions.

"How long have you known?" he asked her.

"A few days," she said. "We were talking, after you got kidnapped."

Stuart turned back to Antonio.

"Why?" He tried to ask as calmly as he could. "What reason do you have for...for...coming here to execute this man?"

Antonio looked pleadingly at Juan for a moment, and then quickly looked back at the Hermit, who was carefully listening to everything that was being said. It was clear that he did not know either why a priest had come all this way to kill him, and he seemed rather curious to find out.

"We could not believe it when you came to see us in Arví Park," Juan said, edging around so he could see both Antonio and Stuart. "We knew the murder of Manuel's family was linked to the cartel." He paused for a moment but Stuart bored his eyes into him. "You needed help and there was no harm in us helping you. The target was the same."

"Unbelievable," Stuart said. "I'm the sidekick in my

own story! I'm like fucking David Copperfield."

"What?" Carolina asked.

"I don't know, I only read the first line."

"We got you your passport," Juan interjected. "We thought we could put you on a flight out of Colombia, but you wanted to help. Clear your name, help us find Sara and Molly. We thought that three heads would be better than just the two of us. Of course, with Carolina, we got four heads."

Stuart suddenly remembered Molly. How could he have forgotten her?

"She's safe," Juan assured him. "We left her with the police, she's being looked after."

"Good. Yes, but what about Sara? She got killed because of all this!"

Everyone looked at Stuart, except the Hermit who rolled his eyes.

"She's quite safe," Carolina said.

"But Julian Reyes said…"

"He lied. She escaped. We left her in the tender care of the Red Widow. I just hope that wasn't a mistake."

"She's fine," Juan said.

Stuart chuckled nervously.

"Well, that's good news. But still! You dragged me and Carolina into this criminal pursuit?"

Juan continued as Antonio was still staring at the Hermit.

"You came along, yes, but no, not on some criminal pursuit. Your intention, which was ours as well, was to clear your name and rescue Molly and Sara. That's why you and Carolina came along."

"That's a fine distinction," Stuart said. "I'll be an accessory to murder now, say what you will."

"No, you're not," Juan said. "You knew nothing of this."

"I do now! So you were on this quest. I was tagging along for my own reasons. I still don't understand why. Why the hell is Antonio here to…to kill the Hermit?"

"That is not for me to say," Juan said.

Stuart scoffed but they all now looked at Antonio. Having arrived at this pivotal question, Antonio was straining his face, trying to focus simply on pointing the gun at the Hermit. Stuart was not sure what demons he was trying to keep at bay, but he felt he deserved an explanation. The Hermit looked up at Antonio, appearing remarkably calm for someone who had a gun in their face.

"Yes, why are we here?" the Hermit asked.

"It goes back a long way," Antonio finally said in a strained voice.

It always does, Stuart thought, but did not say anything. He waited patiently for Antonio to continue.

"You already know why I'm here, Stuart. I told you on the flight from Madrid. Some years ago I met a girl, shortly after I had qualified as a lawyer."

"Yes," Stuart said. "Yes, the girl you met for one evening, who broke your heart. You became a priest because of it." He paused, feeling confused. "How does she come into this?"

Antonio fought back tears. Stuart looked searchingly towards Juan and the Hermit, but Juan did not move and the Hermit shook his head, clearly not having a clue as to what was going on. They all waited patiently for Antonio to continue.

"Her name was Daniela. I don't really know what happened to me when she rejected me. I went into some emotional, spiritual, physical even, freefall. My job seemed pointless and I quit. Spain was collapsing in the recession, so I probably would've lost it anyway, but keeping it did not make any sense to me."

Oh dear, he found God in his depression, Stuart thought to himself, just moments before Antonio said the same thing out loud.

"So I became a priest," Antonio continued.

"You only met her for one night," Carolina said.

Antonio took no notice. Once he got tired of waiting, Stuart again asked how Daniela featured in the current situation.

"I didn't meet her again for many years," Antonio said. "She unexpectedly came to my ordination. It was really strange seeing her again after all that time. We talked for a while." He paused, thinking back to that day. There was a sadness in his eyes which Stuart struggled to understand. "Anyway, she was happy. She had been seeing a man for a few years and had become engaged to be married."

The Hermit was rolling his eyes, losing interest.

"Who was she engaged to?" Stuart asked, just to keep Antonio talking. His sadness seemed to be slowly overwhelming him.

Antonio took a deep breath, steadying his nerves.

"He was a civil servant in Madrid, called Carlos Muñoz."

The Hermit suddenly stirred and looked up at Antonio, finally starting to understand what was going on.

"Why do I know what name?" Stuart asked.

"Muñoz was a civil servant who worked for Spanish customs," the Hermit said calmly, taking over from Antonio, whose face was twisting into a deeper anger. "Including customs inspections at the port of Cadiz."

The Hermit explained that a few months ago, one of his men, the now deceased Raul, had made contact with Muñoz in Madrid. A simple relationship had been offered: a monthly gift in exchange for customs looking the other way when certain shipments came in from South America. Muñoz had said no, but he had been approached a few times to see if he would change his mind. He had not.

"Yes," Stuart said, remembering the outcome. "He was shot dead just outside his home." He then remembered the other detail, which the media had only mentioned in passing. "His fiancée was shot dead alongside him." He turned to Antonio. "That was Daniela?"

"Oh, fucking hell," the Hermit exclaimed angrily. "We're here because of that? Look, Father, it was a business decision, a... my business is growing, we need to make a mark in Europe. I had to send a message."

Antonio did not say anything. He was still pointing the gun at the Hermit's head, and that he still had the strength to keep it up was a testament to his commitment. Stuart was scrambling to think of something to say to defuse the situation, but he could not think of anything helpful. He had never before seen the raw emotion evident on Antonio's face, an expression of anger and hatred. He steered the conversation back to the Hermit.

"Then you killed the civil servant in London. Did he also reject you?"

"Yes, he did," the Hermit said.

"He obviously didn't get the message."

The Hermit shook his head.

"It has not all gone to plan. But that's the ups and downs of the drugs business. Death is a sad part of it. Tragic, but necessary."

"With little thought of the consequences," Stuart added.

The Hermit sighed and continued slowly.

"I do think of the consequences." He looked at Stuart. "I see them, feel them, live them, every day. And I really do care about my people. In the end, though, I'm just a realist."

"That's fair," Stuart said. "You think of the consequences. I should have said that there has been no one holding you to account for those consequences. Until now."

"I wouldn't say that," the Hermit said and turned back to Antonio. "Look, Father, I've done my best to offset those consequences. I pay good wages to my people, good benefits, they lead good lives because of me. I...I give to local charities. I try to be a good person."

"False charity is not a justification for wickedness," Juan said sternly, sounding like the Spanish Inquisition had come back to life.

"Indeed," Stuart said. He turned to Antonio. "I don't think murder is justification for murder either."

"You don't know, you don't understand how I felt, feel, about her," Antonio said angrily and passionately. "He needs to answer for that."

"I'm not religious, you know that, but even I know what the Bible says about murder. You can't think this is justified?"

"I have to do this," Antonio said. "I have to avenge her."

Stuart turned to Juan.

"Is this what Manuel told you when he came to see you, in your church? That the cartel, the Hermit's cartel, was responsible for everything, including the murders in Madrid?"

Juan nodded.

"And why did you tell Antonio?"

"He had a right to know."

"And why are you helping him?"

Juan suddenly looked angry.

"Why wouldn't I? Men like Escaso have wreaked this country. Killed my father. Killed anyone they, or their rich paymasters, thought was undesirable. Sent millions of people fleeing from their homes. Why not go after this…this…directly?"

"This man?" Stuart suggested. "So evil deserves evil in return?"

"Maybe. Maybe we are doing some good, protecting other people from this menace."

"But the army, the police, are right here. Why not just hand him over?"

"It's not enough," Antonio said angrily. "It is not enough."

Juan shook his head. Stuart did not know what else to add. It was clear that the two priests were lost in their anger and sadness, caused by so much death and loss. A part of him could understand that.

"Please don't do this," Stuart said finally.

With nothing else to add, knowing everything now rested on their consciences, he turned around and, with Carolina, walked out of the apartment. Without saying anything, they closed the door and walked slowly towards the lift. They would go down and make sure the Red

Widow had actually called the police. Then he would leave and get away from the madness of this paradise. As the lift arrived, a gunshot rang out behind them.

Chapter 37

"Contact, lieutenant."

Lieutenant Rebecca Hayden walked over to the radar operator.

"Is that the target?"

"Yes, ma'am. It matches the target parameters. It's arriving right on time as well."

"I wouldn't have pegged a Colombian drug runner to be this punctual."

"No, ma'am."

Captain Cranston soon arrived on the bridge and took control of his frigate. He was feeling extremely pleased with their cruise to the Caribbean. They had apprehended one drug smuggler on their very first day, who had led them to a plot to assassinate the Prince. His ship had saluted the Prince on Grand Cayman, and then again in Cartagena, where his crew had helped provide security on land. It was perhaps a bit outside their normal duties, but every one of them had risen to the occasion. The Prince was safe, as was the Colombian President. And now, in their final days on station, they had intelligence of another drug ship heading north towards Mexico.

"What do we know about the target?" he asked.

"Pleasure yacht, sir," lieutenant Hayden said. "Registered in Panama. Goes by the name Red."

"Unusual name for a boat," the captain remarked.

"Reflects the professional name of the owner, sir. The Red Widow."

"You mean the Black Widow?"

"No, sir," lieutenant Hayden said. "The Red Widow. Apparently, she killed a lot of communists."

"Huh."

"The intelligence report says the yacht will be laden with drugs, sir. It sails once a month."

The captain nodded and smiled.

"Well, aren't we the lucky ones! I love it when

intelligence comes together. Now, lieutenant, the Red Widow, you say! With a name like that, do you think their crew will go down without a fight?"

"No, sir."

"Damn right! Plot a course to intercept. Sound the general alarm. Action stations, action stations!"

**

His footsteps echoed in the central courtyard but the civil servants, bustling around, took no notice of him. He ascended the steps and walked briskly down the corridor towards the Foreign Secretary's office. The secretary gestured for him to go straight inside.

"Good morning, sir," he said, stepping into the office.

"Mr Cooth," the Foreign Secretary exclaimed. "The hero returns."

"That's good of you to say, sir."

"You foiled an assassination and took down two drug cartels!"

The Foreign Secretary motioned for him to have a seat in the sofa group. Cooth sat down and pulled out a dossier from his briefcase.

"I'm pleased to say that I've managed to put together an initial report, sir, with great assistance from the Colombian authorities."

"Good." The Foreign Secretary sighed. "You know, back when they thought that Stuart Gleeman and Robert Hughes were behind those murders in Medellín, I had the Colombian ambassador screaming at me, accusing British citizens on going on a murder spree across her country. Now, I hear some men rather enjoy being yelled at by a woman, but I have to say that I'm not one of them. But now, she seems very pleased with everything."

Cooth smiled sympathetically, not knowing how to respond to that.

"Stuart Gleeman has provided an account of what happened," he reported instead. "I spoke to him briefly in

Medellín in the days after the assassination attempt. He was recouping with a, ahem, female friend. She has also provided a statement. I hope to speak to him further when he returns to London, as I have some more questions for him."

"Walk me through the events then," the Foreign Secretary said.

"As you recall, sir, Mr Gleeman was sent to Medellín to deliver a parcel to the family of Manuel Lopez. He found instead that two family members had been killed, and it transpired later that a third one had been kidnapped. Robert Hughes, and Roderic Moylan-Roth, also stumbled onto the scene, apparently trying to assist Mr Gleeman. They were arrested on the spot for the murders. The cartel, through the media, also tried to implicate Mr Gleeman for the murders."

"Ah, the old blame the foreigner trick."

"Yes, sir. Now, Mr Gleeman managed to evade arrest, and he teamed up with two priests."

"Priests?"

"Hmm. I have to say that he was a bit vague on how he found these priests, but all in all, they seem to have been rather effective."

"Fair enough," the Foreign Secretary said.

"There was also a local lawyer involved, Carolina Rojas."

"This is the female friend?"

"Yes, sir. Again, I would like to find out a bit more about her, in due course, but again, she seems to have provided solid support."

"I guess lawyers can be useful."

"Yes, sir. Now, we, of course, knew about the cartel from Manuel Lopez, but we did not inform Mr Gleeman. He was, after all, only meant to do a quick drop. Mr Gleeman and his companions managed to learn that this cartel was responsible for the murders, as well as the kidnapping of Molly Reed and Sara Lopez, and they set about tracking it down. Whilst they were doing so, there was another murder in Medellín, a Guillermo Adler. There was then a shootout in central Medellín, and one cartel soldier was shot. He was killed by one of the priests, apparently in self-defence. There was then a series of murders in Cartagena. Details aside, they are all attributable to cartel violence. Finally, a murder in the town of El Retiro, a Raul Castaño. The deceased was a cartel soldier. It transpires that he was responsible for the deaths in Madrid and London. I have been in touch with the Spanish authorities, and we can close the books on both cases. Raul was apparently captured by Mr Gleeman and the priests and handed to the local police. The police released him and he was then killed by his own cartel, for some reason or other. However, again for unknown reasons, Mr Gleeman implicated the priests in Raul's death."

"Really? How peculiar."

"Mr Gleeman was then captured by the cartel. The priests and the lawyer informed the army, who stormed the cartel base. I was present myself at this event. Unfortunately, senior cartel members managed to escape together with Mr Gleeman and Ms Reed."

"Unfortunate."

"We knew that the cartel was planning the assassination in Cartagena, and it was fairly obvious that this is where they would be heading."

"Of course."

"The Ambassador and I met the priests in Cartagena, and they provided much assistance on the ground, stopping the assassination and finally appending the Hermit. You will have seen the news, of course."

"Congressman Escaso! I had only ever read nice things about him. The Ambassador said he was of great assistance in arranging the Prince's visit. Now we know why, I guess."

"Indeed. He was, in the end, apprehended by the police at a penthouse in Cartagena. To keep a lid on things the authorities did initially report him as dead, but they have now announced his capture and upcoming trial. It has caused quite a stir in Colombia, as you can imagine. However, once again, for some reason, Mr Gleeman asserted that one of the priests had shot and killed Escaso."

"I say!" The Foreign Secretary looked outraged. "What kind of man is this Mr Gleeman? Two priests help him take down a drug cartel and in return he accuses them of murder? Rather un-British, I must say."

"Quite," Cooth said. "As I said, I will interrogate him further when he returns to London. One of the priests, a Father Antonio Posada Velasquez, shot one man in Medellín, as I said, in self-defence. That might have given Stuart the wrong impression."

"Remarkably ungrateful."

The Foreign Secretary sighed.

"Well, he might just be misremembering things, or misunderstood things in the confusion," Cooth offered. "He's not a trained officer, after all."

"True. Well, one cartel down. It's a superb result."

"Yes, sir," Cooth said. "Now, Mr Gleeman provided further information about another cartel, led by someone called the Red Widow."

"You mean, the Black Widow?"

"No, sir, the Red Widow. She killed a bunch of communists."

"I see."

"The HMS Atholl intercepted her yacht a few days ago, sir. They seized many tonnes of cocaine and the yacht was destroyed. The Red Widow, unfortunately, is on the run, but this is hopefully the end of her cartel."

"Further great news."

"Yes, sir. Now, with Congressman Escaso arrested, his cartel is well and truly over. As you'll have also seen in the news, one of his top lieutenants was a man called Julian Reyes. He made a last-ditch attempt to assassinate the Prince and the President, but he was thankfully stopped by his own cousin."

"It's so sad," the Foreign Secretary said. "Senator

Reyes certainly didn't like us, but she definitely died a hero."

"Yes, sir. She sacrificed herself for the Republic, those were her dying words. Remarkably brave, and it has done wonders for her approval ratings."

"Yes." The Foreign Secretary chuckled but then adopted a serious face. "I was pleased that the President was re-elected in the end. It was the narrowest margin I've ever seen, but hopefully he can get the whole country behind him now, negotiate peace with the FARC, end the civil war, and stem the flow of drugs. I'm sure he's guaranteed a Nobel Peace Prize! All in all, a good result for us, for everyone."

"Yes, sir."

Cooth hesitated and fingered the top of the pages. He was not sure how the explain the rest.

"Is there a problem?" the Foreign Secretary asked.

"Yes, sir."

Cooth paused.

"Well?"

"I don't know how to explain this, sir. We received information that one of our own was working for the Hermit's cartel."

"Yes, I know. This Alan David. You apprehended him."

"Yes, sir." Cooth sighed. "This is information that another person was working for the cartel. We have investigated this, and unfortunately, the information is true."

"Who is this?"

"Tara Lawson, the Embassy Head of Security."

"What?"

The Foreign Secretary shot up from his seat and glared angrily at Cooth.

"The one I told you to reassign? The one you vouched for? The one who was in charge of absolutely everything security-related?"

"Yes, sir," Cooth said. "Well, it turned out that Julian

Reyes was her boyfriend. All she told us was that he owned some restaurants in Bogotá."

"I don't know what to say to this."

The Foreign Secretary slowly sat back down in his seat.

"I know, sir. Julian Reyes was arrested after he killed Senator Reyes. He confirmed all of this during his interview."

"Good. Okay, so what are you going to do about Ms Lawson?"

Cooth struggled to continue.

"Ahem, well, we don't know where she is."

"What?"

"We know she was in Cartagena. She was present at the fortress when we foiled the assassination. Somehow she got away."

"This is a disaster!"

Cooth nodded.

"I feel there is more," the Foreign Secretary said.

"Yes, sir. It turns out, well…. She must have been planning for this eventuality. The evidence is that she's the one who killed Robert Hughes and Roderic Moylan-Roth. She must have sensed that the writing was on the wall. She managed to make off with the access details for the cartel's various bank accounts, including a number of secret offshore accounts. When the investigators tried to access these accounts, well, they had been closed down. The money had been moved. It will be a nightmare trying to find where the money has gone to."

The Foreign Secretary looked ashen-faced.

"I cannot believe this! One of our own, working for a bloody drug cartel." The Foreign Secretary stood up and walked over to the window, adopting the pensive politician look. "No wonder that the cartel knew about our warships, and the Prince visiting, and God knows what other sensitive information."

"I know, sir. The only positive is that the cartel has been shut down."

"Do we know why she's done this?"

"At this stage, we can only speculate, sir. It might have been love, I hear it's a real thing. She might have had some reason betray us. We have to investigate."

The Foreign Secretary returned to his seat once more.

"Molly Reed is safe. That is important. Our warship and the Prince are safe, at least from this cartel. This Mr Gleeman needs some telling off for accusing the priests, but he did good work. You too, all things considered."

"Yes, sir. Thank you, sir. All of that is a very good result. We should be pleased."

"Find Tara Lawson."

"Yes, sir. It might not be today, or tomorrow, but we will track her down."

The Foreign Secretary sighed and pushed it out of his mind.

"Right, whilst I have you here, is there anything else?"

Cooth shuffled his papers again.

"Well, sir, there are a couple of things. Firstly, in Buenos Aires…"

**

Stuart was walking through the departure lounge at Bogotá El Dorado International Airport. He saw a sign from the Colombian Tourist Board reading 'Colombia – the only risk is wanting to stay'. He stared at it for a bit and then started to laugh. Murder and kidnapping aside, he had met some really hospitable people, seen spectacular sights, and eaten great food. On reflection, the slogan was probably true. Most tourists would not be asked by their respective intelligence agencies to deliver strange packages.

Moving around the airport, he perused some of the mandatory tourist shops selling expensive knickknacks, coffee and chocolates. He wondered if he should buy something for his boss, but decided against it. Feeling peckish, he gave in to temptation and bought some chocolate for himself. With that, he sighed and sank down on a seat.

He had had a long few weeks since the tumultuous day in Cartagena. He had met a Colonel Zapata, who had arranged for him and Carolina to fly back to Medellín. He had stayed in her apartment. A doctor had advised him to rest. He had refused to read the news or even watch it on TV, knowing it would just upset him. The only news Carolina told him was that the President had been re-elected. She had seemed neither happy nor sad about that. Most of the time he had sat on the balcony, looking out over the city, reflecting in silence. He thought about love and death, but mostly he was just amazed that he, an introvert with hardly a passion in life, had managed to survive this ordeal. It told him that he was stronger than he had ever believed, and though he rarely thought about the future, he now wondered what other opportunities might be out there for him.

Cooth had turned up one day and Stuart had provided a statement of everything that had happened. Colonel Zapata had also come to interview him. He had told his story so many times that he had started to believe it had all been a bad dream. None of that could really have happened, could it? He had been really pleased to see Molly, who had visited before flying back to England. Finally, after a few weeks, he had felt ready to leave. It had been hard to say goodbye to Carolina, but equally, when he had stepped into the taxi to head to the airport, he had felt some relief. He was glad to be going home.

He suddenly realised that he was late for the flight back to Madrid, where he would connect to London. He bolted up from his seat and walked as fast as he could to the gate. Most passengers had already boarded and he quickly headed down the walk bridge and onto the airplane. He realised that once again he was seated towards the rear.

As he moved down the aisle he spotted a familiar face. His heart started pounding in fear, anger, disappointment and disbelief.

"I'm afraid this is me."

"Still apologising, I see." Father Antonio smiled

warmly. "It is good to see you, Stuart. I prayed that we would meet again."

"Yes," Stuart said and sat down.

He had not looked at the news and did not know how anything had played out in Cartagena after he had left the Hermit's penthouse. The fact that Antonio killed the Hermit had shattered him. Carolina had wanted to tell him about some of the developments, but he had refused to listen. In his mind he was sitting down next to a killer, and that Antonio was free to leave the country confused him greatly. Antonio realised as much.

"There is something I would like to say to you, Stuart. But maybe this tells it better."

Antonio handed over a newspaper. Stuart looked on the front page and was taken aback by the headline. The notorious drug baron, Congressman Escaso, outed as the Hermit, had been captured by the Colombian police and was going to stand trial.

"I shot the wall," Antonio said quietly, making sure that none of the other passengers were listening. "I couldn't do it. I came all that way, so consumed with anger." He paused. "I really wanted to do it. But then you challenged me, and I realised that to an outsider, with no personal involvement in the story, I could not justify my actions." He chuckled in disbelief. "I have sinned most grievously. The police agreed that the cartel soldier I shot in San Antonio Park was killed in legitimate defence of your life. So legally I am cleared. Morally, I don't know."

"You shot the wall?"

"Yes, Stuart. And I am so very sorry. I am sorry you got involved."

"What about Raul?"

Antonio looked at Stuart before realising what he was being asked.

"You were told I killed him? No, it was the cartel. I don't know why."

A weight was lifted from Stuart's shoulders. Antonio was innocent.

"Maybe the cartel wanted to poison my mind against you."

"Perhaps."

"I'm sorry as well then," Stuart said. "I misjudged you and Juan. Carolina really didn't like either of you, maybe I was too swayed by that."

"No, she didn't! But I think she came around in the end. Or maybe not." Antonio chuckled and shook his head. "They say that God moves in mysterious ways. He has tested me, and I know I have failed, but who would've thought that He would send, as my moral guide, a lawyer! And one from England at that!"

They both laughed at that.

"I've never been called a moral guide before," Stuart said.

"I think too many sheep never thank their shepherds. So thank you."

The plane started moving back from the gate. Stuart realised there was still something amiss.

"There is one major flaw in this story, though," he said.

"What's that?"

"Our cooperation, me being your moral guide and all, it all hinges on us being seated next to each other on that flight from Madrid. What are the odds of that happening?"

Antonio nodded in contemplation.

"And don't say God," Stuart added.

"I wouldn't dream of it," Antonio said with a broad grin.

They both laughed.

"Major plot hole, I think," Stuart said and shook his head. "Oh look, they fixed the camera."

The small screen in front of them had switched to the tailfin camera, giving them a perfect view of the plane as it taxied down towards the runway.

"Colombian engineers, eh?" Antonio looked out of the window instead, seeing the skyscrapers of central Bogotá in the distance. "I'll be back soon, I'm sure. With my mind cleared from sinister intent, I think I'll enjoy it more. What about you? Will you be back to see Carolina?"

"Yes," Stuart said slowly. He had not given it much thought, but he recalled the tourist slogan and nodded to himself. "Yes, why not? If you discount the dead bodies, it was a paradise of sorts."

"Yes. A place of real wonder." Antonio smiled. "Well, here we go."

They leaned back in their seats and enjoyed the view from the tailfin camera as the plane thundered down the runway and rose in a graceful arc over the snow-capped peaks of the Andes, turning north, for home.

Author's note

I wrote this novel after visiting Colombia during Easter 2014. I was fascinated by its history, culture, the sights and the people. The only drawback, if it can be called that, is the immense heat; even so, I was probably the only one on the return flight who was excited when the pilot announced 'grey clouds and a light drizzle' at London Heathrow.

Colombia was colonised by the Spanish in the 16th century, not least because of the discovery of gold. The indigenous cultures already living there included the Tairona (whose descendants, the Kogi, still occupy the northern Sierra Nevada Mountains) and the Muisca. These cultures were experts at gold, and created all manner of gold artefacts for religious, political, and everyday use. Many Colombian cities today have gold museums. The Spanish took the gold, the emeralds (also found in Colombia) and silver (found in Peru), and began shipping it back to Spain. England, at war with Spain on and off between the 16th century and 1814 at the end of the Napoleonic Wars, began attacking these Treasure Galleons in the Caribbean. English warships also attacked the port city of Cartagena, to disrupt Spanish trade; an event which is still remembered today. The wealth available from attacking a Spanish Treasure Galleon also gave rise to piracy in the Caribbean.

After the United States of America declared independence in 1776, it was perhaps inevitable that the Spanish colonies would do the same. In 1808, during the Napoleonic Wars, the French, under Emperor Napoleon, invaded Spain. King Ferdinand VII was removed from the Spanish throne and replaced by Napoleon's brother, Joseph. This led to a schism in Spain, between those loyal to Ferdinand and those loyal to Joseph. The colonies began questioning why they needed to be loyal to either, and soon an independence movement began.

The colonial wars of independence ran until 1824, when the Spanish were defeated at the Battle of Ayacucho in Peru. The key leader in Venezuela, Colombia, and Peru was Simón Bolívar. He favoured joining these countries in super-Republic, called Gran Colombia. Given the prevalence of gold, emeralds, silver, and other natural resources, such a country could have shifted the global balance of power significantly. However, key national leaders opposed this, including José Antonio Páez in Venezuela and Francisco de Paula Santander in Colombia. Not before long, Venezuela, Colombia, and Peru became independent nations. Bolivia (perhaps ironically named after Bolívar) broke off from Peru and Ecuador broke off from Colombia (Panama broke off from Colombia in 1903). Political battles between federalists, supporting Bolívar, and nationalists, supporting Santander, seemed to have laid the basis for the civil war that was to come.

Colombia has been embroiled in civil war and unrest on and off since the 1830s. In the 19th century, the struggles may have been political in nature. In the 20th century, the struggles have also centred on class. Militant communism arrived in Latin America in the 1920s, after the Russian Revolution of 1917. Communist guerrillas were formed, ostensibly to fight for the workers, including to secure control and ownership of land. The most well-known of these guerrillas was the FARC, which was formed in the 1960s and, under the 2016 peace treaty, is now disbanding. Similarly, from the 1960s and onwards, the general state of lawlessness in parts of the country gave rise to organised crime, which could make a fortune from growing and smuggling drugs. Perhaps the most infamous drug lord was Pablo Escobar, who, amongst other things, was elected to the Colombian Congress and was responsible for blowing up a civilian airliner. The purpose of exploding a bomb on Avianca Flight 203, on November 27, 1989, was to kill a presidential candidate. The candidate, César Gaviria Trujillo, was not on board and was elected President the following year. Perhaps unknown to Escobar, there were two American citizens on board Flight 203. Their death led to President Bush senior, and President Clinton thereafter, to instigate a US law enforcement effort to hunt down Escobar. The drug lord was assassinated at the end of 1993.

Given that guerrillas were fighting against business owners and landowners, and drug cartels were kidnapping for ransom to fund their operations, the business owners and landowners began not just hiring private bodyguards, but forming their own paramilitary groups. In the end, the guerrillas, drug cartels, and paras, were all as bad as the other. One of the roles played by the paras was engaging in 'social cleansing', in which they killed people considered undesirable. This included suspected communist guerrillas, drug dealers, other criminals, but also vulnerable people such as street children and prostitutes. A serious concern were the seemingly close links between the paras and various members of the police as well as politicians. For that reason, there have been objections to the British and US governments providing assistance to the Colombian authorities in the so-called war on drugs. These issues, including the acts of violence perpetrated by the different groups, are explored by Professor Michael Taussig in his book *Law in a Lawless Land: Diary of a Limpieza in Colombia* (University of Chicago Press, 2005) and by the travel writer Tom Feiling in his book *Short Walks from Bogotá: Journeys in the New Colombia* (Allen Lane, 2012). Both books are well worth reading.

There have been many efforts to secure peace. A Justice and Peace Law was passed in 2005, designed to demobilise the paras by offering them lenient sentences if they voluntarily disbanded and returned to lawful employment. Overall, it seems to have been a success, but crime continues (for instance, Escobar's hitman, known as Popeye, who killed at least 300 people, was himself robbed at gunpoint in late 2016), and there are serious questions about justice to the families of those killed by the paras. There have been many attempts to negotiate peace with the FARC, which had all failed. People were understandably sceptical when President Juan Manuel Santos began a new round of peace negotiations with the FARC in 2012. Whether or not the negotiations were to continue was a key factor in the presidential election held in May 2014. President Santos was re-elected with 50.95% of the national vote, thus getting a (small) mandate to continue the negotiations. It is difficult to image a smaller margin of victory. Nonetheless, a peace treaty was finalised with the FARC in 2016. In the same year, President Santos won the Nobel Peace Prize. As with the Justice and Peace Law of 2005, serious questions remain about justice for those affected by the FARC's guerrilla campaigns. It is perhaps necessary to balance justice for victims against the prospect of long-term peace. Otherwise, by the end of the 2020s, the Colombian civil wars will have raged for two centuries. In the past decades, millions have been killed, wounded, or displaced from their homes. Perhaps an imperfect ending is preferable to having no end at all.

This novel is set against that backdrop and takes places in the weeks leading up to the important 2014 presidential election. A month earlier, on 8 March 2014, Malaysian Airlines flight MH370 vanished over the Indian Ocean. Whilst pieces of the wreck have been found on Reunion Island, the mystery remains unsolved. At the same time, Colombia was gearing up to participate in the football World Cup for the first time in 16 years, where the country would eventually reach the quarterfinals.

The visit of the English Prince and his wife, the Duchess, is inspired by the real visit by HRH the Prince of Wales and the Duchess of Cornwall to Colombia in October 2014, as part of a wider tour of Latin America. This included a visit to Cartagena. That visit became marred by controversy over the unveiling of a plaque commemorating English sailors who died trying to capture Cartagena in 1741, when it was still a Spanish colony, as mentioned above. This attack was part of the so-called War of Jenkins' Ear, fought between 1739 and 1748 between Britain and Spain. Locally, the English naval forces were regarded as little more than pirates. The plaque was removed a week after the unveiling.

The HMS Atholl is a fictional ship. However, the HMS Portland and the HMS Argyll are both real Type 23 frigates. They patrolled the Caribbean, and visited Cartagena, in June and October 2014 respectively, the latter to coincide with the Prince of Wales' visit to the city. The HMS Portland, on that patrol, did capture two vessels smuggling drugs out of Colombia, serving as inspiration for both the capture of Manuel's motorboat and later the Red Widow's yacht.

The unnamed politicians in the novel are loosely inspired by their real-life counterparts. The character of British Ambassador to Colombia became much bigger than first intended, and so did not originally have a name. In the end, I decided to keep it that way. He is the Ambassador. What else do we need to know?

When a country has a history like Colombia's, it is easy to reduce the country to the sum of its crime. I have tried to avoid that in this novel. As said, Colombia is a truly fascinating place and well worth visiting (no doubt even more so today, as it keeps working towards peace). The Old City of Cartagena should definitely go on the world-traveller's must-see list. The same goes for the great Rock at Guatapé, which is as mysterious as it is awe-inspiring. Colombia deserves a much better reputation than it currently has.

Lightning Source UK Ltd.
Milton Keynes UK
UKHW03f1014260418
321688UK00001B/1/P

9 781787 197275